Catherine Cookson was born in Tyne Dock, the illegitimate daughter of a poverty-stricken woman, Kate, whom she believed to be her older sister. She began work in service but eventually moved south to Hastings where she met and married a local grammar-school master. At the age of forty she began writing about the lives of the working-class people with whom she had grown up, using the place of her birth as the background to many of her novels.

Although originally acclaimed as a regional writer – her novel *The Round Tower* won the Winifred Holtby Award for the best regional novel of 1968 – her readership soon began to spread throughout the world. Her novels have been translated into more than a dozen languages and more than 40,000,000 copies of her books have been sold in Corgi alone. Four of her novels – *The Fifteen Streets*, *The Black Velvet Gown*, *The Black Candle* and *The Man Who Cried* – have been made into successful television dramas, and more are planned.

Catherine Cookson's many bestselling novels have established her as one of the most popular of contemporary women novelists. After receiving an OBE in 1985, Catherine Cookson was created a Dame of the British Empire in 1993. She and her husband Tom now live near Newcastle-upon-Tyne.

OTHER BOOKS BY CATHERINE COOKSON

NOVELS

Kate Hannigan
The Fifteen Streets
Slinky Jane
The Garment
Hannah Massey
The Unbaited Trap
Katie Mulholland
The Round Tower
The Glass Virgin
The Dwelling Place
Feathers in the Fire
The Mallen Streak
The Mallen Girl
The Mallen Litter
The Tide of Life
The Slow Awakening
The Iron Façade
The Girl

The Cinder Path
The Man Who Cried
The Whip
The Black Velvet Gown
A Dinner of Herbs
The Moth
The Parson's Daughter
The Cultured Handmaiden
The Harrogate Secret
The Black Candle
The Wingless Bird
The Gillyvors
My Beloved Son
The Rag Nymph
The House of Women
The Maltese Angel
The Year of the Virgins

Catherine Cookson

MAGGIE ROWAN

CORGI BOOKS

MAGGIE ROWAN
A CORGI BOOK : 0 552 14081 5

Originally published in Great Britain by
Macdonald & Co. (Publishers) Ltd

PRINTING HISTORY
Macdonald edition published 1964
Corgi edition published 1970
Corgi edition reprinted 1970
Corgi edition reprinted 1972 (twice)
Corgi edition reprinted 1973
Corgi edition reprinted 1974 (twice)
Corgi edition reprinted 1975
Corgi edition reprinted 1976
Corgi edition reprinted 1977
Corgi edition reprinted 1978 (twice)
Corgi edition reprinted 1979
Corgi edition reprinted 1980
Corgi edition reprinted 1981
Corgi edition reprinted 1983
Corgi edition reprinted 1984
Corgi edition reprinted 1985
Corgi edition reprinted 1993 (reset)
Corgi Canada edition published 1995

Set in 10/12 pt. Linotype New Baskerville by
Phoenix Typesetting, Ilkley, West Yorkshire.

Corgi Books are published by Transworld Publishers Ltd,
61-63 Uxbridge Road, Ealing, London W5 5SA,
in Australia by Transworld Publishers (Aust.) Pty Ltd,
15-25 Helles Avenue, Moorebank, NSW 2170,
and in New Zealand by Transworld Publishers (N.Z.) Ltd,
3 William Pickering Drive, Auckland.

Printed in Canada
Cover printed in U.S.A.
UNI   10 9 8 7 6 5 4 3 2 1

To PETER and MICHAEL LAVELLE, my two cousins, without whose technical help and guidance this book would certainly not have been written; to Peter for leading me to the coal face and answering my endless questions; to Michael for supplying me with most valuable data; and to Jimmy Tiplady whose descriptive reminiscences lent colour to my thinking: and to those miners whom I saw working in the bowels of the earth and who evoked so much of my admiration that my fear became lost under it.

Contents

Part One

Maggie

Part Two

Tom

Part Three

Stephen

Part Four

Ann

Author's Note

Felburn is fictitious, as are all the characters in this book. Place names have been used merely to form a background; and pitmatic dialect has been used only here and there to give atmosphere.

Part One

Maggie

1

The Wedding Feast

Maggie Rowan looked out of the scullery window and over the little back garden to the rising land where the allotments began. But her eyes did not see what they were looking upon; for like her ears, which were filled with the sounds of laughter and merriment coming from the room along the passage, her eyes were seeing only the picture of that room . . . her sister Ann, all decked in white, sitting at the head of the table with her husband, David Taggart, and all down one side of the table the members of the Taggart family: his mother, fat, slipshod Kitty, laughing her way through life like a half-wit; his father, Sep, a loud-mouthed blusterer; and his brothers, Pat, Alec, Bert, Fred . . . and Christopher, not to mention the eight-year-old twins; and interspersed between the men, their women. Of the men, only Christopher was still not married; so it could be said they were all married now, for there was no likelihood that anyone would take him, with his hump and his great head and his spindle-legs and big feet.

The Taggarts had always irritated Maggie. As far back as she could remember they had over-flowed from their own house, next door, into this one. If it wasn't Kitty slipping in to see her mother, it was Sep and the lads to see her father.

The thought of her father brought that strange feeling into the pit of her stomach again; and deliberately she lifted her mind from him, and almost ferociously she tackled the dishes in the sink.

She did not turn round when the door opened and her mother came in; nor did she answer when Nellie Rowan said, 'Leave them, lass; I'll see to them after.'

She heard her filling up the emptied plates from the table behind her, and when her mother left the scullery, the laughter from the room came even louder to her ears, and she flung round to close the door. But with her hand on the knob she paused.

The door leading into the scullery was at the other end of the passage from the front door, and half-way along the passage, one on each side, were the doors leading into the kitchen cum-living-room and the front room. From where she was standing she could see part of the wedding table through the open door of the front room. Her father was on his feet toasting the bride, and his voice, thick with the pitmatic, came to her:

'Here's to you both. And may ye be as good a wife, lass, to Davie as your mother's been to me. And may you, Davie, be a better husband than I've been.'

She saw him look across the table towards her mother who had just sat down, her gaze lowered towards her plate, and she wondered, not for the first time, why he should always seem to knuckle under to her mother, even at times seem to be afraid of her.

Sep Taggart's voice put her teeth on edge as he called, 'What's up with thoo, George? Want pat on back? If thoo were half as good a marrer as thoo art husband I wouldn't have to work me bloody . . .'

'Sep, no language! Mind where you are.' Kitty Taggart's voice came from somewhere beyond Maggie's

14

vision. And her husband replied with mock aggressiveness, 'Who's using language! Dost want me to come over there and clout the gob for thee?'

On this the laughter grew louder; the talking and chaffing became an unintelligible noise, vying with the shrill cries of the children's voices from the kitchen where they were being regaled with their portions of the wedding feast.

Her father sat down; and now she could see her sister. To her, Ann looked, in her finery, like a dressed-up doll. For weeks and weeks there had been talk of nothing but that dress; it had been impossible to lay a pin anywhere for patterns and pieces of material. And for what? To show off for a couple of hours. They couldn't even afford a honeymoon and had been able to furnish only two rooms of the house they had rented; and tomorrow Ann would have to bang his pit clothes, because even for his wedding he dared not lose more than one shift. And who knew, next week he might be like scores of others, on half time, or even stood off. Yet that empty-headed noodle could spend her money on a wedding dress . . . and underclothes and nighties!

'Go on; why don't you eat, man?' It was Pat Taggart calling to his brother. 'How d'you expect to get through your first neet, man, let alone the morrer's shift if you don't eat?'

'That's quite enough of that, Pat!' It was her mother's reprimanding tone.

'Aw, it's a weddin', Aunt Nellie.'

'There's no-one more aware of it than me.' Again her mother's stiff tone.

'Take no notice of him, Nellie. Or you, Ann.' It was Kitty Taggart now. 'Look here, me lad, I'll wring yer lug for you, as big as you are, if you don't behave yersel. It's the whisky talkin'. And what's your wife doin' if she can't keep you quiet?'

'Aw, Ma; gi' ower naggin'. Ann can take a joke. An' it's her weddin', isn't it, lass? An' this time next year we'll be gathered for the christening. What d'you say, Ann? . . . Mind, there's triplets run in wor family. Did ye knaa that?'

'Shut the gob!' It was Sep Taggart's order to his son; and on it Maggie closed the door.

Turning to the sink, she flung the dishcloth into the water. Damn them! Damn and blast them all! With their laughing and yelling, with their jokes and innuendoes, the senseless, ignorant lot! Why had she stayed off work? They hadn't expected her to, and it would have been all over when she came home. But no; she must needs torture herself one fraction further. Always it was like this, rubbing salt into her own wounds. Why did she always seek pain? Would she never learn? It was as if in opposition to her own iron will that some stronger force would thrust her where her eyes could see and her ears hear things that would set her blood tingling with desire, until the desire itself would melt in the furnace of her being before hardening into one solid block of pain.

Her head drooped on to her chest. She knew the desire that drove her to be here this afternoon was the same that led her into the back row when she went to the pictures in order to witness and silently upbraid the lovers about her; it was the same desire that drove her into Newcastle on a Saturday night so that she could linger on the streets. Had she lingered on the High Street on a Saturday night in this town she would have been the butt for the jests of every lout in the place and food for scandal among the women. That would be after they had got over the shock of Maggie Rowan, she with the face that would put off any man, being possessed of normal desires. The summing up would have been that she wanted a man badly . . . Could she blame them?

She swung round from the sink as two of Alec Taggart's children came running into the scullery.

'Haven't I told you to keep out of here!' her voice rasped at them. And they stared up at her as if confronted by an ogre, but one to whom they were used. Then they ran out again, leaving the door wide, and Kitty Taggart's voice came, filling the scullery like a buffeting wind.

'I promised myself that suite for years. "Nellie's got a suite," I'd say to our Sep here, "an' a front room set all nice an' proper. And I'm goner have one out of the Store as soon as the lads start workin'." Oh, if only I'd got it then, I might have had some pleasure out of it. But no; I had to wait until these big tykes were courtin' . . . six feet an' fourteen stone each of them, with a lump of a lass on their knees.'

The laughter mounted again and Kitty's voice choked with her own mirth as she went on, 'Remember how you'd toss up for who'd have it on a Sunday afternoon? Play cards they would for that sofa. And mind the night when the springs fell through the middle when you, Bert, and Cissie were on it, and you stuffed them back and let you there, Pat, take Gladys in? Oh my! Oh, the laughs we had over that couch! It was in smithereens long afore I had it paid for. And it was the only suite I ever had, or am likely to now. But what odds! It was the best marriage maker that ever was. Aw, Nellie, we've never had much money but we've had some laughs, haven't we?'

'We have that, Kitty.' It was her mother's voice, almost soft.

'Thirty years we've been neighbours. I remember

the day you moved in. It was Christmas time, nineteen hundred and six. It's been a good test, Nellie, for we've never had a cross word.'

'No; you left that to your men.' Pat Taggart's voice came again. 'If it isn't the pit it's religion; and if it isn't that it's the pigs.'

As if she were telling herself she must bear the burden of their voices Maggie walked slowly this time towards the door and closed it. Pat Taggart was right there; it was either pit, religion or pigs that held first place in the conversation of the house. Discussions on pit and pigs were allowed in this house, but her mother would not condone any talk on religion; it was too risky, the Taggarts being Catholics and they Methodists. It was only by keeping a strict taboo on the subject during all these years that the families continued to remain on good terms. And this was helped, no doubt, Maggie surmised, because the Taggarts were wooden Catholics; at least, so she had thought until David, the quiet, stolid individual, had taken a stand and insisted that he and Ann must be married in the Catholic church. What a schemozzle that had caused! Smiling sardonically within herself, she had waited for the split; but Ann had submitted to the Taggart pressure and persuaded everybody that she didn't mind in the least being married in the Catholic church . . . Spineless creature!

Maggie had been frankly amazed at her mother's acceptance of this; more so because her heart was set on their Tom becoming a preacher. There were a number of things about her mother that from time to time amazed her; not least was her mother's attitude towards her, an attitude of persistent kindness, so persistent that at times it was irritating. She didn't want kindness, she wanted a life such as other women had. Oh why, in the name of God, had she stayed at home?

Quickly she turned from the sink and dried her hands; then opening the door she went out into the passage and up the stairs that wound in a half spiral over the scullery to the floor above. The voices rose with her, milling around her . . . her father chaffing Christopher Taggart about the bicycle shop he couldn't rent.

'What's a hundred pounds, Chris?' he was saying. 'Why don't you ask him to let you have it for a fiver? Let him keep his goodwill and stock. Make some bikes up out of your old scrap and tagger.'

'What about havin'a whip round? I've got three bob, Chris; you can have that.' It was Pat's voice.

But no comment came to her ears from Christopher Taggart. It was as if he had no wit, coarse or subtle, to counter gibes. But she knew this to be wrong; of all the Taggarts, David included, she deemed Christopher the only one capable of any sense or desire above the common range that motivated the family. Yet she had no authority for this opinion, it was merely surmise, as she rarely spoke to Christopher, or he to her.

Three bob! Her lip curled into a sneer at Pat's offer. But it was no jest; that would be about all any one of them would be able to raise after having paid his way. What would their faces be like if she were to walk into the living-room now and say to Christopher, 'There's a cheque for your hundred pounds!' She could do it too, and still have twice as much left. They had speculated, she knew, on how much she had put by, but she judged their surmise never to have amounted to over fifty pounds. She'd had that much before she got her first rise, and she'd had two rises since! But none of them knew, not even her mother. What they didn't know did them no harm. She still paid her mother seventeen shillings a week, as she had been doing since she was twenty. Even when her father was off work she had offered her no more, knowing that she would do this only once and she would be expected to keep it up.

Across the little landing, the door of the room that after to-day would be hers alone was open, revealing a jumble of clothing on the bed . . . Ann's clothing! The last remnants of her presence in the house. She entered the room and looked down on them. When they were removed she'd rearrange this room; she'd get a key for the door and tell her mother she'd see to the cleaning herself. This would likely cause one of those lightning rows with her father. Well, she would survive that, as she had done all the others. But she was determined from now on to have some place that would be hers alone, where, without fear of intrusion, she could relax.

Between the tips of her finger and thumb she picked up a home-made brassiere from the bed. It was constructed of odd pieces of silk fastened together with a neat herringbone stitch, a replica of the one she remembered Ann first making when she was fifteen. She could see her now pushing her breasts into it and smiling a sort of secret, delighted smile at the achievement.

Slowly she put the brassiere back on the bed and walked to the window. She looked out, through the houses opposite, through the next street, and the next, and her gaze seemed to fall into the house where, later to-night, her sister would be with David Taggart. She could see them locked so closely together as to be one whole; she could see him carrying her upstairs; he would undress her – he was the kind of man who would want to do that, quiet, with deep and strange fires needing to be fed. Oh yes, she knew; she knew what men wanted. But my God, how did she know, she who had never been with a man? How did she come by this knowledge inside of her, a knowledge she knew instinctively to be true? Why did she go over and over things, dragging them up from the depths of her mind to act them to the last peak of what should have culminated in ecstasy but which always crumbled into torment?

She turned from the window and stood leaning for support on the dressing table. God, why must she do it? Why must she think these things? They would drive her mad; later to-night they would be worse; but not as bad as in three months' time. Yes, then would be the real hell, in three months' time when Ann would come and stand in the kitchen, blushing and smiling that childish smile of hers, and saying with maddening shyness, 'I'm going to have a baby.'

She lifted her head and thrust her face close to the mirror, so close that her green eyes took on a largeness that was merely a distortion. Why, her mind demanded of her reflection, had she been damned like this, with skin the colour of mud and a face so long and narrow as to appear to be devoid of bone structure, her lips a thin mark across her face and her nose an equally thin mark down it, and her body like her face, thin and fleshless? Yet what of her hair, that beautiful, long, thick brown mane? What of it? Instead of lending a little relief to her ugliness it only emphasised it, for no matter how she wore it, it appeared like a busby on top of a pole.

Hopelessly she turned to the window again and looked up at the sky, now a mass of red and purple streaks from the setting sun. She stared at the fast changing colour until her eyes became blinded with light and she had to press the eyeballs tightly before she could see again. The sun was now a huge orange ball, falling gently behind Brampton Hill. It wasn't often she saw the sun setting over Brampton Hill; and now its colours were touching dark masses here and there and picking them out as groups of chimneys and turrets. She could see most of the tops of the big houses standing out from amongst

21

their trees. They looked to be quite close, as if they were just beyond the allotments instead of a mile away.

Her feelings began to move to another desire, a desire born when, as a child, she first saw the lights shining like stars in the sky from the big houses at night. The longing to live on Brampton Hill had been similar to the fairy-palace desire of the normal child; but whereas the child's fairy palace fades into the picture of a little home, her fairy palace had remained in all its magnificence, to be thrown into relief when at fourteen she went to work at Mrs Thornton's laundry, for it was this laundry that catered for most of those who lived on the Hill: Caffley, the agent for most of the local pits – his house was on the far side of the Hill, with a commanding view of the fells; Saunders, the manager of the Phoenix pit, and Tilsley, who managed the Venus – their houses were nearer the top of the Hill but well shrouded in woodland so that their respective places of employment, which dominated opposite ends of the town, were not visible to them; then there were the Pater-Browns – they had a chain of fruit stores in Newcastle – and the Crosbies – three generations of them lived on the Hill; the old man was said to have started in the puddling mills of Jarrow, but now they had their own building yard, small but large enough to merit their elevated residences.

It was said that the Hill was going down; its downfall being attributed to the bungalows which were beginning to encroach on its foot. Many of the larger houses, it was true, were empty, but enough were still occupied to preserve some exclusiveness and to uphold Maggie's dreams.

When she was promoted to packer and sorter she felt in closer touch with the Hill, and it became a mania with her that every article that passed through her hands for it must be perfect. To this end, back would go one third of the ironing to the ironing room; and it was this fetish, she knew, that first caused her to be hated by the other workers. It was also this that brought her to the notice of Mrs Thornton, who managed her own laundry.

Mrs Thornton was a business woman, and she saw in Maggie a perfect assistant manageress. She saw that she was without a friend among the other workers, that she was hated by them; and she considered this a good thing, for no soap or powder would be passed to a crony. She knew, too, that Maggie was feared, young as she was. This also she considered good, for there'd be little slacking under her. And, as she was without apparent charm, there was little likelihood of her getting married; and once trained, Mrs Thornton reasoned, she would be able to place most of the responsibility on her shoulders. But even in those early stages of planning Maggie's career, Mrs Thornton determined that Maggie must not be given power; she had the idea that once Maggie felt power she would be like the beggar on horseback . . . she'd ride to hell.

Maggie sensed all this, almost clear enough to put it into words. And it did not make her love Mrs Thornton, for after fifteen years she was doing the work of manageress and as yet had received neither the title nor the money for it; and Mrs Thornton laboured under the illusion that she was unaware of this imposition. But it wouldn't go on for ever.

No. Maggie shook her head slowly as she continued to gaze at the Hill. It wouldn't go on for ever. Then her thought and line of vision were suddenly broken by a distorted figure crossing the road; it was Christopher Taggart, a bucket in each hand, on his way to the pigs. He seemed almost on a level with her eyes, for although the Rowan's house was the last on the street that ran steeply uphill, the waste ground where the houses ended rose sharply, and for some distance the allotments were on a slope. This slope cut off the view of the main part of the town, which lay in the valley beyond before rising again to form Brampton Hill.

She watched Christopher lumbering along; he'd had to answer the call of the pigs, who knew nothing of wedding feasts. The weight of the buckets seemed to bend the edges of the scoop, wherein his head usually rested; the wind was lifting his hair, and the sunlight was sending shafts of light through it, turning its fairness to flame. She did not think, poor Christopher; that adjective was Ann's. For all his massive upper body, he was weakly and unable to stand even pithead work, and so was the general object of pity. Yet he did not rouse pity in her.

For years he had earned his board by looking after the pigs; until recently, when he had started to gather old iron. This had brought scorn on him, as already two taggereen men had gone out of business in the town. There was nothing in scrap iron any more. But apparently he had his own ideas on the matter for he went on silently gathering scrap; and out of it he had even constructed a bicycle, not quite to orthodox pattern, yet one that moved; and the young Taggart twins made the street like bedlam with their capers on it.

It seemed that from building that bicycle Christopher had become possessed of one idea, to have a little repair shop of his own; and when only four streets away Harry Seymour put up his shop and goodwill for sale, he had become so animated with the desire to have it that he was the butt for the prevailing family joke.

She could remember only yesterday Sep Taggart shouting across the fence to her father, 'Our Chris wants a hundred pounds, George, to buy Harry Seymour's shop.'

And her father had asked with mock seriousness, 'Is that all, man?'

'Aye; he'll give you a third interest in the shop if you'll lend him it.'

'Will he, man? Just a mo' till I go in an' get it. You're sure a hundred's all he wants?'

She watched Christopher now climbing the stile, a surviving relic of the fields that were fast disappearing, and as he stepped down on to the allotment path one of the buckets tipped over, and the swill fell about his feet. She watched him kick his boots hurriedly against the post. She had long guessed that he did not like looking after the pigs, and the resentment seemed to be evident in the simple action of kicking their food from his clothes. Why did resentment stand out more sharply when portrayed by oddities? she asked herself.

She was well aware that she was classed as an oddity, and that her evident resentment against life, too, was put down to her being a man-hater; yet the very people who put forward this view were also those who would be the first to accuse her of being man-mad should she allow a flicker of natural interest in men to show. She had once heard her father say bitterly to her mother, 'I've got that to be thankful for, anyway, there'll be no trouble with her going man-hunting. Though it would be all the same if she did try it on.'

She wondered whether it was from that moment that she grew to hate him, for hate him she did, and it was only the firmness of her mother that maintained peace between them.

The feeling she had for her father seemed to have

overflowed on to her sister. Yet Ann would have been friendly. But Maggie didn't want her friendliness. Somehow, even since Ann was a baby, she had resented any approach from her. Although in those early days the need for a child was dimly stirring within her, she could not tolerate even the touch of Ann's hand; and should she snuggle up to her in bed the contact was strangely agonising. Years ago she had endeavoured to curb her jealousy of the girl, who, being ten years younger than herself, always appeared as a child; but she had found it useless. It had come as a shock when Ann first walked out with David Taggart – then she was still, to her, the spoilt baby of her father and the rest of the house. And now she was married . . . she was a wife . . . that little dollified, empty-headed piece was a wife! And she would have children. Oh yes, she would have children; she was indecent in her open desire to have a large family. Her numerous dolls would now be represented in the yearly baby, and this house would become their parade ground, and the noise of the christenings would be like the noise that was going on downstairs now . . . laughter, yells, silly jokes.

She couldn't bear it; she just couldn't stand that. She must get away . . . take rooms somewhere. But that would mean paying twenty-five shillings a week for board and lodgings. Her saving soul balked at such a possibility. And anyway, she reasoned, wherever she went she would still know when the babies came.

An old thought rose to torment her again. Why had she not had the courage to take the plunge that night years ago in Newcastle when she had met that man. He hadn't seemed to mind how she looked; he had sat talking to her in that café for hours . . . intelligent talk. Then quite suddenly he had asked her to go home with him. And she had longed with a longing that frightened her to accompany him. She knew that he sensed her need, and in a way was being kind to her. She also knew that his kindness would happen only once, for he was a man of many women. She had been on the point of silently accepting by raising her eyes to his face when, like a picture thrown up on a screen, she had a vision, above all things, of the little chapel where Sunday after Sunday she sat with her family and listened to the reasonable talking of their minister, Mr Fraser. She could have cried aloud at the absurdity of it, for she cared not two hoots for Mr Fraser, or for his reasonableness, or for the Methodist doctrine, or, truth to tell, for even God Himself; they were all just a façade. Yet it was this façade that kept her head down, and she realised later that the veneer of respectability that covered her was of such fibre that it was strong enough to keep hemmed in the passions that flowed beneath it. Yet in the refusal of that one offer had gone for ever the chance that she might bear a child.

She leant her head wearily against the window sash and continued to gaze through the net curtains into the distance. The sun had sunk now, and the afterglow was turning the corrugated shacks dotting the allotments into little houses of rainbow fairydom. From a chimney stack in the distance a thin spiral of dark-coloured smoke rose through the changing hues. She could almost see Christopher Taggart stoking up the boiler to cook the swill, his thoughts meanwhile playing around Seymour's bicycle shop . . . He wanted a bicycle shop, and she wanted a child.

The colours of the afterglow stopped their moving into one another; the noise from the room below faded away, even the smoke from the stack became fixed like a corkscrew in the air; only the thought that had leaped into her mind moved; it moved and spread itself and covered the earth; then it contracted again and came back to its birthplace, and with its impact she flung herself round from the window and stood, her back pressed to the wall, her hands spread out flat against it as if she was being confronted by some gigantic possibility which had taken on concrete form. She heard a voice that she did not recognise as her own whisper, 'But he's weakly.' Then on the whisper, cold and harsh, came her own voice, 'But I'm not!'

She walked slowly to the bed and sat down on Ann's clothes, and when the whisper came again, saying, 'They'll all laugh, the place'll be in an uproar,' she lifted her shoulders, and, as if in advance, the laughter rose through the floor from the room below. She pressed out her lips until their thin line took on a shape. She would pay even that price on the chance that she would be a married woman and have a bairn. Slowly her arms folded themselves over one another, and she pressed them to her with a rocking movement, and she closed her eyes and looked into the future and into the mysterious caverns of her mind, where lay concealed the knowledge that from no man could she expect love, but from a child . . . a child of her own body . . . she might even . . . be adored.

She was not aware of how long she sat metaphorically hugging this amazing possibility to her; it was the concerted cries of the children yelling, 'The twins! The twins! They're going to do a turn!' that made her rise from the bed, irritation flooding her again. How often her fingers itched to wind the ears of the precocious Taggart boys. She suspected that they often used her for their mimics . . . She wouldn't put it past them for doing it now. Her suspicions led her on to the landing, and leaning over the banister, her face grim, she listened. But what came to her was the voice of Sep Taggart ordering his sons 'to do' . . . their mother and the priest.

Amidst the urging cries of the company, Kitty Taggart's voice called, 'Not on your life! What if himself was to walk in! Stop it, I tell you!'

'Go on,' ordered their father. 'The bit about himself coaxing a bit of belly pork out of her.'

There was a medley of laughter and cries. 'Go on, Alan; you do your ma. And don't forget to knock the drop off the end of your nose, mind.'

Maggie's nose wrinkled in disgust, and she thought: And into the flour when she's baking, no doubt. There came to her a call for order, and she heard a voice almost identical with Kitty Taggart's, and another, thick with the Irish brogue, representing the priest's.

Her face expressing her scorn, she was about to turn back into the bedroom, when she heard the back door burst open. For a moment she thought it was her brother Tom; he had gone to work to-day, fearing no doubt that if he lost a shift he'd be stood off, like the Baxter boy who lived three doors down. But it wasn't Tom. She heard a man's voice calling, 'George man! George!'

The footsteps hurried along the passage and the twins' voices were suddenly hushed as the man spoke.

In the moment of uncanny silence followed by the mad rush of feet Maggie knew what had happened. Softly she moved back into the bedroom and to the window. Yes, the street was astir, doors opening and people running. Well! Well! For it to happen at this moment! Her thoughts flew to David Taggart. He was one of the trained rescue workers. A slow smile spread over her face. If this fall was like any of the others he could be there till morning . . . So much for the wedding night.

She turned her head towards the door as quick, light

footsteps sounded on the stairs, but she was looking out of the window again when her sister rushed into the room.

'There's been a fall.'

'So I gather.' Maggie did not turn round, but she heard Ann's quick intake of breath.

'Well, how you can stand there doing nothing I don't know!'

On this, she did turn and look at her sister rapidly divesting herself of the finery it had taken her hours to don. 'What d'you expect me to do, run down to the pithead?'

'That wouldn't hurt you . . . Do you realise our Tommy may be in it; he's still down.'

'He may be. On the other hand he may not. There's no need to go mad until you know. And even then it won't help.'

Ann paused in the act of pulling a skirt over her head. 'Sometimes I don't think you're human.' Her voice broke: 'You could even be glad it's happened, to break up my wedding. Why did you stay off, anyway? I didn't ask you.'

'No, you didn't ask me.'

'Oh, I'm sorry.'

Ann dragged a coat from the wardrobe. 'But don't you see, if anything happens to our Tommy, me mother'll go mad.'

Maggie did not reply, and Ann rushed from the room; and Maggie heard her calling, 'Mother! Where's me mother?'

Again Maggie turned to the window. There was her mother, flying down the street behind the running figures of her father and Sep Taggart in their pit clothes, and there were the wives of the Taggart men shepherding their children home; their men would already have flown on ahead to change.

Soon there was no sound coming from downstairs, or from the streets; a peaceful, soothing quiet lay upon the house. As she was about to turn from the window she caught sight of Christopher Taggart. He was jumping the stile with an agility that for the moment wiped out his deformity. His face was upturned towards the fading light, that abnormally large face, the eyes too big and the mouth too wide and the cheek bones too prominent. It was the face of a giant, and in the changing light seemed to reflect a giant's massive beauty . . . He would have been a handsome man, she mused, had his body been straight. But had his body been straight, then she could never have hoped to carry out the scheme that was growing with startling swiftness in her mind. She watched him running past the window and down the street; and as her eyes followed him she felt in the position of a god who held his future in the palm of her hand.

Nellie Rowan stood at the pit gates with her face pressed close to the bars. The coldness of the iron did not cool the fever of her brain, although the same bars had turned her hands to stiff pieces of flesh. It was nearly an hour now since the gate was last opened, and then only to let people in. During the four hours she had stood there no-one had left the pit yard. But for an occasional light from an opening door or from a swinging lamp the yard was in darkness; but away in the far distance, at the top of the two broad flights of steps, there were a number of lights, which kept going in and out as the milling figures up there blotted them from her view.

There were no whispers or debating talk now from the mass of people pressed about her; the cage was going down, and everyone was waiting again with suspended breath.

It seemed an endless period of time before the whisper passed over the crowd, 'It's coming up!'

Nellie listened to the whisking, grinding sound of the wheel as it pulled up the cage to the surface. So still had the night become that she heard the faint clank of the iron bar that stood in place of a door being lifted from the cage. Then came the sound of footsteps on the ironwork of the top flight of steps. They were muffled on the lower wooden flight, and were lost completely when they reached the coal dust of the yard.

There was still no movement from the crowd, until the measured tread of men's feet was heard on the concrete square that fronted the lamp house, the first-aid post and the group of offices. Then it was only a short, combined sigh.

The gate was torn away from Nellie's hands, and she was forced back as a car moved slowly into the crowd. It was an open car, and the swinging lamps, held aloft by the men in the crowd, showed up the burly figure of Caffley, the agent. He was gazing pointedly ahead as if unwilling to face the looks of pain and resentment which he knew were all about him.

The car moved slowly and silently into the main road. Then a single voice crying, 'Bloody bloodsucker!' seemed to send it spurting away. The voice was echoed from different parts of the crowd, not loudly, but in low growling undertones.

'Why don't he get hissel doon?'

'How would he like to keep seven bairns on forty bob a week, eh? You can't run a bloody great mansion on that, can you? And who keeps him and his like in their fancy houses? We do!'

'You're lucky to be getting forty bob,' said a toneless

voice; 'I've got one lad to keep all of us. And a pound he gets, after starting as a screener at eight and tuppence in nineteen thirty-two. Now, after four years, a pound!'

The woman's voice faded away in hopelessness, and another took its place, thick and harsh. 'They say he's standing thirty off next week.'

'Let him; there'll be a riot.'

'What we want to do is to put our bloody heads together and see Peter Lee and get the union to—'

'Aw, the union! Only dam' good they are is for calling a strike. We had enough of the last.'

'Now don't you shout the union down, missis. Some day it'll be a power. It'll move more than mountains, it'll move pits . . . Aye, pits.'

'Be quiet!' It was a woman's voice thick with scorn. 'Is this any place to open your gobs? And I notice you're all top men who are letting off your wind . . . and the ones who can run their whippets.'

'Look here, I'm only on top because of me accident.' This voice came high and angry. 'And what's whippets got to do with it, anyway?'

'There's got to be men on top or there wouldn't be any down below, missis. And men must have some recreation,' a reasonable voice silenced the men . . . and almost the woman, for she came back, saying, 'Aye they must have their recreation, beer for the whippet if there's nee bread for the bairn.'

No-one took this up, the voices dying away in shame-faced silence, and once more the sound of the wheel dropping its burden into the earth was heard.

Talk. Talk. Men were always talking. And about frightening things, like strikes, victimization, and being stood off. Ann drew closer to her mother and put her hand on her arm as if she might, in the act of giving comfort, draw comfort from her. She had always pitied her mother for having to bear the anxious, rugged, uncertain life of a miner's wife; now she herself was irrevocably linked to that life, and it was going to be even harder for her because she had not her mother's strength; she hated and feared the pit. Her fear was woven like a net about David, and because of it she had even tried to persuade him to look for another job. He had been honestly amazed.

'What! Leave the pit on my own?' he had said. 'Without being stood off? Nobody in their right senses would do that, lass . . . not these days.' His tender laugh had proved her senselessness, even to herself. And now, after only a few hours married, the pit was telling her who was master of her life . . . and David's . . . and her mother's and father's . . . and everybody's in this town. But mostly at the moment it was master of Tom's life. She was forgetting that. Her David was down there; but this time he was on the right side of the fall. But Tom . . .

She cast a glance towards her mother. She was looking stern and forbidding, and you couldn't really tell what she was thinking. But if anything should happen to Tom, it would surely drive her mad; he was the star in her sky, and he shone for her alone. She loved the three of them; yes, she did, even though it was hard to believe that she could have an affection for their Maggie. Yet on Tom alone she poured her adoration; and even her reticent nature could not wholly conceal it.

A short while ago, when she was crying, her mother had admonished her, saying, 'Have faith; he'll come up.'

Yes, but how would he come up? Lying on his back or walking? Oh, she hated the pit, hated and loathed it. What would happen if she had to stand outside these gates, waiting as she was doing now, but for David.

34

Would she be able to keep calm, at least outwardly, like her mother? No, it would drive her off her head.

A woman behind her started to whimper. And another said, 'Go home, Mrs Blackett; think of the bairn.'

The whimper turned into broken words: 'He might never see it.'

'Now, now. It's only a light fall they say.'

And the woman's voice whimpered again: 'That's what they said two years ago. They were nearly through then; and there was another fall . . . Perhaps they're all gassed . . . !' Her voice rose to a point.

'Sh! . . . Sh! Don't talk like that . . . Go home, woman!' It was a stern reprimand from different quarters.

Nellie's fingers tightened on the bars of the gate as she listened to the woman . . . Not gassed. Not that. It won't happen. No; it mustn't happen! She sent her command to the heavens, lifting her head to the skies, black yet alight with stars. Then her head drooped, and she leaned it for a moment against the gate . . . Would he be sitting down there going over in his mind his little sermon for Sunday? Only last night they talked about it whilst she was finishing the baking for the wedding. He had stood by her, his shoulder level with her own, so tall was he already; and he had told her some of the things he was going to say when he took his first service in the tiny village chapel at Lemton. Her face had glowed with the heat from the oven, but more so with pride for her boy. Only seventeen, and going to speak in the chapel! The Reverend Mr Fraser said he had the makings of a minister . . . Oh, if he could only be a minster! He could if he would; Mr Fraser would help him. But he just laughed at the idea, saying he knew what he could do and what he couldn't, and he wasn't up to being a minister; if there was to be any ministry for him it would be down the mine. And now he was down there in his first accident. Would this make him change his mind? . . . What did it matter so long as he was safe?

Kitty Taggart's voice broke in on her thinking, as it had done several times already. Endeavouring to be hushed, it was still strident. Shë was pushing her way through the crowd with more hot tea or broth or food of some kind. Feeding the body was the only way in which Kitty could express her sympathy, and it took a prolific form.

But even her voice was silenced as the sound of bounding footsteps on the iron stairs made themselves heard above the murmur of the crowd.

The footsteps paused once in the yard, then came on, and a man stopped at the gate and held up a lamp. His eyes shone white out of his black face, and the light shone into the red wetness of his mouth as he called, 'They're nearly through, and they're all right.'

The questions came flying at him:

'Anybody hurt?'

'How long afore they're up?'

The answers swept hope through the people. The suppression they had forced on their voices was released. They whispered no longer, but called to each other as if across a great distance.

Nellie said nothing. For a long while after the man had gone back she remained staring into the yard. Then seeming to remember Ann, she turned to her, and her remark was characteristic: 'Davie won't be long now, he'll be up shortly.'

And Ann, in relief this time, began to cry again.

But they were not up shortly. The stars had moved high into the firmament and the dew of the dawn was soaking into the crowd before the first liberated man passed through the gate. The crowd was not so large now as it had been; the emotion seekers from the centre of the town who had helped to swell it had taken to their beds when the night became raw. But it was still large, and each man was soon surrounded and lost in his family.

Through the lifting darkness Nellie saw her boy. He was walking between his father and David. His eyes met hers and he smiled. But when he reached her no words were spoken; as if by common consent Nellie walked on ahead with her son, leaving George and David with Ann between them to follow after.

They had left the people and the kindly pats and comforting words well behind and walked the half mile along the main road to where the colliery houses began before Nellie spoke. And then she asked softly, 'Were you frightened, lad?'

It was a while before he replied, 'No, ma; I don't think I was; just sort of surprised. And then that went off too.'

'It hasn't made you feel you don't want to go down any more?' He laughed, a gentle, mature and understanding laugh. 'No, ma; it hasn't. Don't worry, I'll be all right. You know what they say: the devil looks after his own and only the good die young.'

'Don't! Don't say things like that!' Nellie spoke sharply, as she was in the habit of doing to his father when he came out with something raw. Then she added contritely, 'Oh, lad, you know what I mean. God has been merciful.'

They walked on for some further way in silence

37

before Nellie spoke again. 'What did you do with your time?'

'Oh, we yarned a bit' – he gave a small, embarrassed laugh – 'and I talked.'

'What did you talk to them about?'

'Oh, just anything that came into my head. Bits of Rupert Brooke . . . you know, the poet. And then' – he paused – 'and I told them some of what I am going to say on Sunday.'

'What! And they listened? John Blackett and Findlay, and those Catholics?' There was incredulity in her voice.

'Well' – he laughed quietly – 'I didn't say it like a sermon; I said it like Mr Fraser does and like he told me to . . . I just talked. They didn't think it was anything to do with a sermon, not even anything to do with God . . . A funny thing happened though; I got stuck, and was searching for a word when Flora let out a bray, like she does when she's fed up and wants her feed. Oh, we did laugh.'

'There was plenty of air, then?'

'Oh yes, that was all right. It wasn't a bad do at all. Except for Mr Ferguson copping it in the leg.'

Nellie walked on in silence. Being shut in the bowels of the earth for twelve hours, not knowing whether he would see the light again, had not touched him. It hadn't frightened him . . . It came to her that that was what she had been hoping for, that he would be frightened.

Deep inside her a sadness settled. She had not realised before just how much she had banked on him eventually becoming a minister. Now she knew he would never leave the pit, no matter how Mr Fraser used his influence. His talking to the men, and the fact that they listened, men like the hardbitten Blackett and Findlay, had not pointed out to him that his path lay in saving souls; it had only strengthened his primary idea that more could be got over to them if you worked alongside them, breathing the same air, your sweat washing off the same dust, and in your brain, as in theirs, ever a secret fear that one day . . . the pit would get you.

2

The Proposal

Maggie had not been to bed. After tidying the house she had walked slowly down to the pithead just about the time when the agent had passed through the crowd. She heard the murmurs against him, and any sympathetic feeling she allowed herself on the matter went to the man in the car. From the time she had first started to think for herself she had despised the miners. Perhaps at first this was caused by her father; but now all miners came under her scorn. She thought of them as bigoted, ignorant clods, heaving more coal at the corner ends, in the bars, or on the allotments than they did down the pit; they talked and talked. And what did their talking amount to? A strike, weeks of tightened belts; then crawling back to where they had left off. Look at the Taggarts. If any of them had a shilling or two over, what did they do with it? Played pitch and toss down the quarry, or put it on the dogs, or threw away their shillings on games of quoits. And their wives, what did they do when they had a full week's money? Buy boiled ham and tinned peaches for the Sunday tea! And when a short week came they were borrowing.

In her mind's eye she had tried to see her sister brought to this state, but the picture would not form; Ann had the careful ways of their mother. But David was a Taggart, and they were all thriftless, and through him she could see Ann fighting a losing battle.

And what of Chris Taggart? Her fast-forming plans made her ask this question, but she gave herself no answer. Her eyes had searched for him as she walked on the fringes of the crowd. She saw most of the Taggart family there, but no sign of Christopher. And she had returned home to sit brooding over the fire.

Sitting alone in the dead of the night in the empty house gave her the opportunity to think. At least, she told herself this, for she would not admit that anything that could happen to the family would cause her to lose sleep. She gave no thought to her brother's safety, nor did she chide herself for this unnatural attitude; she was no hypocrite. Like her feelings towards Ann, any towards Tom were of resentment, which in his case revolved mainly about his looks – it seemed part of the unfairness of life that he should be endowed with features almost as delicate as a girl's.

Towards morning she had dozed in the chair; and it was the entry of her mother and brother that aroused her. She mumbled a few suitable words that the occasion demanded, and some small part of her drew comfort from her mother's evident pleasure and her saying, 'It was good of you to clean up.'

She was on her way up the stairs when she heard her father come in, and she thought it was with unnecessary eagerness that her mother related to him what she had done. But she heard no appreciative word from her father.

She drew the blind in her room, and as she had watched the sun going down last night now she watched the light of the dawn lifting each ramshackle hut on the allotments as if out of the earth. They came slowly into view, their chimneys, their roofs, and their patched walls. The Taggarts' chimney was smoking . . . Chris must already be there cooking the pig food. She could hear Mr and Mrs Taggart downstairs talking to her mother and father.

After a long moment during which she remained staring fixedly into the distance towards the chimney, she turned swiftly from the window, and taking a coat from the cupboard, she put it on. She had reached the door when she paused and, turning back, went towards the dressing table, and opening the small top drawer, she took out a new box of powder and broke the seal; and using her handkerchief she dabbed some on to her face. The effect of the pale pink powder was to sharpen her nose still more. She saw this and rubbed the powder vigorously off, and went hastily from the room, censuring herself for her weakness.

They were still talking in the kitchen when she let herself quietly out of the back door. A few steps up the back lane from the garden gate and she was on the steep rise of the waste ground. The allotments were deserted and were an unlovely sight; the rusty iron bedsteads and pieces of corrugated iron which marked their boundaries screamed their ugliness at the fresh delicateness of the morning. Only here and there had a hedge been grown round a plot of land, and the earth of these plots was grooved into neat patches. The Taggarts' double plot was railed in, but wood was the least of its supports; besides hoardings, pieces of iron beds were driven and entwined into use to enclose it.

Maggie paused at the makeshift gate. She was trembling. What would happen to her if he said no? To be refused by an ordinary man would be bad enough, but to be refused by him . . . But he wouldn't refuse; he wanted that shop. She thrust open the gate, skirted a heap of old iron and the two pigsties and came to the door of the hut, and as, without any preamble, she thrust it open, she had the overwhelming desire to find the hut empty. But it wasn't empty. His elbows resting on his knees, Christopher was sitting on an upturned bucket staring at the round black stove. And so sharp was her entry that she caught a dreamlike look in his eyes before his surprise had time to overshadow it.

He lumbered to his feet, upsetting the bucket as he did so. 'What's up? Is anything wrong? What's happened?'

She could see his mind flinging about trying to pin down the particular catastrophe that had brought her, of all people, here. His bewilderment calmed her own turmoil, and she felt herself in command of the situation.

'There's nothing wrong, I just wanted to talk to you.'

'To me?'

'Yes.'

He passed his hand over his unruly mass of fair hair and his whole demeanour continued to show his bewilderment, like someone aroused from a deep sleep and doubting his wakefulness. 'Yes. Yes, of course, Maggie. I'll get you something to sit on.'

He took a box from the corner of the hut and stood it on its end; then looked at her.

He was standing about two feet from her and she had to look down on him. If they were to stand close together she thought his head would reach her chin. This would be only one of the many things at which people would laugh; and all her life even this one thing would be a constant irritation to her, for she couldn't stand short men of any kind. In her dreams her men were always tall and strong and virile.

She sat down on the box, and now his eyes were just above the level of her own, those great dark, sombre eyes. And as she looked into them a strange feeling welled in her, a mixture of weakness and fear and revulsion. The revulsion was natural, she told herself, and she would not admit that the fear was in case he should refuse her offer; but the feeling of weakness was foreign; she could not disown it for she could lay it to no cause. He righted the bucket and sat down, and his head sank into the hollows of his shoulders, but it sank stiffly, showing that he was tensed.

He was waiting for her to speak, and when she did, his whole body suddenly raised itself and for an instant took on a look of normality.

'Do you want the bicycle shop badly?'

'Yes, very badly.' His eyes were opened wide with hope.

'I've got the money; you can have it.'

'Maggie!' He was on his feet, standing close to her, looking into her face, and she had the fleeting impression that his face looked beautiful. 'Maggie, would you?'

He actually took her hand, but she pulled it away from him, saying, 'Yes. But wait.'

'Oh, Maggie! You've got no idea what this'll mean.'

Without taking his eyes from hers, he stooped sideways and pulled the bucket closer, and sat down again with his knees practically touching hers.

'I want something in return.' Her voice was low, almost shy, but she did not move her eyes from his.

'Anything, Maggie . . . anything. I'll give you interest, or half share or partnership, or anything. I'll make a go of it if I get the chance.' He was talking with the eagerness of a boy: the weight of his thirty crippled years had fallen from him.

'I want a partnership.'

'All right, Maggie.' His eyes and lips were smiling, and his large face was moving from one pleasurable expression to another.

'But I want something else.'

'Yes?' He nodded, eager to hear more.

'I want to be married.'

The mobility of his face was halted abruptly, as if governed by a switch. 'Married!' His lips mimed the word and his brows contracted. 'But what's that got to do with the shop?'

As they stared at each other the lid on the boiler of swill was forced upwards by the steam, and potato peelings spurted out on to the floor at their feet; but neither of them took any notice. She did not reply to his question, for to her the answer seemed obvious. But apparently it wasn't to him, for he went on: 'But how can that have anything to do with lending me the money?'

Still she did not answer, and his eyes blinked once with the slow movement of an owl's and he shook his head in perplexity.

'I want you to marry me.'

She rose to her feet as she said this, and his head slowly fell backwards as his eyes travelled up the long, thin length of her to come to rest in utter amazement on her face.

She stood waiting, her jaws hurting her with the clenched tightness of her teeth; then her answer came.

Christopher began to chuckle, a thick, deep sound at first; his head rocked gently with it; then the rocking passed into his body, and his body began to rotate, scraping the bucket on the floor with its motion; then the chuckle dropped into his thin legs, bringing them off the ground. This seemed to be the signal for the release of such laughter as Maggie had never before heard. Each vibrating peal of it cut through her, tearing open the dark privacy of her tortured being. For one suspended moment an emotion, terrible in itself, rose in her, bidding her spring on him and kill him; but,

45

as if in fear of it and of the sound of his laughter, she flung around, groped for the door, and ran out of the Taggarts' enclosure, across the allotments to where the old quarry with its rim of sheltering trees began.

Christopher was on his feet, leaning against the boiler, oblivious of the steaming liquid soaking into his clothes. The laughter in his body was bubbling like the steam, and as the steam bounced the lid, so did his laughter bounce him. He began to be in pain with it, for never had he laughed like this before. Often he had thought if he could laugh at himself as if he were a natural clown then things would be easier. But laughter had rarely come to him, and when it had it was the inward kind, of a gentle quality, aroused by the fecklessness of his mother or the comic art of the twins; but never had he laughed outright at anyone, perhaps fearing that their laughter would be turned on himself.

He had been dreaming about the shop when Maggie came in, imagining it as a thriving business that would, with his hard work, furnish the four rooms above it. He had seen them filled with homely things, some perhaps that he'd even made himself. For a number of years now he had been trying to direct his desires towards inanimate objects, for these had not the power to tear the emotions into shreds. It was after David first took Ann out that his mind turned in this direction. He was twenty-four then, and fully sensible of the fact that his life must be barren of all Ann stood for.

The first year during which his brother had quite unconsciously deprived him of the only female company he was ever likely to have was one of almost exquisite torture, for he wanted, above all things, the happiness of both his brother and Ann. Yet he had protested to himself that Ann could have loved him. Wasn't it to him she had always turned in her every difficulty?

And wasn't she, even in maturity, small and slight, her dark elfishness not contrasting startlingly with his compressed body? So he reasoned that if anyone could have loved him it would have been Ann. And yesterday he had been thrown back into the vortex of that first painful year. But only for a time, for the marriage had been inevitable from the start, and when the final link joined Ann to David, he knew a feeling of freedom, which urged him more than ever to find some opening whereby he could release himself from the monotony of his days. Wild schemes had passed through his mind for purchasing Seymour's shop – he had been sitting here thinking them up – but none were so wild and fantastic as Maggie Rowan's offer.

His laughter rocked itself out, and he stood mopping his eyes. Why, in the name of God, had she made such a proposal? Had he been a straight, ordinary fellow he could have understood it. But would she have asked a straight, ordinary fellow? No; she had asked him because, like herself, he was an oddity. But again why? She could not care for him. She acted towards him as she did towards his brothers and all the men with whom she came in contact, coldly, and often at times in open hostility. Was it because Ann was married and she was feeling lonely? He knew what it was to feel lonely, with the future stretching endlessly ahead and the space inside of you growing wider each day as if to make room for the hollowness that the coming years would breed.

He thought of her face as she said, 'I want you to marry me.' In her eyes there had been grim determination and defiance, but behind these signposts of her usual attitude there glowed dimly the reflection of the loneliness which was forcing itself from the secret reserved depths of her. And he had laughed at her, laughed like a maniac.

He could not imagine why he had laughed, for his feelings now were mainly of pity. He thought: Poor Maggie! To be driven to ask the likes of me to marry her. What a pitch she must have reached to bring herself to such a point! And he had laughed! The very last thing he would have dreamed of doing. Where had she gone, running wildly like that? What if she did anything, killed herself or something? For it must have been awful to have her offer laughed to scorn, and by him!

He passed his forearm over his wet face, more to wipe away the confusion in his brain than to dry the tears of his laughter. He must go after her and tell her he didn't mean it. He would thank her for her offer, and put her mind at rest by tactfully inferring that he would forget it and that no-one in the world would ever know of it.

He ran out of the hut and across the allotment. But when he reached the gate there was no sign of Maggie. She would likely be home by now. Yet, somehow, he didn't think she would go home; she would more likely want to go and hide herself. But where? There was only the quarry.

He made for the spinney that bordered the far side of the quarry. Although it was now daylight, the trees still seemed to hold the night fast in their entwining branches, for once under them he had to stop and peer about him.

He called softly, 'Maggie, are you there?' But he received no answer. He zigzagged across the narrow belt still calling softly. And then, as he was about to retrace his steps, he saw her. Her clothes were making a darker line against the black-brown trunk of a tree. It was the last tree of the spinney, it stood sentinel above the town straggling in the valley below, seeming to be on a level with Brampton Hill; and it was towards the far hill that Maggie was looking. She seemed taller, thinner and

48

straighter than ever; the rebuff had not bowed her, and as Christopher approached he was made to feel further uneasy by the forbidding aspect of her. Whether or not she had heard him he could not tell, and he went forward hesitantly, and stood a moment by her side before saying gently, 'Maggie, I'm sorry.'

He looked at his feet as he spoke, staring unseeing at the wet swill on his boots.

She gave him no reply, but seemed to stretch herself even straighter. And he went on hurriedly, 'You know I wouldn't laugh at you really. Who am I to laugh at anybody? It was because it was so unexpected that you should . . . any one should want to marry me.'

His head remained drooped and her body remained straight, and the silence that was heavy on her fell on him. So still did they stand that a blackbird, leaving its nest, did not rush in alarm along the belt of trees, carrying a warning to the other inhabitants, but dropped on to the grassy slope below them and tugged a worm from the sward.

Christopher slowly raised his head to look up at her, and he was surprised to see no tear stains on her face; it was dry, and in this early light the mottled texture of her skin appeared freckled, and the poignant sharpness of her nose aroused in him further pity. His eyes went to her hair. She was without a hat, and even without the aid of the sun the auburn lights were gleaming in the thick coiled braids, yet he could not but think that it was lost on her.

His pity drove him on to say, 'I'll never forgive myself, Maggie. I wouldn't hurt you . . . and it won't go any further . . . I mean what's happened.'

He followed her gaze to Brampton Hill, and after what seemed to him an interminable time, he went on in tones of bewilderment, 'I . . . I didn't think

49

that you cared . . . well, could care for a fellow like me.'

'I don't . . .' The words came cold and sharp with scarcely any movement of her lips. 'Why should I?'

It was strange how her words hurt. She was hitting back, paying him for his laughter. But he was glad of this attitude, knowing that in retaliating her pain would be eased.

He forced himself to say, 'Then why did you ask such a thing?'

'I want a child.'

'A child?'

As he stared up at her his eyes filled with pain. God, the suffering of people. She must want a bairn badly to take a chance on him and another hunchback, for who could bet otherwise? Poor, poor Maggie.

His pity for her overwhelmed him, and his reasoning was lost under it, and he had no power to prevent himself saying, almost pleading, 'Would you give me a little time, Maggie, to think it over?'

For answer, she turned her head and looked down on him, surprise and hope struggling with the tortured expression of her face. She did not speak; but after a moment she turned away and walked through the trees toward home.

Christopher walked awkwardly by her side, and with each stop his brain threw thoughts at him, like quoits into a ring. He could have a shop and a home of his own; he would earn a living; no longer would he depend on the few shillings that came his way when a pig was sold, or the odd shilling slipped to him by a brother, or the selling of a few vegetables out of the garden on the sly to get himself a packet of Woodbines or a bit of baccy; there would be no more tensing himself up to go and look for jobs; no more turning away from the half-derisive, half-pitying looks of the men who said, 'Sorry, lad; the place has just been taken.' All kinds of jobs were scarce nowadays, so his chances of being set on were even less now than they would ordinarily have been; but if he were to marry Maggie, there'd be no more of this.

His mind flung yet one more thought on top of the others and its effect was almost to obliterate them: marrying Maggie meant living with her! All his days he would have to live with her, with the look of her, with her tempers and her meanness, for it was a well-known fact that she was near with money. Could he do it?

He stole a glance at her, and his question was buried under yet another thought: What if he couldn't give her a bairn? He had no proof of his potency, only proof of desires that left him weak and ashamed.

They were walking across the allotments now, and the sight of his home brought the hot colour flooding to his face . . . What would they all say to this? He knew what they would say: he was mad, and she was a hussy. That's what they'd call her when they knew she had asked him, they could never be made to believe that he had asked her, of that he was sure, and they would never understand her reason for asking him. His thoughts became still for a moment with surprise that he himself understood, yet he did.

At the allotment they parted without a word; and he went into the shed and sat down by the fire again, and became lost in a maze of pity for her and fear of the consequences of his pity.

3

A Man's Past

George Rowan stripped himself of his pit clothes with a
fierceness that suggested that each article was burning
his flesh. He threw them one after the other on to the
scullery floor, all except his shirt, and in this alone he
walked into the living-room. 'You heard what I said?'

Nellie was filling the tin bath that stood on the mat
before the blazing fire; she scooped the water carefully
with a jug out of the set pot by the side of the fireplace;
once she stopped and adjusted the newspapers laid
protectively over the gleaming fender; but she did not
answer her husband. The bath half filled, she felt the
water with her hand, then moved to the other side of
the fireplace and took two towels from the oven top and
laid them on the fender within reach of the bath.

'I tell you I'll not have it! Haven't I suffered enough!
Haven't I paid all my dam' life without having to be
made the laughing stock of the town now!'

He was talking to her back, his voice rising on an
anger that was expressed in every muscle in his body.

'Don't shout,' she said; 'and get your wash.'

His chin became knobbled and square, and his eyes
crinkled as if he were about to cry. Then he swung
round from her and stepped into the bath, and stood
for a moment looking down helplessly at the water. A

film of coal dust spread from his legs over the surface of the water, and his feet became lost beneath it.

Nellie turned and looked at him, and said as if to an errant child, 'Why didn't you wash your head first? It's no use going on like that.'

'Nellie' – his voice was almost pleading now – 'she'll listen to you. Put her off. The whole thing's indecent; Chris Taggart, with his hump, and her nearly twice his size; and looking as she does. Can't you see what people'll say?'

'If she doesn't mind, why should we?'

'Because she's barmy. She's never been like anyone else.' His voice was rising again. 'I know how she got Chris. By buying the shop for him. I bet you anything you like that's how she got him. Because even if he's hunched he's a man, and no man would take her without a bribe.'

Nellie began to set the table beneath the window, laying out knives and forks and spoons. She took a little fat, red vase filled with soft golden primroses from the sideboard and was placing it on the corner of the table when she started violently, and her hand gripped the vase, almost upsetting it, as George yelled at her, 'You'll drive me mad, an' all, woman! Why can't you talk about it and tell me what you think?'

Turning swiftly on him, no longer calm and tolerant, she met him with an anger that matched his own: 'You know what I think; you've known that for years! She's carried enough all her life; it's bewildered her. She's looked at Tom and Ann, and she can't understand why she's different, both inside and out.'

'Then it's time she knew! If Chris Taggart knew, he wouldn't have her. Aye' – he grabbed the soap and started to lather himself furiously – 'that's it! That'll put a stop to her gallop.'

53

'What about your promise?'

'I've kept it long enough . . . too long. I should have told her, and she'd have gone years ago.'

The water splashed on to the mat and on to the paper covering the fender, and even on to the shining black stove; and for once Nellie voiced no reprimand, but going to the top drawer of the sideboard she took out a Bible and stood for a moment looking down on it. Then turning to her husband, she said, her voice quiet once again, 'You wouldn't do that, George!'

'Won't I begod! Just wait and see. I'll stop this farce; she won't make a laughing stock of me.'

'George!' The name was uttered as a command, and it brought him slowly upright to face her. She had the Bible open on her palm, and after holding his eyes for a moment she began to read:

Behold, I am vile; what shall I answer Thee? I will lay mine hand upon my mouth.

Once have I spoken; but I will not answer: yea, twice; but I will proceed no further.

Then answered the Lord unto Job out of the whirlwind, and said, Gird up thy loins now like a man: I will demand of thee, and declare thou unto me.

Wilt thou also disannul my judgment? wilt thou condemn me, that thou mayest be righteous?

She repeated the last line twice, then stopped and raised her eyes to his. And he tossed his head from side to side like an unbroken colt; then burst out, 'It's no use, I can't keep it any longer.'

'All right, then!' The finality of her voice brought him to stillness again. 'If you take away the only bit of security she has, I'll leave you.'

'You wouldn't do that, Nellie?' George's whispered words hardly broke the stillness.

'You know me well enough by now to know I don't

talk for talking's sake. Once you tell her, I leave this house; and Tom goes with me.'

His long thin face seemed to become boneless, and the sagging flesh brought his lower lip to a hanging point. For a moment or so longer they stood staring at each other; then slowly George bent and picked up the flannel, and more slowly still he began to rub the soap on to it.

Nellie replaced the Bible in the drawer. Then she went to the oven, and opening it gently, looked in to ascertain how her Yorkshire was doing. She glanced at her husband. He was still rubbing the soap into the flannel, and she went to him, and without a word he handed it to her; and she walked behind him and started to wash his back. She rinsed it and dried it, and when she was finished she went into the scullery to wash the rim of coal dust from her arms. This done, she picked up the pit clothes from the floor, and going out into the garden and round to the side wall, she banged them, one after other, against it. On her return to the scullery she was again washing her hands when the bulk of Kitty Taggart waddled up the garden path.

Kitty entered the scullery, for once not chattering. She stood blinking her large, pale eyes at Nellie, and when Nellie did not raise her head to greet her she said in a sort of lost way, 'You know, Nellie?'

Nellie nodded abruptly.

'Our Sep's just told me. He's near mad. He heard it at the pit. Harry Seymour's brother told him that our Chris was going to buy the shop and that he was going to marry . . . your Maggie. It isn't true, is it?'

Nellie turned and dried her hands slowly on the roller towel on the back of the scullery door. 'Yes, it's true.'

'But, Nellie' – Kitty shook her head in much the same bewildered way that George had done – 'it isn't de – Well, I'm not saying anything against Maggie, 'cos she's your lass, and we can't all be born . . . Well, what I mean is . . . Nellie, for God's sake, say something! Tell me what you think about it.'

It was the cry that George had made.

'I think they are both lonely. And it'll work out all right if we stand by them.'

'But Nellie,' – Kitty's face gathered up in protest – 'our Chris is a nice lad. Oh, what am I sayin'!' She pulled up the bottom of her overall and began to wring it between her hands. 'What I mean is he's gentle an' quiet. An' he thinks, although you wouldn't believe it. Somehow, he's different to all the others, except Davie. Nellie, why has he done it? Somehow I can't see our Chris havin' the nerve to . . .'

Her voice trailed off, and Nellie turned on her: 'Isn't it natural that she should want a home, and perhaps a family, like everybody else?'

'Yes . . . yes, I know that.'

'Well, if you do, I should let things be. Kitty' – Nellie's voice was entreating – 'make it as easy for Chris as you can. Don't pester him.'

It was unusual for Nellie to entreat anyone, but the entreaty was lost on Kitty at this moment.

'Don't pester him! But we know nothing, only what Bill Seymour told Sep about them goin' to be married. And he hinted, likely in a Methodist church! But there's not truth in that, is there, Nellie?' Kitty took a step towards the woman whom, had her nature allowed her to put it into words, she would have said she loved. And she cried pleadingly to her now, 'You'll not let them do that, Nellie? Why, Father McSweeney'll go mad.'

Nellie stiffened. 'I don't know where they're to be married. But Ann was married in your church, Kitty, and Mr Fraser didn't go mad. And we had to bow to that. And it would be a nice return for you all to do the same.'

'Then it's cut an' dried!' Kitty wrung her hands despairingly. 'Oh, my God!' Her hands became still: 'You know something? It's just seeming to me, Nellie, that you're for the whole thing.'

'I want them to be happy.'

'An' you think our Chris'll be happy with your Maggie?' demanded Kitty in a tone she had never before used to her friend.

It was a question that Nellie could not answer, and Kitty turned from her, saying, 'Well, I might as well tell you; our Sep'll put a stop to it. An' he said George was of a like mind too . . . You hear that?' She turned her head over her shoulder and jerked her thumb in the direction of the scullery window and over the fence towards her own kitchen. 'That's our Sep shouting now . . . he's on to Pat about it, an' he'll never let it happen.'

'Sep's like a lot more,' Nellie said quietly; 'he'll learn that the people who get where they aim to go are the ones who keep their mouths shut.'

Kitty's head remained fixed over her shoulder, and she stared at Nellie for a moment longer before going out and banging the door behind her.

Nellie stood watching that fat figure waddling indignantly down the narrow garden path, and she pressed her fingers tightly to her mouth as if to forbid its trembling. Was it only a fortnight ago they were all laughing and joking at the wedding? And Kitty herself said they'd never had a wrong word. Would this business mean the severance of the bond between the two families? Two brothers marrying two sisters should strengthen the tie; but if this second marriage took place, it would more likely act as a knife cutting them adrift.

As her gaze left Kitty and travelled over the wasteland

and into the future, Nellie felt that she was sure of one thing: it was God's intention that the two misfits who had been brought up together and had remained strangers till now should be married; and it was natural that He would use her to bring about His intention – she allowed no particle of her mind to suggest that in so doing she was finding a legitimate way of getting Maggie out of her house.

4

The Oddities

Maggie had changed her route of going back and forth to work; instead of walking into the town and taking a penny bus to the door of the laundry, she now went across the allotments, through the spinney and down the valley, and so into the town by way of the old quarter. This route was much longer, but she took it because, unobtrusively, she could meet Christopher.

No meetings had been arranged between them during the three weeks that had passed since she startled him with her proposal; but, as if by chance, he would be standing at the allotment gate about a quarter past seven in the morning and again at six o'clock at night, and they would, for a few brief moments, speak together, saying the little they had to say.

Christopher had been there first the morning after they walked back from the spinney, and he had said, without looking at her, 'If it's all right with you, Maggie, I'm willin'.'

She had unfolded a very white handkerchief and blown her nose sharply, and as she walked away had said, 'I'll see about the money.'

But she didn't see about the money for some time. First, she made Christopher go and see Harry Seymour with a view to him lowering his price. But when Harry

Seymour, who had already brought the price down, wouldn't do this, there had been a deadlock for a few days. Then later, she told Christopher that she would agree to the price, and that she was going to see about furniture. She said she was going to Raymond's for it, Raymond's at the foot of Brampton Hill; and Christopher was made dumb with amazement that she had enough money to go to such a shop. She did not invite him to accompany her; nor did he make any protest.

When two weeks passed and still the business had not been settled, he became sick with anxiety lest someone else should snap up the shop from under his nose. So one morning he had gathered up his courage and said to Maggie, 'Don't you think you'd better put the deposit down in case it goes?'

It seemed that she looked at him for an endless time before answering, 'Very well.'

It was then, when they went to put down the deposit, that the cat was let out of the bag, and to use Christopher's own words, hell was let loose in the house.

He had expected an uproar, but the mass attitude of his family, with the exception of David, puzzled him. Only too well was he aware that Maggie was no prize; but then, as God knew, neither was he. Yet it seemed to him that now his people were all blind to his defects. With pathetic humility in the midst of verbal barrage, he had pointed out his main defect, his hump; and he had also pointed out that he was human enough to desire a home of his own. The only effect this had on his father and brothers was to make them repeat one phrase; over and over again they repeated it: 'Man, you must be mad!'

But his mother, once she realised that he meant to go on with this outrage, used more than one phrase. He had listened to her alternate pleading and recrimination untouched, until weeping, she said, 'Who's going to look after the pigs?' This angered him, and he had momentarily silenced her by crying, 'To hell with the pigs!'

The twins, too, had followed their elders, as always, and when he found them mimicking Maggie, he banged their heads together. They were so surprised that they made no outcry, although their heads must have rung from the concussion; and he had been so shocked by the ferocity of his action that for days afterwards he could not face them.

It became evident to him that life in the house, the life he had expected to live until he died, was finished. Whether he married Maggie or not, the easy-going, harmonious family life was over. Most of the time he felt troubled, and all the time vaguely afraid. It seemed as if a brick had hit him, and the impact had awakened a part of his mind he had not known existed. At times, too, he was weighed down by misgivings of the consequences of joining himself to Maggie, for if she did not get what she wanted how would she react?

Yet there were bright patches in his thinking; there was the shop, and only this morning it had been brought so near as to make him feel dizzy. If Maggie carried her plans through, and he never doubted for a moment but that she would, on Saturday they would be married, and the shop would be his. That Maggie too would be his he did not dwell upon; he only knew that his pity for her was such that it would make him tolerant. He was already aware that she stood greatly in need of pity and sympathy, more than he himself did; but he had found that she resented his pity, and therefore he must be careful in what ways he showed it, for pity from him must be gall to her.

She had stopped at the gate only two hours ago on

her way to work, and said, 'It can be done on Saturday morning; have you got a good suit?'

'Aye,' he had answered. 'But you don't mean this Saturday, surely?'

'Yes.'

'But this is Monday; there's only five days!'

She had looked away from his startled eyes, saying, 'The sooner the better! I saw Mr Fraser yesterday, and it can be done by special licence on Saturday.'

He had wanted to exclaim, 'Special licence!' and ask, 'But why the rush now?' Yet all he said was, 'You're bent on Mr Fraser doing it?'

And she had replied in a voice that brooked no persuasion, 'I'll not be married in the Catholic church.'

And as she moved off she had said, 'The Seymours are leaving on Friday; we can settle up things with them on Thursday night. And, Christopher—' She had stopped and turned towards him again. It was the first time she had used his name, and it sounded clipped and strange on her lips. And she paused after saying it, as if in surprise at its having slipped out. Then she went on, 'Don't say anything to anybody.'

'Not Davie?'

'No. He'll tell her, and she'll tell me father. I don't want him . . . or anybody to know.'

There was an odd and unusual note of pleading in her voice, but he said, 'I'll have to tell Davie. He's been decent, and I'd like him to be there. Have you told your mother?'

'Yes, she knows, but she'll say nothing.'

'Well, Davie won't either.'

'He'll tell her, he's bound to.' She sucked her lips in between her teeth.

'I'll ask him not to. I've got to have somebody of me own there.'

She breathed deeply, and dropped her gaze to the ground. And it seemed to him she had suddenly become tired, as if, having been fighting someone or something, the uselessness of the struggle was now becoming apparent to her. But as he watched her walking away along the allotment path, the straightness of her back and the briskness of her step betrayed no faltering, and he thought: Even if she was tired or beaten she'd go on; if she wanted something badly enough, she would get it. And he wondered why he had been blind to the strength of her all these years.

He was on his way now to see David, the only one besides Mrs Rowan who still had a decent word for either him or Maggie. But what would David say when he was told they were to be married on Saturday morning on the quiet? And in the Methodist church, at that! This had seemed, even to him, the last straw.

As he knocked on David's back door, David's face appeared at the kitchen window, and he cried, 'Why, come on in, man. What you knocking there for?'

Christopher walked through the scullery, skirting the tin bath standing at the foot of the wash-house boiler, and entered the kitchen. Ann turned from the fire where she was splashing eggs with boiling fat, her face rosy and happy, and she said, 'Hallo, Chris. Come and sit down. I'll pour you out a cup of tea in a minute. Would you like something to eat?'

'Thanks all the same, Ann, but I've just had me breakfast.' He sat down and looked towards David who, with knees bent to bring his height down to the level of the mirror, was endeavouring to brush his wet hair flat across his head.

'Ever see anything like this?' David spoke to Christopher through the mirror. 'She's fixed this so as she can see in it.'

Ann turned from the fire and smiled at Christopher, and he smiled back; and David said, 'Aye, you can laugh. And what d'you think of me having to wash in the scullery, Chris? We never did that at home, did we? And no pit clothes allowed in the kitchen either, mind. Can you imagine me standing for it?'

'It's about time you were taken in hand, anyway,' said Christopher, nodding conspiratorially towards Ann.

'Oh, is it? Well, what d'you think of the latest? you know what she did on Saturday?'

'Oh, David, be quiet, and come and have your breakfast.'

Ann lifted three eggs from the frying pan and placed them on a dinner plate by the side of a thick slice of ham and two fat sausages.

And David said, 'She doesn't want me to tell you, she's ashamed. By, if me mother only knew, she'd go mad.' He winked at his brother and pulled up a chair to the table; and lifting his knife and fork, one in each fist, he thumped their handles on the table in added emphasis to each word: 'She bought a loaf of bread! What d'you think of that?'

'And it won't be the last!' Ann placed the plate before him and turned to Christopher: 'He eats so much. I baked twice last week. He seems to forget I'm not me mother, or his mother; it's nineteen thirty-six not nineteen hundred and six.'

'And she burnt two loaves and forgot to put the yeast in the tea cakes.' David continued his teasing. 'That's what comes of working in a shop instead of going into service and learning how to look after a man. And now she's demanding a gas stove . . . with a fine modern range like that there!' He jerked his fork in the direction of the stove and nodded gravely at Christopher.

64

Christopher looked from one to the other. They were laughing at each other now; they looked close and entwined, they looked married, they sounded married. And he had never heard David talk so much – his happiness oozed out of him.

Christopher felt an ache within him for this comradeship that would never be his; for no matter on what plane his life with Maggie fell, he could never see himself teasing or chaffing her.

Ann left the kitchen to answer the front door, and he leant across the table and whispered to David, 'Can I have a word with you?'

'Now?' David raised his eyes from his plate. 'I'm just off to bed, man.'

'Couldn't you come as far as the gate with me?'

'Aye, I suppose I could.'

There fell on them now a constrained silence, and when Ann returned the light-hearted chaffing was not resumed.

Christopher stood up saying, 'I'd best be off; Cora's about due.'

'Oh, is she?' cried Ann, her face lighting up. 'Oh, I hope it's a big litter.'

'Aye, I hope so,' Christopher replied. But he knew he did not care whether it was or not, for this was the last of Cora's prolificities he would attend, and like his mother on any occasion for thanksgiving he added, but mutely, 'Thanks be to God.'

Ann watched the brothers walking down the narrow strip of garden to the gate. As David moved his shirt was drawn tight against the muscles of his back, and his height was emphasised by its relative contrast with Christopher's; and alongside the ever-present feeling of pride in her man there was renewed in her a deepened sympathy for Christopher. Poor Christopher. She watched him now talking rapidly and urgently; then she saw David's head jerk upwards and shake emphatically, and she wondered what it was Christopher could be asking. Likely something connected with this other business. She referred to the proposed marriage as the other business; she would not refer to it as a wedding, for the thought of it shocked her; she was heartily in sympathy with the Taggarts' reaction to it. Her mother's sympathetic attitude she could understand up to a point, for perhaps underlying the desire to see Maggie married lay the fact that her mother would be glad to be rid of her. But David's attitude she couldn't understand at all, because he liked Chris and he knew what Maggie was; yet, practically from the very first, he was in favour of her marrying Chris. She couldn't understand it.

But now she could see by his motions that he was refusing Chris something. She turned from the window in case they should think she was spying on them, and set about clearing the table. Her small, pointed face dropped into thoughtful lines, and she wondered why such happiness as was hers could not obliterate all the unpleasant things in life.

Marriage, she was finding, changed one completely. It was as if it released a mature self and life was met through this new being; and life was brighter and yet at the same time darker; darker for her, because the possibility of something happening to David down the pit was fast turning into a nightmare; she had been unable to erase from her mind the memory of the accident that had broken up her wedding party. She had been assured by her mother that this feeling would fade with time but she doubted it, for her fear of the pit was bottomless.

When David returned to the kitchen, he went to the mantel-piece and picked up his pipe before remarking,

'It's a grand mornin'; I wish I hadn't to go to bed.'

Ann did not reply, but pushed up the kitchen window to let the smell of the cooking out and the fresh warm air in. Now, because he made no reference to Chris's visit, she was certain something was afoot, and, too, that he had no intention of telling her what it was; and she was piqued into asking:

'What did Chris want at this time of morning? He's never been round so early before.'

David's immediate reaction was to scrape the inside of his pipe with his knife. This startled her and she thrust her fingers into her ears and cried, 'Oh, don't!'

And he laughed and said apologetically, 'I'm sorry, lass. I keep forgetting . . . You know, it's funny, but me ma liked to hear the scraping of a knife inside a pipe.'

'Well, I don't; it goes to my very heart.' She flung her head from side to side.

He laid the pipe down and pulled her to him, and held her close in his arms, and she forgot about Chris and the pipe, and almost everything else for the moment. His lips moved in her hair, and she shivered as he traced them down to her ear.

'Wish you were single again?'

'No – never. Do you?'

'Mm-mm!'

'What?'

The laughter rumbled in his chest. 'Love me?'

'No.'

'No?' He pressed her closer. 'Love me?'

She rubbed her nose through the opening of his shirt and on to his chest; and she nipped at the thick layer of curly fair hair, and he jumped, crying, 'You little devil!' He whipped her off the ground as if she was a child; and she struggled in his arms and pulled at his hair, very much as a child would have done. Then he lowered her gently down, and as if by common consent, they both stopped their playing and became still. And he said, 'I can't believe I've got you.'

She pressed her head against him and whispered, 'Well, you have.'

Then out of the stillness that enclosed them she asked: 'What did Chris want?'

He reached out with one hand for his pipe again. 'He didn't want anything.'

She tweaked his nose, saying, 'Well, what did he want you to do?'

He held the pipe in his joined hands behind her back, and moved his finger inside the bowl: 'Do? Nothing.'

'Oh don't be so close!' She sounded impatient. 'I know he wanted something. It's to do with our Maggie, isn't it?'

'Why, were you listening?'

'David!'

'Well, what makes you think it was to do with Maggie?'

'Because that's all it could do with.'

He flicked the pipe on to the table; and taking her by the shoulders held her away from him, and with his head a little to one side he surveyed her as if at that moment she had been thrust into his life and he was trying to fathom the complexities of her. 'You're so gentle and sweet and tender, and you're so soft-hearted you won't even trap a mouse; yet' – his head shook slowly – 'yet you carry this bitterness against Maggie. I can never understand that in you.'

'Oh, I don't! I don't!' She pulled herself away from him. 'You know I don't. I just don't want Chris to be hurt. I've told you over and over again that you can't imagine what our Maggie's like to live with.'

'But with Chris it'd likely be different; he's so easy goin'.'

'Meaning I'm not?'

'Now, now. Anyway, who knows why she wants to marry? It might be she wants bairns or something.'

'Bairns!' Ann's eyes opened wide and her hand went to her cheek. 'Our Maggie wanting bairns!' She gave a derisive laugh and poked her head forward at him: 'Can you imagine her with a bairn?'

He too laughed. 'No, when I come to think of it. No' – he shook his head – 'no, I can't see her having a bairn.'

'No, nor can anybody else. The top and bottom of it is that she's odd. And it's this oddness that's made her make up to Chris.'

'Oh no, Ann, I wouldn't say that.'

'Well, I would. She's always been queer . . . Oh, you don't know what she's like! You'd have to live with her.'

'Aye' – David rubbed the bottom of his nose, his prelude to humour, and his grey eyes almost disappeared between his narrowed lids – 'aye, I would.' Then he moved one leg against the other in the attitude of a shy youngster and asked, 'And if I did, would you mind me giving her one of the ten bairns that you've booked up?'

'Oh, David Taggart!' She fell on him, and he caught her up, and again they were lost in laughter, until he said, 'Come on.'

He picked up his baccy tin, matches and pipe, and she murmured, 'Let me bolt the back door, then.'

He watched her go to the kitchen door, and he too started when, on opening it, she let out a piercing squeal. In two strides he was standing behind her looking down at the twins lying in a heap at her feet.

'What the . . . !' David was on them before they could scramble up and make their retreat. Simultaneously he lifted them by the collars of their coats. 'What the devil are you at now?'

'We weren't listening; we weren't keeking – we fell; didn't we, Peter? We knocked on the back door afore we come in didn't we, Peter?'

'Aye, we did . . . Aw! Our Davie – stop it! You're choking us!'

'For two pins I'd take your pants down and skelp your backsides! Why aren't you at school, eh? Just wait till your da knows about this.'

Each word was accompanied by a shake, and with each shake the twins jerked out, 'Oh, our Davie, give ower!'

Ann stood looking at them, her hand pressed to her mouth. 'Leave them be,' she said.

And David repeated, 'Leave them be! Aye; but me da won't leave them be when he hears of this . . . peeping through keyholes!' He released his hold on them, and like greased lightning they were off, just missing tumbling into the bath of dirty water in their scrambling exit.

This last incident brought a laugh from David, and he shot the bolt and went back into the kitchen, saying, 'They're the devil's own spawn, those two. I bet you what you like they're playing the nick from school, and they came round here for some grub to take into the country.' He threw back his head and laughed loudly 'Oh, the times I've played the nick! . . . You ever play the nick? No, of course you didn't . . . Come on.' He put his arm about her and drew her out of the kitchen and up the stairs.

But she could not laugh with him; nor could she, when she lay in his arms, respond wholeheartedly to him; for her mind was racing about trying to piece together what they had been saying about Maggie.

If the twins had been there all the time, then it wouldn't be long before they began to pantomime what they had seen and heard. They could pantomime what they liked about her and David, but suppose they repeated what she had said about Maggie. She became sick with the thought; and it came to her that she was afraid of Maggie, that she always had been afraid of her; for Maggie was powerful, and she was afraid of this power being directed against her. Suddenly she shivered and David's arms tightened about her, and to his utter astonishment, she burst into tears.

'Fifty pounds!' exclaimed Kitty Taggart. 'Do you mean to say himself is going to lend fifty pounds?'

'Not out of his own pocket – he hasn't got fifty pence. But he's seen the club committee and put it to them that it'd be a sound investment. And they're goin' to do it. That's what he said.'

'Thanks be to God.' Kitty turned from her husband and addressed herself to the picture of the sacred heart hanging above the mantelpiece. She blessed herself solemnly, and her three sons sitting about the table did not as usual chip her; but they too looked towards the picture as if inwardly voicing her sentiments.

'What about the rest?' Pat looked at his father, who was divesting himself of his pit clothes, preparatory to washing.

'George is going to see a money-lender.' Sep turned towards the fire as he gave this information and reached for the kettle.

'A money-lender!' Kitty and her sons ejaculated the words as by one voice.

'Aye. It just happens he's got an insurance due in two years' time . . . it's for twenty-five pounds . . . he might get an advance on it. And Chris could pay the interest just like he would if he was borrowing it hissel.'

'Eeh! Not that insurance. Why strikes, death or disaster, Nellie's gone without to keep them payments going. Even after George was off them ten weeks she paid every penny up . . . What if she gets to know?'

Sep turned on his wife: 'If you don't tell her, she won't know nowt. Least, not till she finds the policy gone. You keep your mouth shut, and everything'll be all right.'

Pat Taggart reached out for the sugar-basin, and ladled four heaped teaspoons of sugar into his half-cup of tea. He shook his head during the operation and murmured, ''Tisn't natural somehow to me.' He pushed the sugar-basin away from him with an impatient movement. 'It's dam' funny, that's what it is.'

'What's funny about what?' his father enquired.

'About old George,' said Pat. 'It's understandable that we don't want our Chris to marry Maggie, but what I can't make out is all the trouble old Rowan's goin' to to stop her doing it. It's as if he hated her guts; and no matter what she looks like, she's his own flesh and blood after all.'

'Well, perhaps it is understandable.' Alec, who was two years younger than Christopher, spoke up. 'I can see George's point of view; our Chris isn't everybody's cup of tea, is he?' His eyes ranged from one member of the family to another, expecting confirmation of his opinion. But when no-one answered him, he went on, 'Perhaps it isn't that George hates her at all, he just doesn't want her to marry a bloke like our Chris.'

'You look here.' Pat leant across the table. 'Our Chris might have a hump, but he's worth something better than Maggie Rowan! And he's your brother, don't forget.'

'Who you bawlin' at?' Alec glared at Pat. 'You were all for Maggie Rowan a minute ago!'

'I was, like hell! Don't be daft, man; I was just saying . . .'

'Be quiet, the pair of you!' Kitty could be silenced by her husband, but she in her turn could at times like the present still command her sons. She reached to the hob for the enormous brown teapot, and proceeded to fill the cups of the scowling men. 'Be quiet, you, Pat! And no more of it. And go canny with that sugar. If you want to put four spoons in wait till you get home. Now' – she thumped the pot back on to the hob and turned to her husband – 'if you're as sure of the money as you make out, isn't it about time he was told?'

Sep, vigorously washing himself, nodded, and said, 'Aye, you're right. The sooner the better, an' all, for I feel she's up to something by what George says. And he says she's as deep as a drawn well, and cute into the bargain. Aye, he'd better be told. Get the bairns to go and fetch him.'

Kitty went to the back door and shouted, 'You, Peter! You, Alan!'

When there was no response to her call she stumped through the kitchen and up the stairs, and there was the sound of a window being thrust up, and her voice came again, calling over the allotments, 'You, Peter! You, Alan!'

The noise of the window being banged down had hardly vibrated through the house when the twins appeared in the doorway of the kitchen. They looked at the men around the table as if they were fellow conspirators, and of a like age, and they spluttered into their hands, and Peter said, 'We was hidin' under the wash-house table all the time.'

'Go and tell Chris he's wanted. And put a move on! Go on, now!' Sep flung out his arm.

But the twins did not go on; they looked up at their father, and they said together, 'Our Chris?'

'Yes. Whose Chris do you think? Get cracking now.'

The twins looked towards their brothers, two of them with the dust of the pit still on them, and the gravity of whose faces now made them appear as old men, as old as their father. They continued to stare from one to the other, until Pat cried, 'Didn't you hear your da talking to you?' while Sep said nothing but significantly stooped down to the mat and undid his belt from round his trousers.

Even at this the twins did not turn and run, but looked at each other, their eyebrows raised comically. Then Peter said, 'But he's gone!'

Sep straightened himself, and his forehead, blue-marked from the blows of the coal, fell into corrugated lines above his grizzled brows.

'Who's gone?' Their mother was in the kitchen again. 'And why didn't you come when I called you first?' She bent threateningly towards her sons.

'Be quiet and listen.' Sep beckoned the children to him: 'What do you mean . . . he's gone?'

'Well, he went out with his best suit on. He got changed in the hut; we saw him. And our Davie was there. And then they went off.'

The men rose to their feet, their glances flashing back and forth from one to the other.

'Oh, my God, he's done it!' The shock caused Kitty to flop into a chair, and she began to rock herself, crying, 'The fool! Oh, the fool!' Then she put her apron to her face and moaned, 'Oh, my God! And himself will be round like a flash. Oh, Jesus in Heaven!'

'Shut up, woman! Look' – Sep bent to his boys – 'how long ago was it?'

'Oh, a long time, da. Straight after he took the swill.'

Sep straightened and drew in his breath. He rubbed his hands across the stubble of his chin, and for the moment there was quiet in the kitchen, until Pat said, 'Well, that's that.'

No-one seemed to find anything to add to this, and the twins, after staring at one strange member of their family after another, retreated towards the back door, only to dash back along the passage and out of the front door, for they had no desire to encounter their brother Davie. And then there was Chris with him; and they were susceptible to certain atmospheres the family was wont to create, and the present atmosphere said plainly that their Chris was in for it.

Chris entered first. He stood just within the doorway and David stood behind him looking over his head. Sep did not turn and look at his sons, but went on slowly washing himself; but Pat, Alec and Bert confronted their two brothers with looks of hostility, and it was peculiar to the situation that it was mostly towards David that the hostility was pointed.

Kitty, after one glance at Chris, turned her head and stared fixedly at the brown teapot on the hob.

It was Bert who spoke first, and to David. He'd never had much use for David, always having considered him to be too big for his boots; and now he said pointedly, 'Been organisin'?'

'What do you mean?'

'Just what I say.'

'Well, you'd better be careful what you say, else you might have to swallow it.'

Chris pressed his hand backwards on David's leg in an attempt to urge him to keep quiet. Then he took a step forward into the room, and ignoring his brothers, he addressed his father's back: 'Da, I've just married Maggie Rowan.'

75

Sep stepped out of the water and mopped himself considerably with the towel before turning to his son. When he did so, he said slowly, quietly and tersely, 'Thoo's a bloody fool!'

Chris said nothing, but his head lifted out of his shoulders and the pale skin of his face slowly turned red.

'We was getting the money for thoo; we'd uv had it by next week. It was the shop thoo married her for, wasn't it?'

The red deepened, turning to scarlet as Chris stared back at his father.

'It was, wasn't it? George was reet. Oh, thoo bloody fool! And in a chapel too!' His voice was rising now. 'My God! What we comin' to!' He flung round, and grabbing his long pants from a chair, pulled them on with a viciousness that expressed some part of his feeling.

Chris stood befogged; his father's words were amazing him. They were getting the money together to save him marrying her. He needn't have done it! He was tied for life to Maggie . . . and he needn't have done it! Suddenly he felt sick. Had she asked him to marry her without the bribe of the shop, even with his pity for her, would he have consented? No. No! He knew he never would . . . But now it was done, and he must face up to it. And as if he had gained a new courage by his mistake he did face up to it when Bert, picking up his black cap and bait tin from the table, said, 'Well, if you ask me, thoo wants locking up.'

'When I ask you it'll be time enough to stick your neb in!' The retort, flung over his shoulder and the tone in which it was delivered, brought all eyes on Chris. Even his mother stopped her crying to look at him.

The Taggart family was renowned in its own circle for its ready repartee, which would become even swifter

76

during a row; but Christopher had never been included in the aura of this talent, his usual procedure during family quarrels being to walk out or to sit quietly in the corner; and it was never quite known which side he supported.

Bert's derisive laugh as he said, 'She must have given you some spunk anyway; and by God, you'll need it!' made Chris stiffen, but no fresh retort sprang from his lips; for as quickly as his courage and anger had risen, it now fell away, and he felt deflated. What was more, he had no wish to antagonise his family further, for among his conflicting emotions there was a sense of wonderment and gratitude towards them – had they not tried to get him the shop?

He would have left things as they were and gone quietly upstairs to collect his few belongings had not David answered Bert for him.

'I can't see where you've got much room to talk; you're hard set to find your pants sometimes yersel', and you daren't say a word when Doris is wearing them either.'

'Here!' Bert threw his tin back on to the table. 'Who the hell are you getting at this morning! Throwing your weight about some, aren't you? If it's a fight you're after, by God, then you'll get it. As for anybody wearing the pants, you've picked one from a good stock, and you'll soon find it out. Her mother wears the linings an' all! I've had enough of your airs for too bloody long. Come on, out in the yard!'

Bert tore off his coat, preparing to end the quarrel in their usual way, but Kitty, rising to her feet, clutched him by the arms and thrust him into a chair. 'Now listen to me, the lot of you!' she cried. There were no tears about her now. 'There'll be no fighting here. If you want to fight, away home to your own houses, or your backyards, but you won't do it in mine. Now you put that coat on and then get out, off hyem!'

But her words did not succeed entirely in deterring Bert. Grimly he got up and pulled his coat on, saying to her, 'Well, this is not the end of it. He's been asking for it for some time, and he'll get it. Practisin' for a bloody deputy he is . . . or is it an overman? Aye, that surprised you.' He flung round on David. 'Been borrowing books from Harry Taylor, and thought nobody knew. But I'm warning you, don't come no deputy stuff on me.'

Sep took no hand in the row; he could order his wife about as if she was a half-wit, but when it came to the quelling of family squabbles he left these to her. And he had absolute faith in her powers, for never once during their forty years of married life had a blow been struck in the house. The lads had fought it out in the back lanes or in the quarry, and she had bandaged the wounds of their combats and refused to listen to the cause of them; for, as she said, they'd be as thick as thieves the morrer.

But now, as Kitty stood amidst the hot anger of her family, she had an uneasy feeling that in all the to-morrows they'd never be as thick as thieves again; and it was all through Chris . . . him she had always imagined to be the least troublesome of the whole bunch, him who had never brought a penny in – she was purposely forgetting about the pigs. Now he had upset everybody. Just think; for thirty years she had been friendly with Nellie Rowan, and now they were almost like strangers. And look at her lads, like dogs at each other's throats. And there was worse to come, for Father McSweeney himself would be round like a flea the minute he got wind of this affair. And as mad as a hatter he'd be, and lay the blame on her as like as not for letting it happen. And all this, and the fighting, and more to come, through him. She turned on Christopher, angry tears in her eyes and her voice breaking on her words: 'You're to blame! You. Aye, you!' She thrust her finger into his hollow chest. 'All this trouble because of a blasted bike shop. You've started something, you have. You'll have a lot to answer for, you'll see.' The tears were raining down her cheeks again, and her words were cutting into Christopher.

He had never been the one to want or cause trouble in his life, and now it was as she said, because he had wanted that shop he had started something. The weight of all their lives seemed to fall on him. He looked at his mother with pitying, troubled eyes. To think he could be the means of making her cry like this – he had never seen her cry before in his life – and it had all come about because Maggie Rowan wanted a bairn. The thought startled him.

And it was as if his mother heard the thought, for she cried, 'And that Maggie Rowan . . . deep as a drawn well she is. You've tied yourself to something now. There's a pair of you!' In this moment she forgot that, in spite of his deformity, next to David she considered Christopher the nicest of her brood; all she wished to do now was to inflict some hurt on him. And she succeeded when she said, 'The sight of her against you! Can you imagine it?'

'Ma . . . look here.' It was David speaking quietly and soothingly now in an endeavour to calm her. 'It's done and it can't be undone. Give them a chance to see how it'll work out.'

Kitty rounded on David. Her mouth opened to speak but her words were halted by the appearance of Fred in the passage beyond. It was unusual for this son to call in while still dressed in his pit clothes, for he lived at the far side of the town, near the Phoenix pit where he worked.

They all turned as one now and looked at him – his presence augured no good – and Bert, the only other member of the family who worked at the Phoenix pit, stepped towards him, saying, 'What's up?'

Fred walked into the kitchen. There was an air of bravado about him, but underlying it there was fear, and the fear was more apparent to the family than the bravado. He took up Bert's question: 'What's up? That's what I should be asking . . . why the mass meeting?'

For the first time since Christopher had come into the room, Pat spoke: 'Chris there has married Maggie Rowan.'

'No! So you've done it!' For a moment Fred seemed to forget whatever it was that was holding his shoulders back with unnatural straightness yet causing the corners of his mouth to droop pathetically. He stared at Christopher as though he were confronting a stranger. Then quite suddenly his shoulders adopted the lines of his mouth, and he sighed and said, 'Aye, well, she's working; that's something . . . you won't starve.'

'You got the sack!' Kitty almost screamed the words.

'But when, man?' asked Bert. 'You come up with me.'

'Harrison sent for me and told me to go to the office. Jackson gave me me cards. It was just as simple as that.'

'They can't do it! Why, man, what's the union for?'

All the men except Christopher moved forward. 'They can't do it!' All said the same thing, but in different ways.

'They've done it. The union's about as strong as me guts at this minute.'

'It's victimisation. They won't get away with it, we'll come out.'

'What did he say?'

'He said they were cutting down.'

'But you're a puller, man! And there must be pullers. They can't cut down on pullers if they want the pit to stand up. And what about your marrer?'

'He's got it an' all. We're two of the thirty . . . that was no rumour.'

'Well, don't you worry. Go to the lodge and see Buckley. We're with you, we'll come out.'

Fred sat down and the others towered over him, like eagles round a fledgling. Christopher and his marriage and everything connected with it were now forgotten, for the bread of their lives, their very life's blood, was in jeopardy. They all felt they knew why Fred, a key man in his job, had been selected for dismissal, but they would not put it into plain words. It took Kitty to voice it for them.

'Come out; come out; that's all you think about. You made your big mouth go.' Her head bounced at Fred, and his drooped before the avalanche of her tongue. 'I've told you time and again what'd come of it. Now will your talk feed your bairns? You've grumbled about your offtakes, but by God, you'll be wishing you were paying your four bob afore many weeks is over your head.'

On and on Kitty's voice went, and the men stood quiet, listening in a strained attitude as if they were learning something.

Christopher stood outside the circle of them. His father and brothers were joined together by that great welder, the pit. The hate, the necessity, yes, even the love of it, drew them together once again as a family. The power of the pit was like witchcraft; it could embody a community of stubborn, bigoted men into a bond of brotherhood, a brotherhood that stood unchallenged, for no other industry in the world united men as did a pit.

81

For the moment Chris knew he had ceased to exist, even for David, and he was relieved, yet as he turned silently from the room, he felt an added loneliness; he was indeed outside the family now.

Upstairs he gathered his few belongings together and made them into a parcel. He did not look sentimentally around the room in sorrow at leaving it; he had shared it with too many brothers for it to hold any such association; yet it did strike him that perhaps in the very near future he would give anything to be able to return to it.

This thought brought him to Maggie. He lifted his eyes from the parcel and looked at the wall. She was next door now, and likely just beyond there, doing the same as him . . . packing up. Or perhaps she was all packed up before she left the house this morning. Already he knew that one of the trials of living with her would be putting up with her methodical ways. Everything she did was done with method and purpose.

The full meaning of the last word caused him to sit down on the bed heavily, as if overcome by weakness. Maggie never did anything without a purpose. He suddenly felt helpless; he knew he should feel anger, but he felt too inadequate at the moment to feel anything so powerful . . . Maggie had known they were trying to rake up the money for him; that was why she had rushed the business. My God! She had treated him like a bit bairn. And now he felt like a bairn, a twisted, helpless bairn. His arms dropped on to his knees, and his head drooped over them, and his whole body slumped forward, emphasising the hump of his shoulders.

Only a few feet away beyond the wall, as Chris surmised, Maggie too was collecting the last of her things, and her feelings were not so far removed from his, for she too felt utterly deflated.

After the ceremony she had worked herself up to meet her father. For the first time in her life she had felt triumphant, and she had longed to see him, to witness his anger at his plans going astray. She anticipated him yelling, and she had visualised, as she walked home with her mother, the scornful silence with which she would meet it, and the curl of her lip and the loathing that would be in her eyes. She knew from experience that this look of scorn and her silence had the power to madden him more than any retort could. But before she should resort to this usual attitude she had contemplated telling him all the things that had been burning within her for years; she would have said to him, 'You hate me because I look exactly like yourself.' She had long ago come to the conclusion that this was the reason for his hatred, having purposely blinded herself to the fact that those very features that combined to make her ugliness created in him a certain attractiveness: the long face, the sharp nose, and the thin mouth, topped by a mass of thick brown hair, together with his six feet of height, gave him a certain distinction, whereas the only thing that could have relieved or softened these features on herself was a different temperament.

But her father wasn't in; he was away in Newcastle – at the money-lender's.

Like Chris, she did not waste any sentiment on her room; but just before leaving it she went to the window for one last look at Brampton Hill. But this was denied her, for the Hill was covered in sea fret, and she turned from the window abruptly and picking up her cases went down the stairs.

Her mother was standing by the table, which was covered with the best crocheted cloth, on which stood a high glass cake-stand bearing a fruit loaf. And to the side was a tea tray. On Maggie's entry, Nellie rearranged the cups, and asked quietly, 'Won't you ask Chris in for a cup of tea?'

'No; I've told you I'm going straight round.'

'Well, you'll have a cup?'

'All right.'

Maggie took the cup from her mother but did not sit down, and as hot as the tea was, she drunk it almost at once. As she placed the cup back on the table her mother said, 'Are you sure I can't give you a hand to get straight? I'm all done. It wouldn't put me out.'

'There isn't much to do; the place is pretty clean, and the furniture won't be here till this afternoon.'

'Very well, then, lass; you know your own know best.'

Nellie fiddled with the cups again; then turning sharply she went deliberately to Maggie and kissed her on the cheek, saying, 'Remember I'm always here when you want me.'

Maggie's skin flushed to a dull purple. It was the first time she could remember being kissed; even the marriage ceremony had been bare of it. She could find nothing to say; and picking up the cases, she went to the door.

Nellie passed her and opened the front door for her, and stood looking pityingly at her as she went out. But Maggie did not look at her mother, nor did she speak any word of thanks, and they parted in silence. As she crossed the road the touch of her mother's lips still lingered on her cheek, and the feeling the gesture had aroused was pressing painfully into her chest, for although her mother was the only person who had ever shown her any kindness, she could not recollect ever having been kissed by her. The pain seemed to grow with each step. It was a softening pain, breaking into and breaking down the hard core of her being.

She was hugging the pain to her as she turned round the top corner of Nicholson Street, but suddenly it was shipped away to join the other small tendernesses life had deprived her of by the sound of children's voices coming from the chimney place of the gable end.

This recess was a gathering-place for the children; it was used as headquarters for deady-one by the boys; and if the girls could get it on their own they mostly used its shelter to play shops, when the Co-operative store would do rare business, cheques of pieces of coloured paper being handed across the imaginary counter, to be collected and later returned by the recipients who would demand . . . their dividend! their dividend! This game was made more realistic if somebody was minding a bairn, which somebody usually was, and the unfortunate creature would be loaned, to be pushed and pulled and sometimes lugged while the embryo mothers waited in the queue to receive their 'divi', which took the form of a number of pebbles of varying sizes.

But to-day there was a mixed gathering of boys and girls, and the game was neither deady-one nor the Co-op, but one that pleased both sexes, for they were 'at the pictures', the actors being Peter and Alan Taggart. And the sound of their voices and the words they spoke had transfixed Maggie. She stood immobile like a breathing body embalmed in granite, unaffected by the weight of the cases as she listened to David Taggart's voice saying, 'Love me?', and the answer coming so near Ann's voice as to be her own: 'Silly billy! . . . Oh, David, ducky, ducky!'

The children roared at some pantomime that was hidden from Maggie and an iciness penetrated her apparent imperturbable poise as a voice demanded,

'Do the other bit again. Do Maggie Rowan again. Go on Alan. Do that funny part.'

'Aye . . . aye,' came the chorus. 'That part again, Alan.'

The shouted demands and the concentrated interest of the children kept their faces turned from Maggie; and Ann's voice came yet again to her, like a knife in her heart, saying, 'Our Maggie couldn't have a bairn – ha! ha! ha! – cos she's queer. Ha! ha! ha! And it would look like her if she did. Look, like this—' Peter stretched his mouth wide with the first finger and thumb of one hand, at the same time pulling down his eyes by inserting two fingers of the other hand under the first.

'And she's awful to live with, cos she's odd and barmy and up the pole. And she's lanky, like this—' This last came from Alan, who to the sound of hilarious laughter scrambled on to Peter's shoulders.

But almost instantly he slid down his brother's back again, and a whisper ran through the little crowd; and they turned their faces, showing a mixture of fear, insolence and bravado, towards Maggie. Two small girls buried their faces into each other's necks and giggled, while a bigger one admonished them, still with her eyes on Maggie, saying, 'Shurrup! You'll get wrong mind.'

The twins, adopting the ostrich attitude, sat down on their hunkers, and Maggie, her gaze fixed ahead, walked past the staring group. She went down Penelope Street, across the road and into Bush Street. She walked to the end of the street, past the shop now closed and around the corner to the back door. This she unlocked, and entered the yard. Blindly she walked through the jumble of derelict bicycles, for her eyes were almost sightless, so heavily were they misted with the effect of her rage. Mostly by feeling she unlocked the stairway door, and having locked this again she mounted the stairs to her new home.

The stairs led directly into the scullery, and from here she went into the bare kitchen and dropped the cases to the floor. Then she stood near the fireplace, away from the window, and twisted her hands together until the rubbing of the skin became painful. And through her grinding teeth she brought forth words, spitting them like acid on to the empty air. 'Talking about me like that! In front of bairns! My God! But I'll show her! Odd . . . too odd to have a bairn. I'll show her! I'll have a bairn; by all the powers I'll have a bairn! If not by him, then by somebody else. However I do it I'll have one. And more than that, too. I'll get things! I'll make him work as he's never dreamed of doing . . . Barmy, am I? Well, I'll just show her how barmy. You've got to be different to rise, and I'll rise . . . Too odd to have a bairn! Mental defectives can have bairns, but not me. My God!' She held her head between her hands and rocked it slowly.

It never occurred to her to doubt for one moment that the twins could have made up the remarks – too well she knew that they obtained their material from their elders – she would not even allow for any exaggeration; but what she did think was that if they had heard this, then there was a lot more they hadn't heard.

After a while she walked from one bare room to another – stalked would have been a better word – to see where she would put the furniture. But she seemed to be unable to decide, for she could think of nothing but Ann.

Standing in the room that was to be the bedroom, so intense was her feeling that she said aloud, 'She's got everything, and she wouldn't give me the chance even to be like other people.' Her eyes hardened until they looked like pieces of dark-green glass, and she looked down the looming years. She would best her. If it took her lifetime she would best her. She did not know how it would be brought about, but her hate would guide her. And she knew that this hate was not just something that had grown during the last hour, but that it had been there from the day Ann was born.

Slowly now, as if her thoughts were impeding her walk, she moved out on to the landing; taking off her best coat and hat she hung them on pegs on the wall, then went down the stairs that led into the back room of the shop, and at once started to sort and assess the jumble of small stock, the neglect of which, she guessed, had had a more adverse effect on the trade of the shop than the slump itself; but all the while Ann's words were being burnt indelibly into her mind.

As the time drew to half-past eleven, Chris forced home the fact to himself that he could not go on working all night; sometime he would have to go upstairs. He was longing now, with an intensity that he had not imagined possible, to be able to undo the happenings of this day. As the day wore on so many things had combined to strengthen this feeling: first, there was the matter of meals. Saturday, although a scratch day at home, always saw a good midday meal, usually sausages and mash and fried onions, with a couple of mugs of tea and likely a fresh tea-cake afterwards; but Maggie presented him with a piece of blackjack and a pennyworth of chips. She had the same herself, and they had eaten it out of the paper. This latter did not trouble him in the least; it was the meagreness of the amount that both annoyed and worried him.

It annoyed him because, not having paid for it, he felt in no position to complain; his worry was due to thoughts of the future. Apparently it wasn't in Maggie's plans that there was to be much cooking; she had already told him she would have her dinner out, and that he could close for an hour to see what he himself wanted; very definitely, too, she had no intention of ever baking, for already he had made a tea from bought bread and an order had gone in for a daily loaf. He could almost hear his mother's lamentations over this alone, for although her house might not be any too spruce, there was always home-made bread; her cooking was good and plentiful. It had to be to satisfy the demands of her menfolk.

The furniture Maggie had bought for the house startled him. Each piece was foreign to him. It might look all right in Raymond's showrooms; but in those four rooms up the stairs it made him ill at ease. There was no bedroom suite, only what she called a tallboy, and the bed was a double divan – a great flat thing, with no anchorage at head or foot, and consequently there was nowhere to throw your clothes. In the kitchen there was a gate-leg table and two chairs she called wheelbacks; no old saddle where you could put your feet up, and no chairs with the stuffing sticking out and springs that left rings on your skin. And in the front room she had a china cabinet, with thirteen panes of glass in each door, which seemed to make the thing important; and there was a little couch with spindle legs and covered with yellow cloth, so threadbare in parts that the white cotton wool of the packing showed through. There were two chairs to match this, and a group of senseless little tables that slid one under the other. That was all . . . except for a couple of thin rugs with fringes that were to be laid when the floor had been stained. One room she had left significantly unfurnished.

But these irritations concerning the food and the furniture were mere pinpricks to his main trouble, and this was that Maggie seemed more than determined to have the bigger say in the shop. From the moment their so-called dinner was finished, except for the short time it took to direct the placing of the furniture, she had been down here. She had sorted and re-sorted the contents of boxes that had not been touched for years; she had torn labels off and stuck labels on; she had made up puncture outfits from a chaotic jumble of oddments; and above everything she had listed the stocks: hour following hour she had spent adding numbers to lists, each with its own heading, which when completed, she informed him, would be entered into a ledger. She was, he saw, merely following the system she used in the laundry, but her swift reckoning that would by tomorrow night have made an inventory of every article in the shop evoked no admiration from him, for he had seen himself joyfully, if laboriously, spending most of his days for some weeks ahead in doing what she was determined to accomplish in less than two days.

Furthermore, she had already laid down laws: there was to be no tick! She was going to write out a card with the words: PLEASE DO NOT ASK FOR CREDIT AS REFUSAL OFTEN GIVES OFFENCE. The idea seemed to him suicidal. He had put it to her that no fellow these days could fork out thirty bob all at once for a second-hand bike, much less four pounds ten for one of the new ones she was aiming to stock. She had cut him short, saying, 'If they want one badly enough they'll pay. And it'll be up to you to make them want one.'

How in the name of God, he asked himself, could he make a fellow want a bike if he didn't want one? He was realising that when he had dreamed of running the shop, it was in much the same happy-go-lucky way his mother or any other member of the family would have done.

And on top of his irritation and worries there was the night to be faced. He sat down on a box and rested his head on his hands. The blind of the shop window and the door were drawn; there was no light except a weak gleam from the back room. It must be over an hour now since Maggie went upstairs. Was she in bed? Lord God! Why had he done it? He stood up and walked about the darkened shop . . . And there had been no need! They would have got him the money. She had really tricked him into it. Did ever a man feel like this, his loins weak and his stomach sick? He wouldn't have felt like this had it been Ann. He sat down on the box again, and, putting his arms on the counter, he dropped his head on to them.

For life! And he couldn't say a word to her either, for until he made a go of the shop he would depend on her even for the bite he put into his mouth.

'Thoo's a bloody fool!' His father's words rang loudly in his ears. Yes, he was a bloody fool. Besides being weakly in body he was weakly in will; he had no gumption. Had he even a little spunk he would have stood up for himself when she was mapping out their future. But who could have stood up to Maggie? Even big fellows like their Davie or Pat wouldn't have dared She had a way with her that stifled a fellow. All day he had been checking retorts, sealing them down under his tongue.

A singing voice from the street caused him to lift his head. He recognised the singer and the song . . . Roddy Jones, singing 'Get the cans, on, John Michael.'

He listened with a feeling of nostalgia as the voice drew nearer. For how many years had he lain in bed on a Saturday night and listened to that very same song? Roddy would approach his own door on the opposite side of the street, but before he entered he would finish his song. No admonition from his long-suffering wife or pushes from his pals would deter Roddy from carrying the song to its conclusion for perhaps the twentieth time that night. The respectable families in the street turned their noses up at Roddy, saying that he should live down Bogg's End if he couldn't carry his drink better. But all the Taggart men liked Roddy, for he was a good mate and a reliable man down below, and if he liked his bust-up once a week, well, that was his business.

The singing came to an abrupt ending outside the shop, and the footsteps stopped too, and Roddy's voice came thick and fuddled to Chris: 'Chris Taggart's gotta bicycle shop now . . . Aye aye. Did yer hear? Aye, lad. But he's got summack more'n a bicycle shop . . . he's got Maggie Rowan!'

'Sh, man! Sh! Come on hyem.'

'Aye, man, be quiet! Folks is abed.'

His companions coaxed him in loud whispers.

'Leave go! . . . D'ye wanna fight?'

Then Roddy's aggressive note turned to laughter: 'They're gonna give him a month afore he's back with his mother an' the pigs! D'ye knaa Alec Taggart's laid a bet? A quid if he's back, hump an' all, in a—'

Christopher was on his feet glaring at the shop floor. He knew that a hand had been clapped over Roddy's mouth, and the scuffling of feet indicated he was being dragged away. The last he heard was Roddy yelling, 'It was a shabby weddin'. Aye, a bloody dry weddin'! Hoy a ha'penny oot!'

Chris stood gripping the latch of the door. So they were betting on it, were they? He could see Alec, Pat and Bert down at the club. The talk of Fred's dismissal would have worn itself out for the present, and Alec, always the one to bring a light note or a laugh into the proceedings, had betted on him being unable to stick to the bargain he had made.

Anger, hot and searing, replaced the feeling of a moment ago. They would give him a month, would they! Then he'd be back with the pigs, would he! He'd show them. Perhaps there was something in Maggie's businesslike ways after all. They thought, since he was one of them, that if he couldn't make a go of anything with his hands there would be smaller chance with his head. But that was not all. What they were really betting on was Maggie herself, on the effect she would have on him. They knew what they were betting on, did his brothers . . .

He turned and leaned against the door . . . Yet, if he could give her what she wanted, life might be livable. And if she had a bairn it would be his, too; he would be a father, the last thing on God's earth he ever thought of being. To be able to create a bairn! he had never looked at it like this before.

He sat down again, and it was almost as if he was back in the hut on the allotment, dreaming; for in the gleam from the back shop a child appeared, and running towards him it clutched at his knees and laughed up into his face. And its face was very like his own, only better proportioned; round and fair-skinned, with fair curls bobbing on its forehead, and its body was straight. He sat on a long time with the child, and at last, shivering with the cold and not a little with an empty stomach, he mounted the stairs.

The kitchen was in darkness, so resisting the desire to go in in the hope of finding something to eat, he made straight for the bedroom. At the door he knew he must not pause, and his mind seemed to lift his body into the room. There was no light but that from the lamp at the corner of the street. This sent a pale blur through the paper blind, and he could see the slight outline of Maggie on the far side of the bed. He did not expect her to speak, and he had no indication whether she was asleep or awake. With every movement an effort, he took off all his clothes except his long pants and vest, and in these he got into the bed.

He knew that she was lying on her side, her face turned from him, and for the very life of him he could make no move to touch her. The minutes passed, ticked away by an alarm clock somewhere in the room. They mounted slowly to fifteen, and there had not been the slightest movement from Maggie, only the sound of her steady breathing. With a long-drawn sigh of relief, he told himself she was asleep. When five more minutes had passed, each filled with almost prayerful thankfulness, he turned gently on to his side and through weariness was soon asleep.

As Maggie listened to his regular breathing she questioned the force of her emotions. Why, when they had the power to tear her to shreds, could they not impinge themselves on him! Her body was not great enough to house the amount of passion that was re-creating itself within her during every second; it had to pass out and beyond her. Then why wasn't it felt by him, against whom it was directed?

She had prepared herself for bed like a woman about to undergo an operation . . . it had to be faced and got over with. But lying in the dark, she had thought, This is my wedding night . . . and her mind went to the man in Newcastle. Now had it been him coming to her . . . For a space she forgot she was as she was and the woman inside her emerged, a strangely attractive creature, her hair spread loosely over the pillow, not in two tight thick plaits, and the nightgown she was wearing was of silk, replacing the cheap cotton one, and her body was shapely with the breasts pointing upwards; and there was a perfume about her, like a baby freshly powdered.

She was still in her inner self when Chris entered the room, and when he got into bed she shrank inwardly from contact with him. She felt herself like a girl who had been given in marriage to a monstrosity. But as the minutes passed and his hands did not grope towards her, her inner self sank into the fastness where it belonged, and anger and rage and desire and humiliation fought with each other for first place in her mind. And when, after countless minutes, equal in their suffering to painful eternities, she felt him turn on to his side away from her, she wanted to fling round, screaming and clawing at him. But a wave of humiliation, so great as to sweep all other emotions before it, beat her down and she lay motionless, her eyes wide and dry. She lay like this far into the night, while Chris moved restlessly and snorted occasionally.

And once, when his feet touched hers, she had to restrain herself from kicking wildly at them – the bedclothes and the night could not hide their ludicrous largeness, and her hate found a focal point in them. When towards morning he turned unconsciously to her and his arm fell across her waist, she allowed it to remain there, refusing now to be touched by the strangeness of the contact.

5

There Are More Ways of Killing a Cat

It seemed to Ann as she stood in the lamp-house, listening to the never-ending questions of Mrs Thornton's cousin, that she must have walked here in her sleep, that she must have been hypnotized. She gazed about her at the hundreds of lamps hanging from their hooks. They looked like long silver eyes and all seemed to be staring at her, asking her was she quite mad on this lovely sunshiny morning to be going down the pit? Why she, of all people, at any time, should go down?

She had been about to leave the house to go to the Store for the meat when Maggie had come in and asked her to go down the pit. She said she was going down with Mrs Thornton's cousin who was on a visit from the South and wrote for magazines; Mrs Thornton couldn't go with her, and Miss Wentworth, Maggie said, was a snooty piece, and she didn't relish going with her alone, and she'd feel better if she had one of her own kind there . . .

At first she had just stared at Maggie in utter amazement. Then she had laughed, a shaky laugh, and said, 'Me go down the pit! Don't be silly, Maggie. Why, I'm scared to death of the pit. You know I am.'

Maggie had looked sort of down in the mouth, which somehow made her realise that this was the first thing she had asked of her, and she'd refused it! Why, she thought, couldn't she have asked something different? She would have liked to please her, for since she had been married Maggie had tried so hard to be nice, and although she couldn't make herself really like her things were easier all round when there was peace between them. But to go down a pit . . . oh no! Not for their Maggie or anyone else. No. No.

Then Maggie had begun to talk. She talked as Ann had never heard her talk before . . . about the psychological effect of facing up to fear. Somehow she had always known Maggie was clever underneath; she could remember her getting funny books from the library; but she had never imagined she could talk like this – it had been really interesting to listen to her. She said that likely the fear for David's safety would go if she actually saw where he worked. She said a lot more that made sense, about more people being killed on the open roads in a week than were killed in the pit in a year. Things like that. She even made her laugh. Fancy their Maggie making anyone laugh. She had though, when she mimicked her returning from the pit and saying to David, 'Weel, marrer, what's your kebbel like?' Weakly, she had said, 'But what about David? He'll be furious. You know how he feels about women going down.'

To which Maggie had replied, 'We won't be down an hour. He needn't know; it isn't at his pit. And when he sees you have lost your fear I should imagine he'll be thankful.'

Yes, she knew as she listened to Maggie that there was sense in everything she said, for her fear of the pit was becoming something of a trial to both her and David. But now, standing here, she felt she had been stark staring mad to have taken the slightest notice of

97

her; all the talk and reasoning in the world could never make her see the pit differently.

She looked towards the group of men. They were all listening to Miss Wentworth, whose voice, to Ann, was like background music to a walking nightmare, harsh, disturbing and endless. She was asking an old man about the lamp, and it was a relief to hear his guttural, clipped voice as he answered her: 'Yes, ma'm; the main thing is this, this double gauze shield.' He chuckled, a tolerant chuckle. 'Aye, we see they're a'reet . . . a man's life may depend on his lamp burning reet.'

A man's life! The heat was suffocating. Ann pulled at the clean white neckerchief around her neck, then eased up the cloth that covered her hair under the steel hat. She looked down at the short thick stick in her hand and at the long old coat that reached to her ankles. Added to everything else, she must look ridiculous. But looking ridiculous was nothing, it was the way she felt that mattered. She must get out and away, away from even the top of the pit. One of the lamp men had only one arm . . . that was why he was in the lamp-house . . . they gave them jobs like this when they were hurt down below. She must get away!

The old man was still explaining: 'Yes, ma'm, that piece hanging down is the oil vessel . . . Oh, that, ma'm; that's the pricker.'

There was the sound of machinery whirling some-where near, and the sound of the voices began to whirl with it . . . Miss Wentworth's and the old man's, the deputy's, and occasionally Maggie's. She was wanting to attract Maggie's attention, to tell her it was no good, that she couldn't go down, when the party began to move again.

There was a lot of laughter that was not all light-hearted when, coming out of the lamp-house, they were informed that if they were not above ground by nightfall their tallies would still be hanging on the board.

Now they were outside in the yard, and there, towering to the sky, was the pit heap, as if aiming to outdo in height the wheel itself, the wheel that let down the cages into the earth.

'Maggie!' Ann clutched Maggie's arm. 'I can't go. I've got to go home. I'm sorry, but I'm feeling a bit sick.'

Maggie did not look at her; she was looking ahead to where the others were moving towards the steps that led to the wheel-house, and she moved slowly in the same direction, her voice seeming to draw Ann with her as she said under her breath, 'Don't be silly; you can't drop out now and let me down. You'll spoil everything . . . make her embarrassed too. She mightn't go down.' Maggie's tone was soft for her, even placating.

'Why not? It won't matter.'

'Take a hold on yourself. If you ever want to conquer that fear this is the time to do it.'

As they crossed the yard eyes followed them, white eyes in black faces, in which there was neither pleasure nor pain, nor, it would seem, interest. Yet Ann felt their displeasure, even after their owners had passed from sight . . . The men didn't approve of all this; she could see it. Too often she had seen the look in the eyes of her father and of other pit-men.

When she reached the high platform her knees were on the point of giving way, and desperately she tried to take a pull at herself, for all around her were men, and coal. And there, rearing out of the centre of the platform, was the pit shaft; and level with the platform was a surprisingly small cage. For a second it was blotted out by a mist swimming before her eyes, and she groped at Maggie and whispered, 'I can't do it. I tell you it's no good!'

'Don't be a fool! And all them men looking at you!' The softness was gone now from Maggie's voice.

'It's no use, I tell you.'

'Go on!' Unobtrusively, yet fiercely, Maggie pushed her towards the cage, where already crouched in an uncomfortable and unbecoming way was Miss Wentworth.

'It's all right, miss,' said the deputy reassuringly, 'you'll be down in a minute; and it'll go slow. Won't it, Frank?'

The bankman in charge of the cage nodded; and like a marionette Ann stooped and sat on her hunkers, her knees touching Miss Wentworth's; and the deputy moved in with practised ease, calling to a man as he did so, 'You'll come down with the other lady, Willie?' Two iron bars were clipped into place across the gaping open sides of the cage, and they were off.

Ann began to pray as she had never done in her life before, gabbled entreaties that she wouldn't faint, that she would be given strength to see the thing through, that nothing would happen whilst they were down.

As they dropped into the earth, the light from their lamps showed the rough-hewn surface of the walls not more than inches from the sides of the cage. The movement was slow, almost gentle, and in no way to be compared with the drop she had heard the men speak of. And when with a slight bump the cage reached the bottom her terror for a moment was stilled; only to return with sickening force when she stepped out in to the 'road'.

The road. How often she had heard her father speak of the road, when unconsciously she had created her own picture of it: a broad road, leading from a kind of hallway in which the cage landed; the road might narrow later on and men might have to crawl, but at its beginning the road was broad and high. But now she was standing in it, and it was little broader than a passage, about ten feet wide at most and seeming to be filled with a row of small trucks, which stretched away into the blackness and were lost.

She raised her eyes to the roof, about three feet above her head, and could scarcely believe what she saw: criss-crossed pieces of wood holding up huge boulders of rock, and these pieces of wood kept in place by pit props – just pit props – seeming to form a straight wall to the passage as they disappeared in the distance; and behind them lay masses of loose rock, not coal as she had surmised, but rock.

The deputy was some yards away explaining to Miss Wentworth the process by which the coal was taken to the surface in the very cage that had brought them down, when a well-known voice behind Ann said, 'What in the name of God are you doing down here?'

She almost leaped from the ground, and she clapped her hands over her mouth to stop herself from screaming as she swung round to face Bert Taggart. She stood, hardly breathing for a moment, then gasped, 'Oh Bert! I thought it was Davie.'

'What are you doing down here?'

'I'm with Maggie and' – she nodded to Miss Wentworth – 'her. Maggie asked me to come . . . she didn't want to come by herself. But, oh, Bert . . . !'

'Does Davie know?'

She shook her head: 'No, no, of course not.'

'You'll get into a hell of a row.'

'You won't tell him, Bert?'

'Not me . . . But I thought you were scared of the pit?'

'I am; I am. Only Maggie . . . well, I thought if I saw it . . . and she said . . . Well, you know what I mean.'

'Damned if I do.'

'Hallo!' Maggie's surprise, too, on seeing Bert was genuine. She looked at him intently for some time before adding, 'Christopher said you were going with the team.'

'Aye, I was. But it meant losing a shift, and I thought better on it.' He gave a little laugh. 'They've got us scared, you see.'

'We'll be going now,' said the deputy, 'but watch your heads. You'll be able to walk upright for some way, but duck when I call out if you don't want to find yourself sitting on the rails.'

'Aye, keep yer heids doon an' your backsides up, an' ye'll be all right,' Bert laughingly cautioned them. Then as Maggie moved away, he soberly touched Ann's neckerchief, slackening it and leaving it loose around her shoulders – he did so with much the same attitude he would have used with a child. 'Keep it slack until you come up; it'll save you catchin' cold. I'll likely be gone when you come back; I'm onputting this end and my shift's nearly up.'

She nodded and tried to smile, and wondered why Davie and Bert never got on; he could be so nice. But then all the Taggarts had something nice about them. She whispered to him: 'Bert, nothing'll happen, will it?'

He gave her a slight push, saying, 'Why, no, lass. Go on.'

And she moved away in the wake of the others; and her attention was suddenly taken from herself, for, to avoid stepping into pools of water, she had to keep her lamp playing continually around her feet.

They were walking single file in no more than a breadth of three feet, for the coal trucks overhanging the track took up most of the room. But once past the end of the trucks the ground became fairly even and the deputy's voice came to her as if he was speaking through a funnel, saying, 'We'll turn off here for a minute and see the ponies.'

She stopped. Oh no; that was one thing she couldn't do, she couldn't bear to see the ponies. She would let them go on. But this escape was denied her for a man coming up behind said, 'You'd better not dawdle, lass; you'd better tag along. What you trying to do, get lost?'

'No. They're looking at the ponies; I don't want to go in.'

He brought his blackened face down to hers in genuine surprise. 'Why, miss? Why not for? They'd like to see you, they don't often see a lass.'

He took her arm, determined to prove his point, and led her off the main road and along a passage. And she saw the ponies in their stables.

They looked fat and well-kept; but oh, the poor things! Down here all their lives, after having known the freedom of running wild. Oh, it was awful. Never to see the light of day again!

Ann walked silently past the man who had brought her in, and this time he made no effort to impose his will on her. She stood at the corner of the passage adjoining the roadway, and words of her father talking to Tom came back to her: 'Stick to your pony, lad, and it's ten to one you'll escape half the accidents; the pony knows what's afoot minutes afore you do. It's a sixth sense they have. Many's the life that's been saved by a pony.'

Yes; but to keep them down here all the time. Oh, dear God! She looked about her, but her eyes could travel no distance at all before being checked by stones or props. And not only the ponies, but Davie and all those men spent half their lives in this place, and in others like it; and were really terrified, too, of being stood off – so many pits were idle. Yet she wished at this moment from the bottom of her heart that the Venus, and this one too, were idle, for then her Davie would be up above, and he'd get another job somehow. Yet this she knew was a vain hope; he'd always go back to the pit; his dream was of the day when they'd get extra shifts in and earn more money to make living a little easier . . . It wasn't right somehow.

Never having tried to reason things beyond her ken, she could not explain why it wasn't right; she had only her feelings to go by, and they kept telling her that to spend most of a lifetime down here to get money for food to enable you to live in the light for a short while wasn't right.

The deputy, leading the way into the road again, looked at her and asked, half laughingly, 'You're not scared, are you?' And when she didn't answer, he said, 'You'll be all right, there's nothing to be frightened of.'

Miss Wentworth, ignoring Ann, marched ahead on the heels of the deputy, but the man coming out of the passage asked, 'Are you afraid, lass?'

She nodded and swallowed.

'Would you like to go back?'

'Yes.'

'Don't be silly!' It was Maggie speaking, crisp and business-like. Then she smiled at the man, showing her large even teeth. 'She'll be all right. Leave her to me.'

The man walked away, reluctantly, it seemed, and Ann whispered, almost pleadingly, 'It won't work, Maggie,' to which Maggie replied, 'You've never given it a chance,' and without further words placed her hand on Ann's arm and pressed her ahead.

'Keep your heads down now.' It was the deputy's voice again, and Ann obediently bent forward. The rails, now quite close to her, began to sing, a peculiar humming noise, and when the humming grew louder the deputy called, 'There's a set of tubs coming. Now don't worry. Just stand in these little inlets here until they're past.'

Needing no further warning, Ann darted into the hole in the rock side, and Maggie joined her. Alone and seemingly unguided, the tubs came careering out of the darkness, and their noise and proximity almost made Ann scream. And in her terror she clung on to Maggie. At last they were gone, their rumble becoming fainter and fainter, leaving a strange silence in their wake. And in the silence Ann whispered, 'How do they stand it?'

'Who?' asked Maggie, moving into the road.

'The men. All their lives.'

'Well, they survive. Come on.'

'Look, Maggie; I just can't.'

'Are you going to cause a scene?' Maggie asked sharply.

'It's no good. Why are you forcing me? You seem so bent on it. I could go back alone.'

Maggie left her abruptly, and, as if still hypnotized, Ann slowly followed her.

The deputy was now pointing out the pit props, which were no longer brown but white; and this was nothing, he was saying, to what they would see when they got into the mothergate. There, fungi as big as their hands grew on the props.

Ann ceased to listen to the deputy's voice, nor was she interested in those things which were apparently peculiar to this mine, she was weighed down by the overpowering terribleness of it all; but when the party again stopped and the deputy suggested that to see just how dark the mine was they should cover up their lamps, a protest escaped her and she cried, 'Eeh, no';

whereupon Maggie took the lamp from her hand and within a few minutes they were standing in darkness, the like of which she had never imagined possible – thick, heavy, clinging darkness, that hurt the eyeballs, that became alive and pressed on you.

'Don't speak for a minute,' said the deputy.

Now silence was added . . . the darkness and silence of the eternity of the damned. It flashed through Ann's brain that the roaring flames of hell would be preferable to this, for in hell there would be sound and colour; here there was nothing yet everything, everything that was needed to bring the dark terrors of the soul to the surface.

'Oh no!' Her own suppressed scream added to her terror. And as the lamps twinkled again, their small lights appearing brilliant in contrast to the blackness, she wanted to be sick. She turned to Maggie to make yet another protest, but her words and supplicating outstretched hand were checked, for Maggie was looking queer . . . white and sickly almost as if she were about to faint. She stood gaping at her for a moment; then strangely she began to draw comfort from her sister's apparent weakness. She did not feel so alone in her fear now that a person of their Maggie's stamina could be afraid.

She said, 'What's the matter? Are you bad?'

For a moment Maggie seemed to peer through her, then shook her head in a sort of bewildered fashion before walking on, and she, pressing her teeth down into her lip, followed, until the deputy ushered them through a low trapdoor and into a passage, then through a similar door and into the mothergate which led to the coal face.

Here it was even darker and the atmosphere was so moist and warm that the road they had just left was, in comparison, as cool as though it were swept by a sea breeze.

Stumbling along in the rear and bent almost double, Ann followed on the heels of Maggie.

'All clear there?' The deputy's voice ricocheted from the walls.

And the answer came, 'Aye, Peter, all clear and respectable.'

A laugh issued from a section where no light was showing, and it appeared as if the rock itself was speaking.

Ann, still on the outskirts of the group, saw a number of men in trunks and singlets. Even from a distance most of them looked shy and awkward. They continued with their work, just lifting their heads at intervals to take a peep at the visitors.

'So this is where you get the coal?' Miss Wentworth spoke to one of the men.

'Some of it, missis.'

'And how do you get it out? You actually pick it out?'

'He don't; a hard day's work would kill him!'

The humorist, now discerned as a huddled heap doing something in the corner of the road, seemed to be the only member of the workers or party who was enjoying the situation.

'Thoo better shut the gob. What do thoo say, dep?' The man indicated his mate with a nod of his head but spoke to the deputy.

'Divvent ask the impossible, Joe.'

Now the deputy was speaking in the same idiom as the men, and Miss Wentworth, looking from one to the other, made the embarrassing statement, 'There's no master and man; you work as a team, I suppose?'

There seemed to be a rustling of bodies. The deputy

did not answer, and the man said, after a short while, 'We're all workers, miss, one way or another.'

'But some are more other than owt else.'

'Shut the gob, Joe.' It was the deputy speaking now, and for answer the man in the corner began to chuckle.

'Are they going to dig this coal out?' Miss Wentworth pointed to the seam and looked at the men.

'No. These are the stone men,' said the deputy. 'They are advancing the mothergate; they work with the pullers in there.' He pointed to an opening to the side of their feet. It was not more than twenty-one inches high. 'These are the backshift men who get ready for the nightshift and the cutters.'

As Miss Wentworth looked down at the opening she was made to exclaim, 'Not in there, surely!'

'Aye, surely,' said the deputy, now feeling more himself that at last he had astonished this hard-boiled dame. 'Get down and have a look. Get down on you . . . stomach.'

'No, no. I can see all right from here.'

But now Ann, who had been standing on the outskirts of the groups, felt herself compelled to move forward. She must see the place, or a similar place to where her Davie, for nearly seven hours a day lay on his stomach or at best crouched and swung a pick as fast as his strength would allow him.

The deputy said, 'That's right, miss; you want to see?'

Ann bent down. In the gleam of the lamps she saw what she knew to be men, but who appeared like strange, contorted animals from another world. She knew what they were doing; they were pulling out the chocks to let the roof fall.

The light gleamed on a naked arm. She could see it clearly because the sweat running down it streaked it as it went.

The deputy shouted, 'Hi, there, Michael!' and the arm stopped and the body moved round on the ground, and a face showed, all teeth and eyes. It was joined by another, and the deputy shouted again, 'I've three ladies here. Would you like them to come along?'

'Aye. Oh, aye. This is the very place for them.' The men laughed, and into Ann's tortured mind a sense of pride and wonderment forced itself for a fraction of a second. These men working in the lilliputian halls of a living hell were still able to laugh. But the wonderment fled on the thought of her David. He lay like that every day, with nothing but those little pit props to hold up the roof, to keep the thousands of tons of rock from crushing him . . . a few inches of wood defying that mighty weight! It couldn't do it, not all the time; it would give way; it would all give way; it could this very minute, now, while she was standing here! The fear for David became lost in the fear for herself . . . the place was closing in on her; she couldn't breathe . . . My God! We'll all be crushed to death; we'll never get out! Even the whispered words spelt panic, and the deputy said, 'What is it, miss?'

She turned to him and clung to his arm. 'The place'll fall in; I want to get out!'

She clasped one hand suddenly over her mouth, and the deputy said sternly, 'Now, miss, take hold of yourself. It strikes me you should never have come down, but we'll be going in just a minute. The men are showing the lady how a charge is set.' He nodded towards Miss Wentworth

A charge! An explosion! She knew what a charge was: a hole was made in the rock and the explosive put in, and then it blew up.

No power on earth, or under it, at that moment could have stayed her flight. With the fleetness of a stag she turned and ran up the roadway, skipping over the rocks, missing the roof beams as if by a succession of miracles.

The startled deputy shouted to the man who had been talking to Miss Wentworth, 'Bring them along to the cage, Joe,' as he set off after the fleeing figure. He didn't call to her, but ran with practised ease over the boulders. Yet so swift was her flight that she almost reached the trapdoor before he overtook her.

'Now, now!' He caught hold of her arm and pulled her to a stop. 'Steady on.' He was breathing hard himself. 'There's no need to run like that.'

She stood swaying on her feet. 'I want to get out.' Her mouth was hanging loose and saliva was running over her lower lip.

'You'll get out; come on. Only go steady, else you'll likely as not break your legs, and then you'll be in a worse fix. You should never have come down. Hadn't you any idea what it would be like?'

'Yes . . . no. Well, not like this. I want to get out.'

'There now, take it easy. You see, you are in the main road now and it won't be long.'

They passed an old man, a solitary figure, standing as if he was part of the inanimate depth wherein he worked.

Without preliminary explanation the deputy said, 'She shouldn't have come down,' and the old man answered 'No, God fits the nerve to the need.'

They met no-one else until they reached the cage again, and there they saw Bert. He was waiting for the cage to descend, and he turned at their approach and asked with concern, 'What's up? Nowt happened, has there?'

'A bit nervy,' said the deputy tersely.

'She should never have come down,' said Bert. 'I

got the shock of me life when I saw her.' He looked down on Ann. 'These aren't places for the likes of you. But there's nowt to be frightened about, so stop that shivering.' He put his arm firmly about her. 'Come on now, stop it. And cheer up. It would be hard lines about your coal if we all felt like that, now wouldn't it, eh? Why, lass, stop trembling; I've told you you're all right. Here's the cage. Come on, get in.'

He pushed her gently, and the deputy said, 'Will I come up with you?'

'No, I'll see to her, Peter. She's me sister-in-law, aren't you?' He put his arm about her. 'She's all right now.'

Crouched beside her, he hugged her to him, and she leaned against him, clutching at him.

As the cage moved upwards the light from above grew stronger, and she peered at the walls of the shaft, gathering to herself the rays of light . . . Oh, to be out in the light and the sun! The sun. To see the sun again. How many aeons of time had passed since she saw the sun! . . . and David. He didn't see the sun or light for over seven hours of each day, and then in the winter when he came up it was dark . . . Darkness. For days and days, darkness. Oh, David!

The cage bumped to a standstill, and with Bert's hand on her arm she stepped out on to the platform, and right to the feet of David!

Surprise at seeing him made her quite dumb, and fear of his displeasure, for a moment, stilled all her other fears. She gaped at him in a blank astonishment, for this was a David new to her. In all the years she had known him never had she seen him look like this. The coal dust of the pit still on him hid the anger that glowed in his face, but nothing could hide the fury in his eyes and the stretched tenseness of his body.

'What the hell you been up to?'

He stood threateningly over her, and she gazed up at him, frightened now in a different way, for her David never swore at her.

'For two pins I'd . . .'

His forearm lifted as if to bring the back of his hand across her face, and as she shrank from the threat Bert interposed: 'Here, steady on a minute! There's no need for that. You gone up the lum?'

'You mind your own bloody business! I'll see to you later . . . Get off home.' He made a motion with his hand as if to sweep her through the air to the very door. But she was gone, running down the steps so quickly that the men on the edge of the platform held their breath until she reached the bottom.

'Thoo's a bloody fool, that's what thoo are. A swollen-headed bloody fool!'

'Who thoo calling a bloody fool, eh? I'll let thoo see who's a fool! Get the coat off!'

'Here! Here!' The men were gathering round. 'Simmer doon, the pair of you. And you'd better get down to the ground, there's the gaffer yonder.'

'Gaffer or no gaffer,' growled David, glaring at his brother, 'I'll take it out of your hide; you'll not take any more women down when I'm finished with you . . . Did it to get one over me, didn't you?'

'What the hell you talking about?' yelled Bert. They were going down the steps now, their glances clashing. 'You're barmy! I never took her down.'

'Didn't you? Don't tell any damned lies. Thoo's been wanting to get at me for a long time, and you knew she was scared and thought that was one way of doing it.'

'You're barmy. I tell you I didn't take her down. Thoo's up the pole. But thoo's right; I have wanted to get at you for a long time and bash some of the coming deputy ideas out of that big heid of yours; and this is as good an excuse as any. I'll see you in the quarry in half an hour.' His face like thunder, Bert swung off to the lamp-house, while David stalked out of the pit yard towards home.

Long before he reached it the anger had begun to die in him and he felt ashamed, not because it had made him go for Bert, but because it had led him into almost striking Ann. Why in the name of God had he done that! Lifted his hand to her when all he wanted was to crush her in his arms. Why did the damned authorities allow women to go down the pit, anyway? It should be put a stop to. Her poor little face; she looked scared to the very marrow. And he had acted like a blasted unthinking fool.

The house was empty. He ran up the stairs, then down again, taking them three at a time now, and when he reached the back door George Rowan confronted him.

'Where is she?'

'With her mother. I've been for the doctor.'

'Doctor? Why?'

'She's having hysterics or something. Look, Davie . . . did you hit her? I can't believe you did but she keeps on saying . . .'

David lowered his head and said, 'I nearly did. I was near mad. I had just come up and I met Bob Donelly, and he said she was down the Phoenix. He said he saw her with Bert, just before he came up.' David screwed up his eyes and stared at his father-in-law, then went on, 'Her going down a pit when she's always on about it! And trying to get me to leave, in times like these an' all! She's petrified of the pit. And she wouldn't have gone down unless she'd been persuaded; and our Bert's the right one to persuade anybody when he takes it into his head. And it was done to get at me. And I was mad

113

at her because she went.' He rubbed his hand over his face. 'I can't explain it, but when I raised my hand it was with a sort of relief at seeing her safe again.'

'Well, she's your wife and I don't want to interfere, but she's still my lass, and I wouldn't stand for anyone raising a hand to her. But I can guess how you felt right enough. Yet, if you ask me, it wasn't Bert's fault. I haven't got to the bottom of it yet, but you know Maggie was with her?'

'No, I didn't.'

'Well, she was. And between you and me I guess there's more in it than meets the eye. You can never tell with our Maggie. And there's never been any love lost between her and Ann. No' – George looked away – 'there's deep wells in that 'un.'

'But why should she want to take her down the pit? It doesn't make sense.'

'On the face of it, no, but our Maggie always had her own way of working.'

George made to go, saying, 'If I was you I'd leave Ann to her mother for a time; I've never seen her in such a stew before.' He paused and rubbed his chin, and asked diffidently, 'Has anything happened?'

'You mean . . . ?' A redness appeared in David's cheekbones. 'Not that I know of.'

'Well, I only thought. They don't usually go haywire like that, even with going down the pit. Well, I'll be seeing you.'

George walked away, and David stared after him, a feeling of panic now racing through his body. If she had fallen with a bairn and he had raised his hand to her!

He had dreamed lately what would happen when she told him. He saw himself fetching and carrying for her; not that she would want that kind of thing, but she would let him because she knew he would want to share in the burden of it. But it would be no burden to her, for she was quite crazy to start having bairns.

Mechanically he closed the door behind him and walked up the street and along the road towards the allotments, and as he neared them he saw Bert. And they met on the pathway and were forced to walk within yards of each other towards the quarry. And David suddenly thought: This is mad. Life's mad. It's all twisted. You are made to do things you'd never dream of doing; I don't really want to hit Bert no more than I wanted to hit her.

They passed through the spinney and clambered down the rocks, then threw their coats on the ground and faced each other.

If Christopher had been asked what he wanted most he would have answered unhesitatingly to work up a good custom in the shop. To be kept busy all day serving was now his idea of heaven, and although his dream was far from being realised, he had been elated with the events of this particular morning, for hadn't young Stanley Pearson bought a new bike? With cash at that! He had landed a job in Newcastle and he aimed to ride there to save bus fares. His boss was paying for the bike, and he was going to pay him back. That was the kind of job to get. Smart lad, Stanley; no pit for him.

And that wasn't all. He had also sold two second-hand bikes. They were only fifteen bob each, admitted, but he had not before sold two second-hand bikes in one day. Yes, it had been a good morning . . . Until one o'clock, until his mother had rushed in in a tear to say that Bert and Davie had been fighting in the quarry, and that Bert had had to go and have his eye stitched, while Davie's mouth was so swollen and his face so battered he'd not see out of his eyes the morrer. And it was all because Davie thought Bert had taken Ann down the pit. And that was not all. Ann had run home to Nellie and had a dose of hysterics, and the doctor had to be fetched, and he gave her a good talking to. But that didn't do any good, so he gave her an injection; and now she was asleep. And there was their Davie like somebody mad, tearing his hair and walking the floor. And George Rowan was just as bad, for he was blaming Maggie. Now wasn't that a damn silly thing to do.

'I want to be fair,' his mother had said, nodding at him. 'You know there's no love lost between your Maggie and me – we'd get on best in two different countries – but as I said, likely she asked Ann to go down with her to have one of her own kind there instead of being alone with this visitor of Mrs Thornton's. You know how it is with your own kind. But there's George – he won't listen to a word of it. You know he's as stubborn as a mule and he's got some daft silly idea into his head that your Maggie took Ann down on purpose, to give her these hysterics. You know, sometimes I think George Rowan hasn't a happorth of sense. It's as our Pat says, he's a bit barmy where your Maggie's concerned.'

His mother had paused here, and looking at him closely had said, 'It's her I came to ask you about. Why has she gone running up on the fells?'

'Who?' he had asked.

'Maggie.'

'Maggie on the fells!' he repeated dully.

'Yes, your Maggie,' she said emphatically.

He could never accustom himself to hearing the possessive 'your' applied to himself indicating his ownership of Maggie, for nothing could be further from the truth.

'I was coming out of Nellie's – I haven't been in much lately as you know, since your business' – she

116

nodded significantly – 'but hearing Ann go on like that I just had to. And as I was coming out I ran into Singy Baker. Humming away to herself as usual she was, she had just got off the Newcastle bus. And she said they were passing Brampton Hill when she saw Maggie. She was taking the road to the fells and suddenly she started to run as if the devil was after her.'

'But was it Maggie?'

'There isn't two Maggies.'

On this cutting truth he lowered his gaze to the counter.

'What do you make of it?' his mother asked.

What could he make of it? Women didn't run unless they had to. Young lasses might; but married women didn't run, unless it was after a bairn. And why should Maggie want to run across the fells? She wasn't given to taking walks. Why was she on the fells at all? The fells were for courting couples or Sunday-afternoon jaunts.

After his mother left he went into the back shop, and sitting down, tried to make something of the whole business. And this much he did make. Like George Rowan, he believed that Maggie had taken Ann down the pit for some purpose of her own. During the few months they had lived together her hatred of Ann had made itself apparent to him. He had gauged it from nothing she had said or done; it puzzled him how he knew, but know he did. The feeling of bitterness seemed to emanate from her when she was in Ann's presence.

He looked at the clock. Three o'clock and she wasn't back yet. What could she be doing? Surely she wouldn't still be on the fells.

At this point the shop-door bell rang, and he went to serve a customer, and as he handed the man his change the bell rang again and Maggie came into the shop. This in itself was unusual, for she never came in the shop way, but more unusual was the look on her face. His first thought was that she was drunk, for the cold green of her eyes was thawed into an expression he had seen only in the eyes of a drunk – the happy, bemused, glazed expression.

She went into the back shop and he followed the man to the door and slipped the bolt in. When he reached the back room Maggie was standing waiting for him. She did not speak, and he told himself that there was something up with her; she was drunk, or something. For a moment he assumed the right of a husband and asked, 'Where have you been?'

Her lips moved slowly, as if she hadn't full control of them, and then she said, quite softly, 'On the fells.'

'On the fells!' he repeated. 'What for?'

She turned from him and looked up at a shelf piled high with cardboard boxes, and still softly she answered, 'I was running.'

She's going off her head, he thought, and repeated her words again, 'You were running?'

'Yes, running! Running!' Her voice rose and her face widened into a smile as she continued to stare at the boxes, and he knew she was gone from him and this room and was where she had been while she was running. Then slowly she turned to him again and said, 'I was happy. For the first time in my life I was happy, and I had to run and run until I could run no more. I knew what it was to feel joy; I was a woman. Yes, can you believe that?'

Her head bent towards him and her tone changed, and for a moment she became the old Maggie. 'I'll likely never speak to you again in this way. But for these few minutes I'm not Maggie Rowan or Maggie Taggart; I'm myself, and this is my day.'

She swung round from him in the manner of a

young frisky girl, and her voice became thick again and soft. 'It was down in the pit it started. The pit is like me in some ways, or I'm like it, deep and dark, always clutching at something to lighten the darkness, like the white stuff on the props.'

She looked over her shoulder at him with an almost coy look that made her face repulsive. 'You think I've gone barmy, don't you? Don't worry, I haven't. And you'll never see me like this again.'

I hope to God not, he thought. She's off her head in some way; they always say they aren't when they are.

Her mentioning of the pit recalled Ann to his mind, and although he felt it wasn't much use bringing up the matter now, he said, 'Why did you take Ann down the pit?'

'Ann! Ann!' The name seemed to bring her fully to herself, and it was the old Maggie speaking again as she swung round on him: 'Ann! Huh! The wonderful Ann, who's not even fit to be a miner's wife. She hasn't the guts of a chicken. If you could have seen her.'

'You shouldn't have taken her down. She's bad, she's had to have the doctor.'

'Poor soul!' Her voice was mocking. 'But at present we won't talk about Ann, we'll talk about us . . . about me!'

Her voice was dropping again, and he looked at her apprehensively. 'I've got something to tell you,' she went on. 'Anybody but you would have guessed. But you haven't guessed, have you?' Her voice changed suddenly and she bit out the words now. 'You're like her, you didn't think I could manage it, did you? Well . . . I have. I'm going to have a baby. I've been to the doctor's.'

He stared at her, silent and shocked. He wasn't shocked at the fact that she was going to have a baby, although he was amazed that this should have come about through one weak effort, but he was shocked at her reactions.

Now she was standing with both hands inside her open coat, covering her stomach, in an attitude that he was sure no woman, even in Bogg's End, would dream of doing. She looked triumphant and brazen, and for the moment he was appalled that in spurring himself to that effort a seed of life, his seed, was living and growing behind that uncomely and almost fleshless wall of her body . . . Without love, without passion, even without lust, a child had been created.

'You don't say anything, you even look scared.' Her voice was taunting.

'What is there to say?'

The shop bell jangled; and when it rang for the third time, she said, 'Go on, you'd better open it.'

He made no move; and she went on, 'The bargain's more square now. You've got the shop, and I've the child. It'll be my child. You understand that? Mine!'

There followed a silence during which each looked deep into the other's eyes. Then turning from him she said, 'Go on. Open the door.'

He watched her go up the stairs. She was gone, but her words still vibrated round the room: 'My child, mind. Mine!'

The bell jangled violently again, and staring wide-eyed as if awakening from a dream he went to answer it. As he walked through the shop he looked about it with new eyes, and he saw that it didn't amount to much; its glamour, all of a sudden, had faded.

Part Two
Tom

6

Maggie's Son

'Hell, but it's hot.'

'Aye, I bet it is down there.'

'Come off it, Tommy, and don't start preaching at me.'

'You're the last bloke on earth, Davie, I'd dare to preach to. I was only stating a fact. It will be hot down there.'

'You really believe there's such a place?'

'Aye, Davie, I do. If I didn't I couldn't believe in God and His justice. For instance, fancy thinking that Hitler'll get off for what he's done, and is doing, and at this very minute.'

'Aye, there's that in it.' David hesitated with the water-bottle to his mouth. 'I wonder if they've got them all off.'

'Aye, I wonder.'

'They say the trains were crammed yesterday, and with Frenchmen an' all. It's worse for them, I think. Fancy little boats that's done nowt but hug the coast all their lives daring the Channel.'

'And the waters were stilled for them!'

'Aye, an act of God, eh, Tommy?' David knelt back on his hunkers and drew his forearm across his brow.

'I wish an act of God would finish this shift. What's the time, there?'

Tom screwed round and looked along the face to the legs of the men moving in the dim light beyond. 'How's the time going, Will?'

'Ten to four.'

'Ten to four,' repeated Tom. 'Ten to four on a Sunday morning.' He moved to the side of the cutting machine, and David said, 'Preaching the morrow? Or should I say the day?'

'Aye, in Lumley.'

'You should have been a parson.' Only the narrowing of the whites of David's eyes and the furthering of the gleam of his teeth showed that he was smiling tolerantly.

'No. No, I'd be no good as a parson. I'm doing what I was intended to do.'

'You like the pit? You're a funny bloke. If I had your napper I wouldn't stay down the pit.'

'Yes you would, for you know as well as me it's not the pit, it's the chaps – being among your own kind.'

'Aye, perhaps you're right. Well, there's no denying but you've got a way with your own kind.' David laughed again. 'By! They'd want to lynch many a bloke who says the things you say to them.'

'Instead, they laugh at me.'

'Aye, but it's all in good part, man. You don't take any notice of that, do you?'

'No. No, I don't. It wouldn't be any use if I did, would it?'

'No; you're right there.'

For quite a time no more was said. Their tolerant laughter was cut short by the machine starting up, and as the blade tore through the seam even their thinking was made subordinate to the noise. When it again stopped David asked casually, as if the conversation had not been interrupted, 'You ever think of getting married, Tommy?'

Tom reached out and grabbed a small pick and for no apparent reason threw it away again before answering quietly, 'Sometimes.'

'Aye. There's plenty of time. I had to wait years and years afore I could marry Ann. It's a different kettle of fish now though for the young fellows. I had to stew my guts out for years for six and six a shift, and offtakes off that, but now you young 'uns can call the tune; I could have married Ann comfortably on what the screeners are getting now. When I was screening I got eight and tuppence a week. Not that I don't think they should get it, mind . . . and more – it's not afore time – only at times I think life's a bit unfair; not so much to each man but to a generation like, for men will never toil again for a mere existence, like my dad and yours. And now there's money to be made wholesalely, an' more to come, they're nearly past it. Their lungs are so full of dust, they pant like cross-country runners. Ah well, why worry? I bet a few of those poor blokes left on Dunkirk would like to change places with them at this minute.'

The machine whirred again, and when it next stopped David said with a nonchalance that was evidently forced, 'Oh, by the way, Ann wants you to come round to tea the day. Rosalind's coming. Nice lass, Rosalind. Ever think seriously of her, Tommy?'

Squatting on his hunkers his back towards David, Tom remained still, his eyes staring at the bare, blackened flesh of his legs. So Davie knew . . . he must know. That's what he had been leading up to . . . all this talk. Could he have seen him and Beattie together? But how, when they never met except on that desolate part of the fells? Well, what did it matter? All creatures great and small . . . everyone was alike in God's eyes, and if he hoped to follow in His footsteps he must make no distinction either.

'Did you hear what I said to you?'

'Aye.'

'Well?'

'She's a nice enough lass; but not that way for me Davie.'

'What do you want? You'll not get a better-looking girl, or a nicer, I'm telling you.'

'No, I suppose not. But you see, Davie . . . Well it isn't that way with me.'

'Somebody else?'

He turned on David.

'What you asking the road you know for?' Both his voice and attitude were on the defensive.

David ran his forearm over his face, and said slowly, 'Aye; it's better to come out in the open and be above board. The fact is, Tommy, Ann's seen you twice with the Watson girl, and she's nearly worried to death. You're not serious, are you?'

'What if I am?'

David peered at Tom, and in astonishment answered, 'Why, I'd call you a bloody maniac straight away. I told Ann you must be trying your converting business on her, or something. But I can see I'm daft to think any fellow goes out with a lass to convert her. Have you thought what this means?'

'What does it mean?'

'Why, don't be so damn soft, man! You know it'll cause ructions with the family. Have you thought of what your mother'll say? And then there's other people. How long do you think you can go preaching in chapels if you go around with the likes of Beat Watson? You can't stay on the fells for ever. And I can tell you this much straight, the chaps won't stand for any of your philosophy talk when it gets around, they'll send you to hell as quick as lightning. Aw, Tommy, man!' David put his hand on the wet shoulder and gripped it. 'Have your fling, but not with the likes of her. Come on, man, see sense.'

Tom made no answer, but turned sharply away . . . It had started, as he knew it must sooner or later. He had told himself he must meet the inevitable censure with calmness, and here he was boiling inside at the first slight attack. Oh, it was no use applying parables, either to himself or to them, he wasn't out to convert Beattie to God or to anyone else, but to himself. He had fallen for her, and that was that! If they only knew her, as he did. Anyway, he didn't care two hoots what any of them thought, except . . .

His body, without losing its tenseness, lost its firmness and seemed to slump over the loose coal. If he could only make his mother understand the others wouldn't matter.

As a voice shouting 'Up!' came along the face David's hand brought him a playful punch in the ribs. 'End of another, man. Come on,' he said. The matter was closed for David; he had done as Ann urged and spoken to him. Tom would, he hoped, see sense.

They said no more but crawled along the face and into the mothergate. Here they put on their clothes before hurrying to the haulage road, and again in his good-humoured way David nudged Tom with his elbow, saying, 'Come on, man.'

And Tom was forced to respond. He glanced at his brother-in-law and gave a jerk of his head, which signified more than words that everything was all right.

As they arrived at bank Peter was waiting to go down with the incoming shift. 'Hallo, there,' he said, motioning David to one side. 'Here a minute.'

David stepped away from Tom and asked, 'What is it?'

'You heard the latest?' whispered Pat.

'About what?'

'Wor Chris.'

'No. What is it now? Maggie isn't getting him to sell motor-cars, is she?'

'Better than that, by God! He's got one of his own. Well, not a motor-car but a lorry.'

'You don't say!' The brothers stared at each other, David's brows lifting.

'It's a fact. He came round home and told me mother yesterday. It's for to cart the scrap.'

'But who's going to drive it?'

'He's goner learn, but he's hired a bloke for the time being.'

'But how could he?'

'From the Ministry, man.'

'From the Ministry?'

'Aye.' Pat was enjoying David's astonishment as his mother had enjoyed his own. 'Maggie's seen to that. Scrap's priority. I tell you, man, they'll be rolling in it afore the end of the war.'

'Fancy our Chris.' David's voice was hushed with incredulity.

'Aye, wor Chris. Who would have thought it? But look who's aback of him.'

The cage clanked once more, and David said, 'So long. I'll have to hear more of this.'

In the bath-house David imparted the news to Tom, who, although he showed surprise, gave the impression he already knew of it.

While under the shower, David shouted, 'Funny if our Chris beat the lot of us, wouldn't it?' And Tom answered, 'Why should it be funny? If you ask me, a lot of people have underestimated Chris.'

'Aye. It looks as if they must have.' There was no tinge of jealousy in David for his brother, but he could not help being amazed that he, of all of them, should show evident signs of progress. He had imagined that he himself would be the first of the Taggarts to get on, when he got his deputy's ticket . . . or if he got it.

The thought of going home now and having to read up and then write up answers to questions that might be put to him at the coming examination depressed him. He reckoned he knew as much about the pit as the next, and more; but it was this written work and oral business that was getting on his nerves. There was a list as long as his arm to be faced . . . air measurements, gas testing, knowing about the properties of the atmosphere. He knew about the properties of the atmosphere down there all right, but it was getting them on to paper and speaking about them to blokes sitting behind tables up at Chester-le-Street that was giving him the jitters. Ah well, sufficient unto the day is the evil thereof . . . By lad, he was thinking like Tom now. He looked round towards him, but he had gone.

In the yard, Tom stood watching the sun as it came up over the great mound of slack. It was touching the grimy peak with silver and rose. Sunday morning and the sun shining. His spirits rose. After all, life was good. He was going home to a good breakfast, his mother would be waiting for him; he would go to bed and sleep until two o'clock, when she would waken him to his dinner, his Sunday dinner, with piles of Yorkshires, as only she could make them; then he'd put on his best suit and go out.

His heart began to race. At four o'clock he would see Beattie. It would be for only a short while, but he would see her. And then at six o'clock he would stand in a little chapel and talk . . . His heart continued to beat fast. Yes, life was good.

Then, as had happened often of late, his thoughts suddenly flew off along an uncomfortable tangent. Why should men be dying under hails of bullets while he was living this kind of life? He had the urge now, as often, to question God's purpose, but instead, he lifted his head further back to the heavens, and the answer seemed to fall on him. Man fought against man to preserve the life that God had made good, he wasn't fighting against God . . . it was man who caused the Dunkirk beaches, not God. This soothing hand-made philosophy made him at one with the world again.

'Come on; it's too blooming early in the morning to stand there making up poetry.' David hurried past him.

'Who's making up poetry? A fellow can look at the sky, can't he?'

'What I want to look at now,' said David, 'is a plate of grub.'

They were passing out of the gates and into the main road when they were hailed by a group of men on the further pavement: 'Look here, Tom, somebody's come to meet you. Isn't this your sister's bairn?'

Both Tom and David came to a stop and stared across the road in amazement; and the child, who had been looking up at the man and chattering, shouted, 'Hallo, Uncle Tom. Hallo, Uncle Dave.'

Then he darted across the road towards them, and a man shouted, 'He says he's going down the pit when he grows up. Well, he's eager enough, anyhow. But his mother'll likely eager him when she gets her hands on him. Frightened stiff she'll be.'

'What you doing here?' David's voice was harsh.

'I come to meet you.' The child gazed joyfully up, first at one man then at the other. 'You said when I grew up you'd take me down the pit, Uncle Dave. How long will I be to be growed up?'

David glanced at Tom, who said to the child, 'You're a naughty boy. How did you get out?'

'The sun was shining and I put on me clothes by meself, and I crept out. It wasn't dark or anything. An' I turned the key. It stuck though.'

Again the men looked at each other. 'Maggie'll be nearly mad. Come on.' Tom held out his hand and the child took it, confidently offering his other to David, and walked jauntily in between them, skipping every third or fourth step.

'This'll cause a hell of a row. You want your backside smacked.' David looked down on the upturned face, thin and alert and almost a replica of George Rowan's, and the adoring look in the boy's eyes swept all harshness out of him. He loosened his hand from the child's and cuffed his head playfully; whereupon the boy swung round and hugged his leg, and David, stooping swiftly, hoisted him up into his arms.

'You little devil. You know you've been told, haven't you?'

For answer the child chuckled and rubbed his nose up and down against David's, saying, 'You're a rabbit. Can I go and have me breakfast with Auntie Ann?'

'No, you can't.'

David looked at Tom and repeated, 'There'll be a hell of a row.'

'Yes, likely. But what can you do? He can't be tied up; he's kept in enough as it is. That's what's wrong . . . her not allowing him to play on the street with the other bairns. He would come to no harm running wild a bit.'

'Me mother's going to send me to school, Uncle Tom. I'm getting new clothes. They're all green.'

The men said nothing but it seemed as if they groaned together. David thought: She's going to make a cissy out of him if she gets her way; and she'll get her way in this all right. Why doesn't Chris make a stand?

'Your neck's nice and clean, Uncle David.' The child worked his fingers inside David's collar. 'You said one day I'd see you all black. When, Uncle Dave? When?' He brought his face close to David's.

'When you grow up.'

'Oh, I'm going down to get black by meself when I grow up.'

'What can you do?' David said, turning to Tom.

Tom shook his head and laughed. And David hugged the boy closer to him.

Not much chance of him ever going down the pit with Maggie for his mother. But if he was his lad, would he want him to go down the pit? No, by God, he'd want something better for him than the pit. He could understand Maggie in this. And thinking along these lines, he could also understand Ann's fear and hate of the pit.

The boy's soft cheek against his caused a feeling that was akin to pain to assail him . . . five years now and not a sign of one. Why was it that two people who were mad about bairns didn't have them while others did things to prevent their coming? Ann, he remembered, was going to have ten. Now one would do . . . just one. One, he thought, would put her on her feet, for she had never been the same girl since that time she went down the pit; she was quieter, drawn inwards somehow; she didn't sparkle like she had done when they were first married. Oh, why worry about having bairns? It was only her that mattered, and getting her back to where she had been; although he sometimes feared that would be impossible. Anyway, he'd go and hear Tom preach the night; that would please her. Although, by God, if Father McSweeney heard of it, or his mother, there'd be hell to pay.

'Can I go and have me breakfast with Auntie Ann, then?' persisted the child.

'No, I've told you, you can't. You're going home, me lad. And you'll likely get a skelped backside. And serve you right.'

'I won't cry if I do.' The boy's face lost its softness and stiffened into a nearer resemblance than ever to that of his grandfather. 'I got wrong when I went to me grannie's last week, but I didn't cry.'

'Ah-ah,' said Tom, under his breath. 'Look along there. Now you're for it, me boy.'

The child swung round in David's arms and gazed along the road to where his mother came scurrying towards them, and the light died completely out of his face. And he said to no-one in particular, 'Well, I don't care.'

Whether it was anxiety or anger that was blanching Maggie's face David couldn't be sure, but as she came up to them he could see she was in a state, and he put the child down and greeted her soothingly with, 'Now he's all right, Maggie; and don't worry.'

Maggie looked at neither of the men for a moment, but stared down on her son, her throat working in and out and her thin lips lost under their own pressure. The boy stared unblinkingly up at her, and his defiant attitude seemed almost to break down her struggle for composure.

'He's all right; there's no harm done.'

Maggie pounced on her brother. 'No harm done! Not yet. But there soon will be with the lot of you. Getting a child out of his bed at this time in the morning!

Whose child is he, anyway? This is your father's fault!'
She turned on David.

'Me da?'

'Yes. He's always talking to him about the pit.'

'Well, I can't see how you make that out, Maggie, you seldom let him go round.' David's voice was quiet.

'He goes round . . . you know he does . . . when I'm not in. And the lot of you egg him on; then pump him up to keep quiet. I know.'

'He's got to get out some time; you can't keep him in all the time.'

'He gets out.' Maggie again turned on her brother.

'He should play with other bairns.'

'It's my business who he plays with. And remember that . . . Come on here!' She stooped and grabbed her son's hand. 'It would suit you lot to see him running the streets, wouldn't it? There's quite enough around here who do that, and I'll see he doesn't.'

'You'll never tie him to you by force or using your ownership. Give him his head, and you've got a chance to keep him.'

Tom's philosophy maddened Maggie at any time, and she almost spat at him as she said, 'Give him his head! That means let the two families make a lout of him, like the rest of you . . . Well, let me tell you, and you can pass it on to them an' all, he's going the road I choose, and no other. Tell them that.'

On this she swung off down the road, a thin gaunt string of a woman, dragging the child reluctantly after her.

When at last she turned off the main road and she knew the men could see her no more, her pace eased, and with it her temper, and she looked down on her son. And when she spoke to him now her tone bore no comparison with that she had used to the men. 'You know you've been a naughty boy, Stephen, don't you?'

The child did not answer, only tried to tug his hand from her; and she held it more firmly and went on, 'Your mummy has been worried. Didn't you know she'd be worried?'

And when he still did not answer, she stopped and drew him into a shop doorway in the yet unawakened street and, bending down, held him by the arms. 'What did you promise your mummy?'

His eyes as they gazed back at her took on a look that she hated, because it brought her father into his flesh that she deemed entirely hers. But she went on, still soft and coaxing, 'Didn't you promise your mummy that you wouldn't go to either of your grandma's alone? Didn't you? You promised me you wouldn't go, and I promised you I'd send you to that nice school.'

The child's voice too bore no resemblance to the one he had used with his uncles; it was surly now: 'I didn't go to me granny's, I went to the pit.'

'Say grandma, not granny, like I told you.'

'Grandma.'

'Now promise me you won't go to the pit any more. Promise mummy.'

'Well, can I go to me Auntie Ann'o?'

Maggie drew in her breath sharply; then said in an even quieter tone, 'When I take you.'

'Will you take me now, and we can have our breakfast with Uncle Davie?'

'No. Not now.'

'But I want to go now.'

'Mummy's busy this morning.'

'Then can me daddy take me?'

'He's busy too. Now listen, Stephen.'

'No!' He shrugged violently away from her hand and pressed himself up against the shop window. 'I'll go meself. I will go! Auntie Ann's telling me a story about a camel, and it's nearly at the end. I will go!'

Slowly Maggie raised herself up. 'You've been going to your Auntie Ann's then?'

From her voice the child realised he had given himself away, and his lips trembled, then stiffened; and she saw her father more clearly than ever in his face. 'Come on.' She took his hand again, and once more they hurried homewards. This settled it. He had been going to Ann's on the quiet! But he couldn't have gone without Christopher's knowledge. It was one thing him going to the grannies', but entirely another going to Ann's . . . Oh, if only she could be at home all day!

But was it not for him and him alone that she went out to work? And she told herself, she had laid her plans too well in the laundry to let them drop now. With the scarcity of labour and Mrs Thornton's state of health, she could see herself not only manageress, but part owner; she held the whiphand, and both she and Mrs Thornton knew it.

She'd have money, money for Stephen. There was the scrap, and the possibility of making money from that was colossal. If only this war kept on! But there was one snag in the scrap business: legally she had no finger in it. Her lips tightened when she thought where it would have been but for her. It was she who had insisted that Christopher kept it on. If he'd had his way he would have let it drop when he took the shop over. But now he considered it entirely his, although it was her brain that had thought everything out. Well, she'd think out too where the money was to be spent. And that would be on her son, to give him the right background. In any case, this morning's business had made up her mind on one point that had been fermenting for a long time. They were moving! And as soon as possible.

Six months ago it would have been impossible to get even a vacant room in Fellburn, but now, since the scare of Dunkirk, those who could were flying inland, away from a county whose name spelt ships and shipyards, mines and factories.

Maggie's thoughts went to Brampton Hill. The empty houses up there had been requisitioned by the Ministry. But it was all the same, for she knew she was still a long way from Brampton Hill. But at its foot there were bungalows, select little residences; and only yesterday she had seen a number of them up for sale. And although people, even if they wanted a house badly, wouldn't dream of buying one these days, she would buy, because they'd be going dirt cheap, and she'd take the chance of it being bombed or the Germans coming. And in doing this, she'd be on the fringe of Brampton Hill and nearer the dream of her life; and this move would take her son from the influence of the Taggarts and Ann. If only she could take Stephen there alone, leaving Christopher above the shop. But no. She waved the idea away. Left to himself and his family, she could see what would happen to the scrap, and out of the scrap bigger things than she alone could hope to achieve were beginning to loom.

As they turned the corner of the street she saw Christopher hurrying away from the house, and she called to him softly so as not to arouse the curiosity of the neighbours at this early hour. He came back towards them; but Maggie did not stop to give him any explanation; and he looked questioningly from one to the other, then walked by the side of his son. And after a little while he asked, 'Where was he?'

'At the pit.'

Christopher made no comment, but the child and he exchanged glances.

'He knows what he's going to get, he knows you'll give him the strap.'

Christopher raised his head slowly and looked at Maggie, but still he said nothing; and they entered the house without further words, until they reached the kitchen, where he forestalled her orders by saying to the child, 'Go and have a nice wash, son. Take your things off and have a wash, it's dirty down the pit.'

A sparkle came into the boy's eyes at this unexpected game of pretence, and without a look towards his mother for sanction he turned and ran from the kitchen.

Maggie stared at Christopher, and he stared back at her. During the past five years his face had undergone a change; it had lost its wide, gullible look; one would say it had hardened, that it looked almost a door, behind which were locked desires and hates that were foreign to their prison. Maggie was unable to cover the astonishment she felt as he said, 'You think you're subtle, don't you?'

Subtle. She had never even heard him use such a word; she would have said he did not know the meaning of it.

She repeated, 'Subtle! What d'you mean?'

'You know what I mean all right. I'm tired, sick and tired of it, and I'm going to have me say now.'

'Say on.' Her lip curled sarcastically.

'Aye, I'll say on. From the start I've been allowed no say in him.' He nodded towards the door. 'That's right, isn't it? He was yours . . . your bargain!' His teeth met on the word.

'Well, what if he was? You knew what you were taking on.'

'Yes. Yes, I did. But I didn't think you wouldn't let me touch him or look at him if you could help it. You kept me out of the picture, until he started to show you that he wasn't just a doll for you to play with but had a mind of his own. It was then he began to notice me. Yes, go on, you can sneer.

'He didn't see me like you did. I was his da . . . I am his da! And what did you do? You decided to make me a bogey, didn't you? Every time he defied you it was, "Your daddy will punish you, mind".' He mimicked her as he said this. 'You even ordered me to strap him with me belt, didn't you? Yet you used to pretend horror at the ignorance that made women belt their bairns.' He paused as if to give her a chance to say something. Maggie, however, made no retort, her face was stiff and her green eyes were misted, but the mist was like the smoke that covers a cauldron of boiling tar. And he went on, 'I was on to you from the start. You're not as clever as you think, you know. You wanted me to belt him so he'd run to his mummy.' Again he mimicked her. 'Well, I can tell you this. He's never once been belted by me. Aye, you can stare . . . Coo you heard him yelling? Well, two can play at the same game . . . even three. Work that one out. And I'll tell you something else while I'm at it. You'll never keep him. You might as well try to bridle your own father, for he's more him than either you or me.'

Now Maggie did speak. She let flow a torrent of words so rapid that he couldn't follow her flying thoughts. The hate of her father poured out, and the scorn of the Taggart family. The determination to keep the child hers was writ large on every denouncement. And finally she came to Christopher himself.

And what was he before she took him in hand? Keeper of two pigs! An object of pity to all who knew him. Anything he had he had her to thank for it.

He let her go on until she was forced to stop from sheer exhaustion. Then he said, 'Aye. All you say is true. About me, anyway. But this much I've learnt in the five years we've been together. Folks might have pitied me afore I married you, but it was kindly pity; but now they scorn me because I've allowed meself to be ruled and bossed by you. They've seen me kept on one side and not allowed to be a father to me bairn like other men. Me own family scorn me because you've kept me hungry. And I've sat under it all like a mummy for five years. An' five years is a long time. But it's finished! You made a bargain. Well, up to now I've had dam' all out of it, for any money the shop's made you've utilised very cleverly . . . Well, you can have the shop the morrow if you like; I've got the scrap. I had it afore I came here, so I haven't got you to thank for that. And getting back to the bairn. Well, he's yours for as long as you can keep him. And that, I'm warning you, isn't for much longer.'

His head lifted out of his shoulders and his hump seemed to straighten for a second as he squared himself, giving her the fleeting impression, as she had received once before, that he was a normally built man. She watched his open coat gape further as he took in a deep breath before saying quietly, 'Now I'm going to me mother's for me breakfast. I'll get two eggs and a rasher and fried bread and as much tea as I can drink. And if you don't want me to keep this up you'd better see what you can do in the way of grub.'

He was gone. Maggie's two hands went to the table

and, gripping the edge, she pressed herself against it, leaning over it, making it act as a bulwark to her emotions. Now the mist was gone from her eyes and the green was deepening to almost black, and their expression was not unlike that of an enraged and caged beast.

7

Beattie Watson

The fells lay under a shimmering heat, the blue haze deceiving the eyes and giving the impression that the earth was visibly moving, panting slowly, tired with trying to draw breath. The sun was going down but gave no promise of coolness to follow, and Tom sat on the biscuit-coloured grass watching it. On three sides of him was low bush and scrub, and in the open space before him lay a broad stretch of broken ground, with the fringe of the town just visible along its horizon.

From time to time he would stand up and look back over the bushes to where in the distance, standing out against the light, couples were wandering about searching for a sheltered place such as this; and the sight of them once again deterred him from walking to the main road to meet the bus, and Beattie.

Beattie liked this spot – it had become theirs. When, as happened sometimes, they found another couple in possession, she would be annoyed, for she did not like sitting in the open. Yet now, after three weeks of almost daily meetings, he was wondering if her only objection to being stared at was when she was with him, for she would meet him nowhere else but here, and this secrecy seemed foreign to her open, free nature.

At first he had been glad she preferred the quietness

of the fells, for he had not the courage to flaunt her openly. But this he knew could not go on. Soon he would have to face the family with her . . . face his mother.

He snapped off a long dry grass and drew it between his teeth, putting them on edge and causing him to shudder . . . But his mother would like her once she got to know her properly. Who could resist liking her or loving her? He drew his knees up and put his elbows on them, and rested his head on his hands. He had never thought about love until he met Beattie, only the love of God and, of course, his mother. But this feeling was different; it had scorched him like the heat had this grass. Inside he was lifeless and sapped with it; the pure beauty of its first touch had been mangled in the torturous desires it had aroused in his body; the fierce heat of its flame had even thrust up a barrier between him and God.

He rolled over on the hard earth and pressed his body to it. It wasn't sinful to feel like this, it was natural; he was a man. God would understand and help him to keep this thing under control.

His thoughts, turning on God at this moment, created a shamefaced feeling. It was as if he had let someone down and was now crawling back to Him for help. He had lost touch with the feeling of oneness with God that for years now had draped him like a cloak; he lost it when Beattie came into his life. If he could only get back to God, He would understand and help him. He must pray. He would pray . . . now, before she came. He breathed deeply, and began:

'Dear Lord, give me strength to combat this temptation . . . Jesus, You who were a man and knew all the desires of man, strengthen me with Your strength.'

As always when he prayed, he attempted to conjure up the face of Christ. But now he was not successful; so he willed it to come clear before his eyes. And as he willed, a face rose into his vision; but it was the face of his father. Surprise checked his praying, and he flung round on to his back, and in greater surprise looked up at Beattie Watson standing over him.

'Well, I must say! Breaking your neck to see me, weren't you, lying asleep there!'

Her voice was harsh and throaty, but any reproach the words implied was contradicted by the laughter in her eyes.

Tom was on his feet. 'Which way did you come? Why, it wasn't a minute ago I was on the lookout for you.'

'Oh, I got off the bus way down the road – it was so flaming hot I came across the top end.'

'The top end?' he questioned quietly.

'Aye, the top end.' She laughed at him. 'Where the soldiers are camped, you know.'

She was teasing him, yet the sane part of him knew that she was speaking the truth. Likely, she had got off the bus to pass near the camp; but what could be said to anyone so frank as she was?

'Sit down and don't look so grown up!' She pulled at his trouser leg from where she had dropped on to the grass. And he repeated in a puzzled tone, 'Grown up?'

'Aye; and don't keep repeating everything I say. God, but it's hot!' she said, flinging herself back on the ground, her arms spread wide.

He gazed down at her; then lowered himself to her side, and lifted her hand and held it gently to his face.

'Ah!' She sighed and wriggled her body. 'That's one thing I like about you, Tommy. You act like a film star.'

'What!' He dropped her hand, and she let forth a peal of laughter.

'Oh, I wish you could see your face. Don't you think it's a compliment for a pitman to be called a film star?'

'About the same thing as saying I'm a cissy.'

'Come here!' She caught the lapel of his coat. 'Aren't you going to kiss me?'

His face stayed for a second above hers, his eyes flashing from one feature to another before coming to rest on her mouth. Then his own, closed hard and tight dropped on hers. When he finished she lay smiling at him, with an amused tolerant smile like that of a teacher who had watched the clumsy efforts of a favourite pupil.

'You're nice' – she stroked his cheek, and he sought to bring her fingers across his lips – 'but you're funny.'

'Funny?'

'There you go again. Aye, funny. You know, I was thinking the day that you're not like a pitman at all. I've never known a pitman like you, who reads poetry and is a parson.'

'I'm not a parson! I'm what you call a lay preacher. And a poor one at that, God knows,' he added quietly.

'Oh, I think you're clever. There's not many like you. You don't think enough of yourself.'

'You don't know pitmen.'

'Don't I, though!'

'Do you know Ralph Foley and Peter Cremer?'

'No. Who are they when they're out?'

'Ralph Foley does grand paintings of up here on the fells. He gave an exhibition of his own, more than fifty. And Peter Cremer taught himself to play the fiddle and has been picked to join an orchestra in Newcastle. They're doing things.'

'Well, what's that?' she cut in. 'Our Lance can play the cornet, the bugle, and the penny whistle. And he can clog dance when he plays the whistle, an' all.'

Tom pulled at the grass but made no comment on the achievements of Lance, for it was rarely she mentioned her family.

'Anyway,' she went on, 'if I had your brains I'd do something.'

'What would you do?'

'Oh, I don't know. But I wouldn't stick down the pit.'

'I like the pit.'

'Eeh' – she shook her head – 'you're really queer, you know. I suppose it's because you're aimin' to be an Almighty God'a.'

'An Almighty what?'

'God'a . . . a parson. Haven't you heard that one before?'

'No, it's a new one on me.'

'It's really me da's name for them. I wonder what he'd say if he . . .' She stopped and looked past him reflectively towards the sky; then exclaimed, 'Oh God, but it's hot! Mind a minute' – she sat up – 'I'm goin' to take me stockings off. Don't look.'

Obediently Tom turned his head away, and her hands, unloosening her suspenders, became still, and her face for a moment took on a sad, almost regretful expression, to be replaced by her smile as she murmured, 'It takes all types to make a world.'

'What?'

'I said it takes all types to make a world.'

He shook his head. He could not follow her, but he laughed softly.

Then, taking her shoe, she slapped him on the back with the sole of it, saying, 'All clear.'

He turned and looked at her wriggling toes, and she said, 'I've been wanting to do this all day. It was so hot in that dam' factory that I wished somebody would set light to the cordite, and we'd all go up, and that'd finish it . . . No, I didn't, not really; I'd hate to die.' With her swift change of thought she went on, 'Oh, I've brought your book back.'

She reached over the grass and dragged her bag towards her, and Tom said, 'But you couldn't have read it, I only gave it to you the night afore last!'

'I've read some.' She shook her head at him. 'It's no use, Tommy. What's the good of pretending? Them kind of books aren't in my line. And, anyway, I'm frightened it gets messed up or lost. And it's got such a nice cover . . . Oh, don't look so sad, man.'

'I'm not sad.'

'Yes, you are . . . But honest, I read some. And one bit even made me laugh. Where that fellow said: "An' when they gets to feelin' old they ups an' shoots theirsels, I'm told." Lord, I did laugh at that. "An' when they gets to feelin' old they ups an' shoots theirsels, I'm told."' She repeated the lines musingly; then suddenly lay back and laughed loudly. 'It's funny, you know.'

Tom did not laugh with her, but looked broodingly down on his beloved Rupert Brooke, and told himself that this was one of life's lessons to be learned: when you loved someone you had to prepare yourself for him or her not liking the things you did . . . But what matter, so long as she kept on loving him. But did she really love him? What if she left him?

A hot wave, akin to terror, passed through him, and he was impelled towards her by the fear. He put his arms about her and held her closely, and almost immediately she relaxed against him, the curves of her body falling into his.

'Do you love me, Beattie?'

His lips were against her neck.

'What do you think?'

'I don't know what to think.'

'I'll give you three guesses.'

'I don't want to guess; I want to hear you say it . . . Say you love me, you've never said it.'

'Come here, and I'll give you proof.' She brought his head from her shoulder. Slowly her open lips covered his. Then with a swift jerk his mouth was lost in hers, and her soft yielding body became hard and tight against him. For the moment he seemed to become mad and to grapple with her as if she were a wild beast, pressing and pounding at her body in an attempt to push it into the earth. Then with an equal ferocity he suddenly tore himself from her and rolled over on the grass and, shielding his face in the crook of his arm, lay still.

But for the slight twitching of her legs Beattie, too, lay still. Her full lips were drawn close together, and her eyes were no longer filled with laughter. After a while her hand groped for her bag, and, finding it, she took out a packet of cigarettes and lit one, drawing on it with short, quick draws. When after some time she slowly raised herself up she did not look towards Tom but, sticking the cigarette in the corner of her mouth, she pulled on her stockings and shoes again.

With a heavy movement as if his body were packed with lead, Tom turned over and edged towards her. Then he too lifted his body from the ground and sat with his hands hanging limply between his knees for a while, before saying thickly, 'I'm sorry, Beattie.'

With the slightest turn of her head she looked at him coldly out of the corner of her eye, and asked in a flat voice, 'What for?'

He met this new tone with one of surprise, and said

haltingly 'For . . . for nearly forgetting myself.'

If he had misread the scorn in her look, there was no mistaking it now in her voice. 'Ha ha! That's a good 'un. You're too soft to clag holes with, man. I'm going home.'

She was on her feet; and he was facing her. Too soft to clag holes with, was he! He took her roughly by the arms. 'You won't say that to me again.'

'No?'

'No! Listen. Will you marry me?'

Her mouth fell agape; the stiffness left her face and a ripple of laughter slowly moved across it. But on this occasion her laughter found no outlet; it seemed to be checked by an obtruding thought, which she voiced: 'You serious?'

'Aye. Of course I'm serious. You don't ask a lass to marry you for fun.'

His face was grim; the philosophical layman did not exist at this moment; he was a man and he wanted Beattie Watson, and to hell with the consequences! The men needn't listen to him. It had never done them any good what he said to them, anyway . . . people could only be influenced if they wanted to be. And the family? Well, let them take it or leave it. If they wouldn't accept her, then they wouldn't have him, that was all. He'd ask for a transfer to another pit, and him and Beattie would start life together where no condemning eye would be on her . . . Who were they to condemn, anyway? Just because, as most of them had, she hadn't experienced the privilege of a decent upbringing. What chance had a girl, with six brothers and a drunken father and mother? . . . He would make it up to her. Their marriage would be as perfect as a marriage could be.

Yet, as he gazed down into her face, it was borne in on him that, whatever her upbringing, she had been

149

and still was happy in it, and it had left no scar on her. Instead, the stamp of it seemed to be laughter and a capacity for enjoyment. Up to a moment ago he had never seen her other than happy.

She pulled herself gently from his arms and stared away across the moor to where the town was lifting itself out of the heat of the day like a city rising out of the sea. A little breeze swept over the hills, rustling the grass about their feet, and absentmindedly she took the front of her blouse and wafted it back and forward.

'What do you say, Beattie?' There was no pleading in his words, they were more of a demand, and she glanced at him as if he was new in her sight.

She did not answer him directly, but said, more to herself, 'You're the first fellow who's asked me to marry him.'

His heart leapt at her words. He knew she'd had other fellows – a girl like her was bound to have a swarm of men after her – but he'd got in before any of them. 'You will?'

She laughed. Her chin lifted and her eyes swept the endless blue of the sky.

'Beattie, don't keep me hanging on like this.'

He swung her about and took hold of her arms again, and she brought a sobered face down to his. 'You don't know how lucky you are. If I didn't know you were a bit of a sap and I liked you, I'd say yes. Hold your horses a minute!' She raised her hand to check the impetuous flow she knew her words would evoke, and before his eyes she seemed to change from Beattie, the laughing girl, to a woman, twenty years instead of two years older than himself. 'Listen to me, Tommy. I don't want to marry . . . you or anybody else; I've seen enough of it in my time. I don't mind having a bit of fun.' She paused and the light deepened in her eyes for the moment. But as she saw no change in his she went doggedly on, her face hardening with an expression he had never seen before. 'And I'm goin' to have me fun and without the usual consequences either. You understand?' Again she paused, and whether he understood or not she could gain no indication.

'Well, there it is. I've been straight with you. And mind' – her finger jabbed his chest – 'many a one wouldn't. But you're such a . . . sap.' The word was in no way derogatory. On her lips it even conveyed tenderness. 'It's well seen I'm the only lass you've had. And mind, I'm telling you, in one way you're lucky you struck on me. If it had been that other clinging vine, she'd have you hooked up. But I've got me principles, no matter what else I haven't got. You can thank your lucky stars it was me you gave your seat to in the bus and not the lass I was with, or else . . . Well' – she snapped her fingers – 'she wouldn't have let eight months go by and made no move to see you. You would've been hooked by now, me lad.'

She was talking, he thought, as women talked; it was not the talk of a girl. He had been wrong. Her life had left a mark on her; it had aged some part of her. But she was good and square, and as straightforward as even a man . . . She had principles.

His love for her created another plane whereon to spread itself. How many girls would have answered him with utter truth as she had done?

He caught her hands and pressed them into his breast. 'You'll marry me . . . Some day you'll marry me. I can wait; you said you liked me.' He did not insist on the word love, for, strangely now, he accepted the fact calmly that her kisses and passion had not meant love to her. 'That's enough for the time being,' he went on. 'I'll wait.' His voice sounded like that of a settled man. He too seemed to have aged; the responsibility of this love was already lying heavily on him.

Her smile reappeared, flashing into life again, accompanied by a shrug of her shoulders. 'Well, mind, don't say I didn't warn you. And don't start yapping at me when you're left high and dry.'

'Never you fear.' He nodded slowly at her. 'I won't be left high and dry.' He squared himself. 'We're going to start courting in the proper way . . . I'm going to take you home to see me mother and them.' And at this moment he felt it would be bestowing an honour on his family should she visit them.

'Oh no, you're not!' Her smile was gone once more.

'Why?'

'Because I've told you, we either meet up here or not at all.'

'But, Beattie, we can't go on like this. Some of my family know already we're going together. Our Ann saw us up here.'

She turned quickly from him and moved her head impatiently.

'What's wrong in people knowing?'

'Look, Tommy' – she spoke as if she was talking to a child – 'we'd better finish this thing now. It's my fault; I should never have started it. But you were so damned nice, and nice blokes are few and far between. And you talked to me differently . . . about poetry and things. You gave me credit for what I haven't got – a brain; and you didn't just want the one thing. And I'll be honest with you . . . that was your main attraction, that you didn't grab like other blokes. Not that I haven't gone out of my way to make you . . . because, well . . . I'm made that way. See?'

'Oh, Beattie, be quiet!' His voice was imploring.

'No, I won't be quiet, for you're the only bloke I can talk to like this. It's funny, but it's the truth. If I went on like this to other fellows they'd gallop all over me. I've got to stave them off, and egg you on.'

'Beattie!' Now he looked and sounded distinctly shocked.

'Oh, all right. But look, Tom.' She became quiet, her voice, her body, even the restless flashing of her eyes, were stilled for a moment as she said, 'I've got the feeling it'd be better for us both if we break now . . . a clean break. I could go on leading you up the garden; then if I left you flat, which ten to one I will do, it'd be worse for you. You're too nice. That's your trouble.'

'We're not going to break, now or at any time. I've never been more sure of what I wanted in my life. I want you . . . I want to marry you. And I will marry you.'

'Well' – the quietness was sent flying away by her laugh – 'even God Himself couldn't say I haven't tried. But mind, I'm not seeing you in the town.'

'Oh yes, you are. And you're coming to Durham with me. We're going to celebrate the day we met.'

Still laughing, but rather tensely now, she turned from him and looked towards the town again, clear now and uplifted in the first touch of the twilight. But although she continued to laugh, her voice was steely with finality as she said, 'It's up here or nowhere at all!'

So final was it that he had to accept the decision, and he thought: It's because I go preaching that she doesn't want to be seen with me . . . And so great was her power over him that he felt to give that up would be little loss compared with the gain of her.

And as he put his arm about her waist he shut his mind tightly against the voice that cried, 'Tom!' which his imagination suggested was Christ's, but the tone of which held the firm ring of his mother's.

8

By Any Other Name

On one day a year the pitmen from the surrounding towns gather in Durham, bringing their families with them. And on this day they are lords of all they survey; they may listen to their leaders, but there is no hesitation in making their grievances known. Old and young shout for their rights; men who rarely grouse or voice an opinion let themselves go on this, their day. The town is entirely given over to the miners. Only the cathedral standing on its mighty rock high above the River Wear remains untouched by them. Since Norman times it had watched invasions, and it saw little change in the character of man; he still shouted, he still strove – and it wondered at the little achieved in so much time. But knowing that the time past was only a fragment of that time still to come, it gazed down on the milling throngs with the tolerance and complacency of the aged for the very young. And it might be said that it wished for the morrow when the boards would be taken down from the shop windows, the streets and the greens cleared of litter, and the miners, once more clothed in their pit clothes and their right minds, would be striding up and down the hills to the work they cursed and would have denied loving.

But this year there was no invasion of Durham, for

the men who usually thronged it were fighting on land, sea, in the air, down the mines, and in the factories. A few of those miners who were taking a well-earned day's rest had come into Durham, however; but there was none of the zest of the Durham Gala Day, for even in daylight there were signs everywhere of the blackout, and people's emotions seemed too wide apart for any real enjoyment.

Nellie, George and Ann, together with Kitty Taggart and Pat, had come to Durham for the day. It had been an excursion suggested by Kitty on the spur of the moment and backed by George. Tom had not come with them, having left the house before them for a destination known only to himself.

But now in Durham, Nellie stood alone by the river staring at it unseeing. Each year on Gala Day she came to the river and watched the boats full of laughing couples gliding by under the shadow of the cathedral; but to-day she saw neither the boatless river nor the cathedral; all she could see was the face of her lad as she had seen it half an hour ago when, almost with pride, he had presented that lass to her; and not only to her but to Kitty Taggart and Pat. She had been only dimly aware of the unusual silence of the Taggarts, for her mind was numbed with shock. She could not take it in that her lad, her Tom, who was looked up to and respected by everybody, had taken up with such a one as the Watson girl.

She had never indulged in talk or scandal about the people of the town, yet she would have had to be both deaf and stupid not to know that the Watson family were the black spot in Fellburn. That several members of the family had no claim to the name of Watson was common knowledge; it was even vouched for by Mrs Watson herself, who, when in her cups, would tell all and sundry of the joys of her various amours. It was also well known that the only daughter was just a younger edition of her mother.

A spasm passed over Nellie's face. Her lad . . . her lad, above all lads, had to take up with such a one! Now she knew the reason for the change in him during these past weeks. She had worried herself sick on his account thinking he was ill, not so much physically but mentally. She had put it down to nerves – men did get nerves – for she reasoned that he would be more subject to them than other lads because he thought and pondered over things so much. And she had forced herself not to worry him with her questioning, not even when he refused Mr Fraser's most generous offer to him to take on the vacation services in Beckington. It was an honour he should have jumped at; and she had been hurt and puzzled by his refusal and by his stubborn silence as to the reason. But now she knew the reason for it . . . shame! He was ashamed to get up in the pulpit and talk to others about a way of life when his own could not be brought into the open. Yet to-day he had made it open . . . What did this portend? That he was serious? No, no. God in heaven, no! She would rather see him dead.

Out of the depths of her feelings she spoke the thought aloud, and she looked up towards the cathedral and repeated, 'Aye, I would that . . . I would rather see him dead.' And she nodded as if nodding to God Himself, materially present behind those walls. Then up from a chasm within her, wherein was buried a past sorrow, a thought was forced, and the significance of it blotted out the sky, the river, and even the majestic edifice of the cathedral itself. Words swam before her eyes, then doubled and redoubled themselves like an echo. Like father, like son, they said. Like father, like son.

She swung round on the river path and went briskly towards the town. She must get home; she must think; there must be some way to make him see sense . . . Be still and trust in God, she thought; only to refute the suggestion with, God helps those who help themselves. She had prayed to God to keep her lad out of the war, and He had done so; but she'd had proof before that when God answered a prayer He expected you to accept the consequences of the answer, and to learn the lesson it taught. But she could not learn this lesson. From the depths of her heart, she wished at this moment that her lad was beyond the Channel, among those left on the beaches of Dunkirk.

In Silver Street she met George and Ann. George's face was stiff and anxious, and he asked harshly, 'Where have you been, woman?'

She did not look at him, but said to Ann, 'I'm going home.' And George protested, 'Now look here. You've only just come; and going home isn't going to help you, he's not there. We'll talk to him the night.'

Nellie looked at her husband, 'I'm going home,' she said.

After a moment, during which he returned her stare, George said flatly, 'Very well. Have it your own way.'

'I don't want you to come.'

'I'm coming.'

'No, da.' Ann put out her hand towards her father. 'You stay. I'll go with me ma. Say I'm tired and my head's splitting. And it is, it's no lie. Go on' – she patted his arm – 'have a drink with Pat.' She smiled at him, and as her mother turned away she whispered urgently to him, 'Let her be. She'll be better at home. She had to know some time.'

'How long has it been going on?'

'Weeks.'

'Then why didn't you say something afore now?' He too was whispering. 'You could've let on to me.'

'It was none of my business. Look, I'll lose her if I don't go. You go and enjoy yourself and forget about it for the day.'

'Enjoy meself!' He shook his head, and his eyes gave her the impression that his thoughts were turned inwards and that he needed her somehow at this moment more than her mother did. But she swung away and hurried to join Nellie, and together they walked in silence to the bus stop.

And there they were confronted by a prominent member of the chapel, whose greeting was such as to turn a screw in Nellie's heart. 'Ah, Mrs Rowan, off home then, are you? And so soon? But George is staying though, is he? And Tom?' He nodded to her, a sly smile hovering round his lips. 'He'll not be going back yet either. I see he's got himself a young lady. Is that why we haven't been hearing his good advice so much lately?'

Only Nellie's eyes answered him; and after a short and strained silence, he had the grace to bid her good day.

This was but the beginning. Mr Graham had always been jealous of Tom being picked to speak in the surrounding small chapels, when he had a son whom he considered to be more worthy of the honour. And now Tom had proved that he was right. Yes, this was only the beginning, for there were the men in the pit, hard-bitten, dogmatic men. Yet such had been Tom's appeal and Christian living that they were tolerant of him. But now, let him dare open his mouth and they'd throw the . . . Watson whore in his face. Her mind did not jib at using the word, but told her she was right, for her lad had met up with a whore.

* * *

It was dusk when Kitty Taggart came in from next door. She had not yet removed her coat and hat, and the first thing she did was to exclaim loudly at the dishes stacked with neatly folded wet linen.

'You haven't been washing? Why, Nellie! On a day like this an' all. And are you all alone?'

'Ann's not been long gone,' said Nellie. 'I just thought I'd get them done. But I didn't put them out.' This last was uttered in a way as to suggest that she had not violated the propriety of the holiday.

'No, no. But, anyway, you'll be up at four o'clock, and if it don't rain they'll be dry afore breakfast . . . Oh, what a day we've had, trapesing round, and nothing to see. I'm glad to get home, I am that. You know, I was just thinking. Durham's nowt without the gala.'

'No, indeed,' said Nellie.

An uneasy silence fell on the scullery, and Kitty watched Nellie folding and refolding more wet garments, and in a voice that sounded false to herself she began, 'What d'you think those two swine of mine did last night? Did you hear the uproar? With Father McSweeney himself around!'

Nellie shook her head. It was plain to her that Kitty was endeavouring to steer clear of the subject she was wanting most to discuss . . . Tom and the Watson girl.

'It's jailed they'll be, afore they're much older. You know what they did, Nellie?'

Nellie again shook her head.

'They held a funeral on the allotment; and dug a grave they did, and buried young Phil Reeves in up to the neck. Did you ever now! And they turned their coats back to front and read a funeral service over him, in their way. And what d'you think the devils said. That same bit as we used to say when we were bairns: "Ashes to ashes, dust to dust, If the Lord won't have you the

160

devil must." You know. And there they were chanting this when himself passed. And he heard his own voice saying it and he was nearly startled out of his wits, until he looked through the palings and saw the pair of them making game of him – every look and antic to the life. And then what d'you think, Nellie. He saw a head sticking up out of the ground and the tears running down its face, and it yelling, "Let me up! I don't want to be a corpse!"'

Here Kitty's imagination got the better of her and her laughter gushed forth. 'Oh, but I'd have loved to have seen it an' all. You can just imagine, Nellie, how all the lads scattered at the sight of himself – twenty or more there was – and them jumping over the palings like kangaroos. And himself had to dig Phil out. And a sorry sight he was an' all. He brought him to me to clean up. He would bring him to me, wouldn't he?' She nodded to herself. 'And do you know what? He stayed until the twins came in. Yes, there he sat over me. And me wishing him far enough, God forgive me.' She paused and dried her eyes. 'I meant to tell you all this this morning, but you rushed off.' Again she paused and waited. But Nellie offered no comment. And she went on, 'As I was telling you, there he sat. And you should have seen their two faces when they clapped eyes on him. And you should have heard what he said. Blasted them to hell's flames, he did. And there they were, the pair of them, making on they were scared out of their wits . . . But he's got them now all right; at least he thinks he has.' She scratched her ear. 'You know what he's going to do with them? Put them on the altar to serve mass. Every day, an' all. Did you ever? I tried to get a word in, to tell like that it might be a mistake, but all he would say was, "Quiet now. They'll start the day well, anyway. I'll make sure of that. And they'll not make game of anybody in the presence of God."' She held out her hand in dumb appeal to Nellie. 'What can you do? And now I've got to get them surplices and slippers. And look at the expense! . . . And then there's the contrariness of it. It's been me life's desire that one of me lads should be picked to serve on the altar; but devil a one was. And then he has to go and pick them two. Oh' – she clapped her hand to her forehead – 'he doesn't know what he's up to. For there they were, genuflecting to the oven and serving mass on the fender afore breakfast this morning!' The door, opening behind her, pushed her forward, and she was relieved of her effort to keep off the burning subject of Tom, for there he stood, his face grim and tight.

Nellie was in the corner, bending over the boiler and drying it out before replacing the wooden cover that converted it into a table. She did not turn round; only her hand that was swirling inside the bowl became still for an instant when Kitty exclaimed, 'Why, Tom, you're back early! Did you see anything of Pat?'

Tom stood just inside the door, the knob still in his hand. He did not look at Kitty, but at his mother's back as he replied shortly, 'No.'

'Ah well, he'll be dropping in on his way home. He's like death and danger, he's always there. Famishing, like the lot of them.'

Tom stood aside to let her pass, and as she stepped into the yard she looked at him out of the corner of her eye, and she was unable to refrain from asking, 'Enjoy yourself the day, lad?'

Tom stared back at her, and answered unsmilingly, 'Yes, I did.'

'That's right then.'

The door closed, and there was only he and his mother. The air was warm and prickly with the smell of washing-powder, and he sneezed twice and blew his nose as he watched her lifting the dishes of wet clothes and placing them side by side on the boiler top.

'Mum.'

'Yes?' Still she did not turn towards him.

'We'd better have this out.'

Nellie covered the dishes with a sheet. Then her hands went to her apron; as she dried them her eyes flicked around the scullery, making sure that all was tidy. Then still without looking at him she walked along the passage and into the living-room.

Tom stood for a few seconds longer after she had gone; and his face was twisted with his perplexed emotions. Then with something of a blustering attitude he strode down the passage, but at the sight of his mother sitting by the fire, each hand lying in apparent placidness along an arm of the rocking-chair, the bluster left him, and he walked quietly to her side, and, putting his hand on her shoulder, said, 'Mum, can't you understand?'

Now she looked up at him. 'What do you want me to understand? That you've picked up with the lowest of the low? That because of such a one as that your chapel and your God and your family are to be put aside?'

'Look, Mum . . .' His tone was soft, almost wheedling. 'You're not the one to judge hastily. Would you lay the blame of all her family on her? If you only knew her . . .'

'I don't want to know her.'

'There you are!' He made a hopeless gesture with his hands. 'Can you wonder I haven't told you about her before?'

'Tom' – her hands were gripping the arms of the chair now – 'you're not serious, are you? You don't mean to keep this up? Tell me you're not serious.'

Never had he seen such pleading in her eyes. The

pain in their depths aroused an agony of remorse and sorrow within him, and had he the strength he would have put his arms about her and said, 'No, I'm not serious; it's just a bit of fun.' But Beattie did not mean fun to him, she meant life; she had become a cause, a cause for which he was prepared to sacrifice everything. God could be a cause – He had been, with him; the pit could be a cause, and in its own way still was; but no cause could have led him blindly on as did that of Beattie Watson. He firmly believed that beneath the exterior, classed as common, lay qualities surpassing the ordinary; he felt that no woman could be as open and as honest as she was unless these attributes were part of some exceptional character. No woman had the power to arouse such passion and yet inspire him to lift it from its own realm, to sublimate it in love that, at times, seemed to him to be bodyless. How could he give her up and live?

So he turned from his mother's eyes and said, 'I'm serious all right.'

Nellie rose to her feet. 'You've taken leave of your senses! Do you know what this means? Have you gone mad?'

She waited for some reply; but all he did was to put his foot on the fender and his hands on the mantelpiece and rest his forehead against them.

She stared at his bent head, and went on, her voice like her face, sharp and hard now, 'What about the chapel and all the services you've taken, and the things you've said? Remember your last one? Remember how you started? You've got to be able to face man before you can face God . . . Remember?'

Tom moved his head back and forward on his clenched hands.

'What will it be like going down the pit in the morning? The men will spit on you. Even the godless ones listened to you. And because they thought you were good they must have thought there was something in having a God after all. But what'll happen now when Tom Rowan openly shows he has taken up with a whore, and the daughter of a whore?'

'Mother!' He swung round on her, his face blanched white, leaving a blue weal across his temple standing out as if painted on the skin.

'That's what she is.'

'Be careful.'

'She's nothing more.'

His nose was pinched thin and his lips trembled as he said, 'And that's your charity! Carrying out the sins of the fathers.'

Nellie put her hand to her throat, and for a moment her shoulders slumped and her eyes looked at him vacantly. Then she straightened herself. 'The sins of the fathers carry themselves out as surely as night follows day.' She nodded at him. 'But I'm not blaming her for what her mother is or her father, but for what she is. She's a known . . .'

'Don't!' He thrust his hand towards her. 'If you say that again I'll leave the house and not come back.'

Her eyes widened, and the startled look in them was as though she had seen him transformed into some strange being. Her head shook and she whispered, 'Tom.'

But her pleading did not touch him, and she flicked her finger and thumb together, saying, 'It's just like that . . . you've forgot all the years and what we planned.'

'I'm a boy no longer.'

'No' – she looked at him blindly – 'you're a boy no longer.'

Her lips trembled; and her distress was too much for him, and he grabbed at her hands and held them closely pressed against him. 'Mum, try to see eye to eye with me in this. It's no idle fancy. I would do anything on earth not to hurt you, but I cannot give her up . . . Mum!' His eyes bored their pleading into hers. 'See her . . . let me bring her home.'

'No!' Nellie pulled herself away, her face grim once more. 'You want me to give my sanction to a living hell for you? Look. I would rather a bomb drop clean on you and blow you to smithereens. Or I would wish you to be trapped down below' – she thrust her stiffened fingers towards the floor – 'and never see the light again. Yes, I would wish that rather than I would see you joined to a woman of that tribe.'

At this moment George's figure passed the window in the deepening twilight, and his knock came on the front door. And it was repeated before either of them moved. Nellie turned heavily to answer the impetuous summons, and Tom flung himself out of the room and up the stairs, and into his own room.

As of habit he immediately took off his best clothes and put them away; and the movements of his hands as he pushed them into the cupboards or drawers were thrust metaphorically at his mother and anyone else who would try to separate him from Beattie Watson. His clothes away, he stood looking helplessly about the little room as if looking for understanding from some familiar object. But even the familiarity of the room seemed to have deserted him.

With a hopeless gesture he beat his clenched fist into the palm of his hand. If only they would let her speak for herself; if they knew her; the bigness of her. Look at this morning when she was cut by his mother and the Taggarts. Did she storm? No, she laughed. But it was a hurt laugh; and she had looked at him and said, 'Don't say I didn't warn you. And that's only the beginning, mind.'

And then once again she had appealed to him, 'Let's call it quits, Tommy. I'm not worth it, and that's a fact. If you knew everything . . .'

But he had silenced her. Yet now her words came back, pricking his mind and recalling the name his mother had dared apply to her. He began to pace the room in his stockinged feet. If he even harboured the thought he would be as bad as the rest. Women! They were all alike where scandal was concerned. Even his mother had become a ferocious creature under the influence of it.

He was standing in his pants and vest when without any warning knock his father entered.

George looked at his son, and the comeliness of him tore at his heart – his strong thinness, the finely chiselled face without a spot of guilt in it. He was his mother's son all right, and she had fought to build about him a barrier against evil. But just a moment ago she had said, 'He's your son. Never was it more right, like father like son.' By God, that had hurt. Would she never forget? No. And certainly not while the attraction for the harlot type that had played havoc with his own life was rising into action in her son.

He had paid dearly for his weakness. By God, he had that. And he didn't want his lad to land in the same boat. He mustn't land there! If it was only for Nellie's sake, he mustn't land there, for she had suffered enough. It was odd, he thought, how good women acted like magnets for trouble, trouble of this sort that turned them into martyrs. And martyrs weren't the easiest to live with . . . But he must think no harsh word against Nellie. What he had to do was to find a way to prevent her suffering any more, and to save his lad from trouble. But knowing the fever that scorched the blood when desire was loose in it, he was hard set to know what line to take with his son. One thing he must not do, he must not lose his temper. He might not have much sense about some things, but this much he knew from experience, open opposition on a matter of this sort was the quickest way to drive a fellow to the end of the road.

'Can we have a crack, lad?'

Tom turned searching eyes on his father. He had expected some kind of understanding from his mother, but from his father none. Yet here he was, fully aware of the state of affairs, and evidently not going to land out at him about it.

'What's there to say?'

George sat down on the edge of the bed and stared intently at his hands, examining the myriad blue marks covering them. He turned his palms upwards, then downwards again, and went on scrutinising the insignia of the mine for some moments before saying, 'Only this . . . You're old enough to know what you're about.'

Tom looked at the bowed head. This attitude was most unusual. He always thought of his father as a breezy individual, blustering at times, and often trying with his stale jokes; and he had suspected him of weakness, for how otherwise would such a man allow his wife to have the final say in things that were not of her province. He had been very young when he first realised who ruled the house. But this side of his father was quite new; and this understanding and toleration bred new hope in him.

'Dad.' With the eagerness of a young boy about to solicit parental sanction for some beloved scheme he pulled the bedroom chair up to the bed and sat down opposite his father. 'Look, Dad. If only she would see

168

her. If you would talk to her and get her to let me bring her here.'

George's head did not lift, but he raised his lids and peered up at his son as if over the top of spectacles. 'Don't lay any stock on her doing that, lad.' His voice was flat. 'I can't help you there. Women are queer cattle.'

'But, Dad. If only she got to know her, she'd see for herself how . . . I mean . . . well, what a good sort she is.'

'Aye, lad. She may be a good sort – her type often are . . .'

'Her type! What d'you mean?' The polished linoleum squeaked under the movement of Tom's chair.

'What I say, lad.'

George's head was lifted now and his eyes were on a level with those of his son.

'Because her family's rotten you think she's tarred with the same brush . . . I tell you . . .'

George lifted his hand. 'Don't shout, lad. Let's try and keep cool heads about this. Now she's only been back in the town since the war started, hasn't she? And has she told you what she did afore she came back?'

Tom's face tightened. 'What you getting at? She was in Newcastle, she worked in a café. Anything wrong in that?'

'It all depends, lad. Why not ask her point blank what she did there?'

The chair squeaked again across the linoleum, and Tom was on his feet. His chin was pressed flat with the tightness of his teeth. 'It's a good job you're my father.'

George looked up at him. It was funny what a woman could do to a man. It didn't seem possible that this was the same lad of whom he had been just a little afraid because he was so damned good. Strangely, he was finding he hadn't liked the saint as much as he was now liking the sinner.

His voice was even quieter now than it was before, but his words came firm and were weighed with intent. 'You can believe me when I tell you, lad, I know just how you feel. The same thing as is happening to you happened to me . . . Aye, it did that. The only difference is I knew what she was; I did it with me eyes open. There was no excuse for me. And I carried on with it . . .'

He stopped and passed his hands across his eyes, and the room became silent and the air heavy with his remembering, until, with an abrupt movement, he swept his hand from his face and, leaning forward, said bitterly, 'I only know this much: you've got to pay for things like that; you can't have feelings like we have, lad, and not pay for them. I've paid for years . . . your mother saw to that. She put my sin afore my eyes, and there it's been and still is, and likely to be till one of us dies.' He paused, then added, more to himself than to Tom, 'Some men seem to get off with that kind of thing, others don't.'

Tom's brows gathered in perplexity, and George rose slowly from the bed and shook his head. 'I've no right to talk like this; I've said more than I ought. But for your own sake, remember it, lad. And for my sake, forget that I've said anything.'

He stretched out his hand and patted Tom's arm once. 'Good night, lad. Sleep on it.'

The door closed, and Tom stared at it, his brows gathering into deeper ridges. What did he mean? What was he hinting at? He stood for a time in puzzled thought. Then with a toss of his head, like that of a mettlesome horse, he exclaimed aloud, 'Oh, what does it matter, anyway!' He turned and sat down heavily on the bed. His father was an old man, nearly sixty; what could he know or remember of the feelings that a girl like Beattie aroused? Likely, he'd had an affair with some woman before he was married – it would most cetainly have been before he was married, for under no stretch of imagination could he see his father looking at another woman with his mother around. They were old, the pair of them, and both past even remembering what love had been like, and because love had died on them, as it seemed to have done on countless other people, because they had been unable to preserve it, they unconsciously set themselves out to kill it in others. But nothing and no-one could kill the love he had for Beattie Watson. Nothing that anyone could say or do would separate him from her. If God could not do it, then man could not.

9

Mother and Son

Before leaving the shop Christopher gave one more
order to his new assistant. 'Keep those spares for our
regulars,' he said.

In the street, while walking quickly towards his
mother's, he pondered over the strangeness of circumstances which had placed him in the position of a master
giving orders. Only a little over a year ago he had spent
most of his days setting out his wares to attract the
non-regulars. Then the shop had still been his life. But
now, strangely, it had come to be merely a sideline, for
he made more in one day from the turnover on scrap
than he did in a month from the shop.

This morning he was feeling well. He always felt well
now . . . in body, at any rate. And he reckoned it was
getting out in the open air on the lorry that was doing
it.

Two men, black caps ludicrously straight on their
heads, hailed him from across the road. 'How's the
profiteering going, Chris?'

'Not bad,' he laughed back at them. 'I didn't quite
reach me thousand last week.'

'Never fear; you will, lad. And mind, there's many
a true word spoke in a joke.'

'Aye, I hope so.'

'And here's us gannin' done below for a clarty quid a shift.'

'More fool you.'

'Aye, more fool us. But they're still being born every day, you know. So long.'

'So long.'

A warmness spread through him. Only when you had men's respect did they joke with you like that. It was funny. He was the same fellow inside as he had been five years ago, but now, because he had hit on a good thing and was making money, he was being shown a comradeship and respect that he had not experienced before. Sometimes he even forgot his hump long enough to feel the equal of his brothers. Yet was it because of himself the respect was being shown? Was it not because of the money? The light of his self-esteem dimmed then brightened again . . . he had made the money, hadn't he? And about being the same fellow inside – he wasn't the same inside by a long chalk. Five years ago he had been afraid of Maggie, now he was holding his own with her . . . about most things, anyway, even if she had got her own way at last over the move . . . The foot of Brampton Hill! Good God! Who would have thought that he, Chris Taggart, would ever live at the foot of Brampton Hill and have his son going to a fancy school nearby? That was another thing. Five years ago he hadn't been a father. But even now he couldn't think of himself as a father.

The child had been formed by the desire of Maggie, in the same way as a sculptor would take a piece of clay and mould it. Aye, it was just like that. And because the created did not adore his creator Maggie's frustration was greater than before. And her efforts, too, were greater, for with every living breath she tried to extract love from the child.

He remembered the scene of just a week ago. He had returned home to find Maggie behaving like someone demented; for a time he had been afraid she was going off her head; and all because she had found Ann holding the bairn in her arms and kissing him.

At that moment, pity for Maggie rose in him again. The child never kissed her, he always wriggled .and turned from her caresses. God knew that must be awful for her when he was her very life. And his pity swelled when he'd thought: Nobody likes her. He couldn't think of a soul that he knew who liked her; nor yet anybody whom she liked; the only one that mattered to her was her boy; and he hated her. Good God! The revelation turned him cold. Yet it was a fact that she must soon become aware of herself, and when she did who would be blamed for it? Why, Ann. Yes, Ann would get the blame.

Ann wasn't happy either. She had Dave, but she wasn't happy . . . because she hadn't a bairn. It was odd when he came to think of it that Dave couldn't give her a bairn, because he reasoned, surely if a woman like Maggie could have a bairn, Ann could. The blame, if any, seemed to lie with Dave. But then, who dare put blame on anybody for a thing like that?

What was the matter with everyone lately? Was it the war? The whole Rowan family seemed at sixes and sevens. George had been pulled over the coals for shouting his mouth off at the pit – if he wasn't careful they'd be saying he was a fifth-columnist – and Nellie, of all people, had gone for Ann, and told her to stop encouraging Stephen, saying that he was Maggie's son, and Maggie could do what she liked with him. Nellie had always supported Maggie's treatment of the lad. She had definite ideas about mothers and sons, had Nellie. It was a good job she hadn't their lads to deal with. But, anyway, he could understand her being upset over Tom and the Watson business. Who would have thought that could happen to a fellow like Tom, who did preaching an' all . . . the damn fool.

If ever there was a fool it was him. A good-looking, strapping, nice fellow like that wanting to marry a tart like the Watson piece! Now, if a thing like that had happened to him, who could neither pick nor choose, it would have been understandable, but not with Tom.

It was because of him he was going towards home this morning when he should really be on the road to Hebburn with that load. But he liked Tom. Next to their Dave, he liked him better than anybody he knew. And he had a bit of information that might make him see sense, if somebody could tell him. He wouldn't be any good at the job, fumble it, most likely, and make Tom want to bash his head in. No. He reckoned the best one to handle it would be Nellie; women could always deal with women better than men could . . . on this point, anyway.

He decided to go to the Rowans' front door so that his mother shouldn't see him, because she mustn't know about this. He laughed to himself . . . the old girl was as good as *The North Mail* for spreading news; and this was something to be handled quietly.

When she opened the door to him Nellie looked her surprise.

'Hallo, Chris. Anything wrong? Come in. It isn't the bairn, is it?' she asked as he passed her.

'No; he's all right.'

'Sit down Chris. Sit here by the fire; it's a bit nippy this morning. Quite a change.' She patted the hanging pads on the back of the rocking-chair, and he could see she was puzzled by his visit so early in the morning as he was by the best way to make an opening for this delicate matter.

'Thanks, it is nippy.' He sat down, and more for something to do than for a desire for warmth he leaned forward and held his hands towards the bright blaze. 'This is something I'll likely miss when we move,' he said. 'We'll have to buy our coal then.'

'Won't one of the cartmen be able to drop you a load?'

'Too near the nobs, Aunt Nell. And you know how some folks go on about pitmen getting free coal as it is.'

'But it isn't free, they pay for it in more ways than one.'

'Aye, I know. But the old cry is they wouldn't mind a bit being stopped off their wages if they could get a ton of coal for it. And some of them are out to catch a bloke selling his coal, you know.'

'They want to go down and get it.'

'Aye, they do that. They like to make cases in point, as they call them, out of such things. But, anyway, I heard the lads on about the allowance being cut – there might even be coal rationing – and if that's the case me mother'll be hard put to make do, for she can barely manage on the load a month she gets now, you know what she is with the coal. Night and day, summer and winter, there's fires going. I thought she would have stopped it after the lads got washed at the pit; but it's a habit, I suppose.'

'Will you have a cup of tea, Chris?'

'No. Thanks all the same, Aunt Nell.'

In the awkward silence following this remark, Nellie busied herself about the room. Systematically she removed the ornaments from the brackets of the glass-backed sideboard prior to enhancing its shining surface still more with further rubbing. She was well on with this task when Chris spoke again.

'Bit of news about our Fred, isn't it? Fancy him being made a sergeant. Can you imagine it, Aunt Nell?'

'Yes; somehow I can. They say the best way to cure rebels is to give them a bit of authority.'

Chris laughed. 'Aye, well, there's something in that an' all. And he was a rebel all right. Goin' to put the world straight, he was. D'you remember, Aunt Nell? He was stood off the day I was married, and he never did a hand's turn from that until he joined up. And now he's a sergeant!'

Chris moved uneasily in his chair as his mother's voice, yelling at the twins, came to him from next door. Nellie turned and asked, 'Have you been in?' and he replied, 'No, not yet. And if she doesn't come in you needn't say I've been.'

Quietly Nellie asked, 'What is it, Chris? Something's wrong.'

He rose from his seat, and twirled his cap in his hands for a moment before answering, 'Well, nothing's really wrong, Aunt Nell; but there's something I came across, and I thought it might help you . . . I mean help Tom to . . . well, to straighten himself out.'

'What is it, Chris?' Nellie began to dry her hands on the duster.

And Chris, looking at her stiff white face, stammered, 'It's really no business of mine, Aunt Nell, but I like Tom . . .'

'Tell me what you know, Chris.'

'Well, you see, I heard of a woman down Bogg's End way, in Blossom Row, who did a bit of scrap-gathering in a small way, and I went to see if I could do a deal and get her to collect for me. Well, that part was all right. But during the time I was there she got talking, like women do, and she was pretty bitter about her lad. It was him that used to gather the tagger as a sideline. But when the war broke out he was called up and he went into the Merchant Navy, and what did he do but leave his half-pay note to some lass. And then the old woman finds out that the lass is one of the Watson family, and . . . well, Aunt Nell, that's it, she's living with him.'

He stopped, and Nellie, who was now wringing the duster as if it was a dishcloth, asked below her breath, 'And she's still with him?'

'Aye . . . yes. You see, knowing how you were worried about Tom, I made it my business to find out what I could. Not that I interfere with people's lives, Aunt Nell, you know that, because I've got enough to do to manage me own.' His lids drooped for a moment before he went on, 'Well, I found out she lives in one of the Boswell Cottages . . . those ones the council was going to pull down before the war, you know. And what's more, he's with her now.'

Nellie passed her tongue round her dry lips. Then she sat down by the table, and taking the duster she wiped the moisture from her brow, from around the roots of her hair, and from the top of her lip.

'If he knew that, wouldn't it finish him, Aunt Nell?'

Nellie nodded slowly. 'It should do. But he'd have to see for himself, he'd believe no word against her. He's gone mad . . . quite mad.'

Her head moved now from side to side, and Chris said: 'But surely he'll believe you, Aunt Nell. What I had in mind was that you'd go and see her.'

'Me!'

'Well, if he goes she might spin him a yarn. You know what they are. And you could tell her straight.'

Nellie stared across the table towards the fire. Then

she stood up and shook out the duster, and she placed it on the table before folding it into a neat square. 'When would I likely find her in?'

'Any time, I should think. She's working on munitions, but I gathered from the old woman that she's off this week. Supposed to be with a cold . . . but it's funny he should be on leave.'

He watched her fold the duster again, then yet again with studied precision fold it into another, even smaller, square.

He stood up and said, 'Well, Aunt Nell, there it is. I'd better be off now in case me ma comes in. I hope you haven't minded me telling you this.'

Bringing her eyes from the duster, Nellie looked down on him, and her face softened as she said, 'I can't thank you enough, Chris. This is the second time you've done a good turn to my family . . . and to me.'

He made for the door, saying, 'That's all right, Aunt Nell'; but he was puzzled to know what the other good turn could have been. Surely she wasn't meaning him marrying Maggie. Yet it was the only thing he could think of. And as he walked into the street he felt glad that what he had done had, after all, brought happiness to someone.

At half-past two Tom came in and, as was becoming usual now, he threw no cheerful greeting to his mother in the living-room, where she was in the act of taking an earthenware dish from the oven. She placed it on the table, then stood near the fire waiting. It was some moments before he came into the room, and still he gave her no greeting, but went to the table and sat down.

Without a word Nellie helped him to the rabbit and vegetables from the dish, and in awkward silence he started to eat.

After some moments Nellie went into the kitchen and, picking up his bait bag, threw it among the dirty clothes. Then she washed out his water-bottle. And when she had finished she held it tightly between her hands, and her set face contracted before breaking up into twitching muscles. Slowly her head drooped over the bottle and her hands moved around it as if the bottle itself was the source of her trouble; and for a moment it seemed as though the tears were about to rain on it, but a tap on the back door brought her head up and her body straight. And when she opened it to the minister her face was set in its usual immobility.

'Hallo, Mrs Rowan.'

'Good afternoon, Mr Fraser.'

'Is he in?' It was a conspiratorial whisper.

She nodded and stepped aside; and as she closed the door behind him she said, 'He's at his dinner.'

'I'll wait a while then.'

'No. I'd go right in, Mr Fraser, he'll be finished by now.'

'Any change?'

Again she shook her head. And he shook his, too, as he walked away from her along the passage.

His greeting to Tom, whose innate good manners still made him stand up on the minister's entry, was cheery but failed in its attempt to be casual, as the set stubbornness and irritation in Tom's face showed. Always Tom's attitude towards Mr Fraser had been that of an eager pupil towards a loved master, but since the minister had gone over to the other side he had naturally become an enemy – all those who weren't with him were against him, and no-one was with him. He'd had good proof of this an hour ago when they were waiting to come up, and when Ted Fuller had talked to him, saying to his marrer, 'All the Holy Joes are the same. Have you ever read the Old Testament where that old bastard took a piece into his tent? They were all alike, all the bloody lot of them . . . and they still are. And then they expect you to go to chapel. Bloody neck!'

The new fierceness that had been developing like a hot-house plant within him these past few weeks had leapt out and on to Ted Fuller, even before his body made to push through the men towards his tormentor. Only David's silent grip on his arm and the cage opening to receive Ted and his mates checked what would likely have led to an invitation to doff coats in the quarry.

When they reached the top Ted was gone, and not until they were descending the stairs from the wheelhouse did David speak, and then only in terse, abrupt sentences.

'What d'you expect? You can't blame them. I told you what it'd be. And he's right. You preaching types are the worst when you get going.'

Tom paused on the stairs. 'You an' all?'

'Aye, until you get some sense,' said David.

And now here was another of them. Tom rubbed his hand across his mouth. God in heaven! He looked at Mr Fraser and found he was now disliking him, and he hated himself for it, but was unable to check himself from thinking: He's smalmy. Now he'll ladle out his philosophy.

And again he thought: My God! They seem to be right. I've changed clean through.

'Finish your dinner, Tom.'

'I have finished.'

'There's a nip in the air to-day, it gives you an appetite.'

'Aye, it does.'

181

'Your mother always has a nice fire on . . .'

'Look, Mr Fraser, don't beat about the bush. I know why you've come.'

Mr Fraser lifted his round shoulders, and his brown flecked eyes fixed themselves on Tom, and his tone changed. Almost it changed to Tom's own, as if to imply that he was meeting him on the ground of his own choosing.

'All right, we won't beat about the bush. We'd better sit down though, hadn't we?'

He took a chair by the corner of the fireplace and faced Tom as he sat at the far side of the table, and for a moment neither of them spoke, until Mr Fraser plunged in with a statement that acted like tinder to Tom's dry anger.

'You're making a mistake. You don't realise it now, but you're making a stupid and grave mistake.'

'Yes? Well, what about it?' Tom's face was unrecognisable to the minister. 'If I'm making one it's my mistake. It's my business, and no-one's going to pay but me. And who's to say I'm making a mistake? You, above all people, I expected to see the other side of it. What about the casting of the first stone now?'

Tom's tone and attitude were such that, although Mr Fraser was prepared for opposition, he was now shocked by it, not to mention hurt. Who would have thought that this lad . . . no, he was a man now; but he had known him since he was a small boy, a dreamy little boy. He had watched him grow, and he'd had a hand in leading his tastes along their natural lines. He could remember his own delight when he recognised that in the young pit boy lay a born preacher, a boy with a love of God and who saw the good in man even before he understood him in the slightest. The irony of it all was that it was this very God-given quality that

182

had led him into this mess. His inborn belief would not allow him to recognise the bad in the woman.

'I'm casting no stones, I'm only thinking of you and your future.'

'That's past.'

'Yes. Yes, I know it's past; you won't preach any more. I understand that.'

The cool acceptance by the minister, that what had been his pet desire was no more, had the effect of startling Tom. It seemed that in stating the fact that preaching was now beyond him, the minister was himself pushing him into this world where seemingly everyone's aim was to try to stay his entry.

'The future I am referring to is your life, the life you will have to face if you marry this girl. You'll be cut off from your own people; and not only your own people but the Church. You will lose what respect is still yours. And the greatest thing you must face is you will be like a stranger down the pit. Another man could have done this thing and it would have passed unnoticed. But not you; you have said too much. And during the past you have thrown your example far and wide.'

Tom was on his feet. 'All because of lying, spiteful tongues! What do they know of her?'

'Quite a lot.'

The quiet words checked the torrent, and Tom stared down into the set face of the minister, and his fevered brain sent a picture to him of three nights ago when he had gone across the fells to find, not Beattie, but a note from her hidden in the hole beneath the bushes, in which she told him she couldn't see him for a week as she had a bad cold and had to stay indoors. And the last line had ordered him not to try to see her.

He could even now feel the rage and suspicion that filled him; and he had called himself a fool and tried to whip up the courage to disobey her command. But he knew now, as he knew then, that he was afraid of what he would find if he did.

The old adage, there is no smoke without fire, was ever with him, but he would not allow himself to believe that Beattie was bad, for once he acccepted that he imagined she would cease to exist for him. If he believed as others did, he would, he reasoned, act like them and shun her. Yet, he asked himself now, didn't some part of him believe it? Didn't the very fact that he'd accused the minister of casting a stone signify that there was a reason why the stone should be cast?

God! He swung round from Mr Fraser and stared out of the window. And the minister rose and said with compassion, 'Tom, I know how you feel. Will you please believe me? We are all human, God knows. He above all knows just that. There need be no shame in you feeling attracted to the woman . . . it's generally the good men who are attracted by that type.'

'Don't call her . . . that type!' Tom flung round, emphasising each word, and he stared at the minister as if it would take but one more word to bring his arm swinging out.

But Mr Fraser was not to be intimidated. 'If you don't already know it in your heart there will come a time and soon, when you will have to face up to it.'

'All right then. Say everything you say is true and I marry her, what then? She wouldn't be allowed to come to chapel even if she wanted to. That'd be it, wouldn't it? The God-fearing lot would turn their noses up at her, wouldn't they? And I'd be cut off and shunned. That's what you're telling me, isn't it? . . . Well, let me tell you something. If that's the case you have failed.' He was shouting now. 'Do you hear? Failed! All your preaching and your teaching me to preach that life is as nowt unless lived through God's love and justice is all eyewash. You taught me to go into the highways and byways and to take His word with me, His word of love and forgiveness. Aye, forgiveness. You laid great stock on forgiveness . . . And now when I've done it . . . Do you realise that . . . I've done it? If what you think of her is true, I've done it. And what's happened? You're frightened of the result and of what folks'll say.'

Mr Fraser's face was drained white, and he spoke through stiff lips. 'You're confusing sex with love.'

Tom suddenly became quiet. It was as if the quietness had struck him as lightning strikes. His body relaxed; first his face; then his shoulders; and downwards. And his voice was as near to his old manner of speaking as the minister had heard it. 'I expected that . . . I'm not denying that I want her, but I'm going to tell you something else. It's gone deeper than that. I know . . . somehow I know, it's as if God had told me Himself – I know she's the only one for me . . . Aye, you can shake your head. But right in here' – he tapped the top of his waistcoat – 'I know. And you should believe that' – now his voice rose – 'for it was you taught me to search inside to find out what I really wanted . . . to find out what mattered.'

'I thought you had done that, and that it was God.'

A dull red crept up from Tom's collar to his hair. 'He still does, He still has His place.'

'Huh!' The laugh held both amusement and sarcasm. 'His place! You have put Him in His place. His place comes after that woman. And you think He'll be content to stay there?' The raised eyebrows pressed the question, and for a moment Tom stared back at the minister, his body rigid once more.

And he said in a harsh bewildered fashion, 'I know nowt any more, nowt that makes sense. I only know I want to be left alone, to go to hell, if I'm going, in my own way.'

Mr Fraser sighed, and made one last effort. 'Why don't you join up . . . get away? Yes' – he lifted up his hand – 'yes, I know you tried and they wouldn't let you. But if I use my influence . . . I'm on the same committee as Mr Spencer; a word to him might . . .'

'Get me out of the way? That's it, isn't it?' The red had completely drained from Tom's face now, and around his mouth ran a white line as if painted on the flesh. 'Well, I don't want to be got out of the way. I tried once to join up and I'm not trying again. My God, but it's funny.'

The words, used in a form of blasphemy, made the minister's face tighten, and the sickness of his heart was shown in his eyes as he watched and listened to this unknown man.

Tom was shaking his head slowly as if amazed at his thoughts. 'It's so funny, it's enough to make you stop believing in God altogether.' He nodded towards Mr Fraser. 'You, a minister, would have me join up and go and kill men you have taught me to believe are my brothers. You would have me do this just so as I wouldn't marry a lass who, because of her folks, has been given a bad name. You'd have me do this rather than shock the members of the chapel.' He paused, and asked of the minister quietly, 'Don't you think there's a bit of twisting, mind twisting, going on somewhere?'

Mr Fraser picked up his hat from the chair and walked slowly to the door. And there he turned and said softly, 'I wouldn't have believed it. If ever I've seen the Devil at work in a man I'm seeing him now. He's so manifest that at this moment it is hopeless to try and combat him. All I or anybody can do is to pray for you.'

186

'Oh, to hell!' Whether Tom uttered the words aloud he did not know, but he thought them. For the first time in his life he reacted as he had heard other men react to preaching; the jargon of the pit which had never been his supplied him now with words to express his anger and irritation. Yet as he stood in the middle of the kitchen, so taut that his body looked ready to spring through the walls, his form of retaliation forced a disturbing thought into his mind. He had preached in his own way to the men, yet never had it been his lot to receive the retaliation, 'Oh, go to hell!' although he had heard it delivered many times to others; and into his anger flowed the knowledge that the men had liked listening to him, and young as he was they had believed in him and what he had said. But now their reaction would be not such as they would show to some fellow who had a bee in his bonnet about God – and there were a number of such – but they would be violent, as men are when they feel they have been played for suckers.

Into his body again came the stillness he had experienced a few minutes before and which had enabled him to answer Mr Fraser, at least once, with quiet reasoning. And he reasoned again that if there was any truth in what they were saying about Beattie and he gave her up, the men would believe in him again, more than ever, because, having been tempted, he had been strong. They would even like him better for having been tempted as men are. And his mother and Mr Fraser and all those who were praying for him would believe with a smugness that God had answered their prayers. By giving her up he'd please everybody, except . . . himself . . . and God. Yes, and God. He felt now that it was God's wish that he love Beattie, that he stand by her, for she had need of him. Of this latter he was positive.

He straightened his back . . . only by loving her

could he please God. Even if he never touched her body he knew it was destined that he love her always . . . He walked quietly out of the room and up the stairs, and Nellie, after closing the door on Mr Fraser, listened to his steps above. She looked at the clock. She would wait half an hour to see whether he was going out or going to bed. If he went to bed she would go to the Boswell Cottages.

10

Boswell Cottages

Nellie put on her best clothes, her navy-blue melton cloth coat with the neat fur collar and her new shoes, a pair she had bought with part of her last Store dividend, and her hat, a sedate, steady hat that gave way to gaiety only in its coil of navy and fawn velvet set on its flat brim, and lastly, her fawn gloves. These she carried in her hand, and from time to time she would pull at their fingers.

She was walking in the low part of the town now. She went down Barley Yard and across the railway bridge and past Mason's brickyard; then on past the old Ropery. A little farther on she came to another yard with a high wall and iron gates. It bore on its wall a newly painted notice: Christopher Taggart, Scrap Iron Merchant. For a moment she was brought from her worry and distress. Christopher had not mentioned taking this yard; nor had Maggie. By, he was getting on like a house afire. If only he were happy; if only Maggie would be ordinary, if she would stop fighting herself. She was swung back into her worry. Could any woman stop fighting herself? Maggie was fighting for her son . . . for his love. Perhaps she was going the wrong way about it. But who should say how a woman should go about fighting for her son's happiness? Perhaps she herself was wrong in going to this woman to put an ultimatum before her. Some would say it wasn't her business. But whatever touched her son was her business.

She reached a labyrinth of streets that were new to her, and she pondered that she had lived more than thirty years in this town without ever having been to this quarter. She had never roamed far afield from her own home, except to go to chapel or the shops, with an occasional run into Durham or into Newcastle. She thought dully: What have I done with my life? Nothing. Only lived it for the bairns . . . But lived it mostly for him. Yes, she had only really begun to live when Tom was born. And now he was almost dead to her. Had she ever imagined a time when he would come through the door and not greet her? When she would put down his dinner and he would eat it in silence? Never.

She stopped a woman and asked her the way to Boswell Cottages.

'Why, you're nearly standing on them,' said the woman. 'But mind,' she added laughingly, 'don't stamp too hard or else they'll fall down.'

It started to rain as Nellie stood looking at the remains of the row of one-storey cottages, whose neighbours had one by one fallen into ruin, leaving only the small squares of their foundation stones to tell of their past existence. The rain added to the air of desolation, and it drove Nellie nearer to them. And as she knocked on the first door she realised only in this moment that she did not know whom to ask for. Was it likely that the girl would live here with a man under her own name?

The quick answering of the door startled her, and as she gazed down at the child standing there she was lost for something to say.

But the child was not, for she said promptly, 'Me ma's out an' we don't want to buy anything, an' you can't come in.'

Nellie smiled faintly, for the child had recited most of the warning she herself used to give to Ann before leaving her for even a short time.

'It's all right,' she said to the child. 'I just wanted to know if you could tell me the house where—' She hesitated. 'Do you know anyone by the name of Watson who lives here?'

'Beattie Watson, you mean?'

'Yes.'

'Oh, she lives in that one.' The child leant out of the doorway and pointed to the third door down.

The eyes of the little girl followed Nellie in curiosity, and when after a moment of staring at the door Nellie knocked sharply upon it and received no answer, the child shouted to her, 'She's in, 'cos I saw her come.'

Nellie did not again look towards the child, but knocked once more upon the door. And she had scarcely done so when a voice called, 'All right! All right! Wait a minute, can't you!'

The door was pulled open and Nellie's face was forced to show her astonishment. She gazed up at the tousled head of the girl before her. She did not really know in what condition she had expected to find her, but certainly she had not expected to find her doing such an ordinary thing as washing clothes. Her face was flushed, and over a tight-fitting jumper and skirt she was wearing a fancy apron, such a thing as Ann had made for herself before she was married. It was not a thing that any sensible person would wash in, and Nellie's surprise turned to hard criticism. What could you expect from the likes of her!

She looked at the white soap bubbles blotting themselves out one after another on the girl's arms, and again her thoughts momentarily softened. There was nothing about her that openly pointed to the whore. For one thing, her face wasn't clagged up with paint; it looked an ordinary lass's face, almost. Nellie would have said it could have looked a nice jolly face. But now it had taken on a look of sheer fright.

'What do you want?' The question was scarcely audible.

Nellie heard it but she found she could not answer it; and the girl said again, but impatiently, 'Well, what you after?'

Her face was colourless and her lips looked almost blue.

'You're Beattie Watson, aren't you?'

'Yes, you know I am.'

Nellie took a deep breath and drew in her chin, and said, 'I've got to talk to you.' Whereupon Beattie looked around her wildly as if she was surrounded on all sides and could see no way of escape. Then her gaze returned to Nellie, but rested on the top button of her coat. And she said, 'Well, I can't see you now, I'm busy like. You see, I'm washing.'

'It must be now,' said Nellie, and her tone brought Beattie's eyes up to meet hers.

Their eyes were holding each other's when the child's voice came from behind Nellie, saying, 'I told you she was in.'

This interruption caused Beattie to step aside, and with a jerk of her hand she silently motioned Nellie over the step and into a room furnished with a complete bedroom suite. A double bed sporting a pink silk-covered eiderdown drew Nellie's attention, and she immediately thought, the couch of the harlot.

'Go right through.'

She passed into the other room, and two things registered themselves on her mind. First, that the roof was leaking badly; a pail stood to the side of the window and from a large black patch on the low ceiling four drops ran and forgathered before following each other in quick succession into the pail. Second, the place was clean. The furniture was all new and cheap, but it was shining, and the hearth was not full of ashes but tidily brushed up.

Nellie stood for a moment watching Beattie wipe her arms free from suds, and she shut her mind to everything but the essential thing that had brought her here.

'You might as well sit down.' Beattie pushed a chair forward, and because of a sudden feeling of weakness, but much against the grain, Nellie sat down.

For a moment she pulled at the fingers of her gloves before saying abruptly, 'You know why I've come?'

'Yes . . . I'm not daft.'

'No, but you're wicked!' The words had followed on the thought and were out before Nellie could stop them, and they plunged the two women into a barrage of words.

'It all depends upon what you mean by wicked.' Beattie's face was set to match Nellie's own, stiff and hard with anger. 'There's worse than me about. And you chapel lot are among them. Give a dog a bad name and hang him.'

'Do you deny you are living here with a man?' Nellie pointed one finger, taut as a stick, about the room.

'No, I don't. I deny nowt. He's a single fellow, and I'm hurting nobody. And it's me own business.'

'You're hurting nobody? What about my lad?'

At the mention of Tom the anger sank from Beattie's face, and she sat down abruptly as if she had been pushed, and resting her elbow on the table she dropped her head on to her hands and began to mutter unintelligible words. Her head moved restlessly from side to side for some time; then she turned and faced Nellie again.

'I tried to tell him . . . honest to God I did. I tried to put him off but he wouldn't take any notice. I broke it off twice, I did honest, but he wouldn't let me be.'

'He wouldn't?' Nellie's eyes were round and staring. 'You had only to tell him you were living with another man, and I can assure you that would have been enough.'

'But I wasn't. He had gone then . . . I mean back to sea . . . and I was on me own.'

'But you were taking his money as his wife, weren't you? And are still?'

Beattie rose swiftly and looked down on Nellie. 'You know a lot, don't you? Well, what money I get has got nowt to do with you.'

'It's got everything to do with me; it concerns my lad.'

'Oh, my God! Your lad!' There was scorn in Beattie's voice. She stepped back from Nellie as if to give herself greater distance from which to throw the words at her. 'Lad! He's a man! If you'd let him be one, he'd be a man. You mothers, you're all alike. You never let go, do you? But there's one thing certain, you can't keep them for ever.'

Nellie experienced a fresh rush of anger as she listened to the girl, yet she was puzzled at the tangent her defence had taken, until she remembered where Christopher had received the information about her in the first place. It was from the other man's mother. And strangely, too, Beattie's attitude brought Ann before her, Ann saying, 'No mother should think she can do what she likes with a son.'

The recollection added to her fury, and leaning towards Beattie she burst out, 'He's my son, and I'd be a poor mother indeed if I didn't try to protect him from the likes of you!'

'The likes of me! Who are you to say what I'm like? Let me tell you this. There are respectable, or so-called, women in this town who I wouldn't touch with a barge-pole . . . I've had two men in my life. Aye, you can look astonished, but that's the truth. That's all I've had. But I could name some houses in your quarter where even a young gas man daren't go in. They've got to send the old 'uns. And they're your respectable married women an' all . . . chapel-goers!' She stood panting and alert, waiting for Nellie's attack.

But Nellie was silent. Her astonishment was not being registered at the smallness of the number of men Beattie owned to having, but at the frankness of the admission; she had spoken of it as one would speak of having had two glasses of beer . . . How in the name of God had her lad come under this influence! But, why did she ask? They had power, these women, the power of the Devil. Hadn't she suffered from it all her married life? They polluted men.

Beattie was staring at her with eyes narrowed to slits, and Nellie said, 'Your sins won't be lightened by laying the blame on others.'

'My sins!' The derision brought a smile to Beattie's face.

'Yes, your sins. And your last is all the greater because you knew he was preaching.'

'I didn't, not until long after I met him; and then it was too late. What do you think I am to get myself mixed up with a chapelite knowingly? And when I did know I tried to finish it. Anyway, who'd think of a pitman going round preaching?'

'And now you're satisfied because you've stopped him preaching.'

Beattie put her hand to her head and sat down again, and she closed her eyes as if in bewilderment. Then looking at Nellie with a completely changed expression, she asked quietly, 'Can't you give me credit for one decent action? Look, I'll tell you. I knew it wasn't fair, but as I said, he wouldn't take no. Then—' She looked down at the pail with the water now pinging against the side of it and spraying on to the linoleum, and she said softly, 'I got to care for him. I tried not to but I did. And when I knew for sure how I felt I wrote to Bill.' She raised her eyes from the pail and looked down on her hands. 'He's the fellow. I told him I wanted to end it, but he wouldn't take no either. He said if I wasn't here when he . . . Oh well' – she raised her eyes – 'that's how it is.'

Nellie, steeling herself against the pleading in the eyes and voice of the girl, said harshly, 'Well, it must end. And right away. You must tell him.'

'No, I can't do that. No.' She shook her head. 'Look, give me time; I'll get rid of Bill.'

'You'll what!' Nellie rose to her feet, her head nearly reaching the ceiling with the stretching of her body. 'You expect my lad'll have you after living with another man?'

'He needn't know. Well' – Beattie moved her hands helplessly – 'if we start afresh . . . I mean. I'll tell him there's been somebody else . . . but after Bill's gone. Give me a bit of time and I'll manage it.'

For the moment Nellie was too dumbfounded to speak. Then she burst out, 'But you've got a cheek! The cheek of the Devil. You've been with these men and you expect to have my lad, a clean, God-fearing boy.'

'Oh, for God's sake, shut up! You'd think to hear you talk he was still in nappies!' All Beattie's softness was lost again under her anger. 'Let me tell you, from the minute a lad goes down the pit he's a man. I've six brothers and I know.'

'Be quiet!'

'I won't be quiet. This is my house.'

They stood glaring at each other. Then Nellie seemed to lift her body and throw it towards the door. She flung herself through the bedroom, but before she reached the front door Beattie was beside her, and catching hold of her arm, she asked, 'What are you going to do?' The fear was in her voice again.

Nellie looked at her coldly. 'You'll know soon enough.'

'Don't tell him. Oh, don't tell him. Give me this one chance . . . please.'

Nellie continued to glare at the girl. Yet when she answered her her voice was quieter. But it lacked no firmness. 'You know that's impossible; he's bound to get to know. How do you think I found out? Other people know. The best thing you can do is to move away.'

Beattie withdrew her hand slowly from Nellie's arm. She reached out and pulled back the sneck of the door, and then watched Nellie step into the driving rain. She watched her until she had crossed the clearing and became lost in the streets beyond. Then she closed the door, and walking slowly back into the kitchen, she went to the galvanised bath standing on a side table and putting her hands into the suds began mechanically to rub the clothes. Even when the suds became blotted from her sight she kept her hands in the water, as if drawing comfort from its warmth.

*   *   *

The same child who had directed Nellie to No. 4 Boswell Cottages now looked at Tom. She knew he was a stranger to this part; she had seen other strange men about here, mostly in uniform; but they had not stood as this one was doing, stock still and staring. They had gone into the Printer's Arms on the far corner, or to the pictures that loomed its blank back wall up behind the cottages, to which if you pressed your ear you could hear the machinery that made the pictures go. This man was too early for the bar and the pictures. She first noticed him when she was let out to play after the rain stopped. He was standing then as he was now . . . staring. She had passed him to get to the pond, which wasn't really a pond at all, only a puddle swollen with the rain. And she nearly stopped and asked him to shape the bit of wood she was carrying into a boat . . . an Air Force man had once whittled her a sculler out of a littler bit of wood than this.

She had paused for a second by the man's knee, but he hadn't looked down on her; he had kept looking towards the cottages. And he wasn't blinking; his eyes were open, like the blind man who'd had his eyes hurt in the air raid.

She hitched away now towards the water, singing:

The big ship sails through the alley-alley-o,
The alley-alley-o,
The big ship sails through the alley-alley-o
On the fifteenth of September.

Then she pushed her piece of wood towards the centre of the puddle, and lashed the water with a stick until her boat dipped and bobbed. And she became excited and looked about her to see whether there was another child to share her joy and to play at being on the sands at Shields. But she saw no-one, only the man. The sight of him still standing motionless took her interest from her boat, and she left it and walked slowly back to him. She would ask him if he was lost. She was lost once in Whitley Bay, and the bobby took her to the polis station. And one of the bobbies had given her taffie, and she talked to them and they all laughed. And when her mother came for her she didn't want to go home . . . she liked bobbies.

She hadn't reached the man when she saw him move, just his body, not his legs. His body twitched like Ronnie Shelton's did when he was going to have a fit. She followed the man's gaze and saw Billy Cruikshanks go into the house where Beattie Watson lived . . . Her mother said Beattie Watson was no good except in bed, and she was good there. Somehow she couldn't make this out, for she herself was good in bed, she went straight to sleep, and she couldn't see how anybody was no good 'cos they were good in bed. She'd have to ask somebody about this some time.

She reached the man and said, 'Are you waiting for the pictures? They don't start till half past six and you've got to queue. But not if you go in the plush seats.'

He didn't answer, and she walked directly in front of him. And then he moved. He must have known she was there, for he pushed her to one side, and she watched him walk towards the door Billy Cruikshanks had just closed. And she followed him and stood at his side as he knocked on the door. It was a soft knock at first; then he made it louder. And when the door opened, her interest became so intense that she pushed against his legs to get a good look at Beattie Watson. Beattie Watson was frightened; she had never seen anyone so frightened, except perhaps her mother, the day she took her to try the gas masks on.

Eeh! Beattie Watson was swearing. She was saying, 'Jesus! Jesus!' Eeh! The Sunday-school teacher said you'd go to hell if you said Jesus like that and not in a hymn. The man was staring at Beattie, but he didn't speak. Perhaps he was dumb. But he wasn't blind at all, for when Beattie said 'For God's sake go away, and I'll see you later,' and she tried to close the door, he put his foot in it.

Then the door was suddenly pulled wide open and Beattie wasn't there any longer; but Billy Cruikshanks was. He was in his sailor's clothes an' all.

She was very interested in Billy Cruikshanks' sailor suit, because she was on the concert for Christmas, and she was going to do the sailor's hornpipe. And only yesterday Billy had come into their back yard and showed her how to do the hornpipe. And he let her put his hat on. She liked Billy. He was strong and could lift her up with one hand, even though he wasn't tall like this man. He was talking to the man now like her da talked to her ma at times when he was busting for a fight, like as if he was joking but he wasn't.

Billy was nodding his head and saying 'Oh yeah! Now I know. Come to see Miss Beattie Watson have you? And find out how things stand? Chum, I can tell you how things stand. I can tell you all you want to know . . . lugfuls. Shut up, you!' He pushed his hand back into the room.

'I should tell you you're a dirty swine, shouldn't I, sneaking a fellow's lass? A fellow who's fighting for his country mind, and not hiding down the pit! Oh,

I know you're down the pit. Chum, I know lots; you'd be surprised. All right, all right, keep your fists, you're goin' to need 'em. But you're goin' to hear me first; I've been wanting to catch up with you.'

Beattie's voice came to the child, crying, 'For God's sake, Bill, come inside!' And Bill laughed back into the room, 'Aye, anything you say, Beat. Yes, I'll come inside. And he'll come an' all, won't you? Come inside, you poor bugger, and see the home I've got for her.' He flung the door wide, then bent forward to put his hand on the man's shoulder to pull him over the threshold. But it was knocked away, and the sound of wrist meeting wrist was hard, like the meeting of stones. Then after what seemed a long time to the child, during which no-one spoke, the man went into the house and the door was closed.

The child ran to the window, but when she saw the blackout up she ran back to the door and stood on the step with her ear to the large keyhole. And Billy's voice came plainly to her, saying, 'She's had my money: not only the day or yesterday, but since I was a nipper. She gets you . . . don't you, Beattie?'

There followed a stillness and the child pressed closer to the door, when the voice came again, 'You drive a fellow up the lum, don't you? And when you've got him there you vamoose. You're not the first, pitboy. Oh no, not by a long chalk.'

'Don't believe him.' Beattie's voice came through the keyhole, high and thin, like the last vibration of a shrill whistle.

'What about Red MacIntyre?' Billy's voice sounded playful.

But Beattie's was more shrill as she shouted back, 'I was finished with you then . . . you know I was.

And I'm finished with you now, for good! Tom, I am
. . . I am.'

'Tom . . . I am, I am! Hear that? Well, what d'you
think? Do you want this brothel bitch?'

The child waited for the man to speak; and when
he didn't she thought: He's daft. But when she heard
a quick shuffling of feet she thought again, No, he's
not. And as Beattie's voice came to her, shouting, 'No!
No! Stop it!' she dashed away from the door and up
the street. They were fighting and she knew where that
would end . . . in the back lane. But just as she turned
the corner of the last cottage she saw the old woman
again, the one who had been to Beattie Watson's in
the afternoon. She was standing close against the wall
by the far corner.

The child stopped and stared across at her, and for
no reason she could explain she connected her with the
man, and she shouted. 'They're fighting!' before
dashing off again.

Beattie's back door was open and the men were
in the yard. They were hitting each other with their
fists . . . bang, bang, bang! And the man was hitting as hard as Billy. But Billy was very strong, and
his fist hit the man under the chin and lifted him
up, and he fell . . . plop. And she jumped to one
side of the doorway, for she thought he was going
to fall on top of her. She looked down on him now.
Billy had knocked him clean through the opening
of the yard door, and he came and stood over him.
The man blinked slowly, then shook his head. And
before she had time to say 'Jack Robinson' he was
up and they were at it again . . . bash, bash, bash!

And now the man seemed to be real mad, like her
da got when he had a lot of money on a Saturda'

night. He punched and punched at Billy, and she had to dodge this way and that. And she began to shout, egging Billy on. Then she saw the man step back and his fist come up. She could see his knuckles shining white like the bone that stuck out of the half-shoulder of mutton her ma got from the butcher's. As the man's fist hit Billy she closed her eyes for a split second, and before she had time to open them she felt herself lifted into the air. She actually experienced herself sailing through it. Then she remembered no more of the fight.

And now the back lane was full . . . full of faces, and somebody crying. Oh, that was her ma. She could always tell her ma's cry, 'cos she hiccuped all the time.

'You'll be all right, hinny.'

It was Mrs Jamieson from next door looking down into her face. And she meant to answer 'Yes, I'm all right' and raise herself from the ground, but when she tried to move the pain went up her back, and she couldn't say anything. She closed her eyes; and when she opened them again there was Billy. He was kneeling on the ground and he was stroking her cheek, and his face was all blood. Then quite suddenly she forgot about Billy, for he disappeared abruptly from her view as she was lifted in the air. She knew immediately what she was on – it was a stretcher, like they had in the dugout. She was on a stretcher, and when you were on a stretcher you went in an ambulance. She wished she could have sat up to see it better and all the people who were watching her. She tried to smile when she saw the bobbies, but she felt too hazy. There were two bobbies and they were standing by the ambulance. Then her gaze was drawn from them to the man. He was staring down at her, and his face was different, all crumpled and sorry-like. She hoped he wouldn't cry; she got a funny feeling inside when men cried. Her da sometimes cried. Then suddenly she was lifted above his face, and as she went upwards there arose from the murmur around her one clear sentence, 'If she kicks the bucket those two are for it.' And she knew it meant her, and that she was bad and might die.

Part Three
Stephen

11

A Bit of Jollification

Had the war not reached such a point in September 1940 that it could only be continued by the exertion of the limit of the strength of each individual, the affair of Billy Cruikshanks and Tom Rowan and the child, Jennie Forester, would have set light to Fellburn, and the *Newcastle Daily Courier* would have blazoned the story across its headlines . . . Men Fight Over Fellburn Girl . . . Child Flung Against Wall . . . Doctors Fear She Will Never Walk Again. But instead of such headlines there appeared a few lines only, at the bottom of the second page, wherein it said that a child had been injured during a fight, and it was a very regrettable state of affairs.

That was all. With husbands and sons dying, with wives going off with other men, with men stationed in far-off places that seemed like forgotten worlds deemed safe in which to have a bit of fun, fun that seeped through to the wife in Fellburn as if by supernatural means, with daughters joining W.A.A.F.S. or A.T.S. and leaving mothers praying that they keep themselves to themselves, there was little time or inclination to talk about the Rowan affair.

What was the affair, anyway, against the drama of the Battle of Britain? London was ablaze; the country was gasping for its life; many thought it would die; instead pilots and gunners died and planes disintegrated; and the country received its first blood transfusion.

Within a week of Tom appearing in the police court the incident was forgotten by everybody except the members of the chapel and the Rowan family, who, each in his own way, carried the burden of the disgrace. It maddened Maggie; it filled Ann with pity; it stunned George; Nellie for a time seemed to break under it; and its effect on Tom was to change him into a morose man. He talked little and walked a lot; in his turn, he did his firewatching, he put out his quota of incendiaries, and during the latter part of 1941 he worked until he collapsed, helping to extricate twenty-three of his trapped workmates. His efforts were commended by the management. This too was but a pin-prick in the world of catastrophe. During the next year events, depressing and elevating, took place; in February Singapore fell; and on 21 October began one of the greatest battles of all times – El Alamein – and in it Fred Taggart was killed. In 1943 most people were of the opinion that the war would go on for ever; yet on 6 June 1944, everyone saw the war ending within a few weeks; but it was many months before V.E. Day came. And Fellburn, together with the rest of the country, went mad.

It was three o'clock when Tom came up above ground, and he had his work cut out to get through the streets. People were calling to each other; they called to him; strangers greeted him as if he were their kin; a woman caught him around the waist and waltzed him off the pavement, and she laughed and called 'Go on, old sobersides' when he pushed her away.

Already his street was being decorated with flags by the women, and he cut through the lane to avoid their chaffing. Nellie greeted him before he had closed the door.

'It's great news, isn't it? Oh, won't it be grand to buy stuff again! We'll soon come off the ration now. Ann's just gone . . . she's so excited, it's done her good. Now the raids are over she'll be better. And Stephen's been in . . . Chris brought him. Maggie wants us all to go up there to tea the morrow. Not that I'll go, but it's nice of her to ask us, isn't it?' She did not wait for his reply, but went on, 'Come, have your dinner. It doesn't seem real, does it, now it's all over?' She took his coat from him and hung it up. She seemed unable to stop talking, and he listened to her with slight wonder, for rarely did she chatter. As she placed his dinner before him she said, almost frivolously, 'Now we can go back to normal, eh?'

To normal. He looked at her. When had she been other than normal, grimly normal and sensible? And irritating?

On the last thought he attacked his dinner, saying, 'There's still the Japs.'

This statement, or his tone, seemed to take the exuberance from her, and she said rather flatly, 'Yes, you're right; there's still the Japs.'

She went into the kitchen and he stopped eating and stared at his plate. Why must he do it? He just couldn't seem to help it. He pushed the plate away. If only she would leave go of him. Never had he dreamed the time would come when she would irritate him beyond endurance – her very kindness and her solicitude were the worst irritants. Oh, why hadn't he made the break five years ago and taken no notice of her pleading? Why had he allowed it to tear him to shreds? He could feel her yet, crying on his breast, sobbing and entreating . . . sobbing and entreating. And then there was the child too. Yes, he must be fair, it hadn't been she alone who had tied him.

He pushed his dinner still further from him. Somehow the child still tied him, and he still had nightmares in which he slayed children by the score, sometimes beating them on the back until they couldn't move. Yet the nightmares exceeded a thousandfold their cause, for altogether Jennie had lain only a year on her back. He could never recall the relief he had experienced when the doctors found there was nothing structurally wrong with her; all he could recall was the anxiety of that year during which once a week he went to see her. Even when the doctor, trying to lighten his remorse, told him the strangest tale he had ever heard, still his nightmares did not lessen. The strange truth was that the child did not want to walk; she was exceedingly happy as she was. If she walked she would have to return home, and she didn't like her home. In hospital she was waited on and petted, she had numbers of people come to see her, and she amused everybody with her chatter. And she was proud of this last achievement.

When the doctor proposed placing her in a home for specialised treatment under a psychiatrist, he had willingly agreed, although it meant that it would take every penny he made, for he had taken it upon himself to pay for the child during her illness. He remembered now his mother's eagerness to share this burden, but he could give her no credit for it, because he knew she was using it as another invisible cord with which to tie him.

Although Jennie had been walking for the past two years and was now leading a happy normal life, the pressure of her still lay heavily on him. She seemed to weigh on his mind; for he continually found himself thinking, But what if she had died? He could see her dead and he her slayer. Although it had not been his arm that knocked her flying he held himself responsible for being the primary cause. Had he not gone to the house that day it would never have happened; and further, if his mother had not told him he never would have gone. It was this fact that had kept the barrier raised between them. If she had minded her own business the child would not have been hurt; and he would have had Beattie. By Beattie's own choice he would have had her.

Rising, he went and stood near the fireplace. He hadn't thought of Beattie Watson for months now – it was almost like the time immediately after the fight – she had sunk into a pocket of his mind, pushed there by the weight of the child. He was aware of her being there, and her presence hurt him, but consciously he didn't or wouldn't allow himself to think of her. She had stayed fast, secured against thoughts, until the doctor told him about Jennie using her back as a means of escape, and then he knew that he too had used Jennie as an escape. And realising this, his longing for Beattie became as fresh as if he had parted from her but yesterday. Yet during these past few months he knew that time had drawn a curtain between him and her, for he could no longer remember her face clearly, or recall her voice or the sound of her laugh; she was like a poison working out of his blood. And looking at himself now, he saw that he was quite willing that it should go. Only by ridding himself of the poison could he look at Rosemary.

Twice he had gone to tea at Ann's knowing that he would meet Rosemary there . . . Did he like Rosemary? Yes; she was a nice girl. Could he love Rosemary sufficiently to marry her? He swung away from the mantelpiece and went out of the room and up the stairs, and as Nellie called after him, 'Why, you haven't eaten your dinner, lad,' he thought at least it would be a means of escape, a way that would not hurt his mother; in fact it would give her pleasure.

Nellie looked down at the meal she had prepared with such pains, and her head shook pathetically over it. Nothing seemed to please him; the more she did for him the more he seemed to hold her at arm's length. Oh, if they could go back, back to before the war when he used to talk and laugh with her. But no-one could go back. At times she thought he still resented her pointing out to him the kind of woman that Beattie Watson was. But then again she thought no; he must have been glad in his heart that he found out in time. It was hurting that child that had really altered him. And God forgive her, but at the time she had been thankful that the child was hurt, for it had kept him at home. Yes, she should thank God for lots of things. And she did this day: especially that she still had him . . . and whole. Many a poor mother was shedding bitter tears at this moment . . . Kitty had cried broken-heartedly over Fred. Although she still had seven sons left, on this particular day Kitty must have missed Fred as never before. Yes – she took the plate into the kitchen – she had a lot to be thankful for. God had been good, and she would pray that He would be even better and let Tom take up with young Rosemary Monkton. She was a nice lass, quiet, with no airs about her, and a regular chapel-goer. If she got him she would likely get him back to chapel, and, who knew, to preaching again. It would be an ideal match; and they could be comfortable, for he was making fine money. Times had changed. George was making only a pound a week when they were first married, and now Tom was getting nearly twice that a shift. And then there was all the overtime he could put in. It was the miner's day. And not afore time. She nodded at the sink . . .

no, not afore time. Never would things be as they once were. Wars were funny things. They brought sorrow, yet they created chances that a lifetime's struggle in times of peace would never offer. Look at Christopher. Who, in their wildest dreams, would have imagined that he would ever have had the money to buy a house on Brampton Hill? It might have been Maggie who wanted the house, but it was Christopher's money that bought it. And all out of scrap iron. Twelve rooms and a great garden. There again, they would never have got it for the price they had if the war hadn't been on and houses going for a song

Nellie could look back to the day when Maggie had first gone to work in the laundry – like yesterday it was – and now she owned half of it. Fancy that. Maggie owning half of the laundry! And by what she said last week it wouldn't be long afore she owned the lot. There it was, the war again had brought that about. No labour to be had and Mrs Thornton being ill. Of course Maggie had worked like a Trojan – there was every credit due to her. If only it had brought her happiness.

Nellie's reminiscences stopped at this point. She washed the dishes, trying the while to close her mind to the thought that seemed to lead naturally from Maggie's unhappiness to Ann's. But it was of no use. She stopped in the middle of cleaning out the sink and stared through the window. If only their Ann had had a bairn. That's where the trouble lay. She wouldn't have had nerves then; nor would she have had this unnatural love for Stephen; for after all it wasn't natural to dote on the lad like she did. And then there was the lad himself, upsetting Maggie every minute by sneaking off to see Ann. It was getting out of hand, the whole thing. And David didn't like it. No, she could see he didn't like it.

On her thought of David, she saw him walking down his mother's back garden. When he turned to shut the gate he waved and called to her, 'Coming out the night to get blued?'

She leaned towards the open window and shook her head reprovingly at him. He was a nice lad, was Davie. Ann was lucky to have a man like him. It wasn't everybody who would have put up with her nerves these past years, and on top of that this mad affection for the lad.

As David walked towards his own home it was the lad that was filling his mind too. He was telling himself that he would have to pull himself together and not be such a blasted fool as to be jealous of an eight-year-old kid. Not that he didn't like Stephen, he thought the world of him. But not in the same way as Ann did. She was clean potty on him; and he was potty on her. At times lately he had been able to see Maggie's side of the affair. If the tables had been turned, how would Ann have liked a son of hers to give his affections elsewhere? No, Maggie must have her due, it wasn't right.

But what could he do? It would take someone cleverer than him to convince Ann she was wrong. It all came of her not having bairns of her own. Oh, the same old problem. He got tired of it at times. For himself he was now quite content to accept the fact that they weren't going to have any bairns. Not that he wouldn't have given his ears for one, but what had to be had to be. As long as he had Ann he was, to a great measure, content. He wished he could think it was the same with her. Not that she didn't care for him. She did. She had been a good wife in every way. Like with everyone else, there had been bad times. That time a few years ago when she wouldn't come near him. But that was her nerves, and she had got over that. And now that the war was over she'd get over her fear of raids, and her nerves would get better. Aye, she'd get better now . . . Only there was still the lad.

He called out and answered excited greetings as he walked up his back lane.

'Goin' to miss a shift the morrer, Dave?'

'What, and get him to lose his bonus!'

'Deputies don't lose their bonus, man. Do they, Dave?'

'Be hard put to, seein'· they don't get any,' David laughed.

'Aw, go on, man; I bet you make a bit on the side . . . Goner get blued the night?'

'What do you think?'

Laughing and chaffing, he reached his gate and went up the path, and his step was checked when, through the window, he saw the two heads close together – half an hour ago the lad had left his Grannie's with Chris to go home. As he neared the door they came fully into his view, Ann with her arm about the boy's waist, and he kneeling on a chair with his arm about her neck. They were both engrossed in a map spread on the table; and on David's entry Ann jumped and said, 'Oh, you did give me a start. Why do you come creeping in like that?'

She took her arm away from the boy, but he still kept his about her neck.

'Hallo again, Uncle Davie.'

'I thought you had to go home.'

'Father had to go down to the yard and I came to show Auntie Ann my map, to show her what we have won.' His voice was clear and his diction correct.

Ann rose from the chair, pulling herself away from the boy's arm, and he stood up and looked at David with a look that was open yet guarded.

David turned away from it and said, 'Your da told us that your mother was expecting you back. That was why he couldn't stay.'

'Yes, I know.' Stephen jerked one shoulder with a nervous movement. He looked at the shoulder whilst it jerked as if he could see something being thrown off. 'I only called on my way home.'

'But it isn't on your way home, and you know it isn't.'

'David, stop it!' Ann's voice was trembling. She did not look at him as she said this, but went to the fireside box and took out a duster and started to rub the table vigorously. And David, watching her, thought, How like her mother.

He spoke again to Stephen: 'You'd better get home . . . Have you a copper for your bus?'

'Yes.'

'Then off you go, your mother'll be worrying.'

'David!' The note now in Ann's voice made his face grim, and he said, 'We'll talk about this later. Now he's got to go. It's a good step and Maggie'll be wondering.'

'Maggie!' Everything Ann was feeling was conveyed in that one word. She turned angrily away from him, and turning to Stephen, said, 'Wait a minute, I'll go up to the bus with you.'

As she went into the passage to get her coat, quite quietly David said, 'You're not going.'

'What!' She turned on him.

'You heard what I said.'

'Uncle David' – the boy's voice was low and there was a tremor in it too now – 'here's my father coming.'

Both Ann and David turned to the window and watched Chris hurrying up the path; and when he came in neither of them spoke to him, nor he immediately to them, but he addressed his son harshly, 'You'll do this once too often, me lad. Didn't I tell you to go straight home? I dropped him off at the foot of the Hill.' He made this remark to David; and David answered through tight lips, 'It isn't his fault.'

'Yes, it is,' said Chris. 'He just does it to vex . . .' He did not finish, but pointing to the door said, 'Get going. And touch nowt in the car, mind. I'll be there in a minute.'

The three of them watched the boy walk out and down the garden. Although his shoulder twitched slightly he walked slowly and calmly, so calmly that David thought, I'd like to put my toe in his backside, and Chris said, 'What can you do? I got home expecting him to be there. He's due at somebody's party at four o'clock. And there she was, nearly mad.'

David said again, 'You can't blame him.'

'No. Blame me!' Ann was pointing dramatically to herself. 'I rushed to the foot of Brampton Hill and brought him here.'

Chris looked at Ann and shook his head. 'I understand, really. He likes to come . . . I don't blame him. If only the young devil would do it on the quiet. But it seems as if he does it at times just to . . . Oh, what's the use of talking! Well, I'd best be off. Bye, Ann. Don't worry. See you the morrer, Dave.'

David nodded silently, and Ann said nothing, and Christopher went out still thinking, Who can blame him for coming? I come meself. But he's got to be stopped.

As he walked up the lane towards the car, he too, like David, came in for his share of chaff, chaff that was a mixture of fun, envy and derision:

'Goner throw a victory party, Chris?'

'Aye, top hat and tails up yonder, isn't it, Chris?'

'What you goner sell when they don't want scrap, Chris?'

'Why, he'll buy it back and make it into bikes, won't you, Chris?'

'They can all chaff you, Chris, but there's every credit due to you. And you haven't forgotten your own folks . . . that tells the stamp of a man when he don't forget his own folk.'

The last was from a woman; and he turned grateful eyes on her and threw a remark back at the others that was lost in their laughter. And when he reached the car most of his temper had passed, and he said to Stephen, who was sitting behind the wheel, 'Move over, there.' And the boy, sensing his change of mood, said, 'I'm sorry, Father.'

Chris started up the car. 'It's no use telling me you're sorry, you'd better tell your mother that.'

The boy's face closed on the words; and as Chris glanced at him he thought, That's the only time he looks like her, when he puts that . . . shut look on his face.

'Father.'

'Aye.'

'Oh, it doesn't matter.'

Again Chris glanced at his son. He was sitting upright on his seat staring straight ahead; he looked in expression and height a boy of ten, certainly not one of eight. It always surprised Chris anew when he thought, as he was doing now, This is my lad. He never thought, This is my son – son was in the same strange category as father, and he was not even yet used to the boy addressing him as father. There were times when he longed to hear him say da; but the word da was strictly forbidden.

His thinking was interrupted by a hail from the corner of his mother's street. He raised his hand in a return salutation and smiled a grim little smile to himself. Mr and Mrs Farrett breaking their necks to recognise him! The time wasn't far passed when they would not have looked the side he was on. They had always been the nobs of their street because they had a shop in town, and the Taggarts had been beneath their notice. But now, since he had a car and things . . . He ran his hand around the wheel. This was another thing he couldn't get used to. Fancy him having a car . . . and driving it. And going back now to Brampton Hill! Well, they could keep Brampton Hill any day in the week; he wouldn't care if he saw the last of the Hill the morrer. It was bad enough now with hardly anyone on it, but what would it be like when the folks came back, the folks who really belonged there? Maggie thought she was getting her feet well in because she had joined the W.V.S. and so worked with some of the women and was on the child welfare committee. Maggie and child welfare! My God! And her own son hating her guts!

He turned the car cautiously into the main road, which was swarming with people; but although he was careful to avoid them he was doing so more by instinct than sight, for he wasn't really seeing them, he was seeing Maggie, the new Maggie who couldn't, even with all her striving, cover up the old Maggie; neither her new smart clothes nor her visits to the hairdresser could make the desired difference. Who would have thought she would go mad on clothes? She even bought clothing coupons at two bob a time! He could remember when she begrudged having to pay five shillings for a shirt for him; now she even fought with him to get his suits tailor-made. Aye, suits. He had three now besides his working clothes, and all made by a tailor. He had argued that the Store ready-mades were good enough for him, and he could still feel the cruel sting of her reply, 'The Store might make clothes for men of your height, but not of your size!' She might as well have said shape instead of size, for that was what she meant. He had never before wanted to strike her, but he had that day.

Yet she had been right; the fellow did make the suits in such a way that at least, if they did not diminish his hump, they did not emphasise it. It was odd when he came to think of it, but none the less irritating, that she turned out to be right about a number of things – such as the buying of this car, a 1938 Morris Eight which he could now sell perhaps for three hundred and which he got for only a hundred and twenty. Only yesterday she had told him with elation that six months ago she had taken a mortgage on four little houses in the town, all slightly bomb damaged, and that within the next few months she'd be able to sell them for double their cost. It was the first he had heard of the deal. She was cute, was Maggie. That was one thing he had to hand her, she was cute. She could see ahead, whereas he never could; he only saw the thing under his nose. Well, he considered himself, even with that range, as not having done so badly. He knew that he was classed in the category of warm men now, especially round about his own quarter. It was odd that although he had been left home for nearly ten years he still thought of Oswald Street as his own quarter. And that was how, he supposed, it would be till the end. Brampton Hill or no Brampton Hill, he'd feel at home only in his own quarter. And the core of that quarter was his mother's kitchen.

Why was it all the lads of their family were always dropping in home? Look at this morning, the house packed with all but Fred. They still fought and squabbled, but they came back. Was it their mother who kept them together? She made no noticeable claim on any of them that he could see. It wasn't 'Where have you been?' or 'Where are you going?' with her; not like Aunt Nell. Perhaps that was why they all came back. And then there was always something to eat or drink. He didn't know how she managed to get it. It had always been the same, even when money was scarce; but now with money plentiful and food scarce there was little difference; the only difference was in himself. For when he sat eating her food now, he knew that before he left he would slip her something, very likely a note, and she would nod and smile and push it down between her ample breasts; and he would leave the house feeling straight, for the feeling of money in your pocket helped to straighten a man out . . . inside, as did the recognition in the eyes of his brothers that their Chris was a business man – him, the runt of the litter, a business man, him they fought over on his wedding day, the wedding that made his mother shed bitter tears. And now she was proud of him. Oh, she said nowt, but he knew; as he also knew that she didn't, or would never, like Maggie. Yet – he'd admit this only to himself – if it hadn't been for Maggie he wouldn't be where he was the day. Oh yes, he might have sold scrap without her, but she had said truly during one of their many rows 'Any fool can make a little money, but it takes a clever one to keep it and double it.' She was right once more; and he damned her often for being right.

'Father, why didn't you marry Auntie Ann?'

The car swung into the centre of the road and just missed a cyclist by a hair's breadth. They were passing Duke's Park which was only two turnings from the Hill itself, and Chris swung the car into a side road and brought it to a halt alongside the high wall of a house. Then he turned to Stephen.

'What did you say there?'

The boy wriggled on his seat and tucked one leg under him; his shoulder twitched as he looked up at his father. 'I just said why didn't you marry Auntie Ann?'

'What put it into your head to ask that?'

'Nothing.' Stephen looked away through the windscreen up the tree-shaded road. 'Auntie Ann told me she always went with you to feed the pigs, and you used to take her for walks before she married Uncle Dave. It would have been nice, wouldn't it, if you had?' Swiftly he brought his gaze back to his father as if trying to take him unawares.

Chris swallowed, and brought out, 'Now look here, me lad, I want to hear no more of that talk. D'you hear?'

'But I thought you liked Auntie Ann too.'

Again Chris swallowed. 'Everybody likes Auntie Ann.'

'Oh no, they don't.' The leg was slowly withdrawn from under him, and Stephen sat straight up as if stiffened by the meaning of his words.

'Stephen' – Chris's voice was definitely pleading – 'now listen to me. Your mother is trying to do her best for you. You've got to get that into your head. You understand? And things would be better at home if you did what you were told . . . Look. Do this to please me, will you? Have a shot at doing what you're told. If you do I promise you I'll take you along myself to see Auntie Ann at least once a week.'

There, he was on the subject of Ann again when he thought he had cleverly side-tracked it.

'But I don't want to go just once a week, I want to go every day. Why won't Mother let me call every day? Why won't she?' It was a question that demanded an answer by its very insistence, besides the probing steadiness of the eyes and Chris turned from his son and thumped the wheel softly with his fist.

'Is it because of you, Daddy?'

'Because of me!' Chris confronted his son again as if he was a grown man, surprise and amazement in his face at the question. He almost stammered the answer, 'No . . . No. What makes you think that?' My God! the boy had a mind like a grown-up. What did he know? He couldn't know anything, there was nothing to know. Then what was he guessing?

'Well, if it isn't because of you, what is it because of?'

Chris stared helplessly at the boy. He knew his son liked him and trusted him; there was a bond between them, born in the first place through conspiracy against the common enemy; but even with this bond he found this boy at times beyond him, as now, when his approach to anything that puzzled him was almost adult. And for a moment he glimpsed the pain that Maggie must feel after one of her frequent conflicts with him. And he reminded himself that this was a child, who had to be controlled, and he said sternly, 'Now look here, me lad. I want no more of this cross-questioning. You're goin' to do what you're told. And if you don't, then you're on your own, for I won't take your part in any way. Understand?'

The boy did not answer but watched his father start the car and back out into the road. He watched him until they passed through the gateless pillars of their drive, and then he looked ahead again. And when they arrived at the wide steps leading to the house and he saw his mother running down them, his shoulder began to twitch, and instead of looking towards her as she pulled open the car door he looked down at his shoulder as if from it he could draw an answer to all his questioning.

David left the house about half-past seven. He did

not call in at his mother's but went straight into the town. The war was over, everybody was seemingly going mad, it was a night for jollification, and he was feeling as miserable as sin. And all through that dam' lad. Where would it lead? He could only see it getting worse . . . she could think of nothing but him. And it was wrong, for she was taking him away from Maggie; and she couldn't see it. After all, he was Maggie's son. And he could understand Maggie's attitude. But he couldn't quite understand their Chris. He was as bad as the lad at times, never away, and always bringing her something. My God! Was he going barmy, or what? What track was his mind on now?

'Hallo, there, Davie, man. Come and have a game.' The hail came from a side street that was packed with children, and organising a game was one of his men. David stopped and shouted back, 'Why, Phil, this is a new line, isn't it?' He laughed as he moved through the press of children and women, and Phil called, 'Aye, it's harder work than hewing, this.'

'Hallogalee-galee-gle again, Mr Potter. Aw, come on, play it again.'

The children plucked at the man's coat, and he said, 'All right, just one more then.'

He in turn pulled at David's sleeves, saying, 'Come on, do your bit.'

But David backed away. 'No, not me.'

'Come on man.'

'Why, no, man, I'm daft enough.'

It was then he found his hands grabbed from both sides, and amid screams of laughter he was drawn round in the large circle; and he himself laughed as he sang:

'Hallogalee-galee-gle, hallogalee-galo,
Hallogalee-galee-gle, upon a Saturday night-o,

> *This is the way the farmer stands,*
> *This is the way he claps his hands,*
> *This is the way he holds a lass,*
> *And this is the way he dances.'*

David was behind in his pantomiming of the farmer, and the child on his left sat down on the kerb and laughed.

'Let's have it again,' came the cries, and once more he was in the ring, this time with a young woman on one side of him. He merely glanced at her as they started. Her head was thrown back and her mouth was wide open. He liked the sound of her laugh . . . gay, somehow, and free:

> *'Hallogalee-galee-gle, hallogalee-galo . . .'*

He stopped singing and brought his head round to her:

> *'This is the way the farmer stands,*
> *This is the way he claps his hands,*
> *This is the way he holds a lass . . .'*

He turned and swung her round. She was still laughing; but in the press he trod on her foot and she let out a wail and hopped comically, hanging on to him with one hand. And the children near joined in the laughter, and they too started to hop.

When she let go of David's arm she cried to them, 'London Bridge, eh?' And they shouted back, 'Yes. Oh yes. London Bridge.'

> *'London Bridge is falling down,*
> *Falling down, falling down,*

London Bridge is falling down,
My fair lady.

David moved through the press, making his way to the other end of the street. He should know that lass; her face was familiar somehow. What odds. He shook his head, then halted in his stride . . . Beattie Watson! That's who she was. Good Lord! He turned and looked over the heads of the children. Well, who would believe it? But she was changed. She used to be plump, now she was as thin as a rake. And she even seemed shorter than he had imagined her to be. Beattie Watson! What had brought her back? He would have thought after that affair she wouldn't have the face to come back to this town. Still, it was her home . . . What if Tom saw her? He gave an inward laugh. Well, she would have a different Tom to deal with now than she had five years ago. That was certain. There was none of the soft lad left in Tom. Why, lad alive, and he had danced with her. My, that was a good'un.

At the far end of the street another game was in progress, blocking the road and the pavement, and he had to stand for a minute or so. The children, again in a ring, were singing to a smirking girl and the embarrassed boy of her choice:

'Now you're married I wish you joy,
First a girl and then a boy;
Seven years over, seven years after,
Now's the time to kiss and give over.'

'Go on, kiss her, Billy; you won't get out till you do.'
David squeezed by the wall past the players . . . Seven years over, seven years after. He had heard that rhyme from a child. He could remember it since he could

remember anything. But now, for the first time, it struck him as a bit advanced for bairns. Still, they didn't know what it was all about. They would, though, all too soon. Seven years over, seven years after. It was ten years and a month since he and Ann were married.

How people could change in ten years. But he hadn't changed. And Ann hadn't, really. It was just her nerves, and not having bairns when she wanted them so badly. But when she cried on his breast in the night she was his old Ann again.

He suddenly turned in the direction from which he had first come and hurried homewards. He'd make her come out, and they'd have a bit of jollification . . . that would do her good.

But when he reached home the house was locked. He opened the coalhouse door and saw the key was on the ledge. She had gone to her mother's. He felt piqued and hurt. She had refused all his entreaties to come out with him, saying she was going to lie down; but she had gone to her mother's. Well, he wasn't going there for her. Not that they said anything; it's what they didn't say that made him feel awful, as if he was to blame for her nerves or for her not having a bairn! Well, perhaps he was to blame. Their Pat had advised him to go and see a doctor. Go and see a doctor about a thing like that! No fear.

He made his way to Pat's now, having decided against going to his mother's because one of the Rowan's would surely see him and he would then have to go in. No, Pat's was the place to go the night; he wanted a bit of jollification on a night like this.

Arrived at Pat's, he found their house closed too; and a neighbour, on her way out, called over the fence to him, 'They've all gone up on the fells. There's a band and dancing, and they're making a big bonfire.'

He walked disconsolately back into the town again. It looked, in the failing light, like a seething ant-heap, except that these people lacked a direction, being content, for the present, to laugh and jostle and be jostled.

He made his way out of the town square to where he knew was a little public-house in the hope of finding it less crowded than those surrounding the square, but this too was full to overflowing, and it was impossible to force his way into the bar. He went round the side to the best end. Here was the same press of people, and he was just about to turn away when the voice that had hailed him not an hour before hailed him again from the centre of the room.

'Hi, there, Davie! Are you lost the night?'

'Oh, it's you again, Phil. Any chance of getting anything?' he asked across the heads of the crowd.

'Aye, man, if you can crush in.'

David did as he was bid, apologising, as he went, to the women he had to shoulder, but feeling, as he did so, that they had no right to be there. Best end or no best end, he didn't hold with women in bars. It was all right for them to have a bottle in the house, but bars were no place for them. Yet, when he reached Phil, who greeted him with 'You haven't met the wife, have you?' and he shook the little barrel of a woman by the hand, he had to admit she looked a decent body.

'Where are all your lads?' asked Phil.

'That's what I'd like to know,' said David. 'I think this is the first time I've ever been in the town in me life and not run into one of our lot . . . What you going to have?'

'Oh, I'll have a little drop of hard while it's going,' said Phil. 'It's about the only place in the town that's got any the night.'

'And you, Mrs Potter?'

'Well, I'm much obliged, Mr Taggart, but I always have a small port.'

'Aye, and the number of small ports she can carry would sink a battleship,' laughed her husband, 'so look out for your pocket, Dave.'

It was some time before the men got their whisky and Mrs Potter her port wine, and when they were brought Mr Potter, making sure of the next round, ordered again; and before David, making his apologies to the Potters, left the saloon he'd had two whiskies and two beers and was feeling quite warm and mellow inside.

Pushing through the laughing, gabbling crowd filling the passage, he had almost reached the door when a concerted movement from the press pushed his bent arm sharply, and his hand swung forward and knocked against the hand of a young woman, tipping up her glass. The electric bulb of the passage still sported its blackout shade, and David bent above the woman as she brushed the liquid from her coat. 'Oh, missis, I'm sorry, it's the crush. Has it spoiled your coat? Look, I'll get you another drink.' He peered down at her coat. 'Is it spoiled?'

The face that was raised to his bore a sad look that dissolved into a smile under his astonished gaze.

'Why, it's you again!' she said.

He jerked himself upright.

'Hallogalee-galee-gle. Mind, you've got big feet.'

'Aye, I have.' He returned her smile weakly. 'I'll order you another drink. What was it?'

'Gin and it. But don't bother, I've still half of it left. And I was going, anyway.' She lifted the glass and finished the drink, and having asked a woman to pass the glass to the counter, she looked up at him and smiled again; and he found himself opening the door for her, and they were in the dark street standing side by side.

For a moment the situation sobered him completely. God alive! He had only to be seen with her and his number was up.

'It's a lovely night,' she said, 'and the town's going mad. Have you been up on the fells?'

'No . . . No. I'm looking for my brother; I've got to meet him. I'm sorry about that drink. I hope it hasn't stained your coat.'

'No, that's all right.'

'I'm glad of that . . . Well' – he backed away from her – 'good night, then.'

'Good night.'

She made no move to accompany him, and as he turned round and hurried away he felt foolish; but he had his work cut out to stop himself from running. Phew! Lord! What if she tagged on to him! He cut through side streets to avoid the main crush, and took the road to the fells.

It was a good two miles to the fells proper, but now the press of the people, their noise and their laughter, instead of impeding him, seemed to be carrying him there in a matter of minutes, and although he would not admit it, at the back of his mind he was wishing that the distance was ten times the length, for on no account did he want to run into her again.

It was close on nine o'clock before he met up with Pat and his family. Alec too was there, and Bert. And they hailed him as if it was years since they had met.

'Where've you been?'

'Where's Ann?' called Pat's wife.

'Do you know me ma's here?'

'No. Where?' asked David.

'You'll never believe it. Dancing with the old man in that crowd.' Alec pointed to a large whirling group, looking like demons as they danced to an accordion band in the light of the bonfire.

'Never!'

'She is.'

'Aye. By lad, she's enjoyed herself. It's made her forget this morning – we had a job to get her out – it's no use sitting crying now.'

For a moment no-one spoke, and the silence was seen by the closed lips rather than felt, for the voice of the crowd was deafening.

'Had a drink?'

It was Bert shouting to David. The breach between them had been healed for years now.

'Aye, two.'

'I bet you haven't had a drop of this.' Bert triumphantly brought a flat bottle from his pocket. 'Real Scotch! Where's that glass, Betty?'

Alec's wife handed Bert a glass from her bag, and David said, 'Not for me; I've had two, I tell you.'

'You've had nowt like this; it's the real Mackye. Get that down you.' He handed David a small tumbler full to the brim.

'No, man,' David protested, 'that's more than a double. D'you want Ann to throw me out? Here, you take half, Alec.'

'Not me. Get it down you; we've all had a go. And I've another bottle.'

'Well, not the lot, I couldn't carry that with what I've had.'

'We'll carry you home. Go on, man. You'd think you were a nipper and had never had a drink.'

'Never four whiskies in one night, that I haven't. Whisky isn't my drink.'

'For God's sake shut up and drink it! . . . Look out!' yelled Bert as a young couple racing madly round the groups, jostled Betty and pushed her against Alec, who in turn just saved himself from falling against David.

'Get it down you,' said Bert, grimly. 'It would break my heart to see that spilled.'

So David threw back the whisky, gave a mighty shiver, and laughed. And as the night wore on he continued to laugh, at everything and everyone; at Bert and Alec doing the sword dance; at them all standing in a ring, their arms about each other, singing everything from 'Sweet Adeline' to 'The Eternal City'; at them sitting on their coats on the grass watching the twins – young men now – doing a turn; at the whole family dancing away into the crowd for one final fling.

He sat now, his back against a hillock. He was too fuddled to dance; all he wanted to do was to sit where he was amid the coats and belongings of his family and be glad that everyone was happy. He did not even think of Ann. He knew he was wearing a perpetual smile; and the smile was not only on the outside of him, it was on the inside as well. It was a long time since he had felt like this, the feeling that nothing mattered, not a damn thing in the world. And he began to think of his achievements with a smugness that flowed like oil over him. He was a deputy. Who would have thought that a few years ago, him a deputy? And he would rise higher than that . . . overman next. And there'd be no more slumps, no more dread of being stood off; Bevin would see to that; and no more working five shifts for one pound sixteen; no, by God! It took a war to straighten things out. Would they nationalise the pits if they got a Labour government? No, that was all talk; he could see the companies standing for that . . . not them. But they wouldn't get off with things as they had before the war. No, by God; they'd be made to put some of their millions back into the mines . . . and give higher wages. Aye, higher still. When he was young he didn't know what he knew now . . . too full of fear to open his mouth, anyway. But everything would be put right now, they only had to stick together.

'Well, you certainly look happy. Do you feel it?'

'What?' He raised his head and looked up as if through a haze at the speaker, and his hands, which had been dangling between his knees, went to his sides on the grass to support him.

'We seem fated to meet.'

He nodded stupidly.

'Some crowd here, isn't it? You'd think you couldn't possibly meet the same one twice in this town the night. Yet here we are, three times!'

He nodded again.

'It's heavy on the feet . . . mind if I sit down?'

'No . . . yes.' With an effort he stood up and shook his head violently, trying to clear it. If they came back and found her sitting with him! God in Heaven! They were broad but they weren't that broad, not where the Beattie Watsons were concerned. He'd better tell her flatly to get to hell out of it.

He shook his head again and his vision cleared, and he saw her face. It had on it, as if lightly painted, a little smile, a lost sort of lonely little smile, and he found himself saying, instead of 'Get going, lady', 'How is it you're on your own?'

The smile seemed to shrink, and she answered, 'Sometimes one wants it that way. Times like the night I feel I can't be jolly. I keep thinking of other things. Yet when there's nowt to laugh about I laugh.'

Her face wore a sober look as if she had just given him a confidence, and he nodded at her; and suddenly she smiled again, and, looking down at the backs of her shoes, said, 'These aren't heels to walk in.'

The suggestion in the words that she might sit down spurred him into action. He buttoned up his coat, saying, 'I was just going.' He moved a few steps across the grass and added, 'Coming?'

He was still making great play with his coat, and she watched him as she hesitated. Then, with a laugh that had no trace of softness in it, she said, 'Well, I'm making for home, anyway, if my feet'll let me.'

In silence they cut through the crowd. But David's mind wasn't silent, it was in a muddled turmoil. How could he give her the slip? What would his mother and all of them think when they found him gone and perhaps half their clothes and things gone too?

'You going by the main road?'

'No, by Tollis's Cut.'

He may be half seas over, but he was no fool to go on the main road with her. Perhaps they wouldn't be noticed very much in this crowd where you were walking with Tom, Dick and Harry half your time, but on the main road . . .

'You live round Brampton Hill way then?'

'No . . . Aye, yes. Yes, round Brampton Hill.' He laughed at the thought.

'The nobby end of the town?'

'Yes, the nobby end.'

'Well, I can go that way. I turn off at the foot of the hill. What's your name?'

'Dave.'

'Dave what?'

'Oh, just Dave.'

'You don't want to know mine?'

He didn't answer, and she said, 'I'm Beattie Fuller.'

'Fuller?'

They were now on the road, and he stopped under a lamp, and in its dim light peered at her. 'They call you Fuller?'

'So you know who I am . . . or was?'

He made no reply, and she shrugged and said, 'Well, I'm Fuller now . . . Mrs Fuller.'

'Mrs Fuller?'

'Yes, Mrs.' Her voice was testy. 'Anything surprising about that?'

'No . . . No. Where's your husband?'

There was both relief and apprehension in his voice – he was glad she was married, but he didn't want any husband tackling him.

'Somewhere in the desert.'

'Oh . . . You'll soon have him back then.'

They had walked on again for some distance before she said, 'He was killed.'

'Oh, I'm sorry.'

'Are you? . . . I believe you are.' She looked up at him, and he caught the sad look again. Then she began to talk slowly and quietly as if, he thought, to herself. 'Nights of jollification like this always make me sad. Yet I love a bit of fun and a good laugh. But I couldn't get Stan out of my mind the night; and that made me worse . . . He was my husband.' She paused, and David nodded in the dark. 'I could have had piles of company but I didn't want it,' she went on. 'Funny, you always like people better when they're dead, don't you?'

'Do you?'

'Yes, I think so. Not that I didn't like Stan; he was all right, jolly an' all; but I've often wondered if it would have worked out in peacetime. People are funny, you know. They change in a war . . . they put up with things better . . . Have you lived here all your life?'

'Aye . . . yes.'

'I did too until 1940. I suppose you know all about me.'

'I know a bit.'

'That's why you tried to dodge me?'

'Oh no.' He was profuse in his denial of the truth and amazed at her easy acceptance of it. 'No, that wasn't why. You see, I had to meet my folks . . .'

'And you didn't want to be seen with me.'

'No. No.'

'Yes, yes. Oh, I know.' Her tone was peremptory. 'It's the worst thing anybody can do, to come back to their own town, especially after they've blotted their copybook. There's nothing so damning as half the truth!'

David peered down at her profile. It was shadowed by a tam-o'-shanter, which gave her a girlish appearance . . . Funny, she was most ordinary and sensible in her outlook. Perhaps she had a worse name than she deserved. There was something about her . . . something canny; and for all her experience she still looked so young. Here, here! Voicelessly, he pulled himself up. This was likely exactly the way Tom had thought before he started.

'You know I can't think of myself as a bad woman. Do I look one?'

She turned towards him with a silly embarrassed laugh. 'It's funny what little things it takes to make a lass into a bad woman.'

His laugh joined hers; but she checked it by saying seriously, 'But you know what, I'd rather die than do some of the things some women do, mean, petty, rotten things; yet they wouldn't look the side I was on. And it's funny, once you get a bad name you can have any man you like. Oh yes, you can laugh. But you can. You wouldn't credit the men in this town who made up to me after that case. Toffs, too. There was

236

old 'uns that you wouldn't touch with a barge pole, and young 'uns, respectable married young 'uns an' all. And I don't suppose you'd believe it, but at that time, gay as I was, many of the supposed young ladies of Fellburn had had more men afore breakfast than I'd had in me life. But I always liked men better than women, and I was always ready for a lark . . . Why, what you laughing at? I see nowt so funny in it . . . not so funny as all that, anyway.'

David had stopped and was leaning against a wall for support, and his laughter, deep and resonant, shook the night. Never had he heard a woman talk, as this one was doing, with the naiveness of a child coupled with the knowledge of a whore.

She was laughing herself now, spasmodically. 'What's the matter with you anyway? You're tight. Listen. There are folks coming. Shut up!'

Attracted in their direction by the laughter, a group of young men and women came towards them. Arms around each other's waists, they were singing the dream-song of 1939, 'Hang out the washing on the Siegfried Line.' Still singing, the young people formed a half-circle round them. 'Have you any dirty washing, mother dear?' They nodded towards Beattie as they sang, and she, associating their question and her reminiscences, was broad enough to laugh at herself, and as her laughter joined David's a young Air Force man on the end of the line caught her round the waist and pulled her into the company, and on to the road; and she, still laughing, cried, 'Wait a minute, we can't leave him,' and the half-circle swung in again; and she caught hold of David's arm, and, laughing as if he would never stop, he allowed himself to be borne away like a giant feather. Down the road they went, the night ringing with their song, and as Beattie sang she looked up at David whenever the opportunity of lamplight afforded, and he, singing now, looked down on her. They were linked close together and everything but this crazy enjoyment was lost to him.

'I love a lassie, a bonnie, bonnie lassie.
She's as pure as the lily in the dell.'

Their glances caught and held, and David's singing became choked as laughter bubbled in him again. When they came to Tollis's Cut they were forced to go in single file, and Beattie broke away from the airman and allowed the singers to go on while she, still with her arm about David, said, 'I should be flaming mad at you.'

His laughter eased, and he asked between gasps, 'Mad? Why?'

'You know why. It tickled you, didn't it . . . pure as a lily in the dell!'

She sounded hurt, and he said, 'Oh, I wasn't meaning anything personal; I've laughed at things all the night. I've had a few, you see.'

'Aye, I see. But it hurts, nevertheless. Some folks think people like me can't be hurt. Hell! Why did I come back?'

She was about to tear herself away from him, but he held her. 'Look, I didn't mean to hurt you; why should I?'

'Yes, why should you?' She spoke dully now, all the laughter had gone. 'It's this place. Everybody's the same, out to put a knife in you. In London or any big city, even Newcastle, I'd be an ordinary lass; nobody would take any notice of me; but here, in this little hotbed of a town, I'm pointed out as a bad lot. And it makes me flaming wild!' Her face took on a look of the wildness, and she brought out defiantly, 'You can believe it or not, I've had nobody since Stan went away. And you can bet your bottom dollar you can count the women on one hand here who can say the same thing.'

'Yes. Yes. I believe you.' He was quiet now. She wasn't such a bad sort . . . he could see quite plainly how Tom had cottoned on to her. And it was a rotten shame, everybody down on her. And she was right in what she said about this little one-eyed town – you only had to make one mistake to be in the pillory.

'Anyway, why the devil am I making excuses for myself to you. It's got nothing to do with you. What's up with me the night, whining me head off? . . . Let go.' She pulled away from him.

'No . . . no, take it easy. Come on, cheer up.' He smiled down on her, and she looked up at him, her face serious.

'You're nice.' She reached up and patted his cheek. 'I'm all prickles the night. Too much thinking. Thinking's no good to anybody, not when it's about things that's done and cannot be undone.'

'You're right there.'

'What do they call you?' She smiled fully at him now, and as he looked down in her face and answered, 'I've told you . . . Davie,' he thought: She's bonnie, real bonnie. You wouldn't think it until she laughs . . . or smiles. She's got something, somehow. Tom must have felt like hell when he gave her up. I never understood it like this before. Just to see her in the street, you wouldn't think she could get you.

'I know you said Davie, but what's your other name?'

'Does it matter?'

'No . . . not very much . . . I just thought I'd like to know, that's all.'

Against all the common sense in him, against the small still voice which said get going while the going's good, against Ann's face whch flashed for a second in front of

Beattie's, against the fact that to all intents and purposes she had stripped a fine fellow like Tom of his natural gaiety and youth, his arms tightened about her, and he heard his own voice, soft and silly sounding, saying, 'Would you like me any better if you knew?'

Her breast was pressed close to him, and she dropped her head on to his neck and her body rippled with her laughter.

'Here, what's got into you now?'

He tried to see her face, but she went on laughing. When she did raise it it was wet, and she said, 'Oh, it was funny to hear you take that line. You're not used to it, are you?'

Before he could protest one way or the other, she went on, 'And it was all the more funny because you're scared of me . . . Oh yes, you are.'

'Scared of you!' His arms tightened about her and he brought his face closer to hers. 'Me scared of you? Now that is funny.'

'You can't even lie properly.'

His retort was stilled; her face came and went in obedience to the shadow cast on them by the swaying branch of a tree in front of the lamp at the corner of the cut, and his eyes focused on her lips, their softness more remembered than seen in the dim light. They were wide with laughter, but slowly they closed until they fell on each other gently. His head moved downwards, no pause, no hurry; steadily his lips went to hers and he could have stilled the ocean's obedience to the moon sooner than curb the desire that was burning his loins. As he kissed her his being was lit with something that seemed to him beyond the body; he visibly shook with its force, and all he desired was to go on shaking. So when he felt her lips trying to withdraw from his he drew them even closer into his own.

When at last he released her the flame within him was burning white, and it had touched her, for she no longer attempted to draw from him, but leant on him and sighed; she was quiet, and outwardly he was quiet; his chin rested on the top of her tam-o'-shanter, and his eyes moved from the lamp to the cut, all vague and dim, yet too light; and he looked beyond the lamp to where he knew was the high wall that surrounded part of the garden of the Bensons' house. Without a word he moved towards it, practically carrying her with him, so tight was his arm about her. And she offered no protest, until, her back against the wall, his hands moved over her, and then she exclaimed, 'No, no! Not that.'

'What!' His voice was thick and unrecognisable to himself.

'I've told you . . . not that! What do you take me for?'

He became perfectly still. The baulking of his desire filled him with sickness, but it could in no way quench the fire. Perhaps because of his prompt obedience to her protest, she unbent and said, 'Well, you were asking something, weren't you?'

And when he did not answer she gave a shaky little laugh. 'Your best plan is to make straight for home, laddie; and I think mine is, an' all.'

It was that laugh . . . it was like a prod in a fellow's stomach. His body was about her, pressing her into the wall, and his lips were searching to pin hers down as she moved her head from side to side.

'No, no! Look . . . look, not here, anyway.' Her whisper was urgent. 'Let's go to my place first . . . No, I tell you!' Her protests became weaker, and suddenly they stopped altogether and her attitude changed; and almost instantaneously the fire that was in him was met and overshadowed.

He had heard about women who could love with this kind of love better than a man knew how to; but to him it had just been hearsay, like stuff one read about but was untouched by, save that it aroused a kind of disturbance in the stomach and a feeling of envy. He had loved one woman in his life, and he had wanted only her. Whether she gave him bairns or not, there had remained only her. The essence of his love was to give ... she must be happy, for only then could he be happy. In all ways his giving had mounted with the years, she had taken all he had to give, accepting with a placidness that left a want in him. Yet, no matter how his giving was received, he knew he would never cease to give. But with this woman his feelings were completely reversed.

As the force of her passion met his he felt that here was a well he could draw on and which would never empty; he would give nothing, only take and take again. He felt as naked as the day he was born, and as unashamed, for no thought could penetrate the rising ecstasy. If thought could have pressed through the white furnace in which he was being welded to this woman it would have told him that in this one moment he was justifying his existence, that all life had been a mere building up to this point when he should feel his burning body shot into space, balm-filled space, pressing on him as if with myriad soothing palms ... His body lay in space, heavy and relaxed, and his sigh of contentment ran through it. And his contentment made him gurgle like a baby, and when the gurgle was answered he began to fall.

They leant on each other, laughing; her tam was on the ground, lying where it had fallen beside his cap, and a gust of wind, coming from nowhere, lifted them together and tossed them, tumbling and still close, into the gutter. And the wind blew Beattie's hair against his face, and as he caught it between his teeth a light shone on them, blinding them. It was the headlight of a car swinging suddenly into the cul-de-sac to enable it to turn. For a second they stared into it, then blinked rapidly. But before it swung away they turned their backs to it, and, still joined together, continued to lean against the wall.

Christopher himself would never have managed to evade the wall. It was Maggie's hand gripping his that steered them within an inch of it, her hand that swung them on to the road again, and again her hand that switched on the light in the car.

'Look where you're going!'

Christopher brought his shocked and bewildered mind back to his driving; and after a moment he cast a look towards Maggie. He could not see her eyes, but the corner of her lip was turned up as it did when she had scored over somebody, and the sight of it made him say grimly, 'If you mention of this, I'll . . . I'll kill you!'

She turned and looked at him, her eyebrows slightly raised, but she did not speak. And after a space he said, 'It could have been somebody else, anyway. You can never be sure in the dark.'

She made a little sound that jerked her head as she emitted it, and he growled, 'Well, mind, I'm telling you.'

Whereupon she said with a quietness that gave added emphasis to the words, 'Everything comes to him who waits . . .'

'Maggie!' He made to bring the car to rest near the kerb; and she, ignoring the entreaty that was now in his voice, said sharply, 'Let's get home!'

He pressed his foot on the accelerator, and the car sped along the road and up the hill, and into the drive of his house. And for once when he ascended the steps to this stately 'gentleman's residence', which he now called home, he did not feel ill at ease, because, for the first time, he was not conscious of his entry. He followed Maggie through the hall and into what she was pleased to call her drawing-room; and he took off his coat and cap and flung them on to the couch. Maggie walked to the fireplace, which contained a large electric fire, resplendent with imitation logs, and as she stooped down to switch it on she called over her shoulder, 'Put your things in the hall.'

'Dam' me things! Now look here, Maggie. If you make anything out of this it will mean trouble and . . .'

'Oh, definitely,' she interrupted him airily.

'You think you're clever, don't you? . . . Well, it won't only mean trouble for other people, it'll mean trouble for you. And I mean what I say.'

'And I mean what I say.' She swung round and faced him. 'If she had looked after her man instead of my son this wouldn't have happened.'

He moved a step nearer to her: 'If you say one word of it, I'll walk out.'

'That would be a tragedy!'

He ignored her gibe.

'Aye, it would. For you it would, because this'd have to go.' He waved his large head in all directions about the room. 'The laundry and your few houses wouldn't keep this up.'

'You would have to keep me wherever you went.'

'Oh no. I'd make a home for you, my kind of home, and if you didn't come that'd be your look-out.'

Her face darkened. 'Don't think that will stop me.'

He turned away, and, picking up his coat and cap, said casually, 'I think it will. You lay great stock on aping the swells.'

He had reached the door, when he was stopped in his tracks. Her words seemed to hit him in the back of the neck. 'I'd have thought you would be glad to see Davie go. Then you could throw your cap in . . . you've been practising long enough.' In her fury she slipped into the common metaphor.

He turned slowly towards her; his fair skin was scarlet. And his mouth opened and closed a number of times before he brought out, 'You're a nasty-minded bitch!'

'But you don't deny it.'

He gave her one furious look, then went out, banging the door after him.

On the first landing he paused. Why hadn't he denied it? And, as she said, why was he breaking his neck to keep this from Ann? If there was a rift he could step in. But Ann was Davie's wife, and Davie was a Catholic . . . there'd be no hope of a divorce. But divorce could be sidetracked – there were ways and means. My God! He spurted forward. What was he coming to? Was he a blackguard altogether? That was her, putting things in his mind.

He reached his room, a narrow, plainly furnished room, and as of habit he sat on the bed. This was the way money made you think – he would never have thought like this before the war – break up Ann and Davie! Already his son had gone quite a way to forcing a wedge between them. Was that why David had taken up with that piece? He dropped his head on to his hand. Could he really have seen the picture that was in his mind, Davie and Beattie Watson, dishevelled and hatless, locked together as if they were drowning? Yet radiant in their drowning. Beattie Watson, her of all people! And after her breaking up Tom. And then Davie . . . Davie was steady, moderate in all things. He would have sworn that never in his life had David looked at any other woman but Ann. Then how? Why? His head rocked . . . It was beyond him. And now there was her downstairs planning how best to use this knowledge.

He rose slowly to his feet. Well, let her try it on, that was all, and she would experience the result of her efforts and fighting to mould him to her pattern . . .

The artificial logs burned steadily yet without diminishing in size, the supposed flame moving round and round them. Every twentieth second it would light the top of the central log, giving to it the silvery hue of ash. It had reached its two hundredth flicking of the main log when Maggie stirred. She had been sitting on a pouffe, staring unseeing at the fire, and now she bent forward and switched it off. Then, rising, she looked around her drawing-room as she always did last thing at night, switched off the candelabra of lights and went upstairs.

Her room was on the opposite side of the large landing from Christopher's, and she walked through it and into an adjoining room, separated from her own only by a curtain. The fact that the room was in darkness made her head flick with annoyance and brought her thoughts from their dark dwelling. That was the worst of foreigners . . . the Overmeers were always pretending they did not understand her orders, he outside the house and she in. And now the nightlight was out. It had never been lit! She would not allow herself to think that Stephen had put the light out, for he had promised her never to put it out again. Years ago she had been surprised that he preferred to go to bed in the dark, until one day she heard him talking to a boy as he came out of school. He was telling him that he played going down the pit in bed. She thought now of the look she had seen on his face that day . . . anger because he had given away his secret and, mixed with the anger, a kind of fury that she should again have come to meet him to make sure he did not go to his Auntie Ann's. He had not tampered with the light since she told him that if he did it again they would move away from Fellburn. So she now repudiated the idea that he had once again put the light out. No, it had never been lit. That Mrs Overmeer couldn't be trusted to see to even the lighting of a nightlight.

When the candle was steadily glowing in its rose-coloured bowl she lifted it up above the bed. Stephen was sleeping in a contorted heap, one knee drawn up almost under his chin, the other pressed down on top of the bedclothes; his pyjama coat was open and rumpled up his back, and his whole appearance suggested he had gone to sleep fighting.

Maggie did not immediately cover him up, but stood, her body bent over the bed, gazing down on him. Her eyes roamed back and forth from his narrow waist and thin chest to his equally thin face, until finally they rested on his face. And as she had done countless times before, she asked herself, why should his features so like her own, combine together to make him beautiful . . . beautiful and maddening, for he was becoming as maddening in a way as her father. Yet the more he annoyed her the greater became her determination that he should obey her. But above all these arbitrary feelings there stood her love for him, her love full of pain and gnawing, which, together, filled her mind with suggestions and ideas that put into practice would, she imagined, gain for her the love of her son. She wanted to bend now and gather him into her arms and fondle him . . . always she wanted to fondle him.

The lines of her face stiffened as she thought of his taut body whenever her arms went about it . . . And who had she to blame?

She put down the light, covered him up and returned to her room and slowly began to undress. All she had ever really wanted in life had been a child, someone to belong to her and her alone. The desire for money and power had been a secondary thing. It had taken its own place in the scheme of things after Stephen was born as a means on which to build his environment, education and future. When its power had enabled her to move on to the actual Hill – although at times this made her physically weak with a feeling she termed joy – she looked on this success mainly as a background for her son, the son through whom lay her only means of expression . . . some deep-ingrained honesty told her that she herself would never acquire an importance that would make her stand out from the crowd. Her present success might have made her the envy of those people among whom she was reared, but she had found out, and bitterly, that this did not guarantee acceptance, even with the camaraderie of war, by the remnants of the class on whose ground she had dared to tread. Another woman might have used her charm to force the wedge, but she had to accept that this means was entirely beyond her power. She often drank deeply of gall when she saw Christopher, with his deformed body and tongue littered with homely phrases, being treated as an equal by them. At these times, she confronted herself with the thought: 'They can hardly do anything else . . . fire-watching together.' Yet when she found herself in the same position with the . . . ladies, the same excuse could not be applied. So if she were to rise, it would have to be through her son. Her expression must come through him.

For a long time now she had been thinking of a prep. school, and beyond, on the glorious horizon, a university . . . Oxford or Cambridge. She felt that, left to herself and without interference, she could make Stephen turn this dream into reality. But only if he was left to her, and not if his emotions were being constantly worked on. She closed her eyes wilfully to the fact that her own attitude towards him came under this last heading. Her actions, she encountered, were the natural outcome of mother-love. It was . . . that one who caused the conflict. Her mind, which was never really free of Ann, now swung open to the devilish joy she had experienced on seeing David lust-bemused with that woman . . . Mrs Fuller, or Beat Watson, as she once was. Strange, wasn't it, how things worked out?

She paused in the act of pulling a nightdress over her head. It was a month ago since she had sat in her office and looked at Beattie Watson asking for work under the name of Mrs Fuller – the woman who had caused so much trouble in her family. Not that she cared two hoots for Tom's lacerated feelings, but she had cared, at the time, for the scandal. Although the woman had changed considerably she had recognised her; and only because she was very badly in need of workers had she taken her on, warning her that she would have to accept being moved on to any job, even in the wash-house. And she could remember being annoyed at the airiness of the reply, as Beattie Watson said, 'Oh, I don't mind what I do. I might look thin, but I'm all right. I had to leave the munition factory because the cordite got on my stomach, that was all. You can send to Hereford and ask them . . . they'll tell you.' And now here she was, having an affair with a man, you might say, of the same family, so closely were the two families connected.

If she had schemed for a thousand years never could she have brought about anything so liable to strike at her sister . . . The good David, the solicitous husband, the upright man, the man who even pretended he didn't mind not having bairns so as not to hurt his dear wife, and all the time he was 'playing away' on the quiet. The despised sayings of her people seemed to fit perfectly such events as this, and for once she didn't chide herself for thinking them.

As she stooped to throw the bedclothes back a knock came on the door, one distant rap, and she cast towards it a look of irritation not unmixed with astonishment. The Overmeers slept above the coach-house, it couldn't be her; it could only be . . .

The door opened, and she turned on Christopher a cold look but one which still held her surprise.

'You could have knocked, couldn't you?'

'I did.'

'Well, you could have waited.'

'Why should I?'

Now her eyes widened and her back straightened, and for a flicker of time she thought what it might have been like if that voice that now had a ringing note of command in it and was the voice of her husband could have issued from another body. But the thought was merely a flicker, for her eyes seemed to dwell longer than usual on his braces, which, she knew, were arched like a bow across his back.

'Well?'

His lips tightened and his head made quick little movements from side to side. By lad, if she was some men's wife and she spoke like that to them they would skelp her gob as quick as look at her. Once upon a time he had put up with her manner because he was sorry for her, thinking that she was made that way; but since he had come to gain the respect of men he had resented more and more her attitude towards him. And now he lifted his head out of its scoop and said, 'It'll pay you to remember it isn't a dog you're talking to. I've had about enough of it, I'm nearing the end of me tether.'

Only her silence showed her surprise. She stooped and picked a green dressing-gown from off the chair and put it on, throwing her long thick plaits, first to one side then the other as she folded the lapels of the gown across her chest. And as he watched the quick smooth actions he, in his turn, thought, If only that hair had been on some other lass. Its gleaming brown against the green cloth was right bonnie. The contrast brought him to notice the dressing-gown. It looked classy. He didn't know she had things like that for indoors, no more than he knew what she had in this room of hers, for if he wanted to visit the boy in bed he went in by the landing door. Queer, when you came to think of it, a room in your own house, your wife's room, and not knowing what was in it. He cast his eyes quickly about it . . . Aye, she had done herself well . . . all green and yellow hangings and rugs, and brown furniture . . . a nutty brown.

'I've got to get up early in the morning. What do you want?'

'What do I want?' His eyes became as hard as her own. 'Just to say this. You want him to go to a posh school, don't you?'

She made no answer, and he went on, 'You've got it all planned out – a prep. school, and finally a university. It'll take getting on for two hundred a year at Conifers, won't it? Of course, that includes everything—' There was mimicry of pseudo-refinement in his last words, and her expression caused him to say, 'Aye, I could talk like your Mr Maitland Byrnes if I wanted to, but it'd be a fake, just like him being headmaster of Court College is a fake. If you knew owt about human nature you would see he's all wind and water. No. But as clever as you think you are, anybody can put one over you if they talk refeened . . . blah!' His hand, nose and mouth combined to make a deprecating movement, and Maggie actually cried out, 'You haven't dared to go to the school?'

'Dared to go?' He became quiet. 'Why shouldn't I? Who pays, I'd like to know? But put your mind at rest; I didn't go to the school. But your mighty Mr Maitland Byrnes actually sought me out . . . Aye, that surprises you. But you see I've got what Mr Maitland Byrnes wants . . . money. And his tinpot college is going to need money when the proper schools come back and take their own again . . . Aye' – he nodded at her – 'he left the crowd of councillors in the Town Hall lobby and made himself known to me when I was getting me permits. All over me, he was. Said I must go to Speech Day.'

He could see her body tightening under the dressing-gown, and he laughed, and the sound was even painful to himself.

'Don't worry, I won't go. But let me tell you this. You'll bring him more harm than my hump or my pitmatic voice could do.'

Her expression did not alter, and he went on, 'Well, all I came to tell you was that you'd better lay stock to what I said earlier on the night. If you tell Ann or anybody else what you saw there'll be no posh schooling for him other than what you can provide. And your gold-mine of a laundry will be like Mr Maitland Byrne's school shortly, it'll be up against big competition. Perhaps you didn't know that before the war Cannings bought the ground behind the Square to build a modern laundry. The ground's still there. But, anyway, one thing's certain, you can't play the big bug on your own' – he flung his arms wide – 'not in this way, you can't, for long.'

Maggie looked at his large, square face, at his great brown eyes, now almost black with feeling, and her eyes travelled from the tremendous width of his chest down his thin legs to his feet, big feet in thick boots, feet that were a match for his head and chest but ludicrous as attachments to his legs.

She had hated his feet almost as much as his hump. Seeing them, or feeling them, it was the same. For the short time she had felt their proximity in bed she had been maddened by them. In his sleep they had floundered about as if in futile search. To-night they looked even bigger and seemed to her the symbol of his commonness, and the commonness of the other members of his family and their associates. The commonness seemed to spread over all but a few of the residents of Fellburn. And he would see that his son should know nothing but this commonness if she dared to use the knowledge she had gained to-night. The very fact that he had come to this room proved he would go to any lengths to save Ann from being hurt.

As she stared at him she realised what she had not known before, that part of her hatred of Ann was because he loved her. And she was surprised at the pain the words evoked when she said, 'You would sacrifice the boy's future for her?'

It was some time before he answered, 'Aye, I would . . . for her peace of mind. If it's the only way to check the devil in you, I'll do it.'

She gave a twist to the belt of the dressing-gown. 'You talk as if I'm the only one who saw him. What if someone else tells her?'

'That remains to be seen. There's nobody going to run to her with that kind of news, nobody but you. And it's my opinion, anyway, that the thing's a flash in the pan – he was tight or something.' He shook his head at this point, being almost unable to believe himself what he said, for he could not imagine David to be tight enough to go whoring in the street. 'But,' he went on, hitting on the truth in his fumbling to find an excuse for his brother, 'he was likely only out for a bit of jollification and he met up with her.'

'Jollification!' Her lip curled. 'Well, jollification or no jollification, I'm going to tell you this. Unless you find some way to keep her off my boy I'll risk all you say you'll do.' Her lips parted in the imitation of a smile. 'And won't I delight in telling her that while she's been neglecting her husband for my son he's found solace somewhere else.'

Christopher ran his thumbs down each brace, pulling them away from his chest, then letting them snap back with a crack that held its own significance.

'All right' – he turned – 'try it on, and we'll see who comes out on top.'

She watched him go out, and waited for the door to be banged. But it was closed quietly, and she realised that the whole of their conversation had been quiet, tense and quiet, so as not to wake the boy.

Slowly she got into bed, and as of habit she picked up a book from the bedside table. But she didn't read, for a tiredness was assailing her, not the tiredness of sleep, but the tiredness that was in some way connected with the feeling she used to have before Stephen first moved in her womb, the tiredness which was bred of her fight against loneliness.

12

The Thinnest Strand

Stephen walked down Brampton Hill on his way to school. Until recently Friday had been the one glorious day in the week for him, because on this day his mother did not drive him to school; on this one day a week her time was completely taken up with the laundry – it was pay day and accounts day and bank day – and he was free . . . until four o'clock.

The sun shone hot on the back of his neck; the birds were flitting swiftly to and fro on the branches of the trees behind the high walls that guarded the privacy of the houses on the Hill. It was just the day for going over the fells. If he could dash round now to his Auntie Ann's and say, 'Come on, on the fells,' she would come. He could see them both running and laughing and falling on their faces on the grass. His mind tried to carry him back to one Friday last term when they had done just that. But it failed, and, instead, dropped him into the middle of the morning, to the point of time when he must show his arithmetic to Mr Newman. He didn't like arithmetic and he hated Mr Newman.

Mr Newman had only recently come on his horizon. Last year, and even the year before, he could remember vaguely hearing stories of the White Devil. But then the second form had seemed thousands of years away.

But on the first day of this new term the years had vanished as if touched by a magician's wand, and within a matter of hours he knew precisely why Mr Newman was called the White Devil. He was fat and pale-skinned, and the paleness was emphasised by his hair, which was black and wiry and which, of its own accord, jutted straight out from above his ears; and when rage swayed him, which it did at least once a day, his hair took on the appearance of horns.

From his very first day in this form Stephen had continually encountered the real devil in Mr Newman, and the devil seemed to pick him out to be the recipient of his spleen. This was remarked on during the first break of the term by his form mates, who, with the cruel candour of youth, plus patent relief at their own escapes, told him, as one wit put it, he was to be the chosen of the God of the Underworld.

Stephen soon learned too that Mr Newman was a homework devil. He would fling examples on to the blackboard, bark 'Got that?', rub them out before the flustered minds had even begun to sort out the jumble of figures, then he would call out a succession of numbers, each denoting a terrifying example in the textbooks, which were to be done as prep.

Of the ten examples of yesterday's homework Stephen had completed six, and of the six only one gave him any comfort. This he had managed to work out, the others he had merely guessed at. He dug now into his satchel and brought forth an exercise book, and looked into it in troubled perplexity. It was no use . . . he would never be able to see any sense in them . . . he must be stupid. But he wasn't stupid. Mr Rankine, the English master, knew he wasn't. He hadn't said so, but his eyes had looked nice at him when he read his composition aloud to the class. And after class he had asked him what he wanted to be; and because he wasn't afraid of him he had dared to tell him the truth . . . a miner. And Mr Rankine had laughed and cuffed his ear in a nice way . . . He knew he wasn't stupid. But Mr Newman and . . .

'Steve!' His name coming hissing through the hedge startled him so much that he jumped off the kerb and into the road. He stared at the thick hawthorn hedge, and his name, called again and accompanied by a suppressed laugh, made his face light up and his eyes sparkle, and he dived across the pavement and bobbed this way and that to see through the dense growth.

'I know it's you, Dennis. Is Jimmie there?'

'Aye, I'm here.'

'Come on out.'

'No, you come in.'

'How?'

'Further down, there's a hole at the bottom. You needn't go down to the gate . . . just a bit further along.'

Stephen ran down the hedge until Dennis's voice called, 'Here, man. Down here,' and, crouching down, he lay on the grass verge and was immediately pulled into the field.

'We saw you comin',' said Jimmie, 'and we dodged in here.'

'Where you going?' asked Stephen. 'Aren't you going to school?'

Pat's sons looked at each other. There was a year difference in their ages, but they were so alike as to be often mistaken for twins, being very like their young uncles at an earlier age.

'We've got a holiday,' said Dennis, 'haven't we, Jimmie?'

Jimmie nodded.

'Holiday? We haven't. What for?'

'Oh . . . well . . .' Again they looked at each other then burst out laughing, and Dennis said, 'We'll tell you if you don't split.'

'No . . . honest, I won't.' Stephen shook his head, his eyes wide.

'We're playing the nick.'

Stephen knew what playing the nick was; Dennis and Jimmie often played the nick . . . and they continued to live. Imagine anyone playing the nick in their school and Mr Newman finding out. Stephen could see death, instantaneous, descending on the culprit.

'D'you know whose field this is?' he asked.

'No, and we don't care.' They laughed again. 'But over there there's a wood. It's grand. Nobody knows about it but us. And it's crammed full of blackers.'

'Blackers?'

'Blackberries, yer dafty . . . whoppers. As big as that—' Dennis made a circle with his first finger and thumb that would have encompassed a golf ball.

'And there's a hole that stinks,' said Jimmie.

'Like a poke of divils,' added Dennis.

'And there's big trees with nests in them. Nothing in the nests though. We climbed fifteen last Thursday.'

Stephen's eyes sparkled in genuine admiration. His cousins always evoked admiration in him, and he longed in his innermost heart to be like them. It didn't matter which one, his admiration was shared equally between them. His eyes still sparkled as he said dolefully, 'I wish I could come.'

'Come on then.'

'But I'm going to school.'

'Give it the slip.'

'You mean . . . play the nick?'

The last words were whispered and Stephen's finely arched eyebrows slowly rose towards his hair. The vista of escape, which held such delights, was here close at hand . . . trees with nests, holes with smells, and blackberries; and by indulging in these delights he could escape Mr Newman's lesson. And by Monday, he, Mr Newman, would likely have forgotten about the sums. Or, anyway, he'd have time to have another go at them over the week-end. He might even be able to take them to his Auntie Ann's, whereas when he asked his mother . . . His mind closed down on this avenue of thought and swung eagerly back to the proffered joy of the moment. Its acceptance was already decided in his mind.

'But what'll I say?' he asked.

'Oh, say your ma was bad,' said Dennis.

'No, she's never bad,' said Jimmie, with emphasis on the she, 'and she goes to school to meet him.'

The boys surveyed each other thoughtfully, and Stephen burst out, 'But not to-day . . . it's Friday.'

'That's right,' said Dennis. 'But the ma excuse has worn thin, they don't believe it. What about having toothache?'

'But I never have, all my teeth are good.'

'Well, you could say . . . No, I tell you what,' cried Jimmie. 'Say you had nightmares and slept in.'

'I do have nightmares.'

'Well, then' – the boys beamed at him, great innocent beams, it was as if his statement had draped their scheme in a white veil of truth – 'what we waiting for? Come on.' They both touched him on the arm before turning and running across the field.

Stephen hesitated for one second, then he too ran, jumping and leaping in their wake, over the hillocks towards the wood.

It was nearing eleven o'clock when Mr Rankine closed

the front door of his cottage and set out on his journey to school. His breath came in short wheezing gasps, and he told himself he was a fool, and he consigned Mr Maitland Byrnes to where he considered was his proper dwelling place. Ringing him up to tell him Steele was away with hay fever, and he'd be obliged if as soon as possible . . . ! Asthma, to Mr Maitland Byrnes, was merely an excuse for mornings in bed.

He walked slowly to the end of the lane, through a gateless opening and past a board nailed to a post and bearing the words 'This Wood is Private Property, Keep Out!' And within a few minutes he was lost to view in the belt of trees.

Ah! He tried to sigh a deep sigh of satisfaction, but the effort was checked by his breathing, and he stood for a moment looking up at the naked trunks and the bushy-headed tops of a group of pine trees. What he should do was to stay here, right here, and sit beneath these trees all day . . . sleep under them and inhale the balm of their scent, and damn Mr Maitland Byrnes. Why did he stick him, anyway? Him and his tinpot college! Oh! He made a gesture of futility to the trees, and with a final nod towards them walked on.

He had been walking for five minutes when he heard the noise, a noise that only boys could make . . . barbarous sounds of glee and joy and bravado; and although it meant leaving the path and tackling the wooded incline to the right of him to observe them, he did so, because he loved boys, but mostly he loved the sound of them at play. He knew where these boys were; they were in the stream that leapt down the little valley. Only last week he had sat and dabbled his feet in that stream. Wouldn't Mr Maitland Byrnes have been shocked at such loose behaviour on the part of his English master? Again, damn Mr Maitland Byrnes!

He closed his eyes for a moment when he reached the summit of the hill, and when he opened them there were the boys, framed as if in a picture. They were naked, and one boy was lying on the bed of the stream that was not much wider than his own body, and he was pretending, in about six inches of water, to be swimming strongly, while the other two were splashing each other with scooped handfuls of water that sprayed like jewels over them. The little stream was full of shadows and sunbeams, mixing with each other as if stirred by a giant hand. The shadows and the sunbeams dappled the boys, and the scene brought a feeling of envy to the man as he watched. He stood perfectly still, until the smallest boy move into a patch of sunlight, when he took a step forward and exclaimed aloud.

Whether in some way the boys sensed they were being watched or they heard the strange voice even above their own noise, they stopped their play, and the two who had been sparring stood still for a moment. And then they knew something had stopped their fun, for a voice came to them from the top of the bank.

'Taggart!' it said.

Stephen's head jerked upwards so quickly that the back of his neck made a cracking sound.

'Come here.'

Stephen stepped out of the stream and grabbed at his shirt; and as he walked towards the master he pulled it crazily over his head.

'What's this, Taggart?'

'Please, sir.' Stephen stared up into the long, straight face of the little man. 'Please, sir.'

'Yes?'

Stephen's head swung in all directions on his shoulders. It swung round and he looked down the bank to where Dennis and Jimmie were staring up at him and at the same time trying to scramble into their clothes; it swung down to the bottom of his shirt, and he looked at his wet bare legs; then it swung back to the master's face, and his eyes, although he was not aware of it, were full of pleading.

'Go and put your things on.'

He scurried down the bank again, and Jimmie, with his eyes still on the man on top of the bank, asked out of the corner of his mouth, 'What's up? Who's he?'

'Master,' whispered Stephen.

'Come here, you two.'

'Us?' the boys both asked at once.

'Yes . . . you.'

They left Stephen and scrambled up the bank, and when they reached the man they were in no way intimidated, for, besides fearing no-one, they found they were nearly as big as this chap.

'Who are you?'

'This is Jimmie,' said Dennis, pointing to his brother. 'And that's Dennis,' said Jimmie.

'Stop trying to be funny,' said the master. 'Jimmie and Dennis what?'

'Taggart.'

'Taggart?'

'Yes. He's our cousin.' They nodded to where Stephen was now coming up the bank.

'Your cousin? Well, well.'

They both laughed at the little man . . . he was funny, he wheezed when he talked, and he seemed to spit his words out.

'How old are you?'

'I'm nearly fourteen,' said Dennis. 'And he's nearly thirteen.' He pointed at Jimmie.

'Why aren't you at school?'

They looked at each other, their eyes smiling quizzically.

'We're playing the nick,' said Jimmie with slightly bowed head and raised eyes as if he was imparting a joke and wondering just how it was going to be received.

Something passed over the little man's face, like a ripple. His wheezing became louder. Then he asked, 'Do you do this often?'

Again they looked at each other, and Dennis nodded, while Jimmie said, 'On fine days.'

'And what excuse do you give?'

Here they laughed out. 'None now, the teacher just canes us. And once,' prompted Jimmie, 'we were really sick through tinned herring, and we still got the cane.'

'Splendid,' said the little man. 'How many do you get?'

'Four . . . sometimes six.'

'Which is your school?'

'St Agnes's.'

'Well' – the little man seemed to grow bigger before their eyes – 'if you are not in St Agnes's within half an hour, when I shall phone your teacher, I'll ask him to give you ten. Do you understand? . . . Off now!' His voice swelled – it seemed bigger than himself.

With just one quick glance at Stephen the boys were off, running through the trees, pushing at each other as they went, their very heels saying, 'We're going but we're not scared.'

'Now, Taggart, are we ready?'

'Yes, sir.' There was a distinct quiver in Stephen's voice. He wouldn't have felt like this, he was telling himself, if Mr Newman had caught him . . . not this sorry feeling, anyway. But now Mr Rankine would no longer call him out to the front to do things on the board, or speak to him nicely, or cuff his head.

'It's a beautiful morning, Taggart.'

'Yes, sir.'

'Do you like woods and trees, Taggart?'

'Yes, sir.' Stephen tripped over a rut in the path as he spoke, and Mr Rankine's hand stopped him from measuring his length on the ground. 'There you are,' he said, steadying Stephen, his hand still on his shoulder. 'Now tell me. Why did you play the . . . join your cousins this morning? Because it was a nice morning, eh, and you wanted to play in the wood?'

Stephen did not immediately answer . . . Mr Rankine didn't sound really mad at him. Although his voice was stiff, he still seemed the master a fellow could tell things to right out. So he said, 'Yes, a bit, sir. But I didn't want to go to school because . . . well, I hadn't got my homework done, sir.'

'Ah.' Mr Rankine wheezed once or twice. 'Did you try to do it?'

'Oh yes, sir, for a long time . . . even when I was in bed.'

'Let me have a look at your work.'

Stephen fumbled in his satchel and proffered the homework book. And Mr Rankine looked at it as he walked slowly on . . . ten sums for one evening. God! That was Newman all over . . . never missing the smallest chance to vent his spleen against life . . . Of course it was life that had twisted Newman, not Newman himself who had done so. No, the big, fat leech couldn't be expected to see 'The fault, dear Brutus, is not in our stars, But in ourselves, that we are underlings.' Was ever a school made up of such teachers? Maitland Byrnes, with his ego vying with space in its endlessness; Newman with his ulcer, and his frustrations, and his middle-class rancour. Once he had thought, Poor Newman, but not now, not since he learned that his main outlet was the goading of boys, mostly ones like young Taggart here who came from working-class people, whom Maitland Byrnes was being forced more and more to take into his college . . . College! A third-rate educational establishment staffed by men who had failed. Yes, that was the truth of it . . . men only fit to give out ersatz education, including himself. But at least he was human. Whatever damage his own upbringing had wrought it had not smothered his humanity.

He looked down on Stephen. When he first saw and heard the boy's mother, his own had been brought vividly back to mind, and he remembered wondering whether Taggart, too, would develop asthma. And he had watched the boy as one follows the development of a specimen, feeling something of a prophet when he saw Taggart's head jerking to the side, and he had waited for the twitching of the shoulders to follow. And it came – he could remember when he himself twitched – and he decided he would keep an eye on the boy, and, if possible, prevent the development of the scourge from which he himself was suffering now.

He had often looked back to his own schooldays and thought that the understanding and a little personal attention of even one teacher might have been enough to counteract the destroying influence of his mother . . . It might. On the other hand, it might not – his present philosophy added the cynical touch.

'Let's sit down here and see what we can do about these, eh?' He tapped the book and walked towards the shade of a tree, and Stephen, his mouth gaping with relief, followed him, and sat down at his knee, his legs curled under him.

'Now what have we . . . ? Well, if we do it this way.' The pencil moved slowly until the answer was reached. 'There now . . . you do the next one.'

After various licks at his pencil, Stephen, to his great delight, brought off the sum.

'There. That's all there is to it.'

After the last sum had been completed and Mr Rankine had deftly altered three of the others, he said briskly, 'Well, now, no more loitering, or else we'll both get it. Come on.'

Almost gaily, they walked through the wood, and it wasn't until they neared the school that Stephen was brought sharply down to earth by the question, 'And what excuse are you going to give Mr Newman for being absent?'

Stephen looked up at the master, and the choice between toothache, his mother being ill, and him having had a nightmare was instantly dismissed from his mind. It was funny, but although Mr Rankine was only a small man, not even as big as his father, he made you think of big things . . . like doing brave things. He could see Mr Rankine, if he had played truant, marching into Mr Newman and saying, 'I've played truant.' So, with a tilt of his chin, he said, 'I'll tell him the truth, sir.'

The statement brought Mr Rankine to a halt . . . Good lord! For any boy to tell this kind of truth to Newman would only have disastrous results for the teller . . . but much more so when he was Taggart.

It was on the tip of his tongue to say, 'Don't be such a fool,' but the boy's face was bright with heroism. And he walked on again, saying, 'Mm . . . mm. You know you'll be caned?'

'Yes, sir.' The tone was bright, as if the prospect of the cane was even pleasing.

Well, it was impossible to tell the boy to give Newman any excuse but the true one. Whatever the boy said he would get a lashing, both with the cane and the tongue.

The latter, he knew, many boys dreaded more than the former.

They reached the drive leading to the Schoolhouse and as they approached the main door Mr Rankine, after a number of wheezing coughs, said, 'Should you find yourself stuck at any time, Taggart, come along to me.'

'Oh, thank you, sir.'

He coughed again. 'I often take a walk on the top playing-field during break. You understand?'

Inside the glass door he stopped and smiled down at the boy, and Stephen, his heart full of admiration for this man, who, at the moment, appeared like a god to him, smiled back and tried to put all he felt in once again saying, 'Oh, thank you, sir.'

As Mr Rankine's hand brought him a cuff alongside the ear he turned and ran along the corridor, his body buoyant with gratitude and courage. Perhaps if his momentary feeling of courage had not been so great his fear would have lent him caution and the disastrous incident would never have happened. But he almost flung himself into the classroom, and not until Mr Newman turned his opaque eyes from the blackboard and let them rest on him did his courage recede; and then only a little, for the import of Mr Rankine's words shone like a beacon before him. Even when, without a word, Mr Newman turned his attention to the blackboard again and left him standing foolishly, the object of rows of curious and excited eyes, even then his courage was high, and he was fully aware, like everyone else, that this seeming ignoring of himself forebode dire results.

The example was finished with a wide sweep of Mr Newman's arm across the board, and he stepped on to the dais and seated himself at his desk. The air of the classroom was still, the bodies of the boys were still, there was no movement other than of their eyes, which travelled backwards and forwards from the boy, in whom dwelt some part of themselves, to the great black-cloaked deity who had the power to rain on each one of them terror, terror that affected their bladders to such an extent that the agonies never came singly.

Minutes passed. Mr Newman wrote. He wrote with a flourish, but without bending his head, so that his entire face was ever present before the class. Only his eyes were cast down on his work; and he never raised them until Stephen, his voice sounding like a squeak, said, 'Please, sir, I want to tell you why I didn't come to school.'

Still without lifting his eyes, the master said, 'You came in without knocking, Taggart. Go out and come in the correct way.'

It was some seconds before Stephen moved; then his head gave a jerk, and, blinking rapidly, he walked out of the room, closed the door after him, then knocked . . . waited . . . knocked again . . . waited . . . knocked for the third time, and when the sound of a grunt came to him he entered the room again and walked slowly up to the desk. Now his courage was definitely ebbing, and he knew that if he did not say what he had to say right away he would revert to the 'nightmare' excuse, and in some way that would, he felt, be letting Mr Rankine down and spoiling everything. So he stood below the desk and looked up at the white face with the lowered lids and said, 'Please, sir, I played truant, and I'm sorry.'

Mr Newman's lids lifted even slower than they were wont to fall . . . it was as if the effect of this preposterous utterance was weighing them down with leaden incredulity.

'You what!' The question was quiet; there was even the feeling of sensuousness about the words. As they came, wrapped in their soft thickness, they deceived Stephen; and he went on, 'I didn't mean to, and I won't do it again.'

Mr Newman moved out of the desk and off the dais as if he was borne on air. He looked down on Stephen through misted eyes for quite a while before he said, and still quietly, 'You have the effrontery to come and tell me you have played truant?'

Stephen only heard the words, he could not be expected to recognise the deeper meaning which said, 'You fear me so little that you can tell me the truth?' or to recognise that behind the meaning lay the knowledge that never before in his teaching career had a boy voluntarily spoken the truth to him – he arrived at the truth only after whacking it out of their hides.

Something inside Stephen's stomach suddenly became loose, it shook and trembled, making his shoulder twitch and his head jerk. He turned round slowly to watch Mr Newman as he glided to the cupboard to take out the cane. He had seen that cane only twice before. Once he had watched Mr Newman push a boy along the corridor, and his imagination had given him a picture of what happened in the 'Black Hole of Calcutta'. The boy was called Miles, and he was eleven and was a boarder, and he had cried and said he would write and tell his father, who was a Commando.

'Bend over.' Still quiet, Mr Newman pointed to a chair. Stephen gasped as if he was about to choke, but he did not move.

Then Mr Newman emitted a roar, which broke the stupefied silence of the boys and actually made Stephen jump from the floor.

'Over!' it said. The cane whisked the air until the sound resembled the rush of seagulls' wings.

Stephen was not conscious of bending over the chair – it seemed as if the bellow had lifted him off his feet and thrown him over it. He felt he was losing his balance and grabbed at the chair legs. Then his arms were flung wide and his legs jerked out behind, and a scream tore out of his being as the cane, like a red-hot poker, struck his buttocks. The breath had hardly returned to his body before a searing pain lashed him again, seeming to cut him completely in half. He made a series of animal sounds and tried to rise, but a hand like steel held the back of his neck; and once again his body was set alight in agony. As the cane, this time, lashed the flesh beneath his trousers, so violent was the kick of his legs that he was propelled forward. The grip on his neck was released, and he found himself on the floor against the dais. Through the mist of his flowing tears he saw Mr Newman's hand righting the chair, then saw his arm stretching out to its full extent and his finger point to it. The twin emotion of his fear rose to him; it swelled up, blotting out the fear completely for a moment; his eyes became red with his hate. Never taking his eyes from the master, he scrambled to his feet and stepped back on to the dais.

'Taggart . . . come here!'

'No!' His voice was no longer a squeak – it was like no voice he was conscious of having used before. He stretched his thin neck out of his flaming body and looked across the desk at the approaching face.

'No!' It was the defiance of Dennis and Jimmie speaking, it was the indomitable spirit in the face of his two grandfathers, it was the stubborn independence of all the Taggart men, it was the cry against injustice, and its very sound brought courage to himself.

The face came slowly nearer, and as if anticipating the hand that would, in the next second, flash out and lift him through the air, his own hands flew to the desk, lifted the large, oblong, metal inkstand, with its two wells of red and black ink, and hurled it, with a strength drawn from a source other than his body, right into the large white face.

The gasps of twenty-two boys was like the moaning of the wind through the treetops. No sound came from the master; he was leaning back against the front desk, his hands held to his face, and his fingers were coloured with three coloured fluids . . . scarlet and crimson and black. The sight was dreadful, past description; it sapped the courage that was born of hate; and fear returned to Stephen. He leaped from the dais to the door and, tearing it open, fled along the corridor and out through the main glass door, beside which only a matter of minutes ago he had stood in happiness. He raced down the drive and on to the main road, on and on, until, gasping like a trapped animal, he found himself at the gate of the field, the same field he and Mr Rankine had crossed, and through whose hedge he had been dragged so happily earlier that morning.

Now, stumbling and running, he crossed the field and entered the wood. He was still running when he began to loosen the buttons of his trousers. Panting he climbed the bank that hid the little valley, and, rolling like someone drunk, he descended to the stream, where, without hardly a pause in his walking, he stepped out of his trousers and sat his lacerated buttocks in the gently flowing water. After a while, he staggered out and moved towards the clump of bracken, and putting his head on his arms he began to sob.

13

The Full Circle

To Maggie there was always something very satisfying in paying out the wages; not that she considered that the women had earned half of what she paid them, the satisfaction lay in that she, once Maggie Rowan who began at the very bottom, was now at the top . . . at least of this particular world.

There was left in the laundry only one other woman of the original group Maggie had started with, and she had risen to the position of forewoman. She was standing now at Maggie's side, at the sorting-room table, calling out the amount due to each woman, and from time to time Maggie would glance up at a woman whose name was called and look her disapproval at, perhaps, the make-up or the clothes . . . some of them came to work as if they were going to a party!

'Mrs Stringer . . . three pounds two,' said the forewoman.

Three pounds two for an ironer! Maggie counted out the money and pushed it across the table. Before the war, it was five shillings a day, and offtakes off that. With their morning tea and their bus fares, they were very lucky if they cleared a pound a week.

'That's the lot. Except Mrs Fuller. Hers is three pounds fifteen and eight.'

'Where is she? Why isn't she here?' asked Maggie.

'She's not feeling too good,' said the forewoman.

'What's the matter with her?'

The forewoman gathered up the money. She wasn't going to tell the bitch what was the matter with Beattie Fuller, she had a down on her already – sticking her on those machines! Although, she must give the devil her due, if she'd known what was wrong with Beattie she likely wouldn't have shoved her down the wash-house. 'She's had a bilious attack.'

'She'd better get home then, and put Mrs Tingley in her place. The machines should be empty now, anyway, for the cleaning.' Bilious attacks had to be paid for if they took place in the laundry.

'Tell her to go home? But she's all right now.'

'Then why isn't she here?'

The forewoman hesitated, then said, 'Well, she wanted to get a load in . . . a machine was empty and she didn't want it to stand idle.'

Maggie looked straight at her forewoman. The woman was even too stupid to lie properly – she was covering up in some way for that Fuller piece. Trust any of them to trouble their heads about a machine standing empty! Without further comment she gathered up the bag and the time-sheets from the table and went into her office.

The office was glass fronted and looked down the length of the laundry. Her eyes travelled expertly over the five-roller calender, over the single-roller Tullis past the collar machine to the ironing tables, and then to the arch, through which she could see one of the washing-machines and the figure of Beattie Fuller bending over it.

Maggie walked out of the office and up the calender room and into the wash-house. She made the pretence of examining one machine after another; she spoke to an old man who was loading one with sheets; and she stood in front of the other two that were in motion, clanking and rattling when the gears changed, revolving the drums first one way then the other; then her eyes casually came to rest on the fourth machine, and she walked slowly up to it.

Beattie Fuller's head and shoulders were lost inside the drum. One arm was raking the cold water with a stick, and with a swish she brought the stick up and slapped the small square of linen on top of the wet bogie load of washing. And she gasped as she straightened herself; and Maggie said, 'I hear you're not well.'

Over the top of the load of washing Beattie looked at Maggie and said, 'I'm all right.'

She had known for a long time now who Maggie was, and she guessed Maggie knew who she was. Nothing had been said, but more than once she had caught a look in Maggie's eyes that spoke volumes, which she interpreted to mean that if hands weren't so hard to get she would have short shrift. One thing was a constant puzzle to her, that Tom Rowan could have a sister like this.

'If you're sick you'd better go home.'

'I'm not sick. I do my work, don't I?' She gave the bogie a jerk, and it swung slowly and heavily round, and with a great effort she got it moving towards the hydro.

As Beattie moved away, Maggie's eyes became fastened on her hips, and a feeling akin to a thrill passed over her. She watched Beattie manoeuvre the bogie up to the hydro, and her eyes fell to the coarse apron covering Beattie's stomach. It bulged slightly . . . But that could be the rubber apron beneath it. No, that was no rubber bulge . . . And she'd had a bilious attack. You were usually only sick up to three months, though . . . The sickness could be anything. Yet . . . She walked nearer and stood at the bogie as Beattie hauled the wet linen into the hydro. She watched her ram it down, and she was about to say, 'You haven't got it even, you'll not get the machine to start packed like that,' but what she said was, 'Are you pregnant, Mrs Fuller?'

Beattie stopped lifting the linen and brought defiant eyes to meet Maggie's. 'Yes, I'm pregnant.'

Maggie drew in a long breath, then after a moment said, 'Isn't this work too heavy for you, then?'

'When I can't do it I'll pack up.'

'How far are you gone?'

The question sounded excited, even eager. It surprised Beattie, or the manner in which it was asked did, and she answered slowly, 'Over four months.'

Over four months . . . Although Maggie still stared at Beattie she wasn't seeing her, she was looking back and reckoning . . . from May. It was now the end of September . . . Over four months . . . Of course, it could be any man's. But it wasn't . . . it was Davie Taggart's.

Without another word she left Beattie and, back in the office, she sat at her desk and a surge of satisfaction so sweet as to be sensual swept through her.

It was now many months since she last saw Ann. It was in her kitchen, where she had gone yet once again to fetch Stephen away, and Ann had dared to come out into the open and say, 'Who's to blame if he prefers me to you?'

She had thought it impossible for her hate of Ann to find a yet deeper level, but on that occasion it had bored into regions of her being not hitherto dreamed of.

The sensation that was warming her showed in her eyes; she felt them to be sparkling. Beattie Fuller was carrying David Taggart's child! She was not mistaken, she felt as sure of it as she was of sitting there. David Taggart had begotten a child. What would Ann do when she knew that, for had she not, voicelessly, laid the blame for her childlessness on David? Here would be proof positive who was at fault . . . And Christopher had threatened what he would do if she spoke!

Her lips formed into a mirthless smile. What would he say to this? Would he try to hush it up to save his precious Ann? God! What did men see in her, anyway? Her father . . . David . . . Christopher . . . and . . . She would not even think her son's name. Anyway, one of them at least had grown tired and taken unto himself another woman. And what a woman! Oh, it was many years since she felt as she was feeling at this moment; not since her son was born had she glowed like this.

The phone on her desk rang, and she lifted it, and when the voice spoke she smiled and said, 'Oh, yes, Mr Maitland Byrnes, this is Mrs Taggart speaking.'

She listened, her elbow resting on the desk. Then the smile vanished and she rose to her feet, her mouth agape. And when Mr Maitland Byrnes asked, 'Hallo! Are you there?' she brought her lips together with a snap, and said, 'I don't believe it. Stephen wouldn't throw an inkwell at anyone. Let alone a master.'

'But, Mrs Taggart, I can assure you he did. And not only the inkwells, but the metal stand with them. The master is now at the hospital having his eyebrow stitched.'

'Stitched?'

'Yes, stitched!'

'What have you done with Stephen?'

'What have I done with Stephen?' Mr Maitland Byrnes's tone was very unlike the usual suave one Maggie was accustomed to. 'I have done nothing with him, as yet. The young man thought it best to fly after he had made his attack.'

'You must be mad,' said Maggie.

'Madam!'

As the syllables vibrated along the wires, Maggie thought of what Christopher had said about this man and she knew his judgement to be right. She had known it then, though not for worlds would she have admitted it. She glared into the mouthpiece, and her tone too was unlike the one she kept for Mr Maitland Byrnes. 'I know my boy, and he wouldn't have done such a thing unless he was driven to it.'

'If you know your boy so well, are you aware that he played truant this morning? And just before lunch he marched into Mr Newman's room and coolly stated the fact.'

After a time during which Maggie held the receiver away from her as if afraid of what next would issue from it, she said again, 'I don't believe it.'

'Then you had better come here and meet the twenty-two witnesses of the scene, Mrs Taggart.' He paused. 'You will understand that I cannot possibly have the boy back here.'

Again there was a pause. 'When I took him I told you we were accustomed to receive boys only from homes which had. a certain social status, and I fear now that in breaking the rule in your case I have laid up trouble for myself. What are the parents of those boys to think? . . . And then there's the master It'o yct to be seen whether he makes a case of this . . .'

Maggie banged the receiver down, and her mind acted so naturally under the shock that she cried aloud, 'To hell with you, and the master!'

Without pausing to lock up her desk or to give any instruction to her forewoman, she whipped her hat and coat from the peg and put them on as she ran out of the laundry to her latest acquisition, a two-seater car. She sped out of the laundry yard and through the town and up the hill without giving a thought to any traffic regulation; and she had barely brought the car to a standstill before she was out of it and in the house.

Christopher, after a good lunch, was lying back in an armchair smoking. He, too, liked Fridays. It was funny, but on Fridays he had the best dinner of the week . . . Mrs Overmeer seemed to go out of her way to please him on this day. And while he was eating he would often fancy he was back with his mother. He'd had a pot pie to-day, every bit as good as his mother could make. 'I cook her for four hours, and she's got all the gravy nice through her.' That's what Mrs Overmeer said when she brought his dinner in. All smiles she was, not like when Maggie was at the table; then she was as stiff as her apron.

Only one thing was troubling him as he half dozed, and then it was but vaguely . . . Stephen hadn't come home for dinner. Knowing his mother wouldn't be in, he had likely nipped off to Ann's. Well, he'd tip the wink to Mrs Overmeer not to say anything, and Maggie would be none the wiser.

'Where is he?'

Startled, he looked up into Maggie's face. 'Who? What's up?'

'Stephen.'

'Stephen?' He pulled himself to his feet.

'Where is he?'

'I don't know.'

Maggie went into the hall, calling for Mrs Overmeer, and Christopher followed her, saying, 'Look, what's up? . . . I tell you he isn't here. Perhaps he's gone to . . . to your mother's, or having his dinner at school. You know he's always wanted to.'

Maggie looked down on her husband, and her neck worked in and out like a bellows as she said, 'He's struck a master with an inkstand and split his head open. And he played truant this morning.'

Christopher made no comment on this statement, but he continued to stare up at Maggie as if she had gone mad; and he looked prepared to humour her by listening to her gibberish.

'Are you stupid altogether? Don't you hear what I'm saying?'

'Aye, I hear all right. You're telling me that our Stephen has hit a master and that he's been playing the nick.' It was seldom he referred to the boy as 'our Stephen'.

'Have you seen him?'

'No, not since this morning . . . He's not here. I told Mrs Overmeer not to bother keeping his dinner hot. Where are you going?'

As Mrs Overmeer appeared in the hall Maggie was already running down the steps again, and Christopher from the hall door, called, 'Wait a minute, can't you? Let's get me coat and I'll come.' But by the time he returned to the door Maggie was gone, and not even the sound of her car could be heard.

He let out a good round oath and got into the Ford and set out for Ann's. She must be up the pole. And yet if she was going up the pole her madness wasn't likely to take this particular line regarding the boy. More likely she'd see him as the Prime Minister, or some such.

When he reached Ann's it was to find Nellie entering the house on the same errand as himself. She was wearing her apron, which in itself was unusual and told its own tale, for she never 'walked the street' in an apron.

She greeted him with 'Maggie's near mad. What could have made him do it?' But before he could answer they were both confronted by Ann.

She looked quickly from one to the other. 'Something's wrong, Davie?'

'No,' said Christopher. 'We're looking for the boy. Is he here?'

Ann shook her head slowly; and her mother said sharply, 'Now it's no use hiding him; he'll only have to face the music some time.'

'What are you talking about? What's happened to him?'

'He's not here?' It was Christopher now asking the question.

'No, he's not here. Haven't I told you! Don't stand there looking mazed, tell me what's happened.'

He told her what he knew, and she used the same words as Maggie, 'I don't believe it.'

'I'd better get back and tell her,' said Nellie.

'Wait a minute, Mum, and I'll come.'

'No!' Both Nellie and Christopher spoke together. Then Nellie turned and went hastily out – and Christopher added, 'It'll be better if you don't until . . . later.' He didn't have to say 'Until Maggie's gone.'

Ann sat down by the table and looked at Christopher with the childlike stare that always made him want to put his arms about her. And he said, 'Don't worry.' He gave a small laugh. 'He's going to be like our lads. We all played the nick, you know.'

'But the master.'

'Aye, that bit's odd. As big as our fellows were, not one of them had the spunk to hit a teacher. There's something fishy about it . . . I'd better get along, Ann, but as soon as I know anything I'll slip back.'

His hand rested on her shoulder for a minute, and when he lifted it away it seemed accidentally to touch her short fair hair where it curled round her ear.

The door closed on him, and she watched him disappear down the garden; and for a moment her thoughts left Stephen and she murmured, 'Poor Chris.' His money, his car and his rise in the world had not lifted the adjective from his name – to her he would always remain 'Poor Chris'; in fact, anyone who was unfortunate enough to be in touch with Maggie qualified for that adjective of poor.

Chris loved her – she knew that – and she often wondered what there was in her to evoke love. But of those who loved her, only one mattered – Stephen. Yet a few minutes ago, when the sight of her mother in her house apron had made her think that something had happened to Dave, there had been only him, and she had been flung back to the days when her love was full of worry and fear for him. Perhaps it was coming back, not the fear and the worry, but the love, as it was before they were married. A number of times during the past few months she'd had similar thoughts. But whether it was she herself or Dave who was resurrecting the past she did not know. She thought it was Dave, for he was different – not that he had ever been other than good to her, too good at times, but during these past months it was as if the tables had turned; instead of her leaning on and sheltering behind him, he was now in that position. He rarely left the house except to go to work; and it wasn't as if he was trying to keep her company, but as if he wanted to be mothered and protected, like Stephen.

She had once read that the only successful marriage was that in which the woman was equally wife, mistress and mother, and that the outstanding marriages were those in which the mother part was most active. She did not believe any of this, particularly the latter part, for from her own observation of the families about her she saw that the sons did not want to be kept. Once they felt the mother trying to hold them, they strained away. Look at their Tom. Because her mother would not let him go he was like someone in a trap. Then look at all the Taggart lads. Kitty laid claim to none of them, and they were never off her doorstep. If she herself had had a son she would have . . . What if Stephen had really been her son? Would she have let him go? And would she have minded had he preferred Maggie to her?

She refused to pursue the matter, and jumped to her feet, chiding herself for sitting thinking useless things, worrying things, as she was always doing. Stephen was lost and in trouble and likely wanting her – it wouldn't be his mother he would turn to. The thought lent wings to her feet, and she sped out of the house and to her mother's.

At six o'clock Stephen had not been found. The police had known of his disappearance now for some hours, and as yet had not the slightest clue to his whereabouts.

Maggie, like someone demented, had driven the car around the nearby countryside until she was on the point of collapse. She had spoken to more strange people to-day than she had done in the whole of her life; and in spite of her cast-iron armour, she had found that the kindness and helpfulness of entire strangers forced its way through a chink and warmed her. Everyone had wanted to aid her; even Christopher had showered on her the pity that had lain so long dead.

He had returned to the house again, and, finding her pacing the floor, had said, 'Sit down, lass, you're all in.'

He had never before called her lass. And he actually took her arm and led her to the couch; and, what was even stranger, she allowed him to do it.

'I'll get you a drop of brandy,' he said. 'Sit yourself there.'

After she had drunk the brandy she looked up at him and asked, 'Where have you been?'

It was as if they were an ordinary couple who were being drawn more closely together by their joint anxiety.

He answered, 'Nearly as far as Bencham.'

'Nobody seen him?'

'No . . . One thing I found out, though.'

'Yes . . . ?' She stiffened with eagerness.

He moved from one big foot to the other before saying, 'Pat's lads . . . they said they took him along with them this morning and they played in a wood. It was the Cobb's place.'

Maggie was on her feet, her old self to the fore. 'Those two! They're the cause of it all then. They should be horse-whipped!'

'Here, here. It's done now, and it's no use going on like that. Pat's taken the hide off both of them.'

'What about that wood? He might be there.'

He caught hold of her arm as she made for the door. 'Tom and Pat and me have already scoured the place from one end to the other.'

She drew in a deep breath as she went back to the couch; but she had hardly sat down before she was up and pacing the room again like a caged beast. Christopher sat watching her; his hands hanging listlessly between his knees. He was only now beginning to worry, for all afternoon he had thought tea-time would see him back . . . empty bellies had always brought their lads home. And he could see Stephen being driven by the same urge and slipping into the house, and they coming back and finding him, likely in the kitchen stuffing himself. But now it was well past tea-time. And his disappearance was beginning to take on a seriousness; and he thought: What if he's so terrified about hitting that master that he goes and does something? The something began to assume various forms; and he rose saying, 'I think I'll go to me mother's and see if they've heard anything.'

'I'll come.' It was almost as if she had said, 'Let me come', but he said, quite gently, 'No. You stay where you are, the police might ring with some news. You never know what them motorcycle squads picks up. And Mrs Overmeer is useless on the phone, you know that.'

Her usual attitude would have been to oppose on principle any suggestion made by him, but now she merely nodded.

Mrs Overmeer, all solicitude, brought in a tea tray. Mechanically Maggie poured herself out a cup of tea. She was feeling dazed and stupid; her mind was full of a new type of emotion, not connected with the fear, or worry of the moment. Its main ingredient seemed composed of sorrow; it was as if Stephen was dead, as if in this very hour she had lost him. She tried to make herself think that he would be found, and she could see him being found, but her mind still clung to the sorrow.

How long she sat there before she heard the scurry in the hall she did not know, yet before Tom's voice came to her, calling, 'Maggie!' she was at the door.

'You've got him?'

'Yes. Don't worry.'

Her hand went to her throat and passed up over her chin to her mouth; and she pressed it tightly as if to check the show of emotion she might later regret.

'Where is he?' She spoke too quietly.

'With . . . with Chris.'

'Are they coming?'

She looked beyond him, through the open door, to where the drive stretched away into the distance.

'No, not yet.'

It was evident that Tom was uneasy; and she said, 'Well, where is he? He's not hurt or anything?'

'No . . . no. Only upset. Chris is with him. He'll be all right soon . . . You see, one of the masters brought him . . . a very nice chap. He found him hiding near his cottage, and he brought him in a taxi. And reading between the lines he seems to think Stephen did a good job in lamming into that other fellow. But the lad's a bit shaken and he'll need to be kept quiet for a time.'

'But why didn't he bring him home?'

'Well, I never asked the chap that. And we were all too pleased to see the boy . . . Now, Maggie—' He paused. 'He's found; be thankful and don't go off the deep end.' He paused again. 'He's at Ann's. He likely told the teacher to take him . . .'

Maggie's face was mottled and her body had stiffened. 'Why couldn't Christopher bring him back in the car?'

'Well, he was a bit upset and they thought it best to leave him where he was.' Tom didn't say that the boy screamed, as if he was having a fit, at the thought of going home to his mother and to the censure he imagined lay in store for him.

'It didn't occur to any of you how I feel, did it?'

'It did. But it was no use forcing him. And to-morrow he'll likely be quieter; then he can come home.'

'Can he?' Maggie glared at her brother. 'He's coming home to-night . . . now!'

She turned to the door, and he caught hold of her arm, saying, 'Don't be a fool, there'll only be trouble! Be thankful, can't you?'

'Let go!'

So menacing were her eyes that he obeyed her, and she ran down the steps; but at the bottom she turned and asked, ungraciously, 'You coming?'

'I've got my bike.'

He watched her start the car, and his eyes followed its streaking down the drive before he mounted his bicycle.

It was a good twenty minutes later when he reached Ann's, and during his journey he had speculated on what he would find when he should arrive – Ann likely crying her eyes out because Maggie had forcibly removed the boy. And in Maggie's present mood he could see no-one preventing her. He could see no-one preventing Maggie from doing what she wanted to do, in any mood. So he was puzzled as he walked up the garden path at not hearing raised voices – all he heard was a faint moaning sound. Through the opening of the curtains he could see a number of people in the kitchen. The odd thing was that they all appeared to be stationary. The oddness did not strike him fully, however, until he had passed through the scullery and opened the kitchen door. Whatever he had imagined, he was not prepared for the scene confronting him, the scene that was to change drastically the course of his life. It was like a tableau; Ann, with David on one side of her and Christopher on the other, was facing Maggie. All were rigidly still. Only David's eyes flashed towards him as he entered. The tension was so great that it engulfed him, and he too became still. Standing just within the doorway, he looked from one to the other.

As if his presence had quickened the tableau into life Maggie's head moved downwards in the likeness of an animal about to charge. She looked neither at Ann nor at Christopher; it was at David she looked. Then she said, with terrible emphasis, 'You'll be sorry.'

And David, shaking his head as if emerging from a trance, replied sharply, 'Have some sense, woman. Do you think we're keeping him here on purpose? I can assure you I'm not. You've seen yourself how he is. Listen to him now.'

He became silent for a moment and the moaning from above pressed down on them. 'It's as Chris says, if he has some sleep he'll likely quieten down by the morrow, and he can go home.'

'Are you going to let me have him? I can get the police.'

'You forget that he's got a father.' David nodded sideways towards Christopher. 'He's got as much say in him as you.'

Maggie tossed her head up and made a sound that was midway between a laugh and a snort. Still addressing David, her voice thin and piercing, she said, 'Huh! Do you think he's keeping Stephen here for his own good? It's to please her.' Maggie's eyes seemed to fling themselves on Ann. 'If she wanted Stephen drowned, don't you know he would do it?' Now she asked of Ann directly, 'Wouldn't he?'

As though supplied by the one channel, the colour mounted into both David's and Christopher's faces, and Christopher took a step forward, saying, 'Why, you!'

'Deny it.'

The words were fired at Christopher, but Maggie still looked at her sister, and as Ann's eyes stared defiantly back into hers Maggie's venom rose. The sight of Ann standing there protected by two men, both of whom

287

were willing that she should also have her son, was not to be endured. If a bottle of vitriol had been at hand nothing would have prevented her from hurling it into her sister's face. But, driven by the intensity of her hate, she hurled something equally destroying.

'Do you know your husband's got another woman? . . . No, you don't, do you?' Amid the paralysed silence of the moment words gathered on her lips. Then, like arrows dipped in the poison of her hate, she sped them home: 'And she's given him a bairn. You didn't know that, did you? No, you've been so concerned with my son you had no time to bother about what your own man was doing.'

Again it was as though life had departed from the group, but now they had the appearance of puppets whose strings were being held stationary by their operator.

Tom too became transfixed by Maggie's words. His eyes darted to David and saw that within a matter of seconds his face had become grey and pinched, and an unnameable sensation filled him when he realised that no vehement denial would be forthcoming, for his brother-in-law had guilt written all over him. Yet what was more baffling, his eyes were widening in a stupid way, as if the denouncement had surprised him.

Christopher's face, too, was a study in surprise but overlying it was anger, black anger. Tom found he could not look at Ann; he knew she was looking at David, and that her suffering would be in her eyes; and he could not bear to see it. Then something happened that wiped them all from his mind like a sponge as it passes over a slate; it brought the past into the room and opened the sealed door in his heart; it was as if the actual door had banged violently against his ribs, so great was the start Maggie's next words evoked.

'Beattie Watson's determined to be in this family in some way.'

Ann's voice, like a scream, ran through the kitchen: 'You're lying! You're wicked!'

And as Maggie cried, 'Ask him. Ask him where he was V.E. night. Standing in the open like a . . .' Christopher took a step forward. His arm swung across his chest until his hand was behind his shoulder; then it swung outwards and up, and the back of his hand came full across Maggie's mouth, and the force sent her staggering back against the wall; and there was an eerie quiet in the kitchen. Christopher moved forward again and, pointing to the door, said, 'Get out!'

Although rage was blinding him and he could, without the slightest compunction, have throttled her at this moment, he fully expected her to come sweeping back at him. But neither by word nor action did she retaliate; she eased herself from the wall and her hand did not even go up to her mouth where the blood was showing on her lip, but for one long second she looked at him; then without another word she turned about and slowly walked out of the room. No word of Stephen – she might not have been fighting for him – it was as if she had obliterated him with the words which had created this scene.

Christopher watched her go. Except for that time years ago when he had cuffed the twins, never had he lifted his hand to man, woman, or child. And now he had hit her. He had always been afraid of her, he knew that; even when he had stood up to her he had been afraid; but he'd be afraid no more; he had hit her.

His anger was giving way to a feeling of shame and surprise when his thoughts were lifted from himself by Ann crying, 'No! Don't come near me!'

He turned and saw her backing away from David who, like someone dazed, was swaying on his feet, his head rolling on his shoulders as if he were in physical torment.

'It was only the once, Ann . . . God! . . . Believe me, I tell you I was drunk.'

He looked wildly, first at Tom, then at Christopher, as if they could, if they would, substantiate his statement.

With eyes seeming to spread and encompass her face, Ann was saying, 'Beattie Watson. Beattie Watson.' The name rolled round her tongue as though she were tasting it. She too looked towards Christopher and her brother; and then she made a sound, an inhuman sort of noise, half grunt, half moan that had about it a dreadful weirdness; and suddenly it broke and changed into a laugh, composed of low, staccato sounds, which increased in volume until it burst on a shrill scream as David came towards her: 'Don't!'

His supplicating hand waved the air like a conductor's baton, but helplessly. Then it dropped to his side as he watched her back away from him. At the door she turned swiftly and fled from the room. Only her flying feet could be heard on the stairs, there was no sound of her crying.

David passed his hand across his eyes. Well, it had to come. Hadn't he known it would come? For weeks now he had seemed to be waiting for it . . . That car. Why was it some fellows could carry on with a woman for years and get away with it, yet he could trip up once, only once, and his life lay in fragments, tormented fragments? His head rocked again.

That had been part of his torment . . . because it could only be once; and because deep in his heart he could not regret that night, or forget the woman who had made it possible. He had even to stay in the house in case he should meet her, for in that one night she had moved permanently into his life . . . as she had into Tom's. He lifted his dazed eyes to where Tom was standing staring at him, and greater misery was piled on his head . . . he hadn't forgotten her either. He was looking like murder.

David's eyes dropped before the wild glare in those of his brother-in-law. God, what had he done? Just that one night, and now this. And above all and everybody there was Ann . . . Ann. If only he could talk to her and make her see. But what would he be able to make her see? that he wanted another woman? Jesus in Heaven, what had happened to him? He loved Ann. Yes, yes, he loved her. The other thing was different . . . like a craving for drink, or something. If only he could make her see. She had been so nice to him lately. He had felt like a bairn at times, wanting to be comforted, and she . . . The word bairn brought Maggie's words racing into his mind. She had said there was a bairn coming. But it wouldn't be his . . . that one night! . . . Fool. That one night had had power to create a thousand bairns . . . and he knew it.

His head swung again. She could have been with anybody. But that night she was with him! And if there was a bairn, it was his, because he had taken her unprepared. No joy came to him at the thought. Apart from his having been with another woman, what would the fact of him being able to give her a child mean to Ann? In his heart he knew that Ann had laid the blame of their childlessness at his door. Now what he must do was to convince her it was only she who mattered. He must, even though he no longer convinced himself.

He went out blindly, groping at the door, and Christopher listened to him mounting the stairs and to him calling, 'Open the door, Ann.' He listened until the pleading became unbearable, then he turned to Tom and said, 'Don't think too badly of him, Tom, he was tight.'

'Is it . . . Beattie Watson?'

'Aye.'

'And . . . and the bairn?'

'You know as much about that as me.'

Tom looked up at the ceiling, and Christopher said, 'Look, lad, don't get bitter about this. It's not as if you still knew her or anything. And you know what she . . .'

His voice trailed off as Tom's eyes came down to him, daring him to go on; and he lifted his huge shoulders in a helpless gesture and turned away.

Tom stood still. Stephen's moans were faint now; but David's voice was getting louder as he pleaded with a note of desperation, 'Ann, say something . . . What you up to in there? I'll bash the door in, mind.'

As if escaping from the voice, he turned and rushed from the house. But the voice went with him, the voice of his mate, deputy or not, the tolerant voice that poured oil on the turbulent tempers of his own particular workmen, the voice that would come down the face, making him pause to wipe the sweat from his eyes, 'Dodging the gaffer again? You've never been the same man since I left you,' or some such chaff, the voice of his sister's husband, and now the voice of the man who had held Beattie Watson in his arms and given her a child.

His walk through the town was on the verge of a run. Once on the fells he let himself go. Although it was quite dark and there was no moon, he did not stumble; over the years since he had last seen her the unmarked road to the place that had served as a rendezvous for him and Beattie had become as familiar as his own street.

* * *

Christopher had memories still vivid in his mind of sleepless nights when 'Jerry' had strafed the town, when in the sandbagged cellar of his house he had sat with Maggie and the Overmeers and watched Stephen peacefully sleeping in a bed as comfortable as the one in his own room. Maggie had seen to that. There was the memory of a week when night after night he had helped to fight incendiaries and put out fires, and worst of all, to carry maimed bodies from wrecked buildings. But these had become memories without pain, for he had lost no loved one in the war. True, his brother had been killed, and for a time he had been sorry; but between being sorry and feeling sorrow there was a wide gulf. Yet the memory of last night, with its weight of anxiety and sorrow, would remain with him all his life.

Twenty-four hours had passed since Maggie had revenged herself, and so much had happened that life would never be the same again, not for him, or David or Stephen, or Tom . . .

Maggie . . . and not for Ann.

He was driving slowly past the actual gate through which Stephen and Mr Rankine had walked so happily yesterday morning when he stopped the car and got out, and leaned on the gate. He looked across the peaceful field to where the trunks of the trees were blackening and their foliage was seeming to bend under the flame of the setting sun. He did not consciously see this, or even think about it, but he felt that beauty persisted, even seemed more beautiful, when the mind was in pain. He wanted to lay his head on his arms and give vent to his crying, for all his body was crying and only his eyes were dry . . . Where was Ann now? Was she frightened? Perhaps it would be as well if she was, for then she'd be feeling and speaking, giving voice to her hurt. Never had he imagined how terrible silence could be when imprisoned in the human body. To see someone you knew, and loved, unable, or refusing, to utter a syllable was more torturing than to see that person writhing in pain.

As he said he would do, David had bashed the door in, and there he had found Ann lying on the bed, stiff and wild-eyed and silent. Only when he touched her did she move, and then it was more in the nature of a convulsion . . . nervous hysteria the doctor afterwards called it. And now they had taken her away to that place. They could say it wasn't an asylum – nerve centre, they called it. Then why was it attached to the asylum? My God, it was unthinkable, Ann in that place. And what was even more unthinkable, she had seemed quite willing to go.

He had stood in the kitchen with Nellie while the doctor talked with David, and his own sorrow had been dimmed for the moment by the sight of David's face as the doctor said, 'It had to come, you know; she's been leading up to it for years.'

Christopher thought now of that last sentence, but it did nothing to shift the blame of this terrible upheaval from Maggie. Nor did the fact that if Beattie Watson was going to have a bairn to David it would have been bound to leak out sooner or later. No, to his mind Maggie was responsible for it all.

And then there was Nellie. He knew that her real anguish had not begun when they took Ann away but when she realised that once again Beattie Watson was tearing at the vitals of her son. He had stayed out all last night, coming home only to change for work. That, to her, was all the proof she needed.

Christopher left the gate and got back into the car, and proceeded slowly up the hill. He had said he would leave the house if Maggie dared to open her mouth about this affair. Well, this was one time he would stand firm; he was going now to collect his things and tell her. But in spite of his resolve it wasn't going to be easy. Had he been leaving the boy with her he would have had no hesitation in walking out; but like Ann, the boy had broken. It was strange that their collapse had occurred on the same day. He wondered again what the doctor had said to Maggie to-day that had prevented her from coming tearing to his mother's and snatching her son from the coarse proximity of his family. It must have been something strong, whatever it was, to keep her away. Yet, surely, he would not have dared to say to her what he had said to him . . . 'if you want to keep that boy sane, keep him away from his mother.' Surely no man could find an assortment of words to soften that blow. 'Let him run wild,' he had said . . . 'tear his things . . . get dirty. Send him to a school where he'll mix with the rough-and-tumble, or that twitch of his will go here.' He had tapped his head significantly; but in his brusque way he had remarked, 'Don't worry unduly; I'll do what I can with her.' And as he went to go out he asked, 'Why don't you come down into the town again so that the boy will be near his people. Hill's no good for any of you. His Grannie Taggart and the lads will be the best medicine for him.'

Well, Stephen was with the lads now; but how long would he be allowed to stay there? What worlds could be overturned in twenty-four hours! His home such as it had been was broken up.

He brought the car to a standstill at the bottom of the steps, and as he entered the house he thought: I'll sell it, and quick. She can get a place of her own.

He paused outside the drawing-room door . . . His hand went out to the knob. Then he turned abruptly away and went up the stairs. He'd pack his things first and tell her on his way out.

His packing did not take long; two suitcases held all his belongings; and he carried first one then the other out on to the landing. And as he placed the second down a man's voice, shouting from downstairs, came to him. He paused with his back bent, listening. The words were unintelligible, yet they plainly conveyed anger.

His brow puckered with his thinking . . . that was George's voice. He had intended to take the cases down one at a time, for even now, with all his improved health, he still found his strength taxed when he lifted a heavy weight, but the voice, louder now, impelled him to lift both cases, and stumbling hurriedly down the stairs he dropped them with a thud at the foot.

The drawing-room door was open, and standing sideways to him was George Rowan. Maggie was facing him.

Last night he had seen Maggie's face look almost inhuman with temper. Since first knowing her he had seen it express many-emotions, but none in such a way as it was doing now; it was livid, with a startled, almost frightened lividness. George was leaning towards her. His face, in contrast, was red, and his words almost choked him as he said, 'You've hated her since she was born. And now you've driven her mad.'

Christopher moved into the room, and George jerked round towards him. He was wearing his flat pit cap and his pit clothes, and Christopher remembered that he was down below when they took Ann away, and that he would not have learned about her until he arrived home.

'It's you, is it? Well, you might as well hear this.' George tossed his head in Christopher's direction. 'She's your wife, and I pity you for it. I've always pitied you. And if I'd had me way she'd never have brought it off.' He turned towards Maggie again; and more quietly now but more ominously he went on, 'As I said, I'm going to put you back where you came from . . . the gutter. You may make money and live in your big house, but this'll stick in your mind till you die, it'll cover everything you do. It's been bad enough for me, but it'll be a hell of a sight worse for you, because you've got the idea that you're somebody, that you're a cut above us lot. That's right, isn't it?' He waited, and when no muscle of Maggie's face moved he went on, 'If I'd had me way you'd now be in the backwash of a Liverpool slum where you were spawned. A bob a time your mother used to charge. Aye . . . your mother.'

George smiled a slow smile with his lips alone: 'I can see you believe me. Now you know why I hated your guts . . . I fell for your mother. No, not Nellie; but a prostitute. I was a daft young lad, and I thought I could save her; and I took her out of the mud to a respectable street. But even when you were filling her belly she was supplying gentlemen at a shilling a go.'

Christopher, looking at Maggie's face, felt he could not bear it. God! God, it was awful! She didn't deserve this. He put his hand tentatively on George's arm and murmured, 'You've said enough.' And George, with a sweep, swung it off, crying, 'No, by God, I've not! Not by a long chalk. I've waited years to tell her this.'

His eyes, filled with a mixture of pain and hate, turned back on Maggie. 'You're wondering how you came to look on Nellie as your mother, aren't you? Well, I'll tell you I met and courted and married her all in a flash. It was the rebound, the full swing of the pendulum from the gutter to the church. But after a few months the gutter pulled again and I went back . . . And there you were, an unwashed brat, lying in a box in a windowless room; and there you would have remained for me, only Nellie found out what I was up to, and she found out about you. And you became her trump card. Nothing would stop her but she would have you to bring up. Oh, she was clever in her way, was Nellie. She put my sin before my eyes, for the ugliness of the gutter never dimmed as long as you were there; you grew more like it every day . . . dark, ugly and mean.'

'George . . . here, steady on!' Christopher's voice was a command, and George swung round on him. 'Steady on, you say. You can tell me to steady on when you've been through just a bit of what I have . . . years and years of that!' He thrust his finger in utter contempt at Maggie. But still she made no move. 'Years and years of her high-and-mightiness; her sneers, and her treating Ann as if she were a halfwit. And then there was that time of the strike, and we all had tight belts and hungry bellies, and she with her money in the bank – but would she give Nellie a penny over her board, the board money that wouldn't keep a school bairn? That got me. And but for Nellie she'd have been in the same trade as her mother. Things like that rankled. And you tell me to steady on? Why, I'd have told her this years ago if I'd had my way, and shown her the door.' He paused, and his eyes left Maggie and Christopher and they seemed to look inwards. 'If only I'd defied Nellie I'd have saved my lass. Aye, I know I would. But now . . .' His shoulders lifted slightly and his eyes saw Maggie again, and he said, 'There was nothing you didn't try, was there? That time you took her down the pit, it was to scare the wits out of her. And now you've succeeded . . . you've robbed her of her reason. And what have you got out of it? What have you got, I ask you?' His voice rose to a shout. 'Nowt! Nowt! Nowt, d'ye hear! For you haven't got your son; he hates the bloody sight of you. And you'll never have him again. D'ye hear that? The doctor says just a few more months of you and he'll be put away an' all. Now how do you like it?' He moved a step nearer to her, his face almost touching hers. 'How do you like your own medicine, eh?'

Still there was not the slightest movement from Maggie. George might have been spurting the suppressed bitterness of years on to a plaster cast, so little response did he get. But he was not deceived by her immobility; and he went on, 'You've got nowt; you haven't got a soul that'd give you a kind word. You've got no mother and you've got no son; and your man's goner leave you. And he's left it nine years too long. So there, me fine lady who aimed to live on the Hill, what d'you think of that?'

Again there was a pause, during which George pulled his cap more firmly on to his head. 'You don't say nowt, but I know what you're thinking. I've hit you where it hurts. Now I'm going, and I'm leaving you as you left my lass, with nowt.'

He moved backwards a step. His head nodded at her. 'It was ninety-nine chances out of a hundred she'd have never heard of Beat Watson if you hadn't made it your business to tell her.'

Again he waited for some response. But when none came he passed Christopher and walked towards the door, and there turned, saying finally, 'But I'll leave you one thing . . . your mother. If you have a fancy to look, you'll likely find her in the same place, or what's left of her . . . Pinwinkle Street. Ask anyone. Ask any sailor – or anyone, for that matter – where Polly Harkness lives. They'll show you.'

Christopher listened to George's slow tread across the tiled hall. He could not bear to look at Maggie.

He went to the window and stared out on to the drive. George was now walking into the dusk of the evening. He looked an old man, bent and unsteady on his legs; it was as if the weight of bitterness he had thrown off had left his body without support.

Christopher put a bewildered hand to his mouth and rubbed it slowly, pulling his lips first one way and then the other. How was he going to walk out on her now? It seemed as if in one fell swoop she was being stripped of everything . . . . As ye sow so shall ye . . . No, he wasn't going to do any preaching. But what was he to do?

As if only she herself could tell him, he turned towards her. She was still standing in the same place. The only difference in her position was that she held one arm across the level surface of her chest, and her hand, gripping her other forearm, was showing up the knuckles like bleached bones.

She looked so utterly alone, so desolate, standing there in the middle of the room, that the dead pity he still housed began to resurrect itself. It urged him to go to her and say something, but he shook his head . . . he couldn't. If he hadn't hit her last night he might have been able to act differently now; but under the circumstances it would smack too much of the hypocrite. No, he could offer her no word of sympathy; but there was something he could do; he could stay on for a while; he needn't go off right now; a day or two wouldn't make much difference either way. He would stay until she got herself pulled together.

With averted eyes he passed her and went into the hall, and, picking up the cases again, made for the stairs; only to be brought to a stop by her voice, 'You're going the wrong way.'

He stood still a moment before turning round. She was standing in the doorway, and in the dim light she had the appearance of a corpse. Her eyes looked lifeless; almost they appeared to have vanished, leaving the sockets to emphasise the dead expression of her face.

He wanted to say, 'There's no hurry; I'll stay for a while,' but he found he could say nothing. His pity for her rose, yet so strong was she that he could only do as she bade him.

As he walked towards the door, the weight of the cases pulling at his shoulders, he had the idea that once again he was carrying the swill to the pigs, and an intense longing came over him for the days when he had done just that, before the lure of the bicycle shop filled his horizon, and before Maggie had thrust herself into his life . . .

As he had watched George leave, so Maggie watched him. She stood well back from the window, and she could see only his head and the top of his shoulders as he heaved the cases into the back of the car. She saw him slowly close the door on them; then still slowly wriggle himself into the driving seat. She watched him without thinking of him.

So much had happened during the past two days that her mind should have been awhirl with the conflict of her thoughts, but, as if like a thing apart it realised the impossibility to bear the weight of the sum total of her troubles, it dealt with only one thing at a time. All day it had worked around Stephen, one minute bidding her to fly to the Taggarts and tear her son from that slovenly, slipshod woman, only the next to recall the terrible burden the doctor had laid upon her . . . 'If you want him to remain normal you'll leave him where he is for a time. His only chance is to be allowed to run loose; and he's in the right place for that.' When she had reared up at him and said, 'I'll not! I'll get other advice,' he had answered, 'By all means. By all means. I have already seen Mr Spence – your husband suggested it. Very likely he'll order the boy away.'

This last statement had checked any further protest . . . Her son to be taken away. And they would say it was because of her. She knew the doctor was against her. They were all against her.

Afterwards, the day had worn slowly on its endless way. She had wandered about the house like someone lost. Christopher hadn't come back. When she attempted to think of him her hand had gone to her lower lip, swollen and sore inside where her tooth had cut into it. She felt no anger against him; it was almost as if he did not exist for her to apply her anger to. But behind the seeming indifference towards him she knew that presently she would have to think about him, and more than she had done before.

A short while ago when she had heard the heavy steps across the hall, she had thought it was him returning, but it had been her father.

Like a grown girl who had suddenly been told she was adopted, she asked of herself now 'Who am I?' but with a difference . . . she was not asking who her parents were, but from which of them she inherited most of her complex self. And the answer was with her before the question was ended . . . him. The conflict that was for ever warring inside her was of him; the censor that had watched her every reaction was of him, as if through her he was making reparation for his moral slackness. But there was still the other side. However small, there was the side that knew life, life that was bred purely of desire. Now it was plain how she had come to the knowledge of men's actions and reactions, of men's demands and desires; there was no necessity for her to have experienced or seen anything of the darker side of life, for it was part of her, she had been born of it.

She gazed with blank eyes out into the empty drive, and without any warning she retched. Clapping a handkerchief over her mouth, she groped behind her for a chair and sat down . . . Polly Harkness . . . a bob a time! The retching came again, and she sprang up and staggered out of the room and up the stairs and into the bathroom.

When she came out there was no semblance of colour left in her face, even the mottle had paled into the dead whiteness. She stood on the landing uncertain which way to go. Never in her life had she felt as she was feeling now. She was well acquainted with loneliness, but not with this isolated feeling. There was no-one left to turn to. She had never before, even in the very depths of loneliness, longed for someone to whom she could fly, someone to whom she could pour out all her misery. If she had, it would surely have been her mother. The thought of Nellie brought a trembling sensation into her throat. If she had loved anyone before she loved Stephen, it had been her . . . mother. But now she was no longer her mother. But she was still Ann's mother.

Was this why she had hated Ann from the very day she had seen her lying in the crook of Nellie's arm? In the subconscious layers wherein all truth and knowledge were stored she had known all there was to know, and it had bred her hate, and the hate had never lessened.

Her father had poured out his venom because he blamed her for Ann's breakdown – they would all blame her for that; people always blamed the last straw. She did not hold herself responsible for it, yet had she accepted the responsibility still not a spark of sorrow would have touched her. Did any of them ever think to blame Ann for the sleepless nights and tortured days she herself had suffered? They could not all have been blind to Ann's tactics. No. She was not sorry for anything she had done to Ann; she had taken her son . . . and her husband.

She made her way slowly along the corridor. To her mind Ann had always been silly and babyish; there was not a thing outstanding about her, neither in looks nor brains. As women went, she was a nonentity. Yet she was loved. David loved her . . . or had; Stephen loved her – the knife turned in her heart at the admission; her father loved her; and Christopher – he had loved her from the time she could crawl. Looking back, she could see that he had never stopped loving her.

She passed her own door and moved towards Christopher's. Here she paused; then slowly she pushed the door and went in. Already the room had a deserted look. The sweet, thick smell of his tobacco pricked her nostrils. Her head lifted . . . why was she here? He was gone. Hadn't she told him to go? But he would have stayed.

Under the foot of the bed she could see a pair of his boots. With her toe she moved one into full view. If there was anything that could bring her back to the normal way of thinking about him it would be his boots. The enormous boot with its thick welt and bulbous toecap looked abandoned, the stiff leather, moulded with use, falling away in small ripples on each side of the lolling tongue. She was not given to fancy, but at this moment she thought the boot looked like a dog pining for its master. Whereupon, with a quick movement of her foot, she kicked it under the bed again. There was a dull clatter as it hit its partner; then the room was as it had been, quiet and desolate.

Whether the added desolation of the room seeped into her or her own feeling of desolation flowed over into it she did not know; she only knew that she could not bear this misery. Never, even in the depths of her loneliness, had she allowed herself the relief of tears – tears were for senseless women, women like Ann – but now the avalanche of her emotion drove her, not towards the chair, but towards Christopher's bed, and, dropping on to it, she thrust her face into his pillow, and, putting her hands under it, she pressed it to her mouth to still the terrifying sounds of her weeping.

Part Four

Ann

14

The Law of Opposites

Nellie's world had been lying in fragments about her for months now. There seemed not a splinter left to fall, yet each day as she covertly watched Tom eating his meal in feverish haste with never a word to her, then changing and speeding away on his bicycle, she experienced anew the tearing pain she felt when first she knew that his haste was speeding him to that woman. She had no actual proof he was going to her; she had heard no whisper; and she had not spied on him, although more than once she was tempted to do so. No, she knew without any evidence where he went. And she cried out hourly, 'He can't do it. God won't allow him to do it . . . a woman who is having a child to his brother-in-law, who has broken up his sister's life and turned her mind . . . he can't do it. It is an evil thing.'

But he did it. He went to her each day, even when he was on nights and finished at six in the morning, he would mount his bicycle and away. Which way he went she did not know; but she guessed by the condition of his shoes that his journey took him beyond the town.

She looked now out of the window at the snow blowing like smoke clouds on the wind . . . the first snow of the year. Vaguely she hoped that it wouldn't lie. But what if it did? Nothing mattered any more. Christmas was a week away, but there'd be no jollification in this house . . . Ann in that place; Maggie separated from Christopher, and her child taken away from her for the second time; George going about like a man deprived of his spine, no will to live left in him; and all because of that woman. It couldn't be! It mustn't be! She clenched her fists and pressed them on to the draining-board . . . But it was. All these things had already happened; all that could happen had happened, except that her son had yet to tell her he was going to leave her. When he should tell her that there would be nothing more that could happen to her.

She looked down on her clenched hands, red and toil-worn with work that had been done as a duty to her husband and for love of her son. If or when he should tell her that, there would be something she could do . . . she would curse the woman; she would curse her in the name of God, and she would pray night and day for her to wither and for all she should touch to do likewise . . . even if it should mean the main thing she touched . . .

The snow had changed from a thin spray to thick heavy flakes before Tom left the town. The flakes clung to his eyebrows and to his narrow moustache, and the front of his overcoat took on a breastplate of white. It was only half-past three, but already it was nearly dark.

Before reaching the fells he took the track forking sharply right. It was so uneven that the cycle bounced and lurched as on a switchback. But after some distance it smoothed out and widened. He passed a farmyard, where a heap of fresh dung steamed through the snow, and the smell and lowing of cows all suggested warmth. A farm hand gave him a muffled hail and he hailed back. About a mile further on he dismounted, and, pushing his bicycle through a gap in some treacherous hawthorn bushes, he made his way through a little copse of young birch saplings. Where the saplings ended a wood began, thick with naked trees and snow-sprinkled undergrowth; and here he left his cycle, pushing it into a dry hollow. Then banging the surplus snow from his clothes he went into the wood. Beneath the trees it was almost impossible to see, for besides the falling snow the canopy of entwined branches was like a curtain across the sky. But without hesitation he kept to the narrow path until it bore sharply left. Then he moved away from it in the opposite direction. The path he now took, through the undergrowth, was singularly clear. But he moved with more caution, until he neared the wide girth of an oak; and here he stopped, to peer through the gloom before slowly moving on again. Within a few yards from the tree he was standing by the broken fence that marked the boundary of the wood, and beyond was the road he had left earlier on.

Through the snow he could just make out the fuzzy outline of the cottage on the far side of the road. No light gleamed even dully through the little window; and he pulled his lower lip between his teeth, and stood, his hands deep in his pockets, gazing at it . . . Was she bad? Where was the old woman? . . . He hadn't seen either of them for a week now. What if they were both bad and in there alone? His hands inside his pockets opened and shut. There was no way he could find out . . . none, except to go and knock. He stepped backwards, as if checking himself . . . Well, what was he to do? His mind derided him with the answer. Do what you seem pretty good at doing . . . stand and watch.

How many weeks had he been watching now? He had lost count. Six? Eight? He didn't know. If he hadn't seen her again perhaps it would have been all right; and if his mother hadn't asked him to go with that message to Maggie he would never have seen her. How would his mother feel if she knew it was she herself who had started him on this game? He knew that she guessed where his daily trips were taking him; she had suspected him long before he had taken to following Beattie.

It had all come about because Stephen, who had been back with Maggie only a few days, came crying to his Grannie Taggart, his twitch worse than ever, and stammering so much that he was incoherent, and no amount of coaxing would make him return home. Kitty had come to Nellie, wondering how she was to let Maggie know, for Christopher was away at work, as also were Sep and the twins. Nellie had turned to him then and said, 'Would you go to the laundry and try to explain to her?' And reluctantly he had gone.

It was weeks since he had seen Maggie. He knew, as who didn't, that she had left the Hill and was now living in a little house not far from the laundry. He knew the house; it had been built just before the war and was privileged to have the wall of the new electric components factory on one side and on the other two a high cypress hedge, which gave it seclusion. Personally, he considered it a great advance on the mansion on the Hill, but what Maggie thought no-one knew.

The news that she was only his half-sister had at first surprised him and given him the reason for her difference. He had never been able to like her; yet on that day he had stood in her office and looked into her drawn face and deeply sunken eyes he had been sorry for her. He had fully expected her to jump down his throat when he delivered his message, yet her reception of it had been strange; she had turned away and sat down at her desk, and after a while she had said, 'All right. Let him stay.' She had even added, 'Thanks for coming and telling me.'

In that moment he had glimpsed a little of her suffering, but he could do nothing to help her; there was no link or ever could be between them; he didn't understand her.

A wooden trolley full of sheets had blocked his way at the top door, and rather than stand amid the curious glances and laughing eyes of the girls he had turned abruptly and made his way out through the washhouse. It was then he had seen her; across a bogie load of wet linen their eyes had met and held in startled recognition. Hers were the first to fall away, and as she turned to push the bogie he saw the shape of her, and his anger had almost choked him. The anger stayed with him for days; but it wasn't levelled totally against her; of the two, David came in for the greater part.

It was nearly a week later that he followed her to her home. She took the bus, and at a distance he followed it on his bicycle. He was surprised to find she was living so far out of the town. The cottage was just off the main road; but he made it his business to find another way to it. And now his watching had become almost an obsession. He watched her leave early for the laundry; he waited her return in the evening, listening for the bus to stop on the main road and knowing that within a minute she would come round the bend and pass so close to him he could almost touch her, and he would watch her enter the gate of the cottage and walk slowly and heavily up the path.

Why did he watch? Was he hoping to see David go in or come out? If he were to see him, what would he do? He knew what he would like to do . . . kill him. Nothing was deep enough or strong enough to describe the loathing he now felt towards his brother-in-law. Once it had been even possible to say that he loved David; but now his hate was so great that when he was forced to meet him down the pit he wanted to spring on him and throttle him. As his hate of Beattie had lessened, his hate of David had grown; it was as if the amount could not diminish.

A sound coming from the direction of the cottage brought his body up taut; it was the door opening and the latch dropping back; and when the blurred bent figure in the long coat showed through the snow he could not distinguish whether it was her or the old woman. He listened to the rattle of the windlass lowering the pail into the well . . . Whoever it was would have to pull that bucket up . . . His own hands were freezing inside their gloves and coat pockets. The windlass handle was of iron . . . He made a forward movement; but again checked himself. He was now standing level with the hedge, and the person at the well had only to look across the road and he would be seen, even through the falling snow, for the light here on the road was considerably lighter than in the wood.

But the woman did not glance in his direction. Laboriously she wound the bucket to the top of the well, unhooked it and stood it on the ground, then straightened herself as if to gain breath before stooping again to pick it up.

She had become almost lost to him when he heard her cry out sharply. There was a dull thud and the clatter of the pail as it rolled on to the stones of the path. When he reached her she was turning on her side in an effort to rise. Even when he put his hands under her arms and brought her to her feet he still did not know which of them she was; not even when the voice coming from the depths of the shawl said, 'That's the last straw,' not even then did he know; for the voice was merely a broken croak, which told of a severe cold.

When she was standing firmly again he withdrew his support and said, 'Go inside, I'll get the water.' And when he had filled the pail and turned towards the house again, to see her still standing where he had left her, then he knew which of them she was.

'What – do – you – want?' Each word was uttered as if it gave her pain.

He did not answer but walked towards the door with the pail and waited. Before reaching him she stopped again and said, 'Did you hear? Get yourself away.'

But he still stood. She began to shiver violently, then she swept past him and turned swiftly to close the door. But quite gently he kept it open. And when she released her pressure he followed her inside and closed the door behind him.

At first he could not see her but her voice came hoarsely to him: 'Will you go away!'

It was then he discerned the dark bulk of her moving back from him.

'Do you hear? Go away.'

A fit of coughing seized her; and when it passed he said, 'I'll go soon enough. Why don't you light the gas?'

She did not answer, and he moved a step further into the room, careful because of the huddle of things he sensed about him.

'Do you hear me? I don't want you here.'

He lit a match and held it above his head, and her face, a changed strange face, wavered in its flickering light. As the match died out he saw her sink on to a sofa, on which, judging by the jumble of clothes, she had been lying. He lit another match, and it showed him the old-fashioned stalk lamp in the centre of the table and the fire in which sticks were smouldering but with no sign of igniting. As he moved cautiously round the couch towards the table, she croaked, 'There's no use going there; there's no oil in it.'

'Where's it kept?'

'I told you to get out.'

'Where's your oil and your wood?' His voice was almost a growl.

Only silence answered his question, and he muttered, 'You're ill. When I've fixed up the fire and light I'll go, never fear.'

Still she said nothing.

'Where's the oil? You may as well tell me.'

'There isn't any.' She was seized by more coughing, and he waited; then asked tersely, 'Any candles?'

'There's only a bit left. Up there.'

He groped along the mantelpiece until he found the candlestick with the short stump of candle. He lit it, and when the light strengthened he did not look at her but towards the hearth, and with his back to her he asked, 'Haven't you any coal?'

When silence again greeted him he took the candle and made for the only other door in the room. Beyond, he found a rough stone-floor wash-house and scullery, in one corner of which there was a pile of wood neatly stacked against the wall, and an old tin bath beside it full of coal.

Placing the candle on the floor inside the room, he then carried in coal and wood, and within an amazingly short time he had the fire alight.

During this process neither of them spoke; nor did he look at her; but when the fire was roaring he turned and asked gruffly, 'Is the can handy?'

'What can?' Her voice squeaked, and she began to cough again. And he stood and watched her press her hands into her chest.

'The oil can.'

Her head was bent over her knees, and she swung it back and forward in a hopeless gesture. He said no more but went out into the scullery again, and with the aid of matches searched for the can. Eventually he found it in a little wooden shed outside the back door.

In the room once more, he asked brusquely, 'How are you off for food?'

She looked up at him now and straight into his face. Stonily he returned her stare, showing no sign of the mad racing of his heart nor of how shocked he was at the change in her.

'Tom Rowan . . . listen . . . to me.' She was speaking in gasps. 'I don't want you here . . . now or any other time . . . Is that clear?'

After a moment he said, 'Yes, clear enough.'

'Well, then.' She drew a blanket up round her shoulders.

'I'm going for the oil. Is there anything else?' His voice could have implied that his self-appointed errand was being done under protest.

'I can get oil . . . One of the girls'll be coming in on her way from work.'

'That won't be till six and the shops'll be closed. Where's the old woman?'

She looked up at him again, surprise showing in her red and swollen eyes. He could see the question there, 'How do you know about her?'

'She's in hospital,' she said.

'Why don't you send for your mother?'

Her head waved in the fashion of a mother's who had grown weary of the questions of a precocious child. 'She's been dead for years.'

'Isn't there someone of your . . . ?'

'Mind your own dam' business!' She pulled herself to her feet by the head of the couch and stared into his face, now not more than a foot from her own. Then she tried to shout at him, 'Are you clean mad?' But her voice broke and her words became an unintelligible gabble. She sat down abruptly and ended slowly, 'You never had any sense.'

'Have you had the doctor?'

'Oh, my God!' She turned her face into the pillow.

'I'll phone him.'

She raised her head and addressed herself with slow laboured words to the back of the couch: 'He's been. I've only got cold. I had a woman coming in, but her man took bad . . . But one of the girls will be calling in after work. I've got all I want . . . trouble an' all; and if you want to lessen it, stay away from me.' Her head sank back on the pillow and he turned from her and left the cottage.

Once out of the gate he ran like a hare down the road. The snow was still falling steadily and the night had come down without the usual twilight. But as if drawn by a magnet, he turned into the hedge almost opposite to where his bicycle was hidden, and within ten minutes he was in the town.

Not more than fifteen minutes later he was pushing his bicycle up the short path of the cottage. He leaned it against the wall under the low hanging roof and went to the door. But it did not give under his hand; and he pushed against it twice before realising that it was locked. His lips opened, but he checked the call they were about to make; nor did he knock, but he groped his way round to the back door. And it did not really surprise him to find that this too was locked. Next he tried the wash-house window, but it would not give. It was a square window, almost as big as the one at the front of the house. He struck a match and the light showed him the old-fashioned sneck similar to the one at home. It had been his job, as a young lad, to get through such another window as this when his mother forgot the key.

Within a matter of seconds his pocket-knife had forced back the sneck and he had raised the lower half. He experienced some difficulty, however, before he finally stood in the scullery. After closing the window he went into the room. Beattie was sitting on the edge of the couch, her hands pressed tightly between her knees. She did not speak when he went past her to open the front door and bring in the can and carrier-bag. Silently he went about filling the lamp.

After lighting it he filled the oil stove in the scullery and stood the tin kettle on the ring; but search as he might he could find no tea. The tins he opened showed him a variety of things, but not tea; and when the kettle bubbled he was forced to go and ask her, 'Where do you keep the tea?'

For a while she neither moved nor spoke, she might have been unaware of his presence so near to her, then with a helpless gesture she pointed to a polished wooden box on the mantelpiece; and when finally he brought her the cup she took it from him without comment.

'Are you hungry?'

She shook her head.

'There's bread in that bag.' He nodded towards the carrier-bag.

She lifted her eyes to his, and the pleading in her voice forced its way through the croaking. 'For God's sake go away! If you want to help me, stay away. Don't you think there's been enough damage done?'

'You're afraid he sees me.'

'Who?' The question was asked in genuine surprise.

Then slowly the dark gleam from his eyes made her aware to whom he was referring, and with her open palm she beat her knee, saying, 'Men! Men! Look' – she waved her hand despairingly – 'I don't want to go into all this. I've had enough. I'm asking nothing from anybody . . . help, sympathy or money. All I ask is to be left alone.'

'Does he leave you alone?'

'I've never seen him!' Her voice rose, crackling and squeaking. 'What do you take me for? The only thing I'll tell you is this: I didn't know who he was . . . I didn't know he was your relation. And as I see it there's been enough harm done, so don't you come here looking for more. I can't stand it. So there.' She paused and leant her head to one side as if listening. 'That's the bus.' She looked up at him again. 'For God's sake go! If you're seen here . . .'

'I'll wait outside until she's gone.'

He turned from her and picked his cap from off the table.

'You're mad.'

'Don't bolt the doors again.'

He let himself out of the front door and, taking his bicycle, pushed it round to the back of the cottage; then, coming back, he crossed the road into the wood and waited.

After ten minutes, since no-one had passed him, he returned to the cottage again. Beattie was now lying down, and he stood at the foot of the couch listening to her laboured breathing for a moment before saying, 'There was no-one on the bus.'

She lifted her hand to her head, and he saw that it was shaking. And he moved nearer, standing stiffly above her. 'Are you cold? Will I get you a bottle?'

She opened her mouth to refuse his offer, but her teeth chattered so that she had to clench them.

'Where is it?'

Her hand moved under the clothes and she brought out the water bottle and handed it to him; and when he returned with it filled she was lying with her hands covering her face.

'Here.'

She did not take the bottle but turned heavily on to her side away from him. Her body was trembling, and the sound of her crying was too much for him, and he dropped down by the side of the couch, his hands hovering uncertainly over her as he implored, 'Beattie, don't. Don't.'

Her crying mounted and became a source of agony to him. Sometimes there was nothing to hear at all as she held her breath; then when her sobs, weighing on each other, forced their release, he would implore yet once again, 'Look . . . don't. You'll only make yourself worse.' Once he nearly said, 'Think of the . . .' but his mind would not even allow him to harbour the word, even as a thought. Twice his hand almost touched her shoulder; but each time he withdrew it.

After a while, when her sobbing eased and she was lying comparatively quiet, the latch of the door was lifted, and she flung herself round and leaned on her elbow to gaze in startled surprise at the girl now standing in the room. Tom too, from where he was kneeling, gazed at the girl; but their surprise was nothing compared with hers. Her mouth agape, she stared fixedly at Tom. Then when she looked at Beattie she stammered, 'I'm sorry, I'm sure . . . I missed me usual, and I took the through one and got off at the cross-roads . . . Are you better?'

Beattie attempted to say something, but the words stuck in her throat. And the girl went on, 'I got your rations and things.'

She put a bag on the table, still without taking her eyes from Beattie. 'I got your pay.' She placed a small packet beside the bag. 'She's filled your place.'

Her eyes flickered over to Tom, where he was standing now by the head of the couch. The action, slight as it was, betrayed her knowledge of the relationship between her boss and this man.

An embarrassed silence fell on them, until the girl spoke again; 'Can I do owt? Get you anything, like?'

Beattie eased herself into a sitting position and drew in a sharp breath before she made to speak. But even as her lips opened, Tom said, in a flat unemotional voice, 'I'll be seeing to her.'

'Oh.' The girl pushed up her coat collar, and Beattie gasped out, 'Peggy!'

And the girl said, 'Yes, Beat?'

Beattie put her hand to her throat. 'Will you sta . . . ?'

Before she could finish the word, Tom, again in the same flat voice, said, 'Perhaps you'll be good enough to look in the morrow: I'll be here this evening.'

He stared at the girl until her eyes dropped away. Then he turned towards the fire and kicked the tottering log into place.

The girl's answer was stilted with her surprise, 'Yes. Why, yes.' Then she asked, 'What about the oil, Beat?'

Over his shoulder, Tom said, 'I've got that.'

Another silence followed: and when he turned round, the girl was staring at him, and Beattie, her eyes closed, was leaning against the back of the couch.

Again the girl adjusted her collar. 'Well, I'll go . . . We'll be snowed-up . . . Good night, Beat.'

Beattie did not answer, and the girl moved towards

the door. Then with one backward glance at Tom she turned and went out.

Her eyes still closed, Beattie croaked, 'I hope you're . . . satisfied.'

He made no reply.

'Your sister'll know the morrow.'

'That's all right by me.'

She opened her eyes. 'They'll laugh at you.'

'Yes. Well, I can stand that an' all.'

'They'll say it was me again.'

'I'll soon tell them different.'

She raised herself and leaned aggressively towards him. 'I'm going to have a bairn to your brother-in-law!'

To hear it put into plain words was like drawing a steel cord round his throat. The blood pounded in his head, and his teeth ground on the words, 'You don't have to stress that fact!'

'There's your mother; what about her? She'll want to kill me.'

'I've got my own life to live. What I do with it is my business.'

'Look, Tom.' She hung over the edge of the couch. 'You shouldn't need telling. I'm no good . . . never have been. I met your . . . that fellow once . . . just once . . . and this happened. Isn't that enough for you?'

Her eyes never flinched from his, and he thought, with a wave of relief, he was right then when he said it was only the once.

'It wouldn't have happened if I'd had some gumption years ago,' he said.

Slowly she drew herself back and leant against the pillows, dropping her hands helplessly on to the blankets. And her voice was but a whisper as she said,

'You want to thank God you hadn't, I'd have driven you mad.'

He remained looking down on her: 'Aye, perhaps then, but not now. I'm quite capable of holding what is mine now.'

Her eyes came up to his, tired, swollen, weary eyes, that would never again hold the sparkle of youth that he remembered; but they held all his body, soul, and mind craved. He dropped on his knees by the couch. 'Beattie.'

'No . . . no!' She made one more effort, thrusting her hands at him, trying to keep him off. But he took them and gathered them into his chest.

As she strained away from him another fit of coughing seized her, and he had to release her hands, but his arms went about her and he held her. And when the coughing ceased and her sobs broke out afresh, his hands gently stroked her head, and his eyes closed against the pain that he termed 'happiness'.

15

The Hope Block

'Hearts trumps? They would be. Anything in the love line, and trust me to be short of it.'

'Shut up, Queenie, you're giving the show away.'

'Does it matter? I never have any luck.'

'Your lead, Ann. What do you expect? You're always moaning.'

'If you'd had what I've had . . .'

'Look. Are you going to play or not?'

'You're as bad as they are. Occupy your mind . . . use your hands . . . forget yourself . . . think of others . . .'

'Mrs Holland.'

The four women turned their heads in the direction of the door.

'Yes, sister?'

'Come here a minute.'

Mrs Holland hesitated; her heavily rouged lips pouted; then she slowly rose and with a half-defiant air walked up to the sister, and followed her out of the room.

'Well, that's put finish to the game. Anyway, it'll soon be suppertime. Where's my knitting?'

The stout woman moved away and sat down in an armchair before the fire; and as she settled herself she said, 'I can't see her ever really getting better myself. Anyway, I never thought she was really bad; I think it's just the way she's made. I should imagine she's been like that since she was born. You can't blame the men for walking out on her.'

'No.' The young woman with the blonde hair and pastel complexion sitting beside Ann gave a little laugh. 'What amazes me is how she ever gets them to walk in.'

Ann rose, and taking a magazine from a pile on a side table also sat down by the fire and set about the pretence of reading. She found she could escape quite a lot of needless talk that would invariably lead to pertinent questions, by this means. Sometimes she even tried to read, but she would read no more than a sentence or two before her thoughts would be on the page staring up at her, forcing her to go over and over them until the repetition became wheels that would gather momentum and whirl round in her head; and, in their turn, they would fill her with fear, and the fear would make her sick.

Still, she was better. Oh, yes, much better. Did she really want to get better though? That was the question Doctor Dickinson asked her this morning, and she had answered, 'Yes.'

And then he had added, 'But you don't want to go home?' To which she had answered, 'No.'

Five months she had been here now, and they were like five years . . . or fifty, so full had they been of terror and thinking. But now she was better. Oh yes, she was better. Somehow in spite of herself she was better, for here, she was in the Hope Block. She remembered when she first saw Hope Block. It was the day they made her get out of bed and walk down with the others for treatment. There was a nurse on each side of her, their arms linked around her waist; and one kept saying, 'You're doing fine.' And then her legs buckled and she began to cry. They stopped beside a wide window, and through her tears she saw the horse-chestnut leaves falling. The tree was standing in the middle of a great lawn, and about its feet lay a carpet of bronze and gold. And the other nurse said, 'You'll be over there very shortly.' And it was some time before she understood the nurse was referring to the house beyond the tree, the house that was nicknamed the Hope Block.

But it was quite some time before she went to the Hope Block; she continued to go each week down the grand staircase, with its great balustrade and its thick red pile carpet, and along the hall of mirrors to a door at the end, which seemed the dividing line between two worlds, the world of the grand mansion, full of strange and terrifying people, and a world of bare stone steps, leading in a spiral down to a tiled passage, then into a room with wooden benches and a lavatory that stank from over use. When your turn came you were led through a green baize door into a room in which the familiar nurses and doctors were different – the trusted Doctor Dickinson was no longer in nice smelling tweeds, but in a white coat, sitting at the head of a high couch. He placed something on your head; it pressed against the temples . . . then bang. You were shot into nothingness.

But one day she had not been completely shot away, and her body lifted off the couch and she was conscious again, and she heard the doctor swearing. But this had not made her afraid of the electric treatment. Not until she found that she walked with just a hand on her elbow from that couch back to her bed in the ward. And then she became afraid . . . of this thing which made her do what she couldn't make herself do . . . walk . . . walk without aid.

It was some time, too, before she realised how large a place Poynters was, and how stocked full it was of people like herself . . . or worse; and she decided that if she was to go mad then she would prefer it, even try to make it, the sullen, quiet way; for depression was preferable to laughter; even the terrible crying of the woman in the next bed she could stand, and her constant repetition of 'I can't bear it . . . I can't bear it,' but not the laughter of the woman opposite. And the greatest terror she had ever known, and which retarded her progress by weeks, was when, for no apparent reason, a gurgle of strange laughter welled up in her own throat.

It had taken Doctor Dickinson to explain this away. He did so by giving a simple illustration of a very tired child, who would toss itself about, laughing and crying alternately. Her nerves, he said, were very, very tired, and they were asking for rest. So were Mrs Bateman's nerves. Her laughter did not mean that she was going mad. No-one here was mad, or going to go mad; they would all be better through time. And she would be better.

She hadn't believed him. Yet all he said was true. There was Mrs Bateman now, sitting by the fire, quietly knitting, and her laughter was no longer immoderate; and Miss Jackson, sitting at the table playing patience. She was the one who had kept saying she couldn't bear it. And he had also been right about herself: she was better . . . in all but one thing.

Doctor Dickinson had said to her only that morning, 'You're going to be better than you've been for years. And don't worry about not being able to think of your husband . . . that will come. And then you will want to see him and be quite ready to go home . . . Now don't worry; we won't make you go a minute before you want to.' He had patted her hand and said, 'We like having you.'

It was as if she was the only one in the whole place to whom he gave a thought. She knew this was silly, but he made you feel like that.

He had asked, 'How's the dressmaking going?' And she had said, 'Fine.'

'And the thinking?'

And she had said, 'Not so good.'

'That'll come, never fear.'

It was difficult for her to realise that thinking had caused her nerves and that because she hadn't been given a child she had subconsciously determined to have Stephen, for in doing so she would be supplying her mother-hunger and she would also be getting her own back on Maggie. She had not known that her life had been soured by Maggie's power to bear a child. She had never imagined she herself could be sterile, for it would have been quite impossible for her to accept the fact that the fertility of her mind was not matched by the fertility of her body. In her simple way of looking at things she had worked it out that wanting children so much, had it lain with her alone, she would have had them. Yet what she must face up to was that David had given another woman a child. The woman concerned did not touch her; it was strange but she felt no jealousy of her now; the jealousy would seem to be levelled against David's power to create. Yesterday the doctor had said 'Won't you see your husband, he has come all this way? If you will once make yourself speak to him, I promise you that this feeling will go.'

But she had shaken her head and pleaded, 'Don't make me.'

That was the last obstacle – once she could think of David, then see him, she would be ready to go home.

Miss Jackson, speaking to no-one in particular, said, 'This time next week I'll be aboard ship sailing into the sun. Do you think anything nice will happen to me?'

'The men'll be daft if it doesn't.' The two women turned towards each other and laughed. 'With your looks I don't know what you've got to worry about,' said Mrs Bateman.

'I'm not worrying . . . just thinking. Did they give you any idea when you'll be going out?'

'Not for a week or two . . . Doctor Dickinson seems bent on keeping me away from the stove and the wash tub. By' – she glanced around the room – 'I'm going to miss all this. Hotel life isn't in it. What do you say, Mrs Taggart?'

Ann lowered the magazine. 'Were you speaking?'

'I was saying that this is like a posh hotel.'

'Yes, it is.'

'Are you coming to the singsong after supper?'

'Yes.'

'I wonder what's happened to "Moaner",' said Miss Jackson.

'Speak of the devil,' said Mrs Bateman, turning her attention assiduously to her knitting as the door handle rattled.

But it was a nurse who entered, saying, 'Mrs Taggart. Matron would like to see you.'

'Matron?' Ann rose, her eyes widening and seeming to swamp her small face. Matron very rarely sent for you, she generally came herself. And it was nearly seven o'clock.

Her eyes and those of the other two women questioned the nurse; but she volunteered no information; and Ann walked by her side through the main lounge and into the matron's office.

The matron was not alone, the doctor was with her; and he rose as Ann entered the room and said, 'Ah, there you are, Mrs Taggart.'

Ann looked from one to the other; then asked quietly, 'Is something wrong? Is it my mother?'

'No. Not your mother.' The doctor came forward and took her hand. 'It's your husband.' He stared into her face and her eyes became dark, and she moistened her lips and waited for him to go on.

And when he made no further attempt to speak, she swallowed hard and her words seemed to tumble over themselves out of her mouth. 'The . . . the pit. There's been an accident.'

'Yes.'

'He's hurt?'

'It's not known.'

'Where is he?'

'He's still down.'

Still down. It seemed that the whole of her life had tended towards the moment when David would be still down . . . shut in the pit.

'I . . . I must go home.'

'That's right.'

'Now.'

'Yes, as soon as you like.'

Even as the doctor spoke she was turning towards the door; and once in the corridor, her legs began to move faster than they had done for months, until she was running.

16

The Last Extremity

David continued along his district, and as of habit swung his lamp to shine on that part of the roof where the pressure had squeezed the wooden wedge, rammed between the roof and the pit prop, into a circle of splaying splinters. The prop itself was bent but had not cracked, and his hand went out to it in a casual slap. The section had settled all that it was going to settle; there was nothing to fear from her; she was like a permanent invalid who would never die.

He walked on, his eyes moving ahead with the lamp rays, looking for some unfamiliar sign. So used was he to this road that the position of each rock had become part of a pattern: it was settled; it was put. Yet still his eyes searched.

He came to the loading station, but the conveyor belt was not pouring the coal into the tubs, for it was the back shift, the shift in which the face conveyer was pulled yet another four feet six inches nearer the new face and the hazardous job of drawing the supports from the roof above the used face and dropping it was put into operation. This too was the shift when the roadway had to be driven forward and the mothergate trunk conveyor belt brought up, and this was yet another shift when he must face Tom twice.

During the course of his inspection he was of duty bound to visit every man twice during the shift, and now as he clambered over the stationary belt and entered the mothergate the muscles of his body began to stiffen and his jaw bones to give series of cracks, and he said to himself, 'I needn't look at him; I don't really need to go near him . . . he'll be in-by.' Yet he knew that he would go in-by . . . just to be near him. His jaw cracked so hard that it pained him. If only he would speak, go for him, curse him, even try to bash him. He would know where he stood then. Or would he? Would he ever again know where he stood? This kind of life was pure hell. He had not clapped eyes on Ann for months; and it was odd that he had not heard either hers or Tom's voice from that night. The silent house, the irritation of doing for himself – he would not live at his mother's because, although from his brothers he had heard nothing worse than 'You've been a bloody fool', he felt their condemnation was strong . . . he had smirched their respectability – these were telling on him. Above ground he suffered mostly because of Ann, but down here it was Tom who filled his horizon. Had he known Tom still felt like that about her it would never have happened . . . Yes, it would. For the thousandth time the truth reared its head at him. That night he had been bewitched with whisky and then with her. And she wasn't to blame altogether, for she hadn't known who he was. But she knew all right now, and she wouldn't answer his letters. Yet he must do something for the bairn. February . . . it should be born about now.

The sweat stood out on his forehead, and he drew his arm across it. She had returned the last letter and the money, and not a word had she said.

He could not bring himself to go and see her, for apart from the fact that he did not entirely trust himself he was afraid of running into Tom. He had no indication of how things stood between them, for no-one mentioned either of their names to him; the matter was a closed subject; yet somehow he felt that Tom was seeing her. One thing was clear and certain . . . Tom was still mad about her, and mad at him. Mad really did not quite fit the feeling that emanated from Tom towards him, yet he could find no other word . . . he could not bear to think it was hate . . . And then there was Ann . . . it was as if she was dead, as if she had died that night.

When he reached the end of the mothergate, one of the stone men standing near the face conveyer-belt machine said, 'Danny would like a word with you, Dep.'

He nodded and, dropping to his hands and knees, began to crawl along the face. The going was difficult. He passed two men lying on their stomachs in the cutting track, and said, 'Hallo there, Charlie . . . Hallo, Harry. How goes it?'

'OK, Dave, so far.'

'Good.'

As he crawled on he tried to think of Danny to keep his mind from Tom.

Make a good dep would Danny. Then why didn't he try? Said he didn't want to get beyond himself. That wasn't the real reason. It was pen fright, like he himself once had. That was at the bottom of it. Tom liked Danny . . . They were pals. There he was, back on him again.

He rested for a moment on his stomach. The light from his cap reflecting from the facets of the coal made them shine like those of diamonds. His eyes focused on them as if they must stand witness to his thoughts and hold him to the decision he was now making . . . he would speak to Tom when he got through. Once he had spoken he would feel better.

A little further on he stopped again and examined a fault in the roof where it had dropped about eight inches. He let his light play over it for some time; then he muttered aloud before moving on again.

When he came to the place where Danny was pulling at the cable attached to the cutting machine he called, 'Here, a minute.'

Danny, almost naked, dropped the cable and asked, 'What's up?'

And again David said, 'Here a minute,' and turning, crawled back along the face, Danny following. Reaching the hitch, he said over his shoulder, 'Look there,' and he manoeuvred his lamp about the roof.

'She's moved,' Danny said.

After a while they crawled back to the cutting machine, and David exclaimed, 'Don't bore until I've had another look. I'll be back shortly. There's plenty of time. It might be nothing; on the other hand . . .'

He left the sentence unfinished, and his gaze travelled ahead to where a man was starting to withdraw the roof props, and again his jawbone cracked . . . He would have to pass him, with only inches between them . . . What could he say? How could he begin? . . . 'Look, lad, I'm sorry?' Or, 'Tom, can you forget it?' . . . God, he couldn't bring himself to start in any way.

He turned to Danny again, playing for time. 'You wanted to see me. Can't it wait?'

'Aye, I suppose so. It's nothing very much, only . . .'

'All right.' David cut him short. 'I'll see you later, I'll be back afore long to have a look at that.' He jerked his head along the face.

'Oh, I wouldn't let that worry you,' said Danny.

'I'm not; but I'll be back.'

He moved off and came abreast of Tom, and although he kept his eyes straight ahead he was conscious of the black, forbiding profile. He hesitated for a second, but the pause was hardly noticeable before he crawled on again. This was no time for personal issues, he had his work to do. The excuse was apparent to himself.

Every foot of the roof towards the tailgate came under his eye, but nothing showed that could cause him any alarm; roof sections moved continually, then settled into place. If you became windy about every cracked pit prop the pit would never be open: yet better to play safe than be sorry.

An hour later, almost two and a half hours before his usual time for returning, he was back at the tailgate, driven there by a force against which his reasoning was powerless.

The exit was entirely blocked.

After a second of stupefied staring he turned in his tracks and raced to the haulage road. There was the possibility that the fall was at one end only, and that the men at the face, hearing it, would have escaped by the mothergate.

He gathered men to him as he went; but when they reached the mothergate all was quiet, that awful quiet that had the power to turn a man's stomach . . . Where were the others? He knew where they'd be. They had heard the fall at yon end and had gone in.

This end of the face was still clear, and, flinging himself down, he crawled in. He had expected to get no further than the hitch, for he thought it was the fault that had given way; but he was relieved and surprised to find this particular roof section still holding. His conscience wouldn't have the chance to judge him on that. It was beyond, where the cutting machine was, that the fall must have taken place.

He soon came to it, and as usual when actually confronted with the catastrophes that were the sperm of the pit his head became cool and his mind held nothing but that which was needed for the moment.

He passed his hand with a sweep over his eyes, squeezing away the sweat. What now? Only two men could work side by side here, and it was going to be a hell of a job to get this stuff back along the face. And they would have to look slippy too.

He listened for a moment, his head held to one side; and there was no need to order quiet from the men behind. Only their deep breathing drifted on the heavy, pressing silence, and it was not joined by the sound of any tapping signal from the trapped men.

He was turning his head to speak to the man close by him when a sound did come to him. It came out of the earth, almost on a level with his ear, startling him. It was a choking groan.

Like terriers, the man and he began to claw at the rocks and rubble, grabbing and scraping around the place from where the sound had come, and they almost laughed when a well-known voice, choking and spluttering, said, 'My God! I nearly had it.'

'It'll take more than that to kill you, Danny,' called David.

'Why, Dave, man.'

Both David and the man at his side grabbed at the hand that was thrust through the cuttings, and in a remarkably short time Danny's head and shoulders followed.

'Aw, man . . . Dave.' Danny's voice sang the name, and David said, 'Catch on.'

They entwined their hands round Danny's, and with their feet and knees digging into the bottom they heaved until they had him clear.

Once through, Danny clung to David for a moment. 'God alive! I was sure I'd had it then.'

'You're all right, lad. Where's the others?'

'Tom's behind . . . his foot's caught. I couldn't see Joe.'

He did not mention his brother, so David asked, 'And your Bill?'

'I don't know,' said Danny. 'There was a noise towards the tailgate, not like a fall at all, and Bill went through to see what it was. Then we heard him shout. He must have been coming back towards us. Then it really did happen; the whole roof shuddered, and it seemed that most of it came down. When it cleared I couldn't see Joe, and Tom was fast. I tried to but I couldn't clear him on me own, so I made along this way – it looked pretty clear – and I was just here when the second fall came . . . It was like a miracle. It fell behind and afore me, and there I was, in a pocket; and I thought it was me grave.'

'Who's that, dep? How's things?' Another voice came from behind David.

'It's Danny; he's OK . . . Tom's fast and the others further on. Let's get started . . . You want to go out, Danny?'

'No, by God!'

'All right,' said David over his shoulder; 'pass the gear up.'

Now started the almost impossible task of getting the fallen stone and slack out of the narrow passage. With small picks and shovels and with bare hands David, then Danny, passed the debris on to the next man, and he on to the next. They worked as a team, a clockwork team that had been wound up to the limit of its speed. As the slack and stones were pased out props came in and the men supported the roof as they advanced. The fifteen yards to the cutter took two hours to clear, and in the course of those two hours different men came to and went from David's side, among them the overman, the under manager, and the manager. The latest apparatus was at hand, but nothing would answer the purpose of the present moment but men's actual hands and the careful removal of each stone.

David would not allow himself to think of what they would find near the machine. Miracles did happen. Look at Danny. The second fall may not have touched them in there. If it had . . . well.

Long before they came to the machine they heard the metallic tapping that spoke of iron, and Danny cried, 'That's him! That's Tom. He was near the machine. He likely passed out, and that's why he never knocked afore.'

Although it was but a comparatively short time, it seemed hours later to David when he actually saw Tom. He was lying by the machine, almost sheltered by a lean-to of twisted props and loaded boulders, not more than inches from his face. He did not move when the light shone on him, but looking down the length of his body his eyes met David's, and although there was no welcoming gleam in them, the personal issue was waived, at least for David, and he said softly, 'We'll soon have you out of that, lad. Just hang on.'

At first Tom made no response by word or sound, and when he did it was to the sweat-gleaming face of Danny he spoke.

'Joe,' he said, and motioned with his hand to the side of him.

The men, following his pointing finger, saw a face that looked part of the tortured rock itself, and nearby, as if severed and resting there, lay a grotesquely clean forearm.

'It's Joe,' said Danny, quietly, 'and he's buggered.'

'He's alive.' The words seemed to be dragged from Tom, and it was evident to David that he must have attempted the superhuman task of freeing Joe whilst still being trapped himself, and he thought, Oh, Tom lad, Tom. If only things were as they used to be and he could look at him and put into his eyes his pride of him. Words were always futile things in moments like these, but a look between men could convey thoughts that had never yet found expression in sound.

Tom's voice came again, and David knew it was speaking to him although Tom was looking at Danny. 'See to . . . Joe,' he said.

David's hand went out to Tom's arm, but he checked it; he did not want a rebuff, not in front of the men. He turned to Joe, and slowly and with a tenderness that would have done credit to the gentlest of women, he and Danny began to clear the rocks away. But long before they had Joe's twisted body lying on the top of the stones David had administered the prescribed dose of morphia and had the satisfaction of seeing the tortured lines straighten out of the man's face.

Few words were spoken as they strapped him up in preparation for the difficult task of getting him along the face.

'Ben will you go along first and pull?'

'Aye, dep.'

Ben, a scrap of a chap with seemingly no flesh on his bones but with a body that gave the impression of indefatigable energy, lay face downwards on what had become little more than a man-breadth tunnel. His body was pressed on the spike-edged rock, yet he might have been reclining on a couch, such was his unconcern for his own feelings.

'You, Stan.'

Without a word, the man addressed went on to his stomach; and one pushing and one pulling, they started the tortuous journey with their unconscious burden towards the mothergate.

'Hell of a job,' commented Danny. 'Take half an hour or more.'

David made no reply, for his eyes were flashing over the roof on the far side of the machine. He seemed to have to drag them back to Tom, to his foot where it disappeared among the stones.

Tom was lying still, waiting with a patience that betrayed nothing of the turmoil within him.

Danny leant over him, saying, 'Now, fellow me lad, you'll be up and running in a minute. Where's that bloody bar? . . . Are we right, Dave?' Then he exclaimed, 'Sh, there, a minute.' He raised his head and peered at the blocked way ahead. 'Hear owt . . . ? Listen.'

All eyes were now on the barrier of rocks, and as if by a mystical signal the men further back along the face became quiet. It came again, the faint tapping.

'It's wor Bill.' Danny's laughter contained his relief. 'It's him. Thank God.' His laughter rose. 'By, I was getting quite worried. I could see half wor pays going to his widow next week. Why, man, let's get cracking.' He lifted his pick to ease the boulders from around Tom's foot, but David's voice, strained and sharp, came at him, 'Hold your hand a minute there.'

He was again looking towards the sloping roof across which a great slab of rock stretched like a beam, both its ends appearing to be buried in a solid mass on either side.

After a moment, during which the men's gaze had joined his, he said, 'All right, we'll go ahead.'

Taking a lever, he inserted it between the boulders directly to the side of the trapped boot.

'Now,' he said.

Not only did Danny join his strength to the effort but Tom, feeling the momentary relief from the pressure, pulled on his leg. But what followed was mercifully lost to him.

David had not expected the release to come so quickly, or so easily; and realising that Tom had only fainted, he set about strapping the ankle up roughly.

'What's the damage?' asked Danny.

'Broken ankle, I should say. He's lucky.'

'By God, he is an' all,' said Danny. 'Wouldn't have surprised me if the only thing for it was . . .'

'Sh!'

Tom's eyes were open, and David said, 'Here, drink this.' He made to hold the water bottle to Tom's lips, but it was pushed aside, and with the aid of his elbow Tom raised himself a little and peered towards his foot.

'It's a break,' said David gently.

He waited like some anxious woman for a direct word to be addressed to him, but Tom said nothing, and he watched him unaided turning on to his side, and knew better than to offer him assistance. Yet when Tom's body stiffened with cramp, his hands involuntarily went out to him, only to be immediately thrust aside. The rebuke cut into him, and, harsh and rasping, his voice went along the face, 'Give a hand here, Ned.'

'I want no hand.' Tom's voice was levelled against him, but ignoring this retort, David called, 'Go along with him, Ned.'

'Look—' Tom jerked his head upwards, a protest on his lips, and the expression on his face made David want to cry out, 'Man, don't take it like that.' Through the dust that danced and twirled like slowly moving curtains in the rays of the lamps, Tom's eyes shone heavy with pain but heavier still with scorn and loathing.

David watched him crawl away until his body was almost beyond the radius of the lights, when it was abruptly halted. He knew what had happened. The rough splint had caught on a piece of wedged rock. It was necessary that someone should follow on behind him.

He called to the man crouched to the side of Tom and pressing himself against the rock to make his passage easier, 'You go with him, Ned.'

Tom said something to Ned, who seemed to hesitate; but when not more than a few yards on the same thing happened again, Ned made to follow him.

It was Danny's voice that brought David's face from Tom's retreating figure and his thoughts back to the urgent issue at hand. 'All set, Dave?'

'Aye . . . Aye. All set, Danny.'

As, with these words, he turned towards Danny, there came a sound that froze all movement in him, a crunching sound, a sound similar to that he heard three years ago, which had been the prelude to his being shut in for seventy-five hours, the sound he likened to eating cinder toffee, for, like that sound, this went through the bones in your head. He was conscious of yelling something to Danny and of turning on to his back, as if with his hands he could keep the roof at bay. Then a scream filled his head; whether his own or Danny's he did not know. He was conscious only of a terrible weight squeezing the breath out of his body; then there was nothing . .

When the earth shuddered before falling, Tom had pressed his body on to the bottom, his arms covering the back of his head; and the scream came to him. It was like the earth crying out in agony, and he thought, This is it. His lips cried, 'Oh, my God!' but his mind cried, 'Beattie!' Stuff sprayed on him, fine grey dust, black splinters and pieces of rock. There was a heave as if the stratum beneath him was lifting, then a grinding that turned him sick as the earth seemed to settle back into place. He was filled with terror, terror that blotted even Beattie from his mind; he lay still, clutching at the dirt as if he loved it and would never let it go.

He moved first when he coughed; the cough lifted his shoulders through the weight that was lying on them . . . He was still alive, and his light was still on. His relief made him quiver as if with ague. He heaved again and brought his body out of the slack and looked at the props to the side of him. They had held. But focusing his lamp some little way ahead, he saw that there they had given and the outlet was blocked. His heart sank . . . All right if it was only small stuff like this; but if it was rock . . . Where were the others? he remembered the scream. Just behind him would be Ned and Danny . . .

It was no use trying to push back, he'd have to turn. But how? If he could scrape this stuff away and bring his knee up.

He worked at the slack, pushing it ahead of him, to give him a space in which to attempt to turn. Making the space was comparatively easy, but to turn round was, he found, an excruciating business, for the bone of the ankle seemed to be piercing the flesh.

The sweat ran down him, and added to this he was finding it difficult to breathe. When eventually the task was accomplished he had to lie for some time before he could even examine the conditions ahead. When he did he found the way to the cutter, where he and Joe had lain a short while ago, was once more closed. He crawled forward over the heightened level of the floor, but could see no sign of Ned.

He was below somewhere. He was about to scrape when his light fell on David . . . he was lying on his back, his head and shoulders partly covered with slack. But his arms were completely out of it and were shielding his face, much in the same way as his own arms had shielded his head.

An odd sensation passed over him, and he stopped in his crawling for a second. How often during the past months had he wished to see David dead? And now? He carried himself forward with a great jerk, calling, 'Davie! Davie!'

But there was no answer. He unfolded the arms; and the face under the coal dust shone like alabaster in the lamplight.

'Davie!' He began to claw the slack and loose earth away, pushing it along his side in ridges, cursing his foot when it impeded him. 'Davie, man! Davie!'

He uncovered him to his thighs, and there his hands stopped against solid rock. The roof, the end of that great slab. No. No . . . not that way. Madly, he began to scrape. His hands went deeper, moving around David's hips; and again they stopped, and a fear such as he had never before experienced came upon him. And once more he cried out wildly, 'Not that way!'

When at last, whipping up his courage, he shone his light directly on where the legs disappeared, he stared fascinated. Then slowly his head dropped until his face was lying against David's stomach.

'Davie. Aw, Davie.' His tears rained on to the dust. 'Oh, Davie man . . . Oh, God. Oh, Christ, Christ in Heaven.'

'Tom.' The sound was scarcely loud enough to be a whisper, but it whipped Tom's head up.

'Tom.'

'Aye, Dave.'

'Tom.'

'Yes, I'm here, lad.' He caught hold of David's hand. David's fluttering lids lifted. 'My back.'

Tom could say nothing.

'Danny.'

There was no answer Tom could give to this. But he said, 'Joe and them will be all right. And the others'll be through to us in no time.'

David's eyes closed.

'Are you in much pain?' Tom stroked the hand he was holding, but David said nothing.

Then a dull thudding coming from the other end of the face caused him to turn over. For the moment he had forgotten about his foot, and the quick jerk brought him to the point of fainting. When he was sufficiently recovered he listened again. There it was . . . tap, tap . . . tap, tap.

He gave up the idea of trying to traverse the few yards back to the blocked end, and with a stone he beat out an answer on a wedged rock in the shallow wall. And then he waited.

The tapping came again; and he bent over David. 'They can hear me, Dave; they're coming. They'll be through that in no time.'

As he waited again for an answer he was conscious of his own laboured breathing, and the thought came to him, They won't have to be long, either.

'Tom.'

'Aye, Dave.'

David's eyes were wide now and staring. 'My legs.'

'They'll soon get through; they'll have you out.' Tom kept his eyes steady as he spoke.

'Tom . . . I'm fast . . . It's the slab . . . isn't it?'

'Don't talk, lad. There's not much air.'

Tom held the limp hand again; and in the silence came a faint sound, as if of scratching. After a while the tightening pressure of David's fingers made him ask, 'What is it, Dave?' And the look in David's eyes as he said, 'It's all right, I know,' made him want to

346

bow his head again and to cry with the abandonment of a child.

Oh, the suffering. All was suffering. In loving you suffered and in hating you suffered; and in the agonies of others, in the crying of women, and in the dry, burning eyes of men . . . Oh, Davie! Davie!

'Got me ticket . . . this time.' David's lips hardly moved, and each word was laboured.

'They'll fix you up, man. They can do wonders.'

'Without – legs?'

'Aw, man.'

Their faces close, in the eerie light they looked into each other's eyes, and of the two, David's were the less troubled.

'Don't take on, lad. It's funny, but there's a kind of peace . . . Tom.'

'Aye.'

'I wish . . . I could put things right.'

'Don't talk, man.'

'Listen . . . I'm sorry. Never have hurt you . . . Ann.'

'Forget it . . . forget it, man.' The choking in Tom's throat was making his breathing almost impossible.

'Tell Ann . . . will you?'

Tom nodded.

'No-one but her . . . Forgive me, lad.'

'There's nothing to forgive, man . . . Lie quiet now.'

Strange to be able to say there was nothing to forgive. Three days ago when he had looked down on this man's son lying in the arms of the woman he himself loved, he had vowed silently, I'll hate it as I hate him.

And at that moment he had thought of his mother; she had been saddled all her married life with a child that was not hers; yet hating, no doubt, as she did the sin, she had, in some measure, loved that which was sinned against. But never could that attitude be his. For Beattie's sake he might hide his feelings; but there would be no crevice in his heart for a son of David Taggart . . . Yet now . . . His eyes moved down towards David's thighs. The only way they'd get him out of there alive would be to . . . His mind would not imagine it. Far better for him to die here. Yet how many men were living without legs!

After a time he became aware that the tapping had stopped. It had been stopped for some time . . . No, there it was again.

He lifted his drooping head. Had it really stopped, or had he not heard it? This made him bend over David to see whether he was still breathing.

That's how it came. You stopped hearing things and just went to sleep. Beattie! Beattie! He was seized with panic. He didn't want to die . . . he wasn't going to die. She'd be left with a bairn and no-one to see to her, no-one who understood her. Beattie! . . . Look, I won't die!

Don't be a blasted fool! He stopped himself from endeavouring to turn round and make his way to the farther end in an attempt to scrape his way out. That's the quickest way to it! Lie still.

Like a child obeying a firm command, he dropped back and lay quiet; and in the quiet a thought took form and began to torment him. It was ten to one that if they didn't get through in a very short time, then when they did they'd find them both dead. Was he to let Davie die without telling him he had a son? Every man wanted a son. Perhaps it would make dying easier to know that part of you still lived on . . . There was no part of him to live on . . . Beattie! Beattie!

'Dave.' He brought his face close to David's. Funny, he could hardly see him. God! The lamp. It was going. Or was it his eyes? 'Dave . . . Can you . . . hear me?'

'Aye.'

'Listen . . . You should know . . . You've got a son, a fine lad.'

There was no answer.

'Dave . . . She's goin' to call him after you.' This was pure imagination, for the last thing she'd be likely to call him would be David . . . 'Can you . . . hear?'

'Aye . . . Tom . . .'

Tom did not answer; and David's voice came again, slightly louder: 'Tom . . .'

'Aye, what is it?' He roused himself.

'Will you say . . . a bit . . . prayer?'

A prayer? His whisper was made fainter with surprise. How long was it since he had said a silent prayer, never mind praying aloud? He felt shamefaced. Yet this was no time or place to be shamefaced: there was no-one to witness his shame but God.

'Our Father which art in heaven, Hallowed be thy name. Thy kingdom come . . .'

His mind began to whirl.

'Forgive us our trespasses . . .'

There came the faintest pressure of David's fingers on his.

Now I lay me down to sleep, I pray the Lord my soul to keep . . . Bairns' prayer, what he learned at Sunday school . . . And if I die before I wake I pray the Lord my soul to take.

Mr Fraser said he had the makings of a minister but that he must search to find Christ. Some ministers never found Christ, which was why they could never make people believe in Him . . . David was a Catholic. They had special prayers for all occasions, especially for dying.

'. . . as we forgive them that trespass against us. And lead us not into temptation . . .'

No chance of that now, the lamp was going. Beattie had been his temptation; she had taken him from God's service. He should ask for forgiveness . . . forgiveness for loving Beattie? He wasn't going to do that . . . he'd do it all again; aye, a thousand times. But he had hurt his mother.

The buzzing in his ears grew louder and he let it blot out the last thought. Slowly his head drooped until it lay on David's chest.

17

The Child

Beattie looked upon the gurgling laughing face of the child, and yet again pondered that anything emanating so much peace and contentment could have been born of her. Surely the months during which it lay in her turbulent womb, fed by her blood, that in itself must have borne the poison of her mind, poison she manufactured daily with thoughts of bitterness and recrimination mostly levelled against herself, surely they should have contaminated it. But no. A second virgin could not have brought forth anything so peaceful.

During the six weeks of its life it had hardly cried, apart from the first shout at its release; it greeted voices and hands only with an infectious gurgle.

Up to its birth she had given to it no thought that held a touch of tenderness. How could she? – she didn't want it. She had never wanted children; she had been brought up with too many. And hadn't it been conceived out of madness, and hadn't she, in allowing its creation, brought trouble on people who had done her no wrong? Even in the momentary contentment when its burden had left her body and she gazed upon it for the first time, not even then did the natural instinct awaken. The spark did not alight until she saw Tom look down on it; and then she knew that any love it was to have must come from her, for no matter how he might try to overcome it his jealousy would erect a barrier between him and the child.

From that moment her love for her son grew. At first she did not recognise it; she only knew she was sorry that Tom wasn't going to . . . take to it, for her aim in life now was to please him. She felt that in some miraculous way she had been given a second chance – he was back in her life, the only man who had shown her any real respect, the man she began to love years ago and now loved with an intensity that amazed her. For the first time in her life she was sorry for the things she had done; her misdeeds had been magnified out of all proportion by others, but their condemnation was now far transcended by her own. Tom had given her all the proof a man could of his love, and she was determined to make him glad that he loved her. She would live for him, and only him . . . And then her son had lain his fingers on her heart, and she found that her being was big enough to hold two loves. Yet before the child was four days old she almost cursed it.

She was lying in the little room under the sloping roof. The child was in its cot by the side of the bed – and she had been thinking how, when she should get up, she would rearrange this room. She still could not get used to the idea that this three-roomed cottage was hers; it was as if, during her pregnancy, she had paid for her sins and that now fate was bestowing gifts on her in a surprising way; for who would have imagined that the lonely old woman with whom she had come to lodge, mainly to keep clear of the town and its curious eyes, would have taken such a liking to her as to leave her the cottage. When she heard the contents of the will, her first reaction was to think: And I did nothing for her; I didn't even make her laugh.

Mrs Pringle had been a reticent woman; the only thing Beattie knew of her was that she had no family and that her relatives were dead. She herself had told Mrs Pringle little of her own life, yet the old woman must have thought about her a lot, for the will read: I leave you my cottage for a home for you and the child.

And now her cottage was to be a home, not only for her and her child, but for Tom. It would be . . . theirs, something that they owned. She had never before known the difference between renting and owning; and now, besides all the other things in her life, there was this proud feeling of ownership.

It was while she lay thinking of these things that the girl Peggy had come running into the cottage, pounding up the stairs, stopping only at the foot of the bed to lean over the rail and gasp: 'Oh, Beattie! Oh, Beattie!'

She had not asked, 'What's the matter?' A sudden terrible foreboding told her.

She had pulled herself up in the bed, and Peggy, nodding her head as if to throw it off her body, said, 'There's been an accident.'

Beattie's eyes bade her go on.

'Five they say . . . some people say seven. I heard as I came out of work, and me an' Sally went to the pithead. I heard someone say, "That's Mrs Rowan, her lad's down," and I said, "Tom Rowan?" and they said, "Yes. And his brother-in-law's down too . . . They were all coming out and there was another fall." They brought one up, but he's nearly had it – he was one of the first lot.'

Beattie steadied herself by pressing the back of her head against the rail of the bed. 'What time was this?'

'Not half an hour ago. I came straight away.'

'Peggy.'

'Aye?'

'Get me things and help me up.'

'Eeh, Beattie, no!' Peggy hastily tucked the bed clothes under the mattress as if this would ensure that Beattie stayed where she was. 'You'll kill yersel' . . . not four days yet. Look, stay where you are.' She forced Beattie back on to her pillows. 'Oh my! Beattie, give over and stay put, will you!'

The door opening at this moment brought a great audible sigh or relief from Peggy, and she greeted the small fat woman with, 'Oh, Mrs Bailey, she's trying to get up because I told her about the accident.'

'You would!' The woman hastened forward. 'Now don't be daft. Settle yourself down.' Expertly she arranged the bedclothes. 'You can do nothing, only pray. And remember you've got the bairn to feed, and if you upset yourself and get milk fever, you'll know about it me lady.'

She lay back, wild-eyed, watching Mrs Bailey tending to the child. If she hadn't had him she'd be able to go to the pit. Tom down there . . . trapped! Her eyes moved towards the floor as if he were just below it. Oh God, don't let anything happen to him. Let him out. Tom, don't leave me. Oh, don't leave me! . . What could she do, tied here to the bed . . . and the bairn?

Tom . . . oh, Tom. Oh God, keep him safe, and don't pay me out like this . . . Tom . . . Oh, be safe . . . be safe.

'Now stop worrying, it'll get you nowhere.' Mrs Bailey glanced sympathetically towards her. 'I don't think it's a big fall, at least, by what I heard. Anyway, they can hear them.'

God hear me. Keep him safe, will You? Don't let anything happen to him. Why did You bring him back if You were going to let something happen now?

Without looking at Mrs Bailey, she asked, 'When did it happen?'

'Round about three, I think.'

Nearly four hours trapped in the blackness, perhaps hurt . . . perhaps already dead. God . . . Look . . . She turned her face into the pillow. She must pray. But what should she say? She hardly knew any proper prayers, only a bit of the Our Father . . . Our Father, who art in Heaven, Hallowed be Thy name; Thy Kingdom come, Thy will be done on earth . . . Give us this day our daily bread . . . Oh, what was the good talking stuff like that! God, hear me . . . She sat up in bed. She had the room to herself again, for Mrs Bailey and Peggy had gone downstairs; so she appealed aloud, her eyes roving over the ceiling: Tell me what to say. Show me what to do . . . I'll be a good woman. You already know that, but if You want him to go back to the preaching I'll egg him on to it, I promise I will. We'll move away and he can start afresh some place else. Only keep him safe, that's all I ask, and I'll pay in some way . . . any way.

'Here! What are you up to?' Mrs Bailey came panting into the room again. 'Lie yerself down, there. Now listen. I've told our Stanley to come straight here the minute he knows they're up. I sent him to the pithead afore I left. Now the only thing you can do is to wait quietly and keep your soul in patience.'

Keep her soul in patience! If Tom died it wouldn't matter what happened to her soul . . . or her body. Happiness never lasted; there was always a catch in everything; Life worked along the lines of giving you with one hand and taking away with the other.

At this point, the child, who scarcely ever cried, burst into a loud wail, and the sound filled her with foreboding.

An hour later the boy brought the news: the men

had got through and found two just alive and two dead, but he didn't know which two were dead. It was Peggy, enjoying herself immensely, who followed with the details.

'He's all right,' she blurted out. 'His leg's broken, or summat. They just got him out in time. He was near suffocated. And he was lying alongside' – she hesitated; but she couldn't prevent herself from imparting what was to her the romantic part – 'Mr Taggart . . . Davie Taggart. They were holding hands and Mr Taggart's legs were caught; and they could do nothing, and the doctor went in and had to take them off . . .'

It was some time later when Beattie came to herself, and it was nearly three weeks later before she was allowed out of bed; and during this time she never saw Tom. The break of the ankle had not been clean – the bone had penetrated the flesh, and what should have been a simple business of setting became a fight to save a foot.

When, at last, he came to the cottage, his foot bound in plaster, limping on a steel heel, they greeted each other shyly; then silently they clung together; and the added wonder was that he lifted the child and held him. Later, slowly and hesitantly, his eyes cast down, he spoke of David. And she listened in silence, knowing that he must speak. And the relief that there was no bitterness left in him eased the pain of her humiliation. He talked of David's last hours – seventy-two of them after they had got him up, during which time Ann had hardly left him. He spoke of Ann, too, of how she was changed. Everybody had expected her to snap again, but she hadn't . . . The one person he didn't speak of was his mother.

Beattie often thought of his mother; but for her, Tom would not go away each night. She had taken ill months ago, and Tom had said he could not tell her anything until she was better. Yet she could get out of her bed to go and stand at the pithead during the accident. If the bronchial trouble was so bad, getting out of bed and going to the pithead should have finished her. Yet, from what she could gather, Nellie hadn't even returned to bed, but visited Tom daily in hospital . . . She had long doubted the seriousness of this illness.

How long would it go on? Well, no matter how long it went on, it was something she must put up with . . . and silently.

It was strange how mothers could hate the women who took their sons, under the protest that they weren't good enough for them. Even if they were good enough something was always found to be wrong with them. Of one thing Beattie was certain: she knew that Nellie hated her with a deep, unrelenting hate; and this hate would never lessen. Yet the woman who should hate her, whose husband she had taken in thoughtless pleasure, and by so doing had driven her, if not into the asylum, into some place not far removed, this woman did not hate her . . . The situation was too strange to be fathomed.

Last Saturday when Tom came to her she knew he was disturbed, and her immediate thought was: His mother's at it again. But after a lot of humming and ha'ing he had blurted out, 'Would you let Ann see the bairn?'

She had just stared at him. Could a wife want to see a child her husband had given to another woman?

'She's hinted at it two or three times. And now to-day she was waiting for me at the end of the road.' He motioned his head backwards towards the door.

'This road?'

'Yes.'

'But what about me? She wouldn't want to see me. You'd better take him to her.'

'Couldn't she come in?'

'Yes . . . All right, I'll stay out the back.'

'Oh no, you'll do no such thing.' The tone was the one she had come to know which brooked of no arguing. 'Either you stay or she doesn't see it.'

So Ann had come in; and Beattie knew remorse, such as she had not experienced before. Just the appearance of this slight, girlish little figure in black, heaped coals of fire on her head. The great sad eyes that had looked at her sent no message of hate. What they said she could find no means within herself to interpret; she only knew she could not bear to look into them; and she had turned away and gone into the kitchen with the excuse of making tea.

When she returned Ann was standing by the cot and Tom was gazing down into the fire. She nudged him and pointed to the tea tray; and he went to Ann and said, 'Come and have a cup of tea.'

But Ann had turned and looked at Beattie and asked softly of her, 'Can I pick him up?'

'Aye . . . yes.'

Beattie's bewilderment at this woman's reactions made the answer sound curt, and she added more gently, 'Bring him to the fire.'

She watched Ann stoop and pick the child up, and she poured out the tea and placed the cup on the table for her. But she found it impossible to stay in the room – the sight of those eyes in the little white face gazing down on the child was too much for her, so she went into the scullery again and closed the door. And it was while standing there, her hands rubbing her throat to try to ease its pressure, that the payment she could make for Tom came to her, and immediately she rejected it, almost crying aloud, 'No! No! I won't do that! I can't . . . not now. If it had been at first . . . But not now.'

Tom had come in from the kitchen, and, placing his arms around her, held her close, not speaking, and she moved her face against him, murmuring brokenly, 'What have I done? It's hell, feeling like this.'

On that occasion Ann had not stayed long; nor, apart from asking if she could hold the child, had she spoken again until she was about to leave. Then, standing like a lost child herself in front of Beattie, she had asked, 'Will you let me see him now and again?'

Beattie, not trusting herself to answer, jerked her head once . . .

And Ann was coming again to-day.

During the six days since her last visit Beattie had faced the greatest struggle of her life, and in her unreasoning, impetuous way she had cried out and fought against it; but no matter how often she said, 'No-one would expect me to do it!' back would come the reminder, 'You asked to be shown what to do, and this is it; and not only will it be a payment for Tom, it will be reparation for all the trouble you've caused that woman and the whole family. Perhaps even his mother's dislike of you may lessen.'

'But he's so canny. And I've got to love him.' She talked to someone within herself whose logical and ready answers startled her: 'It would be no sacrifice if you didn't love him; you only wanted Tom. Well, you have him. This woman lost her husband before he died. You were to blame for that. Apparently she can't have bairns. It's ten to one you can have as many as you can carry. You could have one by this time next year . . . and it would be Tom's!'

'I can't do it.'

'Well, if you don't you'll never know a minute's peace, you'll never get rid of that face. Every time you pick the bairn up you'll see her eyes looking at him. Just look how it's been this week.'

'I'll get over that.'

She bent over the child now and gathered him up into her arms, and he gurgled at her, and she began to walk about the room with him, his face tucked into the hollow of her neck; and in her pacing she looked out of the window and saw Ann coming in at the gate.

She pressed the child closer to her, and when the small knock came on the door she did not immediately go to open it. When she did, Ann smiled at her warily, saying, 'Am I too early? I hope you don't mind.'

'No. Come in.' She did not offer her the child but kept her arms about him; and Ann said, 'I've brought him this . . . it's only a little woolly dog.' She put the package on the table and stood looking at Beattie in a puzzled sort of way . . . She had not been asked to sit down; nor had she been offered the child . . .

An awkward silence fell on the room, and she murmured, 'Perhaps you're busy. If it's not convenient . . .'

The fear that it wasn't convenient was evident both in her eyes and voice; and Beattie burst out, 'Tom'll likely be here at any moment . . . I want to talk to you.'

'Yes?' The fear was still there.

'Would you like him?'

'Like him?' Ann's voice was without expression, it merely repeated the statement.

'To have him, I mean.' Beattie placed her hands on the back of the child's head and pressed his cheek to hers; and the only sound in the room was his gurgling.

'You mean . . . him?' Ann nodded towards the child.

'Yes. Who else?' Beattie's voice was rough.

And Ann, after staring at her, groped at the back of a chair, and, turning it round, she sat down.

'You can't mean you'd . . .'

'Well, what've I been talking about?'

'But . . . don't you . . . want him?'

'Look. We won't go into that. I asked you would you like him?'

'Oh.'

Watching Ann's already pale face whiten, Beattie thought: She's going to pass out. And seeing her body sag against the chair and her head droop on her neck, she took a step towards her, saying, 'Look. I've startled you. That's like me . . . I can never do anything easily and quietly . . . always like a bull at a gap. But I thought you might like him. Anyway, he's more yours than mine.'

Ann lifted her head, and Beattie found it impossible to endure the look in those eyes. She swung about, still holding the child to her, and began to rearrange the cot with one hand, flinging the clothes right and left over the rails as if in a furious temper.

At this moment Tom came in; and seeing Beattie's actions and Ann with the tears running down her face watching her, his heart sank at the thought that there had been a row.

'What's the trouble?' he asked quietly of Beattie.

'Trouble? Who said there was trouble?'

His brow gathered into a perplexed frown, and he asked, 'What's the matter then?'

'Nothing's the matter.' She moved the child to the other arm and began to fling the clothes back on to the cot.

'Here. Give him to me.' His hands were about the baby.

'No.' Her voice was suddenly quiet. She stopped her

361

arranging and, again putting her hand on the child's head, she walked past him and went into the scullery, saying, 'You would come in when you're not wanted, wouldn't you?' Her tone was flat and without reprimand. And he turned to Ann and asked, 'What's up?'

For a moment she found it difficult to answer him.

'She's going to give him to me.' Her voice was scarcely audible.

'What!'

'I didn't ask, Tom; I wouldn't have dreamed. I couldn't believe it when . . .'

'But she thinks the world of him.'

Ann bowed her head. 'I know.'

'Look, Ann. You can't take him.'

Ann's head drooped lower, and he turned from her and went into the scullery. Beattie was standing looking out of the window into the tangle of back garden. He stood close behind her and put his hands on her shoulders, and he looked down into the child's face as he said gently, 'You mustn't do this.'

'It's settled.' Her voice was calm now.

'But you'll miss him.'

She said nothing; and he turned her about, and they gazed at each other, until she whispered, 'Help me to do it as I want to do it.'

Again they stared at each other. Then Tom brought the child's hand to his cheek and gently held it there. 'All right . . . when?'

'Now.'

'Now?'

'It's better done right away.'

'All right then. Have it your own way . . . I'll move in to-night.'

'Tom! Will you?' Her eyes lost their sadness for the moment, and he said, 'I should have done it sooner.

Anyway, this is it. I'll go now and get my things. I'll have a taxi, then I can take Ann . . . and him back.' He dropped the child's hand and took her face between his palms. 'You're big. I always knew you were. I love you, lass.' Leaning forward, he kissed her on the lips before turning away; and under the pretence of blowing his nose he wiped her tears from his face as he passed through the room; and with just a nod to Ann he left the cottage and went to do battle with his mother.

Nellie and George were sitting, one on each side of the fire, when Tom walked in. He was glad to see his father there; it would be better than tackling her alone. His entry, he saw, had taken them both unawares, for he had not long left the house, and the light that appeared in his mother's eyes hurt him. He knew what she was thinking . . . something had gone wrong and it had brought him back home to her. They never lost hope . . . mothers of sons.

His father said, 'Hallo, lad.' He didn't add, 'What's brought you back so soon?'

Nellie, staring at him, said nothing. And when he went to bring a chair up to the fire she picked up her knitting from her lap and the steel needles began to click briskly. She kept her eyes averted from him as he sat between them; it was years since he had done this, and her heart began to pound against her ribs. And its pounding became louder and louder in her ears. Her relief was pitiable, even to herself; but it was transformed with the swiftness of lightning to cold apprehension when, without moving his hands from between his knees or turning his gaze from the fire, he said, 'I've come to tell you something.'

It was George who, after a moment, asked, 'Aye, lad; what is it?' and with an attempt to resurrect his old jocular self, he added, 'Hast won the pools? I'm down as usual. If it hadn't been for Blackpool and Arsenal . . .'

'I'm leaving home.'

The needles stopped their clicking; George's hand, moving towards the hob to knock out the noddle from his pipe, stopped, and his head turned stiffly to look at his son. Then his hand moved on again, and there was the sound of the knocking of the pipe against the bars. The taps rent the quietness like hammer-blows.

Tom slowly raised his eyes to his mother. She was staring at her knitting. It was a sock, and as usual one of a pair for him. With a movement that startled him she picked it up and flung it into the fire, and in an instant she was on her feet. They were all on their feet.

'Steady,' said George. 'What's got to be will be.'

'Be quiet! Has it got to be that your son has lost all decency?' She addressed herself solely to George, as if Tom wasn't there. 'Has it got to be that he makes us the talk of the town by going to live with a common prostitute? Not enough that she was the means of crippling a child, she has to take his sister's man and drive her into the asylum. And this son of yours . . . what does he do? When she has a bairn to his brother-in-law he goes and keeps her!'

It was evident to both men that the emphasis for the first time in her life was being put on his son, not hers.

'Look here,' said George.

'Yes . . . look here!' she cried. 'See reason! Like father like son, as I've said before. You'll find excuses for him because he's doing the same as you did. The only difference is his woman's worse than yours was.'

'Shut up!' Tom's voice drowned her shouting.

And now Nellie looked at him; and in spite of the anger that was filling him there was room left for amazement – the expression in her eyes he could only

364

interpret as loathing. And he knew that nothing he or anyone else could do or say would alter her opinion. Yet he said, 'You don't know her; you've always condemned her without reason.'

'Without reason!' Nellie flung her head back.

'Yes, you have. She's worth a thousand of your so-called . . . good girls. And I'm telling you . . .'

'You're telling me because you're besotted with lust. Yes, lust . . . Leave be!' She flung off George's steadying hand from her arm. 'Night after night you've been with her. Your clothes have reeked of her cheap scent. And what'll happen when she's finished with you, when her lust is satisfied? You know what it'll be as well as me . . . another man. And then another.'

Tom's face looked like a white mask on which eyebrows, eyes and moustache had been painted black. 'She's my wife . . . we've been married nearly four months; and we haven't lived together yet! So much for your lust. If she had said the word I would have left here months ago; but she wouldn't because you were ill. And another thing; she's done what you nor nobody else would do . . . she's given the bairn to Ann.'

It was George who moved forward, saying, 'To Ann? The bairn? She's given her the bairn?'

'Aye.'

'She wants it?'

'She begged to go and see it. She's crazy for him.'

George turned towards the hearth muttering. And Nellie said with a strange quietness, 'It would have been far better for you if you had gone with Davie . . . History repeats itself.' The look in her eyes now was almost vindictive. 'You married her? You fool! And you're glorifying her because she's giving her bairn away . . .' The words came deep and slow. 'Oh, you blind idiot! Would any woman worth her salt give her bairn away if she could keep it? Ask yourself that. She's got rid of that responsibility; and when she tires of you she'll get rid of you. And even the time she's got you, do you think she'll be satisfied with one man? You'll never know a minute's peace.' Her voice rose rapidly again. 'Every minute you're at work you'll be thinking . . .'

Unable to trust himself, Tom flung round from her and out of the room and up the stairs. But Nellie, in her passion, could not let him be. Her walking was like the stalking of a tigress as she went to the bottom of the stairs and called, 'The truth hurts . . . Once a whore always a whore! I said that if you went to her I would curse you, and I do. Do you hear? You'll rue this day, me lad . . . nothing'll go right for you. I'll put my prayers on that . . . You'll curse the day you clapped eyes on her . . .'

'Here, lass, that's enough of that. Stop it! Stop it now! Come on away.' George, not to be shrugged off this time, alternately pulled and led her back into the room. He closed the door behind them; then pressed her into a chair. 'Calm yourself now.'

Whether because of his stern command or because she was spent, she became quiet. He stood close to her, his arm about her stiff shoulders, saying, 'There now. There now.'

His grip tightened when the sound of Tom's steps came to them from the passage. There was the heavy thump of a case, then his footsteps again on the stairs. Three times he returned upstairs; and as he came down for the last time, the taxi drew up at the door.

On its sound, a vibration passing through Nellie conveyed itself to George, and he pressed her tightly to him. And when the sound of the car starting up told her that her son was gone she shivered and her head moved in little pathetic jerks, until suddenly a cry was torn from her, and she turned and buried her face in George's arms.

Gently he gathered her to him, as he had not been allowed to do since the early months of their marriage. Stroking her hair, he soothed her; and when, between her sobs, she cried, 'What am I to do? Tell me, what am I to do?' he did not answer. Never before could he remember her appealing to him. Nor had she ever clung to him. No, never . . . not even when they were first married.

The jealousy for his son he had kept well in hand over the years, but now his son was gone and she had only him. His arms tightened about her.

Christopher walked towards Ann's for the second time that evening. She was out earlier when he called, and his purpose then had seemed more clear in his mind than now. His intention had been quite plain; he had it all planned out: he meant to look in on her now and again and take her things, but say nothing, of course, for some months yet. In the meantime, he would sound Maggie on the matter of a divorce. This would mean a devil of an uproar in the family, but he'd never been anything but a wooden Catholic, so what did it matter. He had taken the first step in this direction by writing to Maggie to ask if he could see her. And to his surprise he had received what he termed a decent letter, with not even a mention of Stephen in it. The attitude she now adopted towards the boy was quite beyond him; it was as if she had never possessed a son; she did not come to his mother's to see the lad, or waylay him, as it had been expected she would do. She could have been dead for all he and his family heard about her. But she wasn't dead; and knowing her as he did, he often imagined the hell she must be going through. And often too – and this was strange, even to himself – he would gladly have sent the boy back to her if he could have been induced to leave him and his grannie.

That was another thing. His own mother was one of the best, but she was treating Stephen as she had never treated her own sons . . . she was spoiling him. Her handling of him was at the other extreme from Maggie's, and he was now wondering which in the end would have the worse effect. Added to this, he had realised whilst living back at home, something which had surprised him not a little . . . he had grown away from the life he had been brought up to. It had been fine to drop in now and again and enjoy the slipshod, easy-going practices of the house; but to live in it, after the years spent in Maggie's ordered establishment, was, he found, irritating. And this, in his turn, he expressed in his constant censuring of Stephen; which, however, did not create any gulf between them. On the contrary, the boy seemed each day to become more attached to him

He was, he now admitted frankly to himself, fed up with being at home; and in his daydreams he looked into the future and saw himself sitting with Ann at a new fireside. Not hers . . . no – David's presence still lingered about that hearth – but at one he himself would provide. And there, with Stephen, they would begin a new life. But this picture never stayed put. If Stephen was in it, Ann wasn't; and if Ann was there he couldn't get Stephen into the picture at all.

Ann's attitude towards Stephen since she had come back from that place was past his understanding. To put it plainly, it looked as if she wanted no truck with him. But Stephen had not been as upset about this as he would have supposed; likely due to the fact that for months he had been running wild with Dennis and Jim.

When he reached the back gate he could see her light was on, and almost jauntily he went up the garden and tapped on the door. And when his knock was answered by an airy 'Come in,' he hesitated for a moment. Had he not known it to be otherwise, he would have sworn she was laughing; that was how her voice used to sound when she laughed. Passing through the scullery, he came into the kitchen, and if he had found her enjoying love in the arms of a strange man his surprise would not have been so great . . . she was sitting before the fire with a baby in her arms, and the look on her face was ecstatic.

'Come in, Chris.' Her voice was light, like the voice of the girl from the past.

He walked slowly towards the fireside; then halted in front of her.

'Whose?' Why did he feel a dread, even before her answer came?

'Mine.'

'Yours?'

'Yes.' She looked down into the sleeping face of the child, then straight into Christopher's eyes. 'Yes, mine now . . . and Davie's.'

'She's . . . she's let you have him?' His face betrayed his bewilderment.

'Yes . . . Yes.' She shook her head with the wonder of it.

He could only stare at her.

'I've been to see him before. And to-day, just two hours ago, she gave him to me. And Tom brought us home.'

He could find nothing to say to this; but he felt strongly there was something indecent about her acceptance of the child, and of the whole situation. He looked at the child his brother had given to another

369

woman, then again at Ann, and found it impossible to make any comment.

His lack of response did not seem to affect her, for she went on talking. 'I'm going to call him David . . . I think he would have liked that, don't you?'

Suddenly he was bitter and angry, yet he managed to cover it and to say tersely, 'Why, yes . . . I suppose so.' The whole thing was indecent. What had come over her? She wasn't like the same person.

She looked up at him again. 'Chris . . . she's good, she's not bad. I've never been able to hold anything against her somehow, and when I saw her, it's funny, but I liked her. No-one need worry any more; she'll make Tom a good wife.'

'He's not going to marry her?'

'They've been married for months.'

He could only stare and remember the row he had heard coming from the Rowans' earlier in the evening. Poor Nellie. This would about finish her . . . So Tom had done it. My God, what a mix-up!

Ann rose, hugging the child to her, saying, 'He must go to bed. His cot's upstairs. If you've got a mind to wait . . .'

He shook his head. 'No. No, Ann; I'll be getting along.'

'All right then. I'll be seeing you again.' She had already turned towards the door.

Slowly he left the house by the way he had come only a few minutes before. The dream was over; gone; finished; spun into thin air by the child of his brother. There'd be no fireside with Ann now . . . He moved his hand around his face as if wiping away a veil. Somehow he had always known it was just a dream. That child would be her life; she already looked happier than he had seen her for years. And Dave only dead a few weeks.

It wasn't right somehow. No; it wasn't decent. Yet, was it any more indecent than him coveting his brother's wife? His head drooped as he walked down the street.

Dave had never said a word about Maggie's accusation concerning him and Ann. Perhaps it just appeared ludicrous; definitely, he couldn't have considered it worth mentioning, not even to accuse Ann and so help to even the scales against himself.

Now Dave was gone. His death had been a blow; it still lay heavily on him, for he had thought the world of Dave. Yes, he had. But that hadn't stopped him from wanting his wife and from planning how to get her before he had been dead a few weeks. God! Human nature was funny . . . awful would be a better word. And Tom had gone and married a tart like Beattie Watson! This was more baffling than anything else.

He walked on until he reached the fells; but here he turned back; a couple-strewn landscape was no place for him at any time, he'd be suspected of snooping . . . Odd, how love and the need for love was denied you if you happened to be like him . . . and Maggie. Why, he asked himself, should he think of her in that connection? Well, wasn't she in the same boat as himself? Yet, if you happened to be born like Dave or Tom on the one hand, or Ann and that Beat Watson on the other, love came as naturally as the seasons . . . And the consequences of love, an' all. Aye, if you had the pleasures you had to have the pains. But, he told himself, he would have risked the pains for a few of the pleasures.

He had walked, unheeding, for some time; and now he looked about him, wondering where he was. He gazed up at the half-finished building in front of him. This must be the new factory they were putting up, next to the electric component place. He only had to cut round the building and he'd be in Wallace Street.

He had almost reached the street, in fact one of its lights had shown him a heap of shingle he must skirt, and he was doing this when he stepped into a water-filled hollow that lay in the shadow. Muttering to himself, he attempted to step backwards, but his foot slipped, and to save himself from falling face forward into the water he twisted round and fell on to his hands; and in this way pulled himself out.

With a good round oath he moved nearer the light and examined himself. My, but he was in a mess! There must have been lime and cement and God knows what in that water. Why the devil wasn't there a red light near it! His boots and the bottom of his trousers were thick with a greyish plaster, and his hands and coat sleeves the same. This would happen to him! And he'd have to walk through the streets in this sight. On a Saturday night an' all!

The sound of footsteps coming down the street behind him made him move back into the darkness from which he had emerged. He stood with his back to the light and waited for the steps to pass. But they halted quite near him, and a surprised voice said, 'Is that you, Christopher?'

He turned round as if he were being caught in some unpleasant action.

'What's wrong?'

Slowly he walked towards the lamp and looked up at Maggie. He gave a little nervous laugh before saying, 'I slipped into a pool of something round there. I was taking a short cut.'

Her eyes roamed over him; at his coat and then his feet; and she said, 'They should leave a light on that building . . . the place is a by-way.'

The retort seemed characteristic of her; and he said, 'Aye. What they do and what they ought to do are two different things. Well, I'll be making me way home. And the sooner I get there the better, I think.' Again he gave the nervous laugh. He expected her to move on, but she didn't; instead, after an awkward pause, she said, 'Won't you come in and get cleaned up? My . . . my place is just round the bottom of the street.'

'Well, thanks. Thanks all the same, but I'm in such a mess, I'd better . . .'

'You can hardly go through the town like that, the stuff's dripping off you.'

'Yes, I know.'

'And it isn't likely they'll welcome you on the bus.'

He gave her a long, scrutinising look. What had she done to herself? She was different somehow. It wasn't in her manner – that still seemed to be the same, short and abrupt. He could see that she wanted him to go home with her, and he thought he knew why. She wanted to talk about the boy. Well, no-one could say she'd been unreasonable lately. It was only natural that she should want to hear about him. And if he went, he'd kill two birds with one stone, he would talk the other business over with her. She'd want to be free as much as he did; it would only be the custody of the child that would concern her.

He shivered, and she said, 'It's no use standing here with wet feet; the most sensible thing to do is to get them off.'

'Yes; you're right.'

Silently now, they walked down the street and turned the corner; and never had he felt so self-conscious as when he entered her gate and followed her round to the back of the house. Even in the dark he could feel the neat trimness of the place; and when she unlocked the back door and switched on the light in the little kitchen and he saw the blue-squared, shining linoleum, he exclaimed, 'No, Maggie. No, I won't come in. I'll mess up everywhere.'

'Don't be silly; the floor'll wash. And don't stand there in the cold.' She held the door back and he passed her, stepping with ludicrous steps to avoid as much as possible dirtying the floor.

The kitchen was soothingly warm, the heat coming from a stove in the corner. There was a row of cupboards, painted cream and a small table with a porcelain top.

'Sit down' – she pushed a stool towards him – 'and let me have your boots.'

'Look, I . . .'

She made an impatient movement, and he sat down and took off his boots. His stockings too were wet, and she held out her hand for them, and added, 'Let me have your coat, it'll dry in no time on the boiler.'

He stripped himself of his coat, and there he stood, as he knew she hated to see him . . . in his braces!

In spite of all her own evident drawbacks, she always managed, he thought, to place him at a disadvantage.

He watched her open a cupboard and hang up his coat near the boiler, then passing into the next room, she said to him over her shoulder, 'Come in here.'

For a moment he hesitated. Then, walking gingerly in his bare feet, he followed her; and immediately he forgot about the situation between them as his eyes took in the room. By, it looked comfortable. And a coal fire an' all, not electric!

She saw him staring at the fire, and said, 'It's a new type; it stays in all night if you bank it down. It's never been out for a fortnight.'

'No?'

He continued to stare at the fire shining out of its tile surround, and she said, 'Sit down.'

He took a seat by the side of the fire, and then she asked him, 'Would you like something . . . tea, or a cup of coffee?'

'I wouldn't mind, Maggie.'

This was beyond him. As a rule there were no odd cups of tea in Maggie's house.

As he listened to her moving about in the kitchen his eyes wandered round the room. There were still some of the pieces of furniture from the Hill . . . the little pieces, like that group of tables and the bookcase and the armchair in which he was sitting. But here they looked different somehow . . . homely.

His thoughts centred on her again. Something had come over her. But whatever it was, it seemed for the better. Perhaps she was finding life easier, living without him . . . He must have been a great source of irritation to her; he would be to any woman like her, more mind than body; in fact, he supposed, to any woman at all. Then why had he contemplated asking Ann to marry him when he should be free? . . . Oh well – he shook his head at himself – Ann had liked him . . . or he thought she had. But liking wasn't loving. No, far from it. Well, that pipe-dream was over. He could see now it had been nothing but an illusion brought over from his lonely youth, and because there had been no love in his life he had clung on to it.

Maggie came in with a tray which she placed on a side table, but she didn't offer him a cup right away. Instead, she looked at his feet, then went out of the room; and he heard her footsteps in the room overhead. He looked down at his bare feet . . . white, flat, and ugly. They even offended his own gaze, and he tucked them as far from his sight under the chair as he could.

When Maggie returned, without directly looking at him, she dropped a pair of socks on to his lap, saying,

375

'They were in the mending bag. I found them after.'

Slowly he picked up the socks and looked at her. She was now bending over the tea tray. She had kept and darned a pair of his old socks! And after he had done what he did . . . The memory of his hand hitting her mouth made him hot . . . What was it about her? She looked different . . . like folks did after they'd had a long illness. Well, no, not quite like that either. More like as if she had been through some process, or a furnace of some kind, and filed down. She was still Maggie . . . her manner, her voice . . . and yet she wasn't.

'I made tea.' She handed him a big cup. Then taking her cup and sitting down at the opposite side of the hearth, she asked, 'Did you get my letter?'

'Aye . . . Yes, I got it.'

They both drank from their cups.

'You wanted to see me about something?'

He took the spoon from his saucer and stirred his tea; and she said, 'Is there not enough sugar?'

'Yes. Yes, heaps.'

How did a fellow start saying, 'I want a divorce'? If she would give him a lead . . .

'Was it about Stephen?'

'Well, partly.'

'How is he?' She looked into her cup. And he stared across the hearth at her bowed head, thinking: My God, but it must have been hell for her. And still is, if I know owt . . . But she's not fighting any more, she's spent. That was it; the look she had . . . the way she acted . . . she was spent. You could almost say she had died . . . she was dead while she still breathed. She was lonely and lost. Yes, he could see it now. She belonged to no-one, and no-one belonged to her.

He had to moisten his lips a number of times before he could say, 'He's all right. Well, a lot better. The doctor saw him last week and he said he was doing fine.' He could not say to her what the doctor had actually said, that now a gentle curb must be applied to the boy; nor could he say that he himself knew this was necessary or that the boy's grandmother was the last person who could apply it; but to his own amazement he found himself saying, 'I'll bring him round if you like, for an hour or two some time.'

Their eyes met across the distance. Then a surprising thing happened. Her hand shook until the cup rattled in the saucer, and her eyes, heavy with unshed tears, fell away from his, and she rose abruptly and went to the tray.

After a moment or so she asked, 'Will you have another cup?'

'No. No, thanks, Maggie.' He felt embarrassed and at a complete loss. So he said, 'I'll be getting along . . . I'd better scrape those boots.'

'There's no need.' Her voice was tight.

She passed behind his chair as she spoke and went to a cupboard to the side of the fireplace. He turned his head and watched her opening the door, and a painful sensation came into his throat. There, alone, but side by side on a shelf was a pair of his boots and a pair of Stephen's shoes.

She picked up the boots, saying, 'You forgot them' and she placed them at the side of his chair and went into the kitchen again.

His old boots . . . True, he had forgotten them. He had only once gone back to the Hill house, and he had been unable to find them and had concluded she had thrown them out. But she had kept them.

He picked them up. They had been polished, well polished. He'd always had to polish his own boots, even when they lived on the Hill.

He looked towards the kitchen door . . . What could be the meaning of it? His socks . . . and now his boots. And put away in a cupboard, together with Stephen's. Surely, she . . . No. No, that would be fantastic. She'd never had any use for him; the boy was all she cared for; and yet . . .

Slowly he drew on the boots; and then went to the kitchen door. 'Is the coat anywhere near dry, Maggie?'

She was standing with her back to him, doing something at the table.

'I don't think it'll be yet.'

He took a further step into the kitchen, and then stood staring at the table. On it was a paper, and on the paper stood his boots. She was scraping the mud off them with a knife!

'Here!' he said. 'What on earth you doing?'

'They'll be easier to carry,' she said, 'and will dry sooner.'

She did not lift her head, and he went behind her and took one of the boots from the table and placed it on the floor; and when he went to take the other from her his hand gripped her wrist, and they both became still.

The mud-caked boot branched from their joined hands like a gnarled stump. Their eyes focused on it, then slowly raised to each other. And again there were tears in hers. And at the sight of them a warmness came into Christopher's body. Pity for her once again flowed back; but with a difference; the pity he had given her before he would have given freely to any maimed animal, but in this pity there was a tenderness, a private tenderness, for he saw that she had . . . cottoned on to him . . . she liked him. Well, he would call it by that name for the present; no woman of any sort had ever loved him, not even his mother; they had pitied and liked him, but that was

378

as far as it had gone. But she, Maggie . . . Well, dear God!

Slowly he withdrew the boot from her hand, and, picking up the other one, he stood them in the corner by the stove; then turned and looked at her, saying, 'They can stay there; I'll be back for them.'

THE END

THE RAG NYMPH
by Catherine Cookson

In the heat of a late June afternoon in 1854, abandoned by a panic-stricken mother in an all-too-obvious flight from the law, Millie Forester burst into Aggie Winkowski's life like a bolt from the blue. Aggie, who was known hereabouts as 'Raggie Aggie', for trading in rags and old clothes was her long-established business, knew well enough the dangers waiting for such a strikingly pretty girl left alone in this rough and vice-ridden quarter and could see nothing for it, other than to take her in.

But what began as a compassionate expediency led to the establishment of a new relationship that would grow and deepen, moulding Millie's destiny and giving new meaning to the life of Aggie Winkowski.

Millie Forester's advance through the coming years to the threshold of womanhood is the core of *The Rag Nymph,* as gripping and socially concerned an historical novel as Catherine Cookson has ever written. Her superb skills of narrative and characterization provide a spectrum of the good and evil of the Victorian era, frankly confronting the terrible menace of child corruption, which remains a constant issue in our own time.

0 552 13683 2

THE HOUSE OF WOMEN
by Catherine Cookson

Emma Funnell is the matriarch of Bramble House, built for her as a wedding gift. Now, in 1968, she is in her seventies, with the avowed intent of living to be a hundred. And, as she has always done, she continues to rule the roost, for apart from herself three generations of the Funnell family live in the house – all of them women.

There is widowed daughter Victoria, increasingly a hypochondriac, granddaughter Lizzie, who bears the brunt of running the house, as well as enduring a loveless marriage to Len Hammond; and Peggy, her sixteen-year-old daughter, now trying to find the courage to drop the bombshell of her pregnancy into their midst.

This explosive situation provides the springboard for a powerful and absorbing novel that explores, over a period of fifteen years, all that fate holds in store for the dwellers in *The House of Women*, reaching its climax with a frank confrontation of a major social issue of today.

'The author's grip on the novel never flags . . . her crown rests assured'
Sunday Times

0 552 13303 5

FEATHERS IN THE FIRE
by Catherine Cookson

Davie Armstrong watched as his master, Angus McBain, thrashed young Molly Geary for refusing to name the man who had dishonoured her. And yet, not an hour later, Davie saw the two of them alone in the malthouse, and Molly was acting like a whore on market day. In a whirl of disbelieving rage he overheard McBain's plan – to let him, Davie, take the blame and marry Molly, to give the child a name. And he was not alone in witnessing the scene, for with him was Angus's daughter, Jane, Davie's staunch ally.

But it was the birth of McBain's true son Amos that unleashed the course of actions that resulted in violence and tragedy. Born with no legs and emotionally crippled, Amos would wield power of frightening intensity and bring disaster to all at Cock Shield Farm . . .

0 552 14068 6

A DINNER OF HERBS
by Catherine Cookson

A legacy of hatred can be a terrible force in life, over which not even an enduring love and all the fruits of material success may prevail. Catherine Cookson explores this theme in a major novel that will absorb and enthral her readers as irresistibly as any she has written.

Roddy Greenbank was brought by his father to the remote Northumberland community of Langley in the autumn of 1807. Within hours of their arrival, however, the father had met a violent death, and the boy left with all memory gone of his past life.

Adopted and raised by old Kate Makepeace, Roddy found his closest companions in Hal Royston and Mary Ellen Lee. These three stand at the heart of a richly eventful narrative that spans the first half of the nineteenth century, their lives lastingly intertwined by the inexorable demands of a strange and somewhat cruel destiny.

0 552 12551 2

The Catherine Cookson Corgi Checklist

❑ 13016-8	Bill Bailey	$4.95
❑ 13301-9	Bill Bailey's Daughter	$5.50
❑ 13274-8	Bill Bailey's Lot	$4.95
❑ 13576-3	The Black Candle	$5.95
❑ 12473-7	Black Velvet Gown	$6.99
❑ 11160-0	Cinder Path	$4.95
❑ 12476-1	The Cultured Handmaiden	$5.95
❑ 12551-2	Dinner of Herbs	$6.95
❑ 10450-7	Gambling Man	$4.95
❑ 13716-2	The Garment	$4.99
❑ 13621-2	The Gillyvors	$6.99
❑ 10916-9	The Girl	$5.95
❑ 12608-X	Goodbye Hamilton	$4.95
❑ 12451-6	Hamilton	$5.50
❑ 13715-4	Hannah Massey	$4.99
❑ 12789-2	Harold	$5.50
❑ 10780-8	The Iron Facade	$5.99
❑ 13300-0	The Harrogate Secret	$5.95
❑ 13407-4	Let Me Make Myself Plain	$5.95
❑ 09896-5	The Mallen Girl	$4.95
❑ 10151-6	The Mallen Litter	$4.95
❑ 09720-9	The Mallen Streak	$4.95
❑ 11350-6	The Man Who Cried	$4.95
❑ 12524-5	The Moth	$5.95
❑ 13302-7	My Beloved Son	$6.99
❑ 13088-5	Parson's Daughter	$5.95
❑ 13683-2	The Rag Nymph	$6.99
❑ 10541-4	A Slow Awakening	$4.50
❑ 11737-4	Tilly Trotter	$4.95
❑ 11960-1	Tilly Trotter Wed	$4.95
❑ 12200-9	Tilly Trotter Widowed	$4.95
❑ 12368-4	The Whip	$5.95
❑ 13577-1	The Wingless Bird	$6.99

Available at your local bookstore or use this page to order.
Send to: Bantam Books, Dept. FB,
　　　　 2451 S. Wolf Road,
　　　　 Des Plaines, Il 60018 USA
Please send me the items I have checked above. I am enclosing
$ _____ (please add $2.50 to cover postage and handling).
Send cheque or money order, no cash or C.O.D's, please.

Mr./Ms.: _____

Address: _____

City/Prov.: _____ Postal Code: _____

Please allow four to six weeks for delivery.
Prices and availability change without notice.